Watch the Lady

By the same author

Queen's Gambit
Sisters of Treason

Watch the Lady

ELIZABETH FREMANTLE

MICHAEL JOSEPH
an imprint of
PENGUIN BOOKS

MICHAEL JOSEPH

UK | USA | Canada | Ireland | Australia
India | New Zealand | South Africa

Michael Joseph is part of the Penguin Random House group of companies
whose addresses can be found at global.penguinrandomhouse.com.

First published 2015

001

Copyright © Elizabeth Fremantle, 2015

The moral right of the author has been asserted

Typeset in Garamond MT Std 13.5/15.25 pt by Palimpsest Book Production Limited, Falkirk, Stirlingshire

Printed in Great Britain by Clays Ltd, St Ives plc

A CIP catalogue record for this book is available from the British Library

HARDBACK ISBN: 978–0–718–17710–2

TRADE PAPERBACK ISBN: 978–0–718–17711–9

www.greenpenguin.co.uk

For Alice, who would have been Stella had I got my way

Contents

The Duel

Stella, star of heavenly fire,
Stella, lodestar of desire.

Sir Philip Sidney, *Astrophil and Stella*

October 1589

Leicester House, the Strand

The wax sizzles as it drips, releasing an acrid whiff. Penelope presses in her seal, twisting it slightly to make it unreadable, wondering if it – this letter – is folly, if it could be construed as treason were it to fall into the wrong hands.

'Do you think . . .' she begins to say to Constable, who is standing at her shoulder.

'I think you risk too much.'

'I have to secure my family's future. You know as well as I that the Queen is not a young woman. Were she to –' She stops and flicks her gaze about the chamber, though they both know they are alone as they had searched, even behind the hangings, for lurking servants who might be persuaded to sell a snippet of information to the highest bidder. 'There have been attempts on the Queen's life and she has named no heir. If one were to strike its target.' Her voice is lowered to the quietest of whispers. She doesn't need to tell him that there are eyes all over Europe on Elizabeth's crown. 'The Devereuxs need an established allegiance.'

'And James of Scotland is the strongest claimant to the English throne,' he says.

'Some say so.' Penelope closes the discussion firmly. Constable is not aware that this has been discussed endlessly with her brother – and their mother, for that matter, who understands diplomacy better than all of them put together. 'I do it for Essex, not for myself. My brother is the one who needs powerful allies.' She hands him the letter, meeting his eyes briefly.

He runs his fingers over the paper as if it is a lover's skin. 'But should it fall into the wrong hands . . .'

He is surely thinking of Robert Cecil, son of Lord

Treasurer Burghley, the man who holds the reins of England. Cecil has a knife in every pie.

She meets his gaze with a half-smile. 'But this is merely a missive of friendship, an outstretched hand. And it comes from a woman.' She places her palm delicately to her breast and widens her eyes, as if to say a woman's words count for nothing. 'Secret communication with a foreign monarch might see Essex in trouble, but from one such as I . . .' She tilts her head in mock humility. 'Oh, I think I can get away with it.'

Constable laughs. 'From a mere woman? No one would even notice.'

She hopes to God this is true. 'You are sure you wish to accept this mission?'

'Nothing would give me greater pleasure than to serve you, My Lady.'

She doesn't doubt it. Constable has penned near on a hundred poems for her, and he is not the only one. Essex is a magnet for poets and thinkers who cluster round him like iron filings, hoping for his patronage, prepared to go to any lengths to gain his favour. By flattering his sister they think they help their cause. She wonders at the irony that, for all those lines of poetry written in celebration of her beauty, repeating incessantly the same figures of speech – her black starry eyes, her spun-gold hair, her nightingale's voice, her marble skin – the man she is wed to has never got beyond his disgust of her. Beauty may make for pretty lines in a sonnet but it is eggshell thin, and as friable; it does not speak of what lies within.

'You will give it straight into the hands of King James.' She is aware of the danger she might visit on Constable with this secret mission, but so is he, and she can almost hear him panting with eagerness. Besides, he is no stranger to espionage.

'But,' he begins, then hesitates. 'How can I be sure of admittance to the King?'

'You are a poet; use your velvet tongue. My seal will get you into the privy chamber.' She takes his hand and folds her signet ring into his palm. 'After all, I am the sister of England's most favoured earl, the Queen's great-niece; that counts for something, does it not?' Her tone is unintentionally sharp and he looks uncomfortable, as if admonished, so she offers him a smile.

'Keep the seal separate from the letter. And give him this, as further proof.' She opens a gilt box on the desk and takes out a limning, passing it to him. He inspects it a moment, his eyes swimming a little.

'Hilliard has not done you justice. Your beauty is greater than this.'

'Pah!' she says with a sweep of her arm. 'Beauty is as beauty does. It looks like me enough to serve its purpose.' She watches as he caches the miniature carefully inside his doublet with the letter.

Her spaniel, Spero, begins to bark, scratching at the door to get out, and they hear the clang of the courtyard gate, then the din of urgent hooves on the cobbles below and a frenzied bout of shouting. They move swiftly to the window just as the door is flung open and her companion Jeanne rushes into the chamber flushed and breathless, crying out, 'Come quickly, your brother is wounded.' Her French accent with its soft lisp delays the impact of her words.

'How?' Panic begins to rise in Penelope like milk in an unwatched pan, but she takes a deep breath to force it into submission.

'Meyrick said it was a duel.' Jeanne's face is ashen.

'How bad is it?' Jeanne simply shakes her head. Penelope takes the girl's elbow with one hand and, gathering her skirts with the other, calls to Constable, who is already halfway down the stairs, 'Send for Doctor Lopez.'

'If he is wounded then surely a surgeon is what's needed,' says Constable.

'I trust Lopez. He will know what to do.'

They get to the hall as Essex is brought in, supported by two of his men, the broad bulk of loyal Meyrick striding ahead, concern written over his freckled face, eyes darting about beneath invisible eyelashes. He wipes a hand through his hair; it has a smear of dried blood on it.

'A basin of hot water,' she barks at the servants, who have gathered to gawp. Jeanne is shaking, she cannot bear the sight of blood, so Penelope sends her to tear bandages in the laundry.

Essex, his teeth gritted, is heaved on to the table, where he half lies, half sits propped up on his elbows, refusing to succumb to repose.

'Just a scratch,' he says, pulling his cape away from his leg so Penelope can see the slash across his thigh and the blood that has stained his white silk stockings, right down into his boot.

'Meyrick, your knife,' she says to her brother's man.

Meyrick looks at her askance.

'To cut off his stockings. What did you think?' She checks the sharp tone that has appeared from nowhere. 'Here, help me with his boots.' She gets both hands around a heel and gently prises one boot away, while Meyrick works on the other, then takes up the knife and, pinching the bloody silk between her fingers, gently peels his stocking away from the wound. It has stuck where the blood is congealing, which causes Essex to wince and turn away. She then touches the tip of the knife to the fabric, slitting it from thigh to knee, revealing the full extent of the damage.

'It is not as bad as I'd feared – not so deep. You will live.'

8

She kisses him lightly on his cheek, only now understanding how relieved she is.

A maid places a basin of steaming water beside her and hands her a clean muslin cloth.

'That varlet Blount,' Essex spits.

'Who challenged whom?' she asks, knowing it will have been her brother's rash temper that provoked the spat. She dabs gently at the wound. The blood is surprisingly bright and still flowing, but she can see that no serious damage has been done. An inch further towards his groin where the vessels cluster close to the surface and it might have been a different story.

'It was Blount's fault.' Her brother sounds surly. Penelope has seen Charles Blount at a distance once or twice at court. He gave the impression of being careful and measured. He is comely too, enough to give Essex some competition with the Queen's maids – and, most importantly, the Queen herself. She's heard that Blount has been attracting some favour and knows full well what her brother is like. He wants to be the only star in the Queen's firmament. 'He started it!'

'You are twenty-three, not thirteen, Robin.' Her voice is tender now. 'Your temper will get you into serious trouble.' Penelope is his senior by less than three years but she has always felt older by far. She can sense his indignation at having lost in this ill-advised duel, when he supposes himself the foremost swordsman in the country. She wants to point out he is lucky to have got off so lightly, but doesn't. 'The Queen will hear of it. She will not be happy.'

'Who will tell her?'

She doesn't answer. They both know it is impossible to sneeze anywhere in the whole of Europe without Robert Cecil finding out, and informing the Queen, before you've a chance to take out your handkerchief.

'You will need to rest a day or two,' she says, rinsing the cloth in the basin where the blood billows out pink into the clean water. 'And your amorous intrigues will be curtailed for a week or so.'

Their eyes meet in silent amusement as he takes a pipe from inside his doublet and begins to stuff its bowl with tobacco.

Doctor Lopez arrives and, after a brief exchange of formalities, gets to work, tipping a measure of white powder into the gash 'to stem the blood flow', he says, offering Essex a length of wood to bite down on.

Essex refuses it, asking for Meyrick to light his pipe and saying he would rather be distracted by listening to his sister sing, so Penelope begins to hum as Lopez threads a length of catgut on to a needle. Essex blows strands of smoke from his nostrils and appears unperturbed as the needle weaves in and out, pulling together the mouth of the wound.

'Your gifts of stitching rival the Queen's embroiderers,' says Penelope, admiring the tidy sutures.

'It is a gift I learned on the battlefield.' He places an avuncular hand on her back and steps with her to one side. There is something honest about the close crop of his hair and beard, steely with age, and the way his smile reaches up to crease his eyes. 'Make sure he rests and keeps his leg up.'

'I will do my best,' she replies. 'You know what he is like.' She pauses. 'And . . .'

'It will go no further, My Lady,' Lopez says, as if reading her mind.

'I am grateful to you, Doctor.' It is not the first time she has felt gratitude for Lopez. If it were not for him she might have lost her first child.

Later they gather about the hearth, listening to Constable recite a new poem.

> *My Lady's presence makes the roses red*
> *Because to see her lips they blush for shame*

Penelope is thinking of the letter to King James tucked in the man's doublet, imagining him riding up the Great North Road to deliver it, feeling a shiver of fear-tinged excitement at the subterfuge.

The lily's leaves, for envy, pale became,
For her white hands in them this envy bred.

'But you change tense there, Constable,' says Essex, who is seated with his foot propped on a stool. 'It should be "become" and "breed".'

'Don't tease him,' says Penelope. 'He does it so the rhyme scans. It is lovely.' She winks the poet's way.

'It's charming,' adds Jeanne, looking up for a moment, needle held aloft, pinched between thumb and finger. Her hands are delicate, small as a child's, and she has a frame to match. The two women are embroidering a row of holly-hocks on to the border of a shift, had started one at each end and planned to meet in the middle, but Penelope's concentration has wandered off and her own needle hangs idly from its thread. Essex's teasing of the poet has silenced the poor fellow, who now stands awkwardly, not knowing whether to continue his recitation. Odd he has such thin skin, thinks Penelope, given he served as Walsingham's emissary for such a time. And to be part of that man's network of spies takes mettle.

'We'd love to hear the rest,' she says, distracted by Meyrick entering the chamber and handing Essex a letter with what appears to be the royal seal attached.

Constable clears his throat and glances at Essex, who is ripping open the missive.

The marigold the leaves abroad doth spread,
Because the sun's and her power is the same.

Penelope has stopped listening and is watching a flush take hold in her brother's cheeks. He screws up the paper and hurls it into the fire, muttering under his breath, 'I am banned from court. Disobedience. Huh! She thinks it is time someone taught me better manners.'

'A few weeks away from court is probably a good thing,' says Meyrick. 'You wouldn't want to flaunt that wound. People might taunt you for it.'

How good Meyrick is with my brother, she thinks. But then they *have* been close since boyhood.

Essex expels a defeated sigh.

The violet of purple colour came,
Dyed in the blood she made my heart to shed.

A page has popped his head around the door, beckoning Meyrick, who approaches him, listening to something the boy says, before returning to Essex and passing the whispered message on.

'Blount!' exclaims Essex. 'What the devil does he think he's doing turning up here?'

Penelope holds up a hand to silence Constable and turns to her brother. 'I expect he has come to pay his compliments and see that you are recovered. It is only out of respect, I'm sure.'

'Respect? The man has none.'

Meyrick puts his large hand firmly on her brother's shoulder. 'Leave Blount to me.' Penelope can see the tightly packed muscles of the man's neck tighten and a flash of brutality in those invisibly lashed eyes.

'You *ought* to see him, Robin,' she says. Essex brushes Meyrick's hand off his shoulder and begins to heave himself out of his chair. 'What are you doing? You need to keep that leg up.'

'If I am to receive the miscreant I will not give him the satisfaction of seeing me reposed like a milk-livered clot-pole.' He limps over to stand beside the great memorial portrait of the Earl of Leicester, as if to gain strength from his illustrious stepfather. He positions himself, one hand aloft, fingers touching the gilded frame. His eyes are ablaze, which causes Penelope concern; she has seen that look before many times and it often signifies the onset of a bout of deep melancholy. That is Essex: wild fire or leaden heart but nothing in between. 'Send the villain in, then.'

As Meyrick leaves the chamber to fetch Blount, Penelope sees he has not yet washed the smear of blood from his hand.

Blount enters, dropping immediately to his knee and removing his hat. 'Forgive me, My Lord, if I interrupt your peace but I come to salute you and to return your sword.'

'My sword?'

'It was left at the scene, My Lord.'

'So where is it?'

'My man has it outside. I did not think it proper to enter your presence armed.'

'Feared it might provoke another spat?' says Essex, then adds grudgingly, 'You did right, Blount.'

'Of the duel, My Lord,' says Blount. 'It was naught but fluke that my blade caught you. It was you who had the upper hand. It should have been I who took the cut.'

Penelope catches herself staring and quickly pulls her gaze away, picking up her redundant needle, making busy with it.

'Get up, man,' says Essex. 'No need to stay on your knee on my account.'

Penelope thinks she can see the hint of a smile play at the edge of her brother's mouth. She knows only too well how he likes a show of humility. 'Get our guest a drink, and I'll have one too.'

Meyrick pours two cups from the flagon of wine on the table, handing one to his master, the other to Blount, who raises his cup saying, 'Pax?'

'Pax,' replies Essex and they drink back, he a little more

reluctantly than the other man. But etiquette demands that to rebuff Blount's chivalry would occasion another duel.

Penelope's eyes have wandered back to Blount, taking in his halo of hair, dark as an Arab's, and the fine proportions of his face and the warm dark eyes. He is better looking than she'd thought. He doesn't wear a ruff, just a flat lacework collar and a notched satin doublet, quite beautifully understated. He has clearly chosen his garb carefully so as not to outshine Essex. So he is a diplomat too. But a single earring hanging from his left ear adds an appealing touch of dash. She is thinking this man might be a good ally for her brother, makes a mental note to talk to Essex about it later, to make him understand that it is not men like this who are his enemies. It is men like Cecil and Ralegh, who have powerful allegiances and the Queen's ear, men who would see him ousted, that he must be wary of. Besides, she would like to see more of Blount at Essex House. He glances towards her at that moment and she feels herself blush as if he can divine what she is thinking.

'Do you know my sister?' asks Essex.

'I am honoured to make the acquaintance of one who has inspired such poetry.' He is back on his knee now, and reaching out for her hand.

She wonders if he isn't spreading it a little too thickly, the charm, which he clearly has in abundance. She can see why the Queen has favoured this one. But he looks up at her and she can find nothing but sincerity in those eyes of his.

'Sidney's sonnets are unparalleled, My Lady. They have transported me at times.'

'And what makes you suppose me to be the subject of Sir Philip's poems?' She has wondered often at the fame that arose from being the muse of a great poet, how it seemed to have so little to do with her and so much more to do with Sidney. What is a muse anyway, she has asked herself many times – no more than a cipher.

Her brother laughs. 'Everyone knows that you and Stella are one and the same.'

'"When Nature made her chief work, Stella's eyes, / In colour black why wrapped she beams so bright?"' recites Blount quietly. 'I recognize your likeness from his words, My Lady.'

'Now there is *real* poetry,' says Essex, causing poor Constable to shuffle uncomfortably.

'None surpasses Sidney,' exclaims the embarrassed poet.

'Enough of this,' declares Essex. 'Meyrick, fetch me my sword. Indeed, it is the very blade Sidney gave me.'

'And I'm sure he didn't intend that you use it for duelling,' says Penelope, trying to remain light-hearted, but all this talk of Sidney is churning up painful memories, forcing her thoughts back to the girl she was eight years ago. She remembers arriving at court, imagining it to be nothing but romance and cheerful intrigue. The woman she is now, restrained, secretive, political, is as different from that girl as an egg from an oyster.

November 1589

Theobalds, Hertfordshire

The man removes his cap and makes a hunched bow, his eyes darting about, giving him the look of a rodent. He must have been on the road, for he is spattered with mud to his waist and his shoulders are dark with wet.

Cecil watches him from his desk where he adjusts his affairs, the inkbottles each exactly an inch apart, his ledgers stacked from large to small, and he turns his quills in their jar so their feathers all face the same way. He is seated with the window behind him so his features are difficult to make out. The desk is positioned thus deliberately, to put visitors at a disadvantage. Cecil is well aware his person is not sufficiently imposing for the job he is called to do but has learned various tricks over the years to compensate for this lack. 'Shut the door.'

The man does as he is bid.

'I hope you were not seen.' Cecil offers him the seat opposite. The rain must have cleared, for a beam of bright midday sun falls over the man's face so he has to raise a hand to shield his eyes.

'No, sir, I took the greatest care to ensure I wasn't followed. I changed horses at Ware, from there took the London Road and doubled back –'

'I don't need the details,' Cecil interrupts, noticing how the fellow's other hand grips his cap in a fist as if his life depends on it. 'I sincerely hope Walsingham is not aware of our meeting?'

'But I was under the impression that Walsingham was with us.'

'Listen to me; there is no "with" or "against", nor is there an "us". It is simply a case of making sure I know what is going on. My father and I serve the Queen's interests and it requires' – he pauses, adjusting his ring so the large emerald faces forward – 'the utmost discretion.'

'Of course, sir.'

'Now, in your letter you intimated there were some goings-on at the Scottish court. Is the King's marriage properly sealed with the Danish princess? There were no problems with the' – he clears his throat – 'consummation?' James of Scotland's proclivity for young men is no secret and there have been moments when Cecil has thought that might be the very thing that would conveniently set James's claim on the English throne adrift. There are other candidates for the crown that Cecil and his father have had their eye on – ones who might be more amenable.

Cecil notices the man is staring intently at his hands; he folds his arms over his chest, tucking them out of sight. His hands are small with ugly spatula fingers; he has always felt they give the wrong impression. As a youth he longed for the kind of hands that could wield a broadsword, hands like those of the Earl of Essex.

'No indeed, sir. That all seems to have been as it should be. The Princess, well, Queen now, I suppose, appears besotted. I saw the blooded sheet with my own eyes.'

'So you travelled to Oslo for the wedding?' Cecil is impressed, wonders how this weasel of a man, who has such a small ration of charm, managed to inveigle himself upon the royal wedding party.

'Yes, I attached myself to –'

'I know,' interrupts Cecil. He doesn't know, but is aware it will keep the man on his toes if he feels he is being watched.

'But there is another matter.' The man has leaned in close and is talking very quietly now.

'Another matter.' Cecil sifts through the possibilities. 'Regarding?'

'Regarding Essex's sister.'

Cecil cannot hide his surprise. He doesn't like being wrong-footed with information he has not had so much as a sniff of. 'What has *she* to do with James of Scotland?'

'She has made overtures – written letters of friendship to the King.'

'Friendship?'

'It may be more complicated than that. She used coded names.'

Cecil's curiosity is further pricked. 'Go on.'

'She has a florid style but the general impression I have gained – you see, I had a moment alone with the letters – is that she was suggesting that, should it come to it – those were the words she used: "should it come to it" – James can count on her support and by implication her brother's too.'

'Sounds like silly games.' Cecil is careful to remain steady, affecting nonchalance, but he feels his skin prickle, and imagines himself as a hound catching the first whiff of a stag. 'I suppose she remained ambiguous?'

'If you mean, did she incriminate herself by mentioning the demise of our monarch, she did not.'

But the code names speak of something underhand, Cecil thinks. 'And who was her messenger?'

'The poet Henry Constable, sir.'

'Ah, Constable, he worked for *me* once. Poets seem to cluster about that lady like flies on filth. It is a mystery to me. He did it for *love*, I suppose.' His disdain is apparent. Cecil is not a man given to love. But he is being disingenuous, for there is something beyond that lady's obvious beauty that impresses him. He has watched her over the years – they are the same age; have risen at court together. She is a woman with a canny instinct for being in the right place at the right time and has the pragmatism more usually found in a man. She would be perfection had she not that brother, Essex.

The mere thought of Essex raises Cecil's hackles. After

the death of the first earl the boy had been raised in the Cecil household. He has a memory of the young Devereux's arrival, the way he dismounted, leaping to the ground before his horse came to a halt. Essex barely gave Cecil – half his size, though more than two years his senior, and crooked as a set of steps – a second look.

His father had primed him not to get on the wrong side of the cuckoo in their nest. That was when he first learned that Essex had royal blood. Not just the pedigree that runs back in four straight lines to Edward III, but Tudor blood – for it was said that Essex's great-grandmother, the whore Mary Boleyn, bore the eighth Henry a child and that child was Lady Knollys, Essex's grandmother. Cecil's father had it from his own father who was Groom of the Robes, and had the King's confidence. 'When royal blood flows from two sources into a single son, it can mean danger,' his father had said. 'So you keep on his right side, but watch him.'

Cecil *has* watched him, has watched him wrap himself about the Queen like a vine, has watched the Queen soften towards him, favour him like no other since Leicester died. The rumour-mongers call him her lover but Cecil knows better – he is no bedfellow, he is the son she will never have; and a mother will indulge a son where she will not a lover.

But he cannot erase thoughts of the sister. He is thinking of the first time he set eyes on Penelope Devereux, on the day she was presented at court. How her beauty took his breath away. He could think of little else for months, fumbling with himself at night over images cast of her in his mind. She smiled at him that day – he remembers as if it were yesterday the shameful, throbbing flush that smile induced – and what a smile, the kind that would light up the shadows of hell. She had smiled, when every other maid he had ever encountered looked at him with barely concealed disgust. But in the years since, Cecil has come to admire more than that generous smile, for behind her celebrated charms hides a formidable perspicacity. Some might call it a dangerous quality in a woman.

PART I
The Egg

When Nature made her chief work, Stella's eyes,
In colour black why wrapped she beams so bright?
Would she in beamy black, like painter wise,
Frame daintiest lustre mixed of shades and light?
Or did she else that sober hue devise,
In object best to knit and strength our sight,
Lest if no veil those brave beams did disguise,
They sun-like should more dazzle than delight?
Or would she her miraculous power show
That whereas black seems beauty's contrary,
She e'en in black doth make all beauties flow?
Both so, and thus, she, minding Love, should be
Placed ever there, gave him this mourning weed
To honour all their deaths who for her bleed.

Sir Philip Sidney, *Astrophil and Stella*

January 1581

Whitehall

When she had first been fitted for the dress she would wear to be received by the Queen it had seemed an infinitely beautiful thing, but there in the long gallery at Whitehall it had transformed into something wrong – too plain, too Puritan.

The countess was listing instructions as they walked. 'Stay on your knee until she indicates you may rise; do not stare; do not speak unless she asks it of you.'

Penelope wanted to stop and listen to the singing, which she could hear faintly coming from the chapel where the choir were practising. They had worshipped there on the previous day after their journey and Penelope had felt the music burrow deep inside her, expanding until she could no longer tell where she began or ended. She had never heard such a choir. Forty voices – she counted them – each singing a different part, yet marrying as if they were one. That must be the sound of heaven, because nothing on earth can draw itself tight about your heart like that until you might gasp for the sheer joy of it. The Earl and Countess of Huntingdon did not allow music in their chapel; they said it distracted from private contemplation and communion with the Lord.

'Don't dawdle so, Penelope.' The countess's hand was clamped on her wrist, so tightly she feared it would leave a bruise.

They walked swiftly past the line of portraits, too fast for Penelope to see if she could find her family amongst them, the countess barking at the dawdlers to step aside. The women's gowns were cut in a way Penelope had never encountered, waspish pointed stomachers embroidered with flowers and birds, skirts flaring out so wide two could not pass in a corridor without negotiation. Some wore gossamer structures curving up behind their heads, like the wings of dragonflies. She wanted to take a closer look to see how they were fashioned, whether it was wire that held them up, or magic. The countess favoured plain garb and the dark-green velvet gown Penelope wore was testament to that. Finely tailored though it was, it had nothing of the splendour of those other dresses, and even the crimson satin sleeves, a delight only hours ago, failed to make it seem less drab. 'The Lord does not appreciate excessive luxury,' her guardian liked to say.

Penelope yearned in that moment for a flowered stomacher, dragonfly wings and a jewelled, feather fan, rather than a prayer book, hanging from her girdle.

'Do not acknowledge anyone unless invited to do so; your uncles will be there; your stepfather' – she said 'stepfather' with a scowl of disapproval; Penelope had noticed long ago that her guardian rarely called Leicester 'Brother' and wondered why – 'your Knollys grandmother, various of your cousins, but you will not look at them. It must be as if the Queen is the only soul in the chamber.' She stopped then and looked Penelope up and down, removing a thread from her shoulder and adjusting her wrong-shaped cap. 'And whatever you do, don't mention your mother.'

Penelope missed her mother. *She* would not have had her in such a plain dress. *She* would have stopped awhile to listen to the music. She imagined her beautiful mother, Lettice Knollys, the Countess of Leicester, beside her in the place of her guardian. *She* would have lent her a set of jewels and pearl-tipped pins to decorate her hair. But Lettice was not even to be mentioned at court – as if she didn't exist.

Penelope felt the anger spread through her on her mother's behalf – her whole family's behalf – and could hear her say, as if it were only yesterday and not five years ago when news came of her father's death, 'That woman killed your father.'

She remembered her bewilderment, for her father had been in Ireland in charge of the English army when he died of the flux. Penelope had come to understand, fitting all the pieces together, that by 'that woman' her mother had meant the Queen.

Penelope usually prided herself on her courage but she felt it dissolving, like a pearl in vinegar, as the door to the Queen's privy chamber loomed near.

'Listen to me, Penelope. The Queen's goddaughter you may be, but she will not want some flighty girl in her household, however well born. You must pay attention. We shall wait inside the door. Do not approach until she beckons. Address her as "Your Majesty", even if others don't – it shows respect. If she asks about your pastimes, tell her you are fond of reading the gospels and no mention of card games.' She must have been thinking of the pack of cards she had confiscated from Penelope and her younger sister, Dorothy, and flung on the fire. Penelope wished Dorothy was with her but the countess had deemed that she was to stay behind. 'And did I say not to mention your mother?'

'Yes, My Lady.' The anger opened up in her again and she quelled it by turning her thoughts to her father's very last wish for her, which had her betrothed to Philip Sidney, whom she hoped might be behind that door. She tried to conjure up a picture of him in her mind but she had set eyes on him only the once, and that had been six years ago. He seemed to barely notice her then, but why would a proud youth already of age, whose uncle was the Earl of Leicester, notice a girl not yet thirteen, even if she were the Queen's kin? His face, she remembered, was finely carved, with a straight nose beneath an open brow and the faintest scattering of small-pox scars that somehow conspired to make him all the more interesting, as if he had lived and had experiences she couldn't even imagine.

Her father's other wish had been to hand the care of his

daughters to his kinsman, the Earl of Huntingdon, a wish apparently sanctioned by the Queen that could not be broken. When she had begged her mother for an explanation Lettice had opened her palms upwards and shaken her head, saying, 'It was your father's will. I have no say in it. Besides, it is a good opportunity for you girls; the Huntingdons have great influence with the Queen.' There was a crack in her voice. Penelope had had to accept that there were some things she might never fully understand. She glanced down at her plain skirts, feeling suddenly at a complete loss.

'Penelope, your daydreaming will be your downfall.' The countess pinched the back of her hand sharply, just as the great doors swung open.

They moved forward together, waiting just inside. The Queen was dressed from head to toe in gold and Leicester was standing beside her with a proprietorial hand on the back of her chair. Penelope dropped her gaze but couldn't help flicking her eyes over the Queen's maids, who were scattered about all dressed in white like a host of angels. She hated that green velvet then, imagining the satisfaction of ripping it from top to bottom, and set her gaze on a knot in the floorboards that was like an eye staring back at her.

After what seemed an age the Queen said, 'Ah, Lady Huntingdon. Let's take a closer look at your ward.' A countess gave her a shove forward. She fixed her eyes on the Queen's hands, thinking it a safe place for them to rest. The beauty of them surprised her; they did not seem the hands of a woman nearing her fiftieth year – an age that seemed incomprehensibly distant to Penelope. Finally reaching the point, a few feet from the Queen's skirts, where the countess had instructed her was the correct place, she dropped on to her knees, still looking at those hands. That close, she was able to see properly the rings that decorated her fingers: a vast ruby, which must have been the one she was to kiss – if the opportunity arose – a square cut diamond with an enamelwork shank, and, surprisingly, a large domed toadstone, ugly beside its more majestic fellows. She thought toadstones were protection from poison but couldn't remember for certain.

'Closer,' the Queen said, and Penelope shuffled forward awkwardly on her knees, watching as those long fingers reached out to tilt her chin up.

Her breast was festooned with pearls and her face was spread thickly with white lead paste, which had crept into the lines about her eyes and mouth. She smiled then, briefly revealing a row of teeth the colour of mutton.

'Lady Penelope Devereux,' she said, running a pair of hooded brown eyes over her, squinting slightly as if her sight was poor. 'How old are you?'

'I am eighteen, Your Majesty.' Penelope could barely get the words out above a whisper.

'Not so young, then.' The Queen looked serious, as if she was trying to make some kind of calculation in her head. 'We hear you can sing. Is it true?'

'I am told I have a serviceable voice, Your Majesty.' She could feel the room lean in to listen, as if what she had to say was of great import.

'It wouldn't matter if you could or not, given your countenance,' was the Queen's reply. Then she leaned in close enough for Penelope to smell the musk on her – a memory sprang into her mind of her mother rubbing musk over her neck and on to the insides of her wrists on evenings when guests were coming to sup – 'You shall spread envy amongst our maids with that face, and if your voice is even half as lovely, all hell shall be let loose.' Though she cupped her hand close to Penelope's ear, it was only the pretence of discretion for the curious gathering of angelic maids could easily hear. The Queen seemed amused.

A little laugh fluttered up in Penelope; she liked the compliment, more than she should have, and enjoyed the Queen's little game that put her at the centre of something she didn't quite comprehend. Certainly the countess did not approve of that laugh.

The Queen then took both Penelope's hands in her own. 'I fancy I shall take you under my wing, Penelope Devereux. You seem to have a sense of humour and look at these glum girls about me.' She swept her arm to indicate the angel maids and it was true; when Penelope looked again, they seemed, despite their splendid clothes, as dull as Latin verbs. 'Besides, I don't doubt you need some proper mothering.'

Penelope noticed the Queen's hand wander up absently towards Leicester's, resting on the back of her chair, and how their fingers intertwined. It was such a very intimate and easy gesture, which to Penelope seemed an indication of ownership – ownership over her own mother's husband. She felt the flare of anger once more. 'I think you will thrive away from the countess's auspices. She takes pride in raising obedient girls but I can see you have spirit. It seems a shame to dim such brightness.' Penelope heard the countess inhale sharply – that spirit was the very thing she had spent the last years trying to knock out of her.

By 'mothering', Penelope asked herself, had the Queen meant that it was the countess lacking on that front or her own (unmentionable) mother?

'Sit,' the Queen said then, patting a stool beside her. 'Do you play cards?'

'I love to play,' she answered, adding, without thinking, 'It gives me a thrill to risk a wager,' which provoked a loud guffaw from the Queen.

Penelope watched her relatives (all but the countess, whose gaze remained stony) swapping looks of approval with each other, seeming satisfied with her performance. 'You have only one opportunity to create a first impression,' her mother had said. 'Be yourself, my sweet. The Queen may loathe me but I was in her favour long enough to know what it is she likes in a girl, and it is not the tedious piety the countess has tried her best to hammer into you. And, sweetness, once you are admitted, it will benefit us all. God knows I need eyes and ears amongst the Queen's women, and' – she had taken her daughter's hand then and placed a kiss on its back – 'you shall be those eyes and ears. I have no influence these days, no say even in the destinies of my own children.'

Just then Leicester had walked in. 'What witch's brew are you two beauties cooking up?'

'Penelope is to be received by the Queen tomorrow – but I presume you are aware of that.' Penelope thought she detected an edge of bitterness in those last words but she had been so long away from her mother it was difficult to tell. 'I was instructing her on correct behaviour.' Then she turned to Penelope. 'You will love it at court, my sweet. All life is there. You have the temperament to shine brightly in that firmament, and the beauty. But let me warn you: don't ever show weakness or fear – the Queen loathes a fainthearted. Isn't that right, dearest?'

'Indeed it is.' Leicester had stooped then to stroke Lettice's swollen belly and drop a lingering kiss on her lips. 'Has this little fellow been kicking you to distraction?'

'He has,' replied Lettice with a smile. 'He is every bit as active as his father.'

Leicester had taken her mother's hand then, weaving his fingers through hers in exactly the manner he held the Queen's hand now.

Penelope was well aware that the Queen had been angered beyond reason at her favourite's secret marriage to Lettice – the countess's servants had whispered of little else for months in the wake of it. But seeing that small yet intimate gesture replicated gave her a sense that the true situation was far beyond her comprehension. She wondered if she would be required to report back to Lettice on things concerning her stepfather and the Queen, if that's what she had meant by 'eyes and ears'.

The Queen asked for cards to be brought and chatted merrily, pointing people out and remarking on them – 'He is my chamberlain, he will see to your needs,' and 'That curmudgeon there is mother of the maids.' As she shuffled the pack Penelope scanned the chamber, seeking out Sidney, but there were so many young gallants, all of them garbed in a dazzling array of finery, it was impossible to identify which might be the one her father had promised was hers.

Reaching up to her frizz of copper hair, the Queen unhooked a vast pearl drop, set about with coloured stones, and, placing it upon the table, said, 'What is your wager, Penelope Devereux?'

Penelope's belly tightened into a knot, for she had nothing to offer save a lace handkerchief of her mother's that was tucked into her sleeve; but that was hardly a fair wager in the face of such a jewel. The Queen must have been aware the Devereux coffers were empty. Slowly she pulled the handkerchief out, letting it drift to the table beside the pearl.

'It is pretty; the lacework is fine.' The Queen picked it up, inspecting it minutely under a magnifying glass. 'You must know that an embroiderer's hand is as distinctive as a scribe's.'

Penelope did not know such a thing, not until then, when she realized the Queen meant she recognized the handkerchief to be her disgraced mother's work. 'I do, Your Majesty,' she replied, holding her breath.

The Queen raised a single painted brow. 'A fair wager, it is. Best of three.'

Penelope let out a silent exhalation and waited for the Queen to pick a card from those on the table and discard another. She did the same and they took it in turns until the Queen tapped the table calling, 'Vada,' indicating a show of hands, displaying a run of fives. Penelope could feel the room press about them, watching the newcomer undergoing her test. She had heard it said that the Queen was not fond of losing and was glad to find that her own skill was no match for her opponent, for she knew it would have been hard to curb her competitive spirit in the name of tact. So it was an authentic defeat when the Queen revealed a second winning hand and scooped up the wagers with a laugh, saying, 'We shall need to sharpen your game, my girl.'

'I fear Your Majesty's skills will always be sharp enough to scratch me.'

This provoked another burst of laughter from the Queen.

'You could do with a little adornment,' she said, taking the pearl and clipping it into Penelope's hair. 'I will send my tailor to the countess's rooms to fit you for a dress.'

'I do not know how to thank you enough, Your Majesty.' Penelope was imaging the fabrics she would choose, thinking of flying on gossamer wings, when an elderly man with a long face and a silver beard approached.

'Burghley,' the Queen said, 'do you know Lady Penelope Devereux?'

So *this* is Burghley, thought Penelope, looking at the man she knew to be the Queen's Chief High Treasurer, the most powerful man in the land, next to Leicester. He was also her brother's guardian.

'I have not yet had the pleasure,' he said, taking her hand briefly. 'But I know your brother well enough. He is happily settled up at Cambridge these days. You are close, I believe?'

'We are, My Lord. I long to be reunited with him.' She was thinking of how many months it had been since she had seen her beloved Essex.

'We shall invite him to court for the tilt,' said the Queen. 'Now where is your own boy, Burghley?'

'He is here, madam.' A boy moved forward. He must have been about Penelope's age but was smaller by far than her in stature, with one shoulder substantially higher than the other and a bulbous body set upon legs so thin it was a miracle they could hold him up. He reminded her, with his odd bird-boy shape, of a painting of the devil she once saw in a forbidden book and she felt a twinge of the old fear that image had planted in her.

Where the father's face was long, the boy's was longer to the brink of ugliness, with a great domed forehead and his hair sticking up above it like bristles on a hearth brush. Both men were clad head-to-toe in black, each with a stiff snowy ruff; but in spite of their plainness there was a luxury about them that didn't pass Penelope by.

The odd boy gawped her way and she, finding sympathy for one cursed with such a crooked form, smiled at him. He didn't return it, but continued gawping and blushing hotly. His father gave him a tap on the shoulder, which seemed to jolt him from his trance. He dropped sharply on to his knees before the Queen, fixing his eyes on her shoes.

'Getting on here at Whitehall, Cecil?' said the Queen. 'Your father showing you the ropes?' Turning to Penelope, she added, 'Cecil arrived at court just a few days ago, didn't you, boy?'

Cecil mumbled out a response, but Penelope was not listening for she had just spotted, beyond him, with a tightening about her heart, the face that was inscribed on her memory.

February 1581

Greenwich Palace

'Collect your things together, Penelope. You are to take Anne Vavasour's place in the maids' chamber.' The countess uttered the girl's name under her breath as if it might have been a sin to say it aloud.

'I am to be a maid of honour?' Penelope's breath caught in her throat at the idea of escaping the strict rule of the countess, imagining herself in her new clothes – a flower garden of embroidery – at the heart of things rather than hovering about the edges, as she had been those last three weeks at court.

'You are.' Her mouth was a tight line. 'But don't let it go to your head. And mind yourself, Penelope. The maids' chamber is not what it was in my day; now it is a hotbed of debauchery. Just look at what happened to that girl.' She shakes her head. 'That is the result when maids are allowed to gad about.'

Penelope had heard Anne Vavasour's cries all the way from the countess's chambers, terrible bellows echoing through the corridors of the palace. Her guardian was asleep beside her, mouth open, snoring, so she slipped from the bed and out of the room, following the dreadful sounds to their source. Her mind conjured images of all the kinds of horror she might find: a bludgeoning; a stabbing; shattered bones. But when she slid unseen into the maids' chamber it was a bewildering scene; Anne, barely visible at the centre of a circle of women, appeared to be in the throes of some kind of fit. Someone thrust a wad of wool into her mouth, muffling those hollow screams for a moment, but she grabbed it with a fist and flung it away. It landed at Penelope's feet.

'It's crowning,' said one of the women. Penelope couldn't understand why she sounded so calm, when Anne's life was clearly in danger. 'Push!'

Then something happened, Anne's cries died and the place was awash with gore. Penelope couldn't move, just stood horror-struck by the door.

'A boy,' said someone. Then came the unmistakable wail of a baby and Penelope understood. She later discovered that it was the married Earl of Oxford's infant that Anne had birthed there in the maids' chamber.

'That wicked girl is in the Tower with her baby, where she belongs, as is the father.' The countess's expression was puckered with disapproval.

'The Tower?' Just the name of the place struck fear into her, for everyone knew that people who entered the Tower often never left it.

'Let her disgrace be a lesson to you. She has sinned in the eyes of God, she will be damned for it in the next life, and in this life she has to suffer the Queen's wrath.' Penelope wondered which was worse, for she had soon learned the Queen could be truly terrifying. 'That girl is not the first. We all know what happened to Katherine Grey. She was committed to the Tower, when she found herself with child, and was never seen again, starved herself to death with the shame of it . . .' She seemed unable to stop listing the terrible fates of girls who had lost their virtue, was counting them off on her fingers '. . . I remember the Queen breaking Mary Shelton's finger with a hairbrush when she wed without permission, and as for your mother . . .'

Penelope wanted to ask about her mother and all those other women whose names were never to be mentioned in earshot of the Queen, wanted to understand the depths of despair that might have led Katherine Grey to starve herself to death. 'My mother –'

'Was a fool,' the countess interrupted. 'Imagine the idiocy

of marrying the Queen's favourite like that. She lost every-thing. She was the Queen's darling and she lost it all . . . lives in perpetual purgatory . . . no influence . . .'

Penelope wanted to make her stop, to shove a wad of wool into her guardian's mouth like the one Anne Vavasour had spat out.

'. . . So mind you behave, young lady. You will have to prove to the Queen that you are not your mother's daugh-ter in character. I am telling you this: if you incur the Queen's wrath you visit disaster on yourself and your family.'

Penelope managed to hold her tongue while the tirade continued as they made their way to the maids' rooms. All she wanted to think about was at last being freed from the harsh reign of her guardian, but all this talk was unsettling her, as if a single, small slip-up might end in disaster. The countess had reminded her often enough of her wayward streak that needed taming. It was all so perplexing, for she had felt liked all the more by the Queen for it. But then a wager at cards was not an unsanctioned marriage – or, God forbid, a little bastard on the way.

Before they entered, the countess pulled her back. 'Remember this: romantic intrigue is one thing but polit-ical intrigue is quite another. People will approach you as a means to achieve the Queen's ear. Take care to make no enemies but do not forget that no one is truly a friend either, when you are close to the Queen. It is only family you can be sure of.'

So it was with a sinking heart that Penelope entered the maids' chamber. A row of inquisitive faces confronted her and she wished her sister were by her side, lending courage. She missed Dorothy; they were barely a year apart, so alike people often mistook them for twins, and had rarely been separated until they were prised apart so Penelope could make her debut at court. She recognized

Peg Carey, a cousin she barely knew, who was running a pair of bright-bead eyes over her as if she were a mare at auction.

'I am Martha Howard,' said a small, sweet-faced girl. 'I shall make room for your things. Would you like to take the truckle tonight? It is so hot, squeezed into the tester.' She pointed towards the large bed that dominated the chamber.

'Yes, take the truckle,' said Moll Hastings, a young woman Penelope already knew as she was close kin to the countess. 'You will be comfortable there.'

Peg Carey was still looking at her without a word. One of the servants arrived with her trunk and the countess took her leave. Wanting to busy herself, she opened the lid and began to pull out a few things, placing her worn felt rabbit on the pillow of the tester.

'Aren't you a bit old for playthings?' said Peg.

'We are not all made of stone like you, Peg,' said Moll with a laugh. 'Here, Penelope, would you like help undoing your dress?'

Once they were all in their nightclothes and the servants had gone they huddled on the tester bed with the hangings pulled tight about them, passing round a small flask of what Moll called 'water of life', which she had acquired 'one way or another'. Penelope had never drunk such a thing, though didn't let on, and, taking a sip, felt it would strip the skin from her throat. It made her cough and the girls laughed but it didn't matter because her head was swimming, pushing any cares she might have had to the margins.

'I am so glad to be away from the countess.'

'I should think so,' said Martha with a gleam in her eye. 'She is quite the harridan. You will find things different with us.'

'Just don't get on the wrong side of the Queen,' advised Moll.

'There's not much chance of that. The Queen is *besotted* with her,' sneered Peg, talking as if Penelope were absent.

'Peg!' admonished Martha. 'Penelope does not court attention from the Queen; besides, Leicester is her stepfather, so it is no wonder she is shown a little favour.'

Penelope thought it best to remain silent on that point, supposing they were all aware of the circumstances of her disgraced mother. It occurred to her, in that moment, that the Queen's favour might be some kind of revenge on Lettice, to steal her daughter away. Well, I am not so green as to be unable to play at that game, she thought, taking another sip from the flask, feeling the warm fuzz spread through her head.

'So do we know what this Anjou is like?' she asked, to change the subject, talking of the Queen's suitor who would soon arrive in England to win her hand.

'He is half her age and so horribly disfigured by the smallpox no one else in the whole of Europe will have him,' Moll said, which Penelope doubted, given he was the King of France's brother. But they all laughed. Penelope was beginning to like Moll's humour. There was something appealingly wild about her and she was older than the rest, knew the ropes at court. Martha was naturally warm, and sour Peg she would win over; she was a cousin, after all. Penelope imagined herself as a butterfly emerging from its chrysalis, flying on jewel-bright wings into the world of the court with its myriad possibilities. She pushed the countess's unsettling catechism to the edges of her mind, allowing herself to be deliciously enmeshed in the gossip and intrigue.

'Tell me about Anne Vavasour and the Earl of Oxford,' she said.

'Poor Anne, that is the worst thing that can become of a maid. She is in the Tower, you know' – Martha said 'the Tower' as one might say 'purgatory'.

'With her *bastard*,' continued Peg. 'Anne Vavasour is too headstrong for her own good. I do not have much sympathy. Who gives themselves to a married man like that?'

'Wait till it happens to you,' laughed Moll.

'It will not happen to me. I would not be so stupid.'

'You never know. When love grabs you by the waist you are at its mercy.' Moll clasped Peg's midriff, tickling until she had squeezed a laugh out of her.

'Just think,' said Moll. '*I* might have wed Oxford. He was to pick between my sister and me. But another arrangement was made.'

'Lucky escape,' said Martha. 'Though Oxford *is* from an ancient lineage and his estates bring in near on four thousand a year.'

'Since when did you start totting up such things, Martha?' Moll said.

'That man is dangerous,' said Peg in a voice shot through with doom. 'He killed a boy once. And look what became of Anne.'

The countess's words crept back into Penelope's mind: *She has sinned in the eyes of God, she will be damned for it in the next life, and in this life she has to suffer the Queen's wrath.*

'*You* have a brother, don't you, Penelope?' asked Martha.

'I have two, and a sister, Dorothy. But my youngest brother, Wat, is still a child and even Robert is not yet sixteen.'

'So only a year less than me. When will he come to court?' asked Martha.

'When he has done with his studies at Cambridge, I suppose.' Penelope felt adrift, in that moment, far from her siblings.

'What does he look like? I mean, does he look like you?' Martha seemed to come alive at the idea of the young Earl of Essex.

'He is a little like me. But he is dark and already very tall with a fine figure.' It could have been a description of anyone.

She saw him so rarely she wondered if perhaps his skin had burst out in pimples or he had grown fat.

'Essex is the poorest earl in the country,' said Peg.

'Well if you are after riches then he won't be for you.' She held Peg Carey's cold gaze, aware of the importance of standing up to her. 'But I fancy he will want a bride a little more . . .' Penelope stopped then, deliberately, leaving her adversary hanging.

'A little more what?'

'Oh, I don't know,' said Penelope with a shrug.

'Thomas Howard,' interrupted Moll. 'He is newly bereaved. He must be seeking a wife.'

'But his titles were stripped and his father executed for treason,' said Peg. 'He was deemed too high a risk, due to that.'

'He may have them reinstated,' added Martha.

'Perhaps you'd like Cecil instead,' said Moll, turning on Peg. 'He is the son of the most influential man in England and you would never want for anything; their wealth is unimaginable.' She drew out the word 'unimaginable', articulating each syllable.

'That creature – he is small, crookbacked and not even knighted.' Peg's derision was carved into the downward curve of her mouth, robbing her of any prettiness. 'They say he was dropped by his wet nurse as a baby and that is why he is all misaligned.'

Penelope, watching Peg's shadowy hands describe Cecil's shape, felt a little sorry for the poor boy, remembering when she first met him and how he had blushed as if he'd never encountered a young woman in his life before and certainly never had one smile his way. 'He will need his wits if he is to survive at court,' she said.

'Indeed,' added Martha.

'Wits he has in abundance. I am told his father is grooming him for high office,' said Moll.

They continued, passing round the flask, comparing the

various merits of all the unmarried men at court, sizing them up for potential. It was inevitable they would eventually turn to Sidney.

'He is so very chivalrous,' said Martha, softening visibly.

'And impenetrable,' added Moll. 'You simply cannot tell what he is thinking.'

'He can be horribly brusque, but there *is* something about him,' said Peg.

'And he's a poet. Just think, he would write sonnets for you,' mused Martha.

'Mind you, the Queen is not pleased with him since he wrote that letter opposing her French marriage,' said Moll.

'She called him "uppity",' added Peg.

'I don't suppose she will be cross with him for long,' said Martha dreamily. 'Do you know him, Penelope?'

'I . . .' She was about to tell them of her betrothal – wondered why they didn't know it, given the way gossip spread through them like the plague – but thought better of it, fearing it might cause some jealousy amongst her new companions. 'I do not.' Perhaps, she considered, Leicester is waiting for royal permission before it is announced, but he had not even spoken of it to her. 'Well not really. I met him once briefly when I was twelve. I barely remember.' She didn't describe how that meeting had been etched indelibly into her mind and from it she had constructed a thousand imagined scenarios with Sidney at their heart. 'But I do know his connections come from his mother's side so he is not so very well funded.' If she sought to put them off by this she was misguided, for it merely instigated a protracted conversation about Sidney's great expectations.

'But he will come into his uncle Leicester's wealth, for Leicester has no issue.' This was Peg, talking breathlessly.

Penelope didn't mention that her mother was back at Wanstead, about to bear Leicester's child, which, if a boy, would knock Sidney out of the line of those great expectations like a felled skittle. She knew when it was best to keep such information close; she had learned that at her mother's breast.

'I fancy he would make a fine match for *someone*,' continued Peg, clearly hoping that the someone would be her.

'He never gives any of us a second look anyway,' said Martha pointedly.

'He is most aloof, it is true,' said Moll. 'But that is part of his appeal. Let us hope that the Queen's marriage plans come to fruition, or none of us will have permission to wed at all.' She turned to Penelope, adding, 'She cannot bear to have her maids make marriages when she remains single,' by way of an explanation. The humour had disappeared from Moll's voice and Penelope assumed there was more to what she said. Perhaps that was the reason Moll was in her middle twenties and still unwed, her petals dropping, still one of the Queen's maids when she should have been mistress of her own household and birthing babies. A sudden thought surprised Penelope, in spite of Moll's predicament, she wondered if she truly wanted to be married yet, just when her adventure at court was beginning.

'And she doesn't like anyone with even the smallest trickle of royal blood marrying anyone else with the same, for fear they will produce a boy to threaten her throne.' It was Martha who said that.

The atmosphere had dropped and the pleasant whirl in Penelope's mind was turning into the beginnings of a headache.

'Think of what happened to Katherine Grey,' said Moll, which provoked a leaden silence and Penelope was catapulted back to the countess's warning, feeling her unease flooding back.

'We can only hope the Queen's plans to wed the Frog come to something,' said Peg, her voice seething with hopelessness. 'I'm going to sleep.' She turned and folded herself into the covers.

Penelope slipped out of the tester bed and into the truckle, enjoying the smooth chill of the sheets after the hot fug within the bed-curtains, but she could not quite shake off her sense of disquiet.

February 1581

Deptford docks

Penelope sat next to Martha on the royal barge with the Queen's party. She buried her hands inside her gown to protect them from the chill February wind that smacked frozen drops of water from the oars on to her cheeks. Another barge, conveying the French delegation, drew up alongside.

'You have an admirer,' whispered Martha with a giggle, as one of the Frenchmen blew a kiss their way.

'I think it was for you,' Penelope laughed, meeting the man's eyes briefly. 'Those French are so indiscreet. I wonder if Anjou's as ugly as they say.'

'He will be here soon enough, if the gossip is true.'

'Do you think the Queen truly means to marry him?'

'I can't understand why she would. Surely at forty-seven' – Martha mouthed the digits rather than saying them aloud – 'she is too old to make an infant. Oh –' She gasped and turned away, covering her mouth with a hand. 'He made a rude gesture.'

Penelope glanced over at the Frenchman, who was licking his lips slowly with the point of his tongue, and turned away nonchalantly, saying, 'Ignore him, Martha,' with a snort of laughter. 'Perhaps the Queen wants a Frenchman in her bed.'

'The thought.' Martha shuddered.

'I suppose what she really wants from all this is to strengthen England's alliance with the French.'

'We are here!' Martha tugged excitedly at her sleeve.

Penelope looked up to see the great ship towering above – Drake's *Golden Hind* on which he travelled to the furthest reaches of the world, bringing back untold riches for the Queen. The countess had described Drake with a sneer as 'a self-made man. Not one of us. I don't understand why the Queen is so fond of him.' The maids, who were less concerned with such things, had discussed Drake at length, all agreeing it was a shame he wasn't more comely.

The Queen stood, taking Leicester's hand for balance whilst the maids scurried about straightening her skirts and smoothing her veil – fine layers of voile, which caught on the wind and blew up and out, almost lifting right off her head and taking her wig with it. The boat slid and bucked beneath Penelope's feet, causing her to grab the shoulder of one of the oarsmen to steady herself. She was the last of the maids to disembark, taking a proffered hand to help her out, not daring to take her eyes off her own feet for fear of falling into the muddy water below. Once on the pier she dropped the hand, looking up to see whose it was, finding him looking at her, his eyes holding her uncomfortably tight. His face, its sculpted planes printed with that faint constellation of scars, was so close to hers it made her heart jostle.

'Take care, My Lady. Stand still; you are caught.'

She turned, not fully understanding what he meant, to see that the fabric of her gown had hooked itself on to a nail on one of the mooring posts. She watched his hands unhook it; his fingers were slender and one was smudged with ink. 'I am sorry. It is torn.' He held it up so she could see the little rent.

'Oh,' she said, and for an instant he looked at her as if he could see beneath the surface, far into her secret depths. Her breath caught in her throat, and the moment had passed. 'It will mend.'

Then they stood in an awkward silence face to face; she unbearably aware of his maleness, the sense of his musculature where his doublet pulled tight across his chest, the way he held the hilt of the sword, which hung from his belt, as if primed to use it should the occasion arise. Her mind raced desperately, seeking something, anything, to say, wondering how it was that she failed to be intimidated by the Queen, whom everyone was scared of, and yet was lost for words in the face of this inscrutable man.

Looking up, Penelope noticed that the Queen was already on the deck of the ship with the rest of the maids and that a great throng was building up behind her on the gangplank.

'I am most grateful,' she said, unable to meet Sidney's eye, or even look to his face for more than the briefest of glances. He didn't smile, or try to put her at her ease. Indeed, she had the sense that he might, in some way, be relishing her discomfort.

His reply, when it came, was so quiet it was swallowed up by the wind and she felt too timid to ask him to repeat it, just nodded and slipped away. As she pushed past the throng she imagined what she might have said: something witty; something that would have made him remember her. But she had been struck dumb by the proximity of the man who had existed for years safely in the well of her imagination.

The deck was exposed to the wind and all the women were holding on to their wigs for fear they would blow into the water. The Queen was making a speech about Drake's great feats of adventure and how, thanks to him, the coffers of England were full. As the applause went up a sudden almighty cracking sound filled the air.

Penelope looked up, thinking the towering main mast had broken, afraid it would crash down on them. But the mast was where it should be, soaring skyward. A turmoil of screaming and shouting began and she turned to see the gangplank gone, splintered under the weight of the crowd. About a dozen souls had fallen into the mud, where they writhed about shouting for help. One or two were clinging on to the railings, hanging on with white-knuckled fists, waiting to be helped back on to the pier by the guards who had appeared suddenly from nowhere. Those who had escaped the fall stood about laughing at the less fortunate, all but Sidney, who threw a knotted rope down to help pull people on to the pier, heaving them up one after the other, not minding that his pale silk doublet was becoming smeared with black river mud.

Drake, seemingly mortified, was barking orders to his crew and a new gangplank was procured so the French delegation might board. All the while the Queen was watching on with a look of mild amusement until she called Drake over, inquiring about the extent of the damage, and Penelope saw a look of concern break momentarily over her face. But no one had been hurt, save for a few scrapes and bruises and some lost dignity.

As they were being seated, packed in like salted fish, a great fuss was made because the Queen's lace garter had gone astray. The French ambassador, Marchaumont, insisted upon reinstating it himself, which caused a flood of giggles to wash through the maids and a fair amount of quiet harrumphing from the older ladies, who whispered to each other about the loose morals of the French. The Queen herself seemed to relish the episode, laughing and quipping with Marchaumont and Leicester as they took their places at the table. Penelope watched her, unable to relate that lighthearted woman with the one who had treated all those girls so harshly for their romantic misdemeanours. She thought of poor Anne Vavasour in the Tower with her newborn, imagining her fear in that place. She watched as Leicester whispered something in the Queen's ear, they shared a smirk and she couldn't help but think of her mother at home alone, feeling anger or hatred, or something like it, rise up through her like nausea.

Penelope tried to concentrate on the festivities. She had never seen such a spread; Drake had laid on everything imaginable. Dish after dish was paraded up the deck and presented to the Queen by red-faced servants struggling under their weight. There was a pie filled with live doves, which flew panicked to perch on the mast, one anointing the shoulder of the French ambassador's man who merely laughed, brushing the offending mess away with a napkin only to smear his velvet cape further.

'*Mais c'est de la bonne chance, ça,*' he said lightly, but one side of his smile turned down. Penelope imagined he was thinking of his laundry bill and the fact that doubtless it was a new cape, fashioned for the occasion of meeting the English Queen.

A goose with a gilded head was presented and Drake was given the honour of carving, discovering in the carcass, with feigned surprise, a gold ducat that was presented to the Queen who tossed it, catching it with a cry of 'Heads or tails?' to her host.

'Heads,' Drake replied.

'Heads it is,' she affirmed. 'Will a knighthood suffice as your reward?'

'It will more than suffice, Your Majesty,' came his reply. Even Penelope knew it was a jest, for the whole occasion had been designed around Drake receiving such an honour, though it didn't stop the countess from commenting under her breath, 'I don't know, will cowherds be made earls next?'

Other splendid dishes followed and eventually, when the feasting was done, and a sugar replica of the *Golden Hind* had been trooped about to a fanfare of trumpets, Drake presented himself to the Queen to receive his knighthood. The Queen, still in effervescent humour, quipping about chopping his head off, handed the sword to Marchaumont that he might conduct the proceedings. This caused another remark of disapproval from the countess – something to do with the French gaining more privilege than they merited – and the woman beside her pointed out that it was likely done to annoy the Spaniards. Penelope was thinking about how she was supposed to be her mother's eyes and ears, wondering how she could achieve this when she barely understood the ins and outs of what was going on.

'What does she mean?' she whispered to Martha. 'Why would the Spaniards be annoyed?'

'I have no inkling. But more importantly' – Martha nudged her, leaning in closer and cupping her hand over her mouth – '*he* is watching you.'

'Who?'

'Who do you think? Sidney!'

Penelope responded with a shrug, affecting indifference, and wondered if Martha had noticed something, but of course Sidney inexplicably fascinated all the maids, so why should she be different? The idea of his eyes on her made her light-headed and it took all her willpower to resist looking back.

May 1581

Whitehall

It was the first truly warm day of the year and they were fil-
ing slowly out of the tiltyard stands with the crowd pressing
behind them. The Queen was up ahead, arm-in-arm with
Anjou – they looked like mother and son – surrounded by
the French retinue. Penelope's hands were full of the Queen's
possessions – her fan, her pomander, her drinking vessel and
a ferret on a gold chain, a gift from Anjou that was wriggling
and attempting to hide itself inside her sleeve. She was trying
to stay upright in the crush and turned to flash an angry look
at Peg, who had just trodden on her heel again. Martha shuffled along at her side, chatting breathlessly about the spectacle
they had just witnessed.

'Arundel in his crimson and gold cut quite a figure,' said
Martha. 'Do you not agree, Penelope? And Sidney . . .' she
added dreamily, letting her voice trail off as if there were no
words to express his allure.

'They were *all* quite magnificent,' Penelope replied, but
she was only truly thinking of Philip Sidney too, though she
would never admit it out loud. The other jousters, despite
their good looks and finery, had paled beside Sidney when he
cantered into the arena mounted on a quicksilver-grey gelding, his armour catching the sun, ostrich feathers bouncing,
his retinue gathered behind him like an army. The grey,
spooked by something, reared up, ears twisted back, whinnying in fear, causing a gasp to go up from the crowd. Sidney,
firm in his saddle, seemed entirely unperturbed and calmed
the beast with ease.

Penelope watched on in awe, hardly able to believe that
this was the man her father had chosen for her. But since the

banquet on the *Golden Hind* she had barely received a glance of acknowledgement from him and, though she was caught up in the excitement of court – the masques, the feasts, the hunting parties, all put on for the French visitors – her disappointment had begun to gather like dust in a corner. Just a smile her way would have sufficed but she felt invisible to him, as if she never was his intended, as if he had never stopped to carefully unhook her gown on the pier, had never looked at her that way.

'I think there is someone trying to gain your attention,' said Martha, indicating a page struggling through the crowd to get to them. 'He is one of your stepfather's boys, I think.'

'By the livery, it would seem so.'

'My Lord Leicester requires you in his rooms, My Lady,' he said as the three of them stopped, forcing the crowd to skirt around them.

'I have to do something with this creature.' Penelope indicated the ferret, which was now burrowing about her neck, tickling her. 'Perhaps you could take him to the stables and ask them to cage him somewhere.' She smiled the smile that usually had the effect of making young men do her bidding.

'My Lady, I would like nothing more than to render you service,' he said, returning the smile. 'But I am charged with taking a letter to the Queen.'

'Then you can help me by delivering these things to her.' She pressed the Queen's affairs on to him, glad of the opportunity to offload them. He then reached out his free hand to stroke the long back of the ferret but it turned, quick as a snake, and sank a pair of yellow fangs into his thumb. He snatched back his hand with a cry. 'Vicious little creature! Hardly an appropriate gift for Her Majesty.'

Penelope glanced at Martha, whose lips were pressed tightly together to stifle a laugh, taking a breath to suppress her own mirth. 'And what does Lord Leicester want from me?'

'I would not know such a thing.' He was gazing at Penelope as if she were Venus appearing from the sea.

'Do you think I believe that? You pages always have your ears to the wall; you must have overheard something.' She tucked the wriggling ferret into the crook of her arm and, pulling a handkerchief from her sleeve, took the boy's hand and gently began to bind the wound.

'I believe the matter is to do with your marriage arrangements, My Lady,' said the page at a whisper. 'But I am not entirely sure. And I must . . .'

Her heart jolted. 'Yes, go, you must take the Queen her letter.'

'But this.' He held up his bandaged digit.

'My handkerchief – it is yours. Go, go.' He looked astonished, as if she had given him her favour to wear.

Thinking of what he had said about her marriage caused a thrill to reverberate through her but it was abruptly muted by the thought of wedlock, even if it were to one so splendid as Sidney, for in her mind it meant leaving the whirl of court to run a household and birth infants – suffocated by domesticity before her life had even begun. She thought of the dour countess at home, each day a strict round of prayer, overseeing the kitchen staff, stitching shirts for the poor, quiet discussions about theology and begging forgiveness for each small misdemeanour, with her husband coming and going as he pleased. That life seemed airless, like being buried alive. She didn't want to think beyond tomorrow. She would have liked to enjoy the pleasures of court a while longer, to watch the young men compete to gain her hand for a dance, to sing and act her part in the masques, to play cards, to make-believe, enjoy the frivolity of it all; she wanted to be courted, not married – not yet. It had been drummed into her time and again by the countess that these pastimes were vanities and that the road to hell was paved with such false pleasures, but there was time enough to atone later. She had the sense of her youth and beauty as of only a moment's duration, like a mayfly, born in the morning, dust by dark, and could not bear the idea of wasting an instant of it.

'So soon,' Martha was saying, echoing her own thoughts. 'You have only just joined us and you will be leaving to wed.'

'These things can take some time.' She didn't really know if this was true.

'Who do you think they have in mind for you?'

'I cannot imagine.' She didn't want to say it was Sidney, not even to Martha, who hadn't an envious bone in her. They would all find out soon enough. The ferret had begun to struggle once more, so she grabbed it tightly by its collar, taking care to keep her fingers out of range, struck by a sudden affinity with the little creature who also had no say in its own destiny.

Once out of the stands the crowd dispersed and Penelope made her way to the stables. She saw Cecil, stopping a moment to watch his hunched figure scuttling, beetle-like, up the steps to the great chamber. As he passed a group of young men one of them broke away from his friends, hobbling along in jeering imitation of Cecil's awkward gait. The others laughed. Cecil kept moving, his eyes adhered to the flagstones, but they formed a circle around him, ribbing and joking. One of them snatched a book from his hand and threw it to another. It flew back and forth but Cecil refused to react so they eventually tired of their cruel game, leaving their quarry to continue up the steps. Penelope supposed Cecil must have been used to such handling to have responded in so sanguine a manner and wondered momentarily if her brother had treated him that way when they lived together as boys.

Just as Cecil reached the doors he bent to pick up his book, which had landed there, and as he stood he turned, locking his gaze on to Penelope with a look that seemed filled to the brim with contempt. She wished she'd had the courage to say something to those jeering fellows and wanted to explain herself, demonstrate her sympathy, but his look unsettled her and then he was gone, anyway, into the dark interior.

The stables were a hubbub of activity with all the grooms rushing about dealing with the horses from the tilt. She spotted Sidney's mount being led off at a distance, less impressive without its accoutrements, the artifice of the pageant dismantled. A pair of pages walked beside with Sidney's armour, in several pieces. One was larking about, had put the helmet on and was playing with the visor, flipping it open and shut. Penelope went into the nearest block. The smell in there was pungent and she trod carefully around the heaps of steaming dung and damp straw, feeling ill shod for such a place in her embroidered doeskin slippers.

She called over a lad heaving two buckets on a yoke and proffered the ferret, asking whom she might give it to. He seemed quite startled by her presence, putting his buckets down and hastily pulling his cap from his head with a trembling hand. He was just a boy really, not much more than twelve by the looks of his milky skin. She smiled, in an attempt to appear less intimidating, but it only caused him further embarrassment.

'Perhaps you could take me to your master,' she said.

He nodded, seeming quite lost for words until he managed to spit out, 'I will fetch him, My Lady,' before disappearing through an inner door and leaving her stranded. Beyond the door she could hear a prolonged and heated discussion about the ferret and whose responsibility such a thing might be. Just as she was considering attaching the creature to a hook by its leash and leaving it, Sidney himself appeared, seemingly from nowhere, dishevelled and wearing little more than his shirt, hose and boots.

'Goodness, My Lady,' he said, dipping in a small bow. 'What on earth are you doing in the stables with a ferret in your arms?'

It was her turn to be lost for words.

He seemed to remember suddenly then that he was not properly dressed. 'You must excuse me for . . . for, my lack of suitable attire.' He stumbled over his words a little, revealing a surprising awkwardness, which emboldened her. 'I've just removed my armour.'

'I have often wondered what a man wears beneath his armour,' Penelope said, immediately regretting it. She hadn't meant to be lewd. She had truly wondered what was worn beneath those rigid plates that looked so uncomfortable, whether men wore padding to prevent the sharp metal edges from rubbing at the joins.

Unlike some other young men she knew, who might have replied with something suggestive, Sidney just said, 'Let me take that animal.'

She handed over the ferret and, holding it at arm's length, he strode over to the inner door, flinging it open, bellowing, 'What is the meaning of this, leaving one of the Queen's maids alone in the stables, while you argue about the fate of this beast?'

Through the open door, Penelope saw the boy flinch as if preparing himself for a beating and she couldn't bear the thought of him being punished simply for happening upon her in the stables. Without thinking, she stepped forward and grabbed Sidney by the shoulder. He turned abruptly, his face filled with fury, as if surprised by an enemy.

She slowly retracted her hand. 'Leave the lad be. He was only trying to render me service. No slight has been done.'

The rage dropped from Sidney's face as suddenly as it came. 'So there is a kind heart packaged in such a wrapping,' he said quietly so only she could hear.

'What do you mean by that?'

'I have usually found that the more beauty on the outside, the less within.'

Penelope was not accustomed to being called kind-hearted,

even delivered in such an inverted manner. Beautiful was something she had become used to hearing, but beauty required nothing more than a coincidence of chance; she would rather people scratched beneath her surface. She looked at him then, and he seemed entirely unfamiliar, nothing like the person she had conjured up in her mind from their previous brief encounters. Yes, they looked alike but her invented Sidney spoke only in silly romantic banalities like a knight in a ballad, and this one – well, she didn't know quite what to make of his backhanded compliment, but somehow managed to find a little mettle to form a worthy retort. 'Do you speak from personal experience?' she replied. 'What is the state of *your* heart?'

'Well *I* am no beauty.' He ran a hand over his blemished cheek. There was that spot of ink on the inside of his index finger, a reminder that he was a poet. He then turned brusquely away, as if he didn't like talking about himself, and back to the men in the room beyond, who were standing to attention, awaiting his orders.

She wanted to contradict him but didn't and it occurred to her that most men with marred skin would grow a beard to conceal it and that by being clean-shaven he was making some kind of statement. 'The animal was a gift for the Queen. House it accordingly, if you please,' is what she said, managing to take control of the situation.

'Yes, do as the lady says,' Sidney added, handing over the animal and closing the door, leaning back against it. 'I seem to find myself rescuing you quite regularly. Was it not you caught up on a nail at Deptford?'

'I would hardly call it either "rescuing" or "regular".' She was realizing with a surge of indignation that he, this man who had inhabited her thoughts since before she could remember, didn't even know who she was. 'If our acquaintance is so intimate, then what is my name?'

He stared at her, wrong-footed, for what seemed an age,

his mouth twitching minutely, as if trying and failing to think of a response.

'The poet is lost for words.' She meant her voice to sound light and playful, but it carried her resentment quite plainly. Turning away from him to leave, she wondered how it could be possible, if her family were discussing her marriage, that no one had even so much as pointed her out to him. Did he not talk amongst the other men when they compared the various qualities of the Queen's maids? Had he not even noticed her sufficiently to wonder in passing who she was?

As she made for the exit she felt him grasp her upper arm, and pull her to him. 'I confess you are right, but please . . . tell it to me.'

She could smell him, had never thought of how he might smell – it was a pleasant scent, surprisingly clean and dry and summery, like hay.

'What is your name?' He sounded so forlorn, her upset seeped away and she allowed him to prevent her from leaving, wanting to prolong the moment, caught up in a tangle of contradictory feelings.

She thought of the horror on the countess's face, were she to discover them thus, so very close, close enough for her to feel his breath beside her ear, he improperly dressed and still clasping her arm as if he would never let go.

'You knew my father well.' Her voice was odd and husky, a stranger's voice. 'And we met once, years ago.'

'Where did we meet?' He held her with a look. 'I would remember.'

'You barely noticed me, were too busy swaggering beside your uncle Leicester. It was at Chartley.' She was remembering herself at her childhood home, aged merely twelve. He had been twenty-one back then, a man already, and she *still* felt unformed – even at eighteen, when she might have been wed with a couple of infants. She was green in the face of this man who had led diplomatic missions to foreign states and fought in skirmishes overseas; he had been a decade at court, he knew what life was. This was not the boy of her dreams with clichés on his lips.

'Lady Penelope? *You* are Penelope Devereux?' His face broke into a smile. 'The two girls dressed in red velvet at Chartley – see, I do remember.'

'Indeed you do not, for I was dressed in blue that day, it was my sister in red.'

'We were once betrothed.' He reached his free hand out to stroke her cheek, with a single finger barely making contact; then he snatched it back sharply, dropping her arm too and taking a step away, as if he had contravened some inner code of behaviour. Penelope was wondering what he meant by 'once', reminding herself that more often than not the couple were the last to know when a marriage deal had been struck. Perhaps he had not yet been told of it; after all, she only knew the marriage was being discussed by chance from her stepfather's page. 'I held the greatest respect for your father.'

'I must go,' she said, feeling marooned a pace away from him, suddenly aware that she was expected in her stepfather's rooms.

'I have to see you again,' he said.

'I can be found with the Queen's maids.'

'I mean alone.'

She didn't answer, just smiled and walked away across the stable yard towards the western entrance, knowing he would find out soon enough that they were to have a lifetime to be alone.

She took the steps two at a time and wove her way through the warren of corridors to her stepfather's rooms. One of Leicester's men stood on the landing outside, slouched against the panelling, straightening as he saw her approach. She paused to adjust her cap and smooth her skirts before nodding for him to open the door.

'Ah, Penelope!' It was Leicester who said this. He stood at the centre of the room like the sun in his gold brocade doublet; the others around him were like dim planets in his orbit.

She dipped in a curtsy, surveying the chamber. A scribe sat at the table, poring over some papers, and the page from earlier was playing fox and geese with another lad beside the window. The countess was there by the hearth with her husband, Huntingdon, both in stiff black, looking like the king and queen on a chessboard. Next to them stood a taciturn young man with large brown eyes, set so far apart as to give the appearance of each one working independently of the other. His mouth was full and slack and slightly open, as if his nose was blocked, but in spite of this he was rather beautiful, like a boy in an Italian painting she had once seen. He too was dressed in black, and she supposed, given the sheaf of papers he had tucked beneath his arm, he must have been a legal man.

'What kept you?' asked the countess. 'We have been waiting.'

Penelope made her excuses, feeling the curious eyes of the young lawyer appraising her. She had become quite accustomed to the scrutiny of male eyes and gave him a long, hostile stare.

'It is not us you should be excusing yourself to,' said Huntingdon. 'It is our guest, Lord Rich.'

She was momentarily confused. The lawyer stepped forward. His hand was clammy as he took hers and planted a damp kiss on its back. It was all she could do not to snatch it away and wipe it on her skirts. She could feel he was trembling and realized that a room containing two of England's most powerful earls could be an intimidating place for one not accustomed to such company. She smiled to put him at his ease and his mouth twitched briefly in return. For an instant his eyes lit up, their dark reaches momentarily gilded. But there was something about Lord Rich, a gelatinous air, which made her think of frogspawn or raw egg. Rich withdrew back to his place and Penelope noticed him meet Leicester's eye with a nod.

'Well, that is settled, then,' stated her stepfather. 'We were thinking early November before the Accession Day festivities.'

'And the Queen, My Lord?' This was Rich piping up. Penelope was looking from one to the other in bewilderment, wondering when this man Rich would leave and they could discuss her wedding to Sidney.

'You have Her Majesty's consent, Rich. She is disappointed to lose a favourite maid so soon but . . .' He let his words peter out.

Rich's mouth stretched into a moist grin.

Penelope swallowed, not caring about the look of disgust she wore, as the reality of the situation settled on her shoulders like a lead cloak. 'Him . . . you want me to marry *him*?' She pointed at Rich. 'But I am betrothed to Sidney.'

'Mind your manners, girl,' warned Huntingdon, his right arm twitching as if tempted to beat her.

'Sidney – what *are* you thinking of?' said the countess. 'That arrangement is long lapsed. Besides, he no longer has the assets, does he, Brother?' She turned to Leicester. 'Not since you spawned a rightful heir and shunted him out of the running.'

Penelope felt a clog of anger in her throat as she thought of the infant son her mother had birthed only weeks before, understanding that it was this baby, her little half-brother fondly dubbed the Noble Imp, who had got between Sidney and his great expectations – who had got between Sidney and her. The message was entirely clear; Sidney was not sufficiently endowed to wed the impoverished daughter of an earl whose bloodlines traced directly back to the third Edward.

'Rich, how apt a name he has.' She flung a hand in Rich's direction without considering her rudeness.

The countess gasped. 'Apologize, Penelope!'

'You must understand, my dear,' said Leicester, 'that we, your family, have your best interests at heart.'

Penelope was on the brink of spitting out a riposte, pointing out that 'family' was a tenuous term, for she was not related to Leicester by blood, but thought better of it.

Rich had shrunk back behind Huntingdon and was clenching and unclenching his jaw.

'I have seen many a maid rail at the choice of husband made for her and they all assent eventually,' continued Leicester. But Penelope wasn't listening, all she could think of was Sidney and the fact that she was no better off than that blasted ferret.

'I refuse,' she said. 'I have the right.'

'My dear.' It was Leicester's smooth voice once more, but she could see in the way his hands were tightly balled into fists that he was concealing a mighty rage for the sake of politeness. 'I think you will find yourself persuaded. Rich' – he beckoned the young man over – 'why don't you describe something of your estates to Lady Penelope?' Rich inched out from behind Huntingdon and Penelope found, in spite of herself, a little sympathy for the fellow. After all, he was as much a pawn in all this as she. 'Show her that picture you have of Leighs. It is such a charming house and Wanstead lies on its route. It is in Essex, Penelope dear.' His tone smacked of insincerity. 'You shall be able to visit your mother and me when travelling to and from London. You have the priory at Smithfield in town, do you not, Rich?'

'I do, My Lord.' Rich was shuffling through his papers and eventually produced a drawing of a house, which he thrust beneath her nose. It was much like any other large country house as far as she could tell.

'It is a fine place,' said Leicester.

'And with space to entertain Her Majesty, should she choose to grace us with a visit,' said Rich, looking at Leicester as if he had posed a question.

'And I'm sure she shall.' Leicester slapped him on the back, a friendly gesture, but even Penelope, through her anger, could see Leicester's distaste for the young man.

It was clear to her what the bargain was. Rich was in need of good blood, influence and the Queen's favour, which she had in abundance; and she was to be the siphon through which his funds would pour into her impoverished family. Sidney's voice echoed in her ears – 'I have to see you . . . alone' – and a band tightened about her temples. She turned to the countess, whose mouth was pursed tight, and then to Huntingdon. Neither of them would look at her.

'I must take my leave,' declared Rich, who was clearly itching to go. 'I shall tell Mother of the good news.' He reached out for Penelope's hand but she didn't offer it, remembering with a shiver of revulsion the previous damp kiss, and simply gave him a cursory nod.

The instant Rich was out of the door the countess turned on Penelope. 'How could you have shown such insolence? I am ashamed that you are a product of my household . . . marriage is a sacrament of the Lord . . . it is not for you to pick and choose . . . I thought I'd bred obedience into you . . . you are your mother's daughter, that is clear as day –'

'Enough!' barked her husband, raising that twitching arm.

The countess looked chastened.

'Kindly still your tongue, Sister,' said Leicester in a menacing growl. 'That is my wife you impugn.'

The countess mumbled a cowed apology. Penelope found some satisfaction in seeing her guardian at the sharp end of Leicester's wrath, but inwardly admonished herself; for it was surely a sin to delight in another's comeuppance, even one who had treated her so strictly.

Placing a hand on Penelope's shoulder, digging his fingers in, Leicester said, 'The Queen has sanctioned this match and I would counsel you not to risk her disapproval by causing a fuss about it. You must know by now what happens to those who lose her favour.' His look was hostile and an image of Anne Vavasour in the Tower, grey with fear, crept into her mind.

She cleared her throat. 'I am required to dress the Queen for supper,' she said, and dropped into an exaggerated curtsy. 'May I be excused?'

'You may,' said Leicester and she left.

They seemed to have taken her failure to argue further as acquiescence, but as she walked towards the Queen's rooms her resistance burgeoned. It was not natural for a couple to be forced together where there was not even a sliver of attraction. She would not wed Rich and that was that.

Leicester House/Smithfield

The various pieces of Penelope's wedding dress were spread about the chamber. Dorothy and Jeanne were trying to lift her spirits with an irritating chirpiness as they laced her tightly into the embroidered bodice and helped her into the cumbersome layers: hoops, bum-roll, underskirt, overskirt, sleeves.

'I am so very happy to be coming with you,' said Jeanne. Penelope squeezed out a smile. She too was glad that Jeanne, a childhood companion, would be in her household; it was the sole joy to come out of her marriage, as far as she could see.

'Who will be riding beside your litter?' Dorothy asked.

'I don't know. All our Knollys uncles, I suppose . . . and Leicester. He is very pleased with himself for replenishing the Devereux coffers with my wedding.' She didn't quite manage to hide the resentment in her voice.

'Here,' Dorothy indicated for Penelope to hold her laces with a finger while she tightened a knot. 'And Sidney. Will he be there? I hope so.'

'As do I. I have never seen him,' said Jeanne, holding her small hands out, palms up, as if it were an inexplicable loss.

'I don't know.' Penelope's reply was curt. She wished they would stop talking about him, but how were they to know of her feelings for Sidney? It was a secret kept between the two of them, expressed in snatched moments: that first encounter in the stables at Whitehall; hurried exchanges beneath the weeping willow on the river at Richmond; hands held in a dance on a feast day; fingers brushing together as they passed each other in the long gallery at Hampton Court. She was catapulted back to the dairy at Greenwich, the door closing, his hands on her waist, the cool damp wall against her back. Their first kiss, witnessed by the silent wheels of cheese and the hanging bags of curd, which occasionally released a wet plink, the only sound other than their urgent breath. The memory made her insides somersault.

Once out hunting at Nonsuch when her horse was lame, Leicester had sent Sidney to her aid. She'd hoped it would mean a half-hour alone but Peg Carey was sent to join them, as chaperone probably, and couldn't disguise her sour face on seeing Penelope riding pillion with Sidney, pressed tightly up against him.

'I cannot bear to see those poor animals die,' Penelope had said of the hunt.

'You are too soft,' Peg retorted. 'Do you not think she is too soft, Sidney?'

'When I was in Paris I saw things that gave me an understanding of savagery,' he said. 'People slaughtered in their hundreds. If you had seen the look of fervour in the killers' eyes, you would abhor brutality too.' His eyes met Penelope's for the briefest moment and she had the overwhelming sense of being understood.

'The massacre on St Bartholomew's?' she asked. He nodded. 'A Huguenot grew up in our household.' She was talking of Jeanne. 'She lost both her parents on that night. Saw the butchery herself. She was just a child. The sight of blood makes her faint clean away – even now. She told me things . . .'

'There are many such stories.' Sidney's voice was grave, as if his experience had left an ineradicable mark of gloom on him.

'But animals are different. We kill them to survive – they are God's gift to us,' said Peg. 'You like venison, don't you, Penelope?'

'That's as may be, but I still feel a sadness for the creatures when they die.'

'Soft, you see.'

'When I shot my first hart, I cried with grief when I saw the despair in its eyes.'

'What kind of ninny weeps for a dead animal?' Peg said.

'Perhaps it shows character to feel tenderness for the lower orders of creation. They feel fear, do they not, and pain?' Sidney was defending her but she sensed there was more to it than that. It was a rare shared affinity. 'You know what the French King enjoys for sport?' he said, looking directly at Peg. 'He takes pleasure in watching live cats tied into a sack with a fox and suspended over a fire. Little fluffy kittens, like the ones I have seen you playing with in the privy chamber. He enjoys their terror, savours the moment the flames bring the bag down, when they screech as they burn.'

'How could you describe such a scene?' cried Peg. 'That is disgusting.'

'It *is* disgusting,' said Sidney. 'Degrading and disgusting and inhumane. And there is a little of that in the excitement of the hunt. If you cannot see that then you are –'

'Then I am what?' interrupted Peg, bristling with indignation.

'Then you are heartless,' Penelope said. Sidney had squeezed her hand, unseen.

'A penny for your thoughts,' Jeanne said, through a mouthful of pins.

'I dread this wedding,' Penelope confessed.

'Why did you not refuse?' asked Dorothy, positioning her sister's necklace and standing back to survey her work.

'You know how it is.'

'But Mother – couldn't she have . . .' She didn't finish, remembering, Penelope supposed, that their mother had less say than anyone in such matters.

Penelope *had* gone to her, begged her to do something, try

to influence Leicester, try to dissuade Rich. 'But I love another,' she had pleaded.

Lettice smiled. 'Of course you do, that is the way of the world and it will pass. Besides, love and marriage are not always happy bedfellows. I did not think I could care for your father when I married him. I thought I loved another too, but affection developed between us. Children create a common bond. You will grow fond of Rich, I am sure, my sweet.'

'But *you* love Leicester.'

'And look how low that love has brought me. I am ostracized for it and *she* keeps my husband in her thrall, offering preferment, his debts paid off, honours bestowed, as long as he remains by *her* side and not mine.'

'I hate her. I hate the Queen.' Her mother gasped and Penelope slapped a hand over her mouth, but the words could not be unsaid.

'It is not the Queen who makes you wed Rich.'

'No, but it is she who has tried to destroy *you*, and she who destroyed Father; you said so yourself: "He would still be alive if she had properly funded his campaign in that godforsaken isle." That is what you said.' Penelope had never fully understood how her father's death came about. There were so many stories, the servants stifling their whispers as she entered a room. All she knew was he left to lead the army in Ireland – a great honour, it was called, that would bring him glory – and he never returned. 'The Queen is a wicked woman and if it wasn't for her I wouldn't be marrying a man like Rich either.' Lettice opened her arms and Penelope fell into her embrace, breathing in her scent, closing her eyes tight as she tried to imagine herself back into the safety of childhood, far away from the woman she had become – eighteen, and on the brink of wedlock.

'Whatever thoughts you hold in your heart,' whispered Lettice, 'you must never say such things about the Queen, even in private. You never know who may be listening. Mark my words. Think of the family, it will serve us *all* if you keep your favour with the Queen. Do that and you may well find yourself in a position one day to secure the future of the Devereuxs. Keep your wits about you, Penelope, for the Queen will not always be there and we must pin our hopes on to her successor or we will not survive.'

'But who will succeed her?'

'Ah, that is the question. Stay close and keep your influence; all will become clear at some point.' Penelope felt like an infant thrust into a grown-up world for which she was unprepared – the survival of her family, how could *she* possibly shoulder that? Lettice added, 'Your brother and sister will join you at court before long but you are the oldest. It is your job to pave the way. I don't doubt you will become a formidable force.' She paused and a spark of something resembling anger lit in her face. 'And one day you may find a way to have –'

Her mother never finished for the nurse arrived with the baby. 'Look, your new brother!' Lettice took her son from the woman – 'My noble little imp' – holding his round face up to hers and cooing in response to his wet gurgles.

Penelope was left wondering what her mother had been about to say. One day you may find a way to have what – Peace? Power? *Revenge?*

Lettice then thrust the boy into Penelope's arms. Penelope wanted to hate him, this child who had stolen the Leicester inheritance from Sidney, but he looked at her with an irresistible gummy smile and she couldn't stop herself from stroking a smooth fat cheek and lifting the little cotton cap to kiss the milk-scented down on his head.

'You will have one of these soon,' her mother said. 'They will grow up together.' That thought skewered into her, for her children would be Rich's.

'You are miles away,' said Dorothy, breaking her reverie.

'I was thinking of babies. I saw our half-brother the other

day. He is almost good enough to eat.' She smiled, trying to push that unsettling conversation with her mother to the back of her mind.

'Turn around so I can comb your hair,' said Jeanne, smoothing a hand over her head. 'Like woven gold.'

Penelope's heart started; those were the very words Sidney had used once, in the gardens at Richmond. They had lagged behind a walking party and stopped by the river where the rushes grew high, affording enough privacy for a stolen moment together. They had come upon a pool with a lone narcissus growing beside it, upright and proud, its face the colour of egg yolk. It reminded her of that story from Ovid and they talked of those myths, of Echo, Callisto, Icarus, and the cruelty of those pagan gods. Then he had unpinned her hair, letting it fall about her shoulders, buried his face in it and whispered, 'Even Venus could not have had woven gold locks such as these.'

'I am to wed Lord Rich,' she told him, wishing she could take the words back, for she had ruined a perfect moment. What she wanted was for him to tell her he would not allow it, that he would petition the Queen, that he wanted her for himself. She imagined telling him that his loss of the Leicester inheritance was an irrelevance; what did she care for wealth?

But his reply was, 'I know it. Let's not talk of that.'

She felt as if he had slapped her, and as time wore on the realization dawned that he had only been playing, as grown men do with gullible girls.

Thank God I didn't give myself to him, she thought as Dorothy attached her ruff to her collar, a great stiff thing that scratched against her neck, and then tightened her laces a little more. But a part of her wished she *had* given herself, and damn the consequences, because the idea of Rich being the one to claim her maidenhead was too much to bear.

Sadness had crept up on her over the following weeks as Sidney grew ever more distant, seeming to avoid her, spending more time away from court. He'd look away as others jostled to partner her in dances, it was no longer his hand proffered to help her out of the royal barge, and when she hung back while out riding or hawking it was always another who would edge her way for idle conversation – he had slipped to the far reaches of her world. Her heart had opened too fast and it was made tender like a muscle unused to action. But she was driven by hope and invented ever more convoluted explanations for his behaviour, until one day he sought her out. It was high summer in the orchard at Nonsuch and the trees were so burdened by fruit their branches drooped to skim the tops of the tall grasses. He had taken her by the hand and led her there without a word.

He picked a peach for her. Its sweetness invaded her senses, a gluey trickle running down her wrist, which she caught with her tongue. He had got down on his knee and taken her hand, as if he were a storybook knight about to propose.

'I led you on. I shouldn't have wooed you. It was wrong, since I knew we could never wed. And for that I am deeply sorry.' He couldn't look her in the eye. 'I hope you can forgive me.'

She had smiled as if her life depended on it, and chirruped, 'No matter,' then turned before he could notice the hurt smear her face. All the poetry in the world cannot prepare a person for their first broken heart, the relentless yearning, the inner devastation, the utter absence of joy and hope. November bore down on her and she enclosed her heart in a membrane, like a baby born in the caul, so it was inaccessible, even to her.

'Is it true,' asked Jeanne as she pinned a long string of pearls to Penelope's stomacher, 'that you . . .' She hesitated.

'That I what?' asked Penelope.

'That you are . . .'

'Spit it out,' said Dorothy.

'I heard talk' – she had partially covered her mouth and was speaking through her fingers – 'that your mother's mother is half-sister to the Queen rather than just her cousin. Does that mean the eighth Henry is your great-grandfather?'

Penelope swapped a look with her sister. She was wondering if that was why the Queen had drawn her into the fold so readily – it hadn't occurred to her before. 'It *is* said we have Tudor blood, but we are not supposed to talk about it.'

'But many *do* speak of it,' said Jeanne. 'And your mother resembles the Queen greatly.'

'I'm sure Rich has heard it too,' huffed Dorothy. 'He will like the advantage it brings him.'

'It didn't bring much advantage to Mother,' said Penelope. It had dawned on her then that Lettice's marriage to the Queen's favourite was twice the betrayal, given her proximity of kinship, and with that came the realization that such a proximity can be more curse than blessing. But she didn't want to think about that, for it made her feel trapped in a web woven from her illustrious lineage.

'What is Rich like?' asked Dorothy.

'I don't know. I have only met him once or twice; he barely spoke. If *you* stood beside him at the altar, I swear he wouldn't tell the difference.' Penelope clapped her sister on the back and expelled a sour laugh.

'But you two are so alike, even *I* sometimes cannot tell you apart from behind,' said Jeanne.

For an instant Penelope was filled with an intense sense of the separation to come, to think that her sister would return to the Huntingdons so far away, and that nothing would ever be as it was.

'All I know is that he has more money than he can spend,'

she said, beginning to laugh, with the others joining in. 'I will be the rich Lady Rich.' Dorothy snorted at this, and they were all subsumed by guffaws. 'With estates all over Essex.' Penelope stood on the bed as if delivering a speech in a masque. 'And a townhouse in Smithfield, most convenient for burnings, if we are lucky enough to have any. My gardens will be filled with exotic fruits so rare they will need a battalion of men to guard them from thieves, there will be fountains of wine springing from the mouths of marble cupids and there will be goldfish in my ponds made of real gold.'

'But how will they float?' Jeanne was sputtering helplessly. 'And you shall have parties and banquets and dancing and music.' They collapsed back on to the bed, helpless.

'I fear I will have none of that.' Penelope's laughter dropped away. 'For Rich does not approve of the "sinful pleasures". He is a Puritan.'

'But you love music and poetry. You sing like an angel. How will you bear it?'

'I don't know.'

Dorothy's face looked stricken, as if someone had died. 'Will you have to live at his house in Essex?'

'Not straight away. The Queen has asked that I remain at court for the meantime. And Jeanne will be with me there.' She reached out her fingers to touch Jeanne's sleeve.

They were interrupted by a knock and her brother's voice calling out: 'Are you dressed, Sis? May I enter?'

'Robin,' she cried, rushing to open the door, finding her brother, whom she hadn't seen for the best part of a year, smiling from beneath a tangle of inky curls, his right cheek furled into a dimple. He opened his arms and they embraced tightly. 'I am glad you are here – so glad. And look.' She stood back to appraise him. 'Your clothes, they are so fine.' She fingered the plum-coloured velvet of his doublet, which was slashed to reveal some kind of golden fabric beneath.

'It was a gift from your intended. A whole outfit, down to the silk stockings.'

'From Rich? Have you met him?'

'He came up to Cambridge to take me out. We visited his tailor, took a boat out on the river, dined at an inn.'

'How did you find him?' she asked, puzzled as to why Rich would be courting favour with her brother, reminding herself that of course Essex was the head of the family. It was the liaison with the Devereux tribe and their lofty connections that were important to Rich.

'Generous.'

'He is currying your approval already.' She pinched her brother's cheek. 'Barely sixteen and already wielding influence.' Beneath his fine clothes he still carried the gawkiness of youth and his face was smooth and soft-angled, though there was a faint downy shadow on his upper lip.

'He is a good enough fellow. A little sober, but good enough.'

'You know him better than I.' She could not hide her bitterness.

'But Sis, remember this: *you* come first.' He stood straight, separating his legs like a guard, and his mouth twisted into a snarl. 'If he ever wrongs you, I shall revenge you personally.' His boyishness seemed to have leaked away. 'I said as much to him, told him my allegiance depended on his good care of you.'

She felt a welling of love for her brother and a sense that she was part of something strong and meaningful, something that couldn't be broken. Stepping forward, she kissed him softly on the cheek and, holding out a hand for Dorothy to take, said, 'The Devereuxs are tighter than the petals of a new bud and will never be prised apart.'

'My beautiful sisters,' said Essex. 'How lucky I am.'

'I wish Wat were here too, though. The four of us have not been all together since Father died,' said Dorothy, turning Penelope's thoughts to her youngest brother.

'He is coming with Mother,' said Essex.

'So we *shall* be all together,' said Dorothy gleefully.

'But I will be dragged away for my wedding night. How will I bear it?'

'Drink lots of wine and you will be so light-headed you will hardly know anything,' said Dorothy, which made them all laugh, but Penelope's heart remained heavy.

She had done as her sister suggested and by the time she found herself alone with her new husband she was so drunk and exhausted she could hardly stand without having to hold on to something. There had been toasts at the wedding supper, cups raised for England, for the Queen, for the newly-weds, for the boys they would produce. It went on and on, and for each toast Penelope downed an entire cupful of Rich's imported French wine. Then instead of dancing there had been prayers of thanks.

'I can see that you are going to need a firm hand,' Rich had said, opening the door to the bedchamber. He had her by the fingers, holding so tight that her ring dug painfully into her.

'You are hurting me,' she said.

'I'll hurt you properly if you are not careful.'

'What do you mean?' Penelope was trying to make sense of his mood through the swirl in her head.

'You humiliated me in public, at our wedding no less, before both our families. You are my wife now and you will never humiliate me again. Is that understood?' He gripped his fist more tightly about her fingers until she feared he might break them but she refused to give him the satisfaction of even so much as a wince.

'I see,' she responded, reliving the ceremony through the fog of wine.

As she arrived, she had stumbled on her gown and knocked her elbow so hard on the font that it brought tears to her eyes. They were all there, wearing that solemn, wistful look people wear at weddings, watching as she walked slowly in her dress that was stiff as a coffin, barely able to move her head for fear her ruff would decapitate her. Her breath caught in her throat on seeing the group of Sidneys, Philip with them. She felt suddenly faint and feared to lose her footing once more, having to grip tightly to Jeanne for support. But then she saw she was mistaken, it was not Philip, but his younger brother, Robert. She told herself she was glad of his absence, that she couldn't have borne to have him there, but truly she was bereft. She forced herself to remember his treatment of her, how he had led her on, how he had failed her, but she couldn't find a way to hate him.

Rich watched her approach impassively, a slight sneer fixed into the set of his mouth as if there was something about her he found distasteful; but perhaps he was feeling belittled by the occasion, faced by his wife-to-be and her ranks of illustrious relations, all their veins gushing with blue blood. Did he think they all believed him beneath them (which, in truth, most did)? She arrived at his side, attempting a smile, but her mouth was too dry to make it convincing. He swallowed, in apprehension, she thought, and she felt a gush of sympathy for him, but not enough to make her feel better.

The chaplain began the service. She stood, then knelt, then stood again, like a puppet, not listening. She felt as if she was at her own funeral and had a vision of all eternity spent with the stern young man at her side. A tremor of panic passed through her as if she had woken to discover herself trapped alive in a tomb.

'Wilt thou have this man . . .'

The words slipped out of her mouth before she could

stop them. 'I cannot.' She stepped away, back towards her mother, but then saw her stony expression and Leicester's, dark with rage, and beside him the Huntingdons, the earl open-mouthed in horror, the countess clasping the sides of her head with her hands. Her siblings, all three, were round-eyed. The guests seated further back had begun to shuffle and whisper, as they understood what was happening. She dropped on her knees before Leicester and her mother.

'I beg you, do not make me . . .' She found courage swelling in her and she got to her feet, announcing, 'I exercise my right to refuse. I have that right, surely?' She looked out at the ranks of relatives; their faces were screwed up with disapproval, or shock, or anger, she couldn't tell which.

'Am I to understand that you refuse this man's hand?' It was the chaplain speaking. He couldn't seem to hide the edge of impatience from his tone, as if she were a tiresome child who had wasted his afternoon.

'I do refuse.'

It was Leicester who stood and guided her firmly back to Rich's side, growling in her ear, 'For God's sake, girl, behave. I don't know what makes you think you have a choice.'

She didn't dare look at Rich beside her. She was reminded of the young bullocks being herded to the knackers, oblivious until they smelled the fear in the air, which set their eyes a-swivel; much as they shifted and shook their heads they couldn't avoid their fate and neither could she, for where could she have gone? Her family would not have wanted her; she would have been cast out of court.

'I am ready now,' she said to the chaplain. 'I just needed a moment's reflection. Marriage is not to be taken lightly.'

He looked at her with a slight nod. She felt the relatives relax at her back. He cleared his throat before repeating the vows.

When she opened her mouth to speak no voice came out and then when it came it was only a whisper, but the chaplain was satisfied. She had frozen over like a winter pond, where life lurks beneath but it cannot be reached. She felt the ring scrape over her knuckle. It felt heavy, so heavy she feared she might never be able to lift her arm again. Only then did she look at Rich, her husband. His was not the face of a contented bridegroom. No, he looked like a man gravely wronged, his cheeks red with suppressed rage.

'Not "I see"!' barked Rich now, pushing her over the threshold of the bedchamber. 'That is no way to speak to your husband. This spirit of yours will have to be curbed.' He had a hand up to her throat and his face close up to hers. '"I am deeply sorry, My Lord." Say it!'

She was tempted to spit in his face but feared if she did he might strike her.

'Say it!' he repeated.

She formed an exaggerated smile. 'I am deeply sorry, My Lord,' she said, as if she was a player impressing the irony of a scene on an audience to tease a laugh out of them.

He shoved her on to the bed, still gripping her throat. 'You think you are better than me, your family, all that noble blood, but you are mine now, your noble blood is mine and you will be obedient. I can hardly bear to look at you. Think you are the jewel of the Queen's maids? The beauty of the bunch? Well, you disgust me.'

'If I am disgusting then you have made me so,' she replied, looking straight at him, refusing to be cowed, the drink emboldening her. 'You can have my body, but you will never have me.'

'*Your body* . . .' He spat that out with a look of revulsion. 'You are a daughter of Eve!' He unlaced himself with one hand while holding her wrists tight – too tight – with the other. She felt her bones might break but she would never have acknowledged that pain with a cry, nor given him the satisfaction of begging him to stop. Eyes squeezed shut, he muttered out a psalm beneath his breath. 'Praise ye the Lord. Blessed is the man that feareth the Lord, that delighteth greatly in his commandments. His seed shall be mighty upon earth: the generation of the righteous shall be blessed . . .' And without opening his eyes he lifted the stiff skirts of her wedding dress.

She stared at the bed hangings, a bower of embroidered flowers and birds, trying to imagine she was there in that stitched garden amongst the silken vegetation, basking in the warmth of an appliquéd sun. But however hard she tried to escape into her imagination she remained in that bedchamber, in her new Smithfield townhouse, with her new husband, the thought repeating itself like a fugue in her head: *for all eternity*, and waiting for the pain.

'It might hurt a little,' her mother had warned her. 'And do not be alarmed by the size of his member, for that is how it is supposed to be. Just allow him to do what he must.' Penelope had long wondered what she meant by 'what he must' and, lying there with her new husband poking about her nether regions and grunting like a hog, she was unsure what *she* was expected to do, glad to be giddy with wine and glad, too, that Rich had finally loosened his grip on her bruised wrists.

He took her hand and pressed it on to his thing. It was not as she had imagined; it had the waxy feel of an uncooked cut of meat. He gripped, frotting back and forth right up by her privy parts. In her mind she replaced Rich with Sidney, scrunching her eyes tight shut and using the full force of her imagination to conjure up that other man with his cut-grass smell and pale-as-water eyes. He was whispering in her ear. A hot thrill began to rise up through her but a part of her wondered if it was not a grave sin to think of another on your wedding night. Her mother had not counselled her on such a thing. The feeling abated.

Rich was murmuring that psalm again, repeating it over and over, and she tried to put her mind to God but Sidney would not leave her head. Then, with a sudden groan, Rich rolled away from her, sat up, laced himself back into his clothes and left without a word.

November 1581

Smithfield / Whitehall

She had not seen Rich the following morning until the horses had been made ready for her departure. She waited on the threshold of the Smithfield house, her head thick from the previous evening's excesses, wondering if she should send Jeanne to find him. But then he appeared.

'You look tired,' he said, as if it was an accusation.

'I slept like a baby, thank you,' she lied.

'Go and curry favour on my part with the Queen.' He offered a hand to help her into the waiting carriage. Once she was out of sight of the groom he held her by the wrist, holding and twisting until her skin burned and still he would not let go. Then he surprised her by kissing her full on the lips. She had to use every bit of her self-control to not wipe the kiss away.

'Are you going to Leighs?' She wanted to think of him far away and when he nodded she couldn't help but imagine some kind of accident.

Once the carriage pulled away she swapped her bracelet, a wedding gift from Leicester, thick with emeralds, to her other wrist to hide the welt. As she sank back into the deeply upholstered seat she wondered if such luxury might go some way to make amends, doubting it.

'I want to know everything,' said Martha, who had come to greet her in the base court at Whitehall. The place was milling with guards and Penelope wondered why.

'There is not much to tell,' she replied as they walked together towards the privy chamber.

'But your wedding?'

81

'I'd rather forget about it.' Martha couldn't disguise her disappointment. 'Sorry, it's just . . .' Penelope wasn't quite sure how to articulate what she had felt about it all, and how could Martha possibly understand the turmoil in her head, when she knew nothing of Rich, nor of her feelings for Sidney? It was only Jeanne she had felt able to confide in – sweet, loyal Jeanne, who could always be trusted with a secret.

Martha offered a sympathetic smile. 'You will never believe what has happened here since you left. There is a Catholic plot afoot, sponsored by the Pope, to assassinate the Queen and all her advisors.' Her eyes flashed with excitement rather than fear, as she whispered breathlessly. 'Fifty armed men at the ready to snatch her away.'

Penelope felt herself shrivel inside, remembering the horrors of the massacre in Paris. Jeanne had told her so little of that night, when thousands were murdered at Catholic hands, but what she *had* said buried itself deep in Penelope's mind – the shrieks of terror, the stench of blood, the river thick with corpses: an image of hell. 'Here in England?' she said without thinking.

'Yes, here. They want to put Mary of Scotland on the throne in her stead. We are all told we must not walk in the gardens for it is too dangerous.'

'Mary of Scotland?' said Penelope. She had occasionally thought of that Scottish Queen who had festered under house arrest with the Shrewsburys for thirteen years, while her young son, James, sat on her throne. She was another who was not to be mentioned in earshot of the Queen but the maids talked of her often, as if she were from a myth and not a real woman at all.

'The guard has been doubled. Did you not notice?'

'I did question why there were so many at the gates.'

'Wait until you see inside. They are lined all the way down the long gallery.'

It had been no exaggeration and when they arrived at the

privy chamber there were a dozen halberdiers guarding the door.

Martha cupped her hand over her mouth and leaned in towards Penelope. 'A Catholic priest, Campion, has been arrested for treason. Found in a priest hole . . . he is in the Tower now, being questioned.'

'Poor soul,' sighed Penelope.

'But he is a traitor,' replied Martha.

'Even so, he is still one of God's creatures.' Her insides shrivelled at the thought of what might be happening to that priest, traitor or not.

As they approached the door the guards requested they open their over-gowns – 'To be sure we do not carry any threat,' whispered Martha – before allowing them to pass.

Inside, though all appeared as usual, Penelope could sense a tautness in the air. The Queen and Burghley were disputing heatedly. Burghley's boy, Cecil, hovered behind his father, shuffling from one foot to the other as if he didn't know where to put himself. She caught him glancing her way and smiled; instead of smiling back, he averted his eyes, pretending to be fascinated by a nearby wall hanging.

'I will not become a prisoner in my own house,' said the Queen, unable to hide her annoyance with Burghley's cautious approach to the problem. 'Those Spaniards have wanted me dead for years. I refuse to be cowed by a few rumours.'

'I beg of you, madam, be prudent and avoid the gardens until we can ensure your safety.' Burghley was crouched beside her, wringing his hands.

It was only then that Penelope began to understand the realities of the Queen's life. She had merely seen the court as a place of benign glamour and romance, with the Queen at its core, like a bee in a hive, encircled by those who sought her favour, making honey. But she was beginning to see the way each and every one of those bees was grappling for survival, even the Queen herself, and that the glamour and romance were little more than distractions. The threat hanging in the air of the privy chamber on that morning must have always been there. She thought of that time she had blurted out 'I hate her. I hate the Queen'; how shocked she had been to hear herself articulate such a wicked thing, like saying she hated God. But how could she not feel such a thing in the face of her mother's degradation, her father's untimely death and her own miserable marriage with its royal seal of approval? But now she understood that things were so much more intricate than she had ever imagined and her feelings had become a muddle of contradictions. That simple childish hatred had been infiltrated by a kind of admiration, and fear too – always fear – though she would never show it.

It was a sobering thought that the Queen had to live each day in the knowledge that the whole of the Holy Roman Empire and Spain, the greatest powers in the world, as well as many of her own Catholic subjects, wished her dead. She was made ruthless by necessity. But still Penelope couldn't push the thought of the tortured Catholic from her mind, imagining his screams as his body was stretched a further notch on the rack.

She waited by the entrance for her cue to approach, looking towards the window, wondering if a pistol shot could be fired with any accuracy through glass, imagining the chaos that would ensue. Her mind drifted to her husband – the thought of that term, 'husband', a prison of a word, made her heart feel like a stone. He would be halfway to Leighs.

She headed the thought of Rich off, gazing beyond the privy-chamber window. The sky was heavy with dark clouds and slowly it began to rain; just a few specks at first, building to a downpour that rattled angrily at the panes. She could hear people in the courtyard below running for cover, shouting to one another to move things under the arcades so they wouldn't be ruined.

'Ah, Burghley, it would seem God is on your side,' said the Queen, laughing. 'I will not be going out in this weather. Neither will my assassins, I suspect.'

Burghley made an attempt at light-hearted laughter in response but his face was distorted with the effort. His son also managed to contort himself into a polite titter but no one else laughed, they all busied themselves with whatever it was they'd been pretending to do: their sewing or reading or letter-writing.

The Queen cast her eyes about, eventually alighting on Penelope. 'My songbird is back,' she said. 'I am glad to see you; none of these girls can sing as you do and I've had to listen to them ruining my favourite tunes for days. How do you find married life?'

Penelope was unsure how to respond, afraid her true feelings would display themselves on her face. 'It is different, Highness,' she said eventually, immediately aware of how inadequate her statement was, and noticed Peg Carey roll her eyes.

'Different?' replied the Queen. 'I have never heard a bride describe marriage thus.'

'What I meant, Highness, was –'

'No, no,' she interrupted with a wry smile. 'Different will do.' Penelope was impressed at the Queen's poise; nothing in her expression or posture hinted at fear, though the guards outside and Burghley's hand-wringing were testimony to the danger she was in. 'Now I would like a song to distract me from all this.' She waved her arm in the general direction of Burghley and Cecil, who were in a huddle of quiet conversation, giving the appearance in their black gowns of a pair of crows picking over some carrion. Cecil revolved his eyes her way momentarily and Penelope was reminded of something her mother had said the last time they were together: *Keep an eye on Burghley's boy; if he is anything like his father he will not be a friend to us.* She smiled his way; once again he did not return it.

An usher announced Leicester's arrival and her stepfather strode in with his entourage. Penelope saw it then, quite clearly, the look of disapproval on Burghley's face which was mirrored in the son's. Leicester was dressed in a suit of silver with a rain-drenched cape swinging from his shoulders that was dripping water on to the floorboards. As he neared Penelope, he winked at her as if to say he knew what she had been up to the previous night. She felt nauseous at the thought of them all carousing after her wedding and speculating on what was going on in the bedchamber.

He approached the Queen, who patted the seat beside her and took his hand as if they were man and wife. Penelope's distaste simmered. Had the Queen truly caused her father's death? So many questions that were impossible to answer.

Sickened by their intimacy, Penelope looked about the chamber to see, of all people, Sidney with her stepfather's men, dressed in black as if he were mourning. His eyes met hers for the briefest instant before she turned her head away, back towards the window where the downpour had not abated. All she could think of was running from the room, out into the rain, running on and on for ever, never turning back.

'Lady Rich was about to sing for us,' the Queen was saying. 'Someone find her a stool and a lute.'

Penelope recoiled internally on hearing her married name spoken aloud in Sidney's presence. A swell of heat moved up her body and on to her face as she was hustled forward. She kept her eyes rigidly away from Leicester's party, and a lute, fat and round like a baby, was thrust into her arms. She sat, bewildered for a moment, cradling the thing, then managed to gather the disparate parts of herself together and began to pluck, listening, tightening the strings one by one, matching the notes with her voice. All the while she was sure Sidney's eyes were boring into her, though she dared not look up, keeping her mind and eyes trained to the tuning of the instrument.

'Do you have a preference for the song, Your Highness?' she asked, hoping to be told what to play, for there was only a single song in her head and she didn't think it entirely apt for the occasion.

'No, no. Play what you will,' came the Queen's response.

She tried to think of other songs, she knew hundreds but they had all deserted her, so she began.

Who likes to love let him take heed!

Relieved to hear a sigh of approval from the Queen, she kept her eyes firmly on her fingers, trying to focus only on the taut catgut beneath them, sensing the vibrations, feeling out the sound, allowing her voice to fall in with the rhythm.

And what you why?

The song began to envelop her, take her along with it as a river might draw a boat in its currents, and she could sense the rapture of the audience infusing her with a feeling of potency.

Among the gods it is decreed

Looking up, emboldened by the music, she found Sidney to the side of the chamber and, locking her eyes on to his, sang:

That love shall die,

The look he returned was mournful, that of a tragic actor, and Penelope felt a frisson of glee, as if she had broken her lance on his armour and won the point.

And every wight that takes his part
Shall forfeit each a mourning heart.

87

Penelope was in her full stride. Sidney may have been the great champion of the tiltyard, the one men sought to emulate and women swooned over, cheering him on in the lists, but this was *her* arena. She allowed her eyes to dance about the room, playfully alighting on one person or another as she sang through the verses.

> *Complained before the gods above*
> *That gold corrupts the god of love.*

When she came to the end, the room burst into a great foot-stamping applause. Only Sidney wasn't clapping. He was staring into the unknown with a furrow between his brows. She stood, holding her lute in one hand, and curtsied to the Queen, as the audience called for more. A sudden splinter of self-doubt broke her surface on seeing the countess, seated, hands in lap, a rigid, pretend smile drawn on the lower part of her face, reminding Penelope of her own Puritan husband and how he would have hated this kind of merriment, would have called it an ungodly pleasure. But if Rich wanted her to keep her royal favour then he would have to tolerate this. A further realization came to Penelope in that moment; that everyone at court was in a state of compromise, either of their principles, or love, or their beliefs – there was no escaping it – and look what happened to those who refused to compromise, like that poor priest. She had a vivid image of a man on the rack, sweating, teeth clenched, bones wrenched from their sockets with a terrible wet pop, like jointing a chicken.

Someone shouted out a song request: '"Oh Sweet Deceit".'

'I shall need the music for that one,' she said. A songbook was procured and a page ordered to hold it for her, provoking some envious looks from the other lads. She settled back on to her stool, tucking her lute under her arm, beginning to pluck out the tune, finding the key with her voice. The requests came one after the other and she sang, lapping up the admiration, until her throat gave out. A group of musicians took over, and some of the maids lined up to dance, but Penelope, exhausted, went to sit by the window.

Sidney sidled over to her like a shadow, asking if he could sit beside her. She nodded without a word, feeling protected by her newfound strength, imagining her heart wrought of iron and welded with sharp spikes.

'Are you mourning?' she asked, pinching the black velvet of his doublet sleeve between her finger and thumb. 'You certainly have a morose air about you.'

'In a manner of speaking,' he replied, looking at his knees. 'You have heard of the Jesuit Campion who is to be executed?'

She nodded, confused by the serious turn in the conversation. She had not thought him truly grieving and felt suddenly shallow and naive, thinking only of her heart when events of far greater importance were taking place.

'He is a dear friend of mine.'

'But he is a Catholic, is he not? An enemy of the state.'

'Things are never as clear-cut as they seem.' He sounded impatient, angry even, as if trying to explain something to an idiot, and she wanted to express the sympathy she felt for the tortured man, but was held back by the sense of her ignorance of such things. 'I believe people should worship in the manner they choose. Campion is a man of faith, not a political man.'

'But,' she looked straight at him, 'how can you separate faith and politics when there are constant Catholic plots against the Queen's life?'

'Alas, you cannot.' He sighed. 'Campion will not avoid his fate. And by association, I am pushed into the wilderness by the Queen. I cannot seem to do anything right with her. But you don't want to hear my gripes. Besides.' He turned his head away so she couldn't see his expression. 'I am not only mourning Campion.'

'Who else?'

He mumbled out an unintelligible response.

'I cannot hear you,' she said, noticing Peg Carey and Moll Hastings looking at her over their needlework, whispering.

'Who else?' she repeated, ignoring the maids across the room.

'You,' he eventually hissed.

'Me?' Her emotions began to bolt but she reined them in firmly. 'I am still alive.'

'But I have lost you.'

'You never had me. You never wanted me, and what of your pretty speech about how you "led me on" and how sorry you were?'

'I was wrong.'

She felt a knot of rage tighten. 'Wrong? It is too late for that now.' She twisted her body away from him, making to rise, but he took her hand. Peg and Moll still had their eyes on her. 'Don't touch me.'

'Let me explain myself.'

'There is nothing to explain.'

'What is this?' He had pushed her emerald bracelet up, revealing the angry welt on her wrist.

'Nothing.' She snatched her arm back.

'Did he do this?'

'It is none of your business.' She smiled a counterfeit smile, for the benefit of the heads that were beginning to turn their way. 'Now, if you please, I must join my friends.' She held out her hand, with deliberate haughtiness, for him to press a kiss on to its back.

'Let me see you in private.'

His expression was so very tortured she almost relented but remembered her spiked iron heart.

'I beg of you.'

'Don't be silly,' she said, as if admonishing an infant, and walked sedately over to Peg and Moll, feeling like a swan, her smooth surface belying the urgent paddling beneath.

'What was that all about?' asked Peg, sliding her eyes in Sidney's direction.

'He was complaining about his lack of preferment. I don't know what he thinks *I* can do about it. I find grumblers so tiresome.'

Peg emitted a little snort of disbelief. 'So, marriage is "different", is it?'

'Just as I said,' was Penelope's reply.

She settled on to the cushions beside them, offering to help stitch beads on to a hanging, aware of Sidney's forlorn pale face watching her from across the chamber. Burghley and Cecil were close by, talking in low whispers.

'. . . if this assassination were to be successful,' Burghley was saying, '. . . all hell will be let . . . not trust Leicester, he is . . .'

On hearing her stepfather's name, she shuffled along a little in an attempt better to catch their words, making as if to get closer to the warmth of the fire, rubbing her hands together with a pretend shiver.

'But you've said it many times before, Father. She cannot be forced to name a successor.' Cecil was holding tight on to a ledger, as if its contents were of secret import. She noticed his fingers were short and ugly though the nails were trimmed and even. Those were not the hands of a man who wielded a sword, there were no calluses indicating stints at target practice, nor scars mapping past grapples. They were the hands of someone who cared very much about the impression he gave. This strange crooked boy, who people said was being groomed to take his father's place beside the Queen, had pricked her intrigue.

'England's future *must* be secured,' said the father. 'Our future too. We risk too much if we are not well prepared . . .' He paused then, lowering his voice further and continued,

'If that Scottish woman gets her hands on the sceptre then I fear we are done for.' The son was nodding slowly.

'We cannot let that happen.' As Cecil spoke, Penelope saw for the first time in the boy, who had always been too shy to meet her eye or even return her smile, a look of dogged determination. It was the look of someone who would do anything to achieve his ends.

'Our future depends upon it.'

Penelope was reminded of her conversation with her mother before she wed: *Think of the family, it will serve us all if you keep your favour with the Queen. Do that and you may well find yourself in a position one day to secure the future of the Devereuxs.* It had confused her at the time, made her feel far out of her depth; but she was beginning to understand that the safety of everyone in that privy chamber was dependent upon the good will of a single woman and that they were all vying for position and determined to ensure the fate of their kin.

December 1581

Leicester House, the Strand

They dismounted in the yard. 'You go on in and see to the bags,' Penelope said to Jeanne. 'And tell Mother I am here.'

She led the horses to the trough where the young groom lifted Dulcet's saddle away from her back.

'Those saddle sores are still bothering her, Alfred,' said Penelope. 'She could do with a comfrey ointment to soothe the pain. I am heading for my husband's house at Smithfield this evening, I'd like her with me.'

A knot of dismay tightened in her breast, painful as heartburn, at the prospect of seeing her husband alone again in the brooding gloom of the Smithfield house. Rich had been at court often, relishing his newfound status, but without lodgings there he was required to return to Smithfield to sleep, meaning she was available to serve the Queen. It was an arrangement that suited Penelope.

'Leave the ointment to me, My Lady,' answered Alfred.

'I'd like to apply it myself. I'm fond of this girl.' She patted Dulcet's neck and ran a palm over her hogged mane. 'But perhaps you would pound the comfrey root for me.'

Alfred smiled, bobbing his head in assent.

'I shall ask my mother if she can spare you to accompany me to Smithfield. I do not trust the groom there to take proper care of her. I shall only be a couple of days and as it is such a short distance from here you could return if you were needed.'

'If you wish, My Lady.' He seemed pleased. She remembered Alfred coming to work in the stables at Chartley. He was just a child then too, but he had a way with horses even then. She once saw him calm a wild pony just by blowing in its ear. 'It is barely a ten-minute ride from here.'

'How are the stables at Smithfield?'

'They are quite adequate.'

'It must please you to have an opportunity to see your husband, My Lady.'

She nodded and smiled but the knot tightened a little more. She tried to imagine herself back into her childhood and pretend she was not a grown woman with a husband, having to walk the knife-edge of court. Alfred disappeared into the barn, returning with a fistful of comfrey root, a pestle and mortar and a jar of goose fat. He balanced the mortar on the trough and began pounding away, whistling as he went. Penelope watched him work, wanting to delay going into the house for as long as possible.

Her mother would want to quiz her about everything going on in the privy chamber – *Leicester and the Queen: how is he with her? What of Burghley, what is he up to with that deformed son of his? You must take care to watch them . . . too powerful for their own good. Which of the ladies are in favour? Who has new jewels? A sure indicator of preference* – and then, of course, there would be questions about her monthlies.

Her courses had come as usual and though she was disappointed she also felt unsure about the idea of a child conceived on that wedding night. How could a baby made of such a loveless episode ever thrive? But if she *were* with child Rich would leave her alone. She felt as if she was in one of those puzzle drawings that don't quite make sense from any angle. And there was the undeniable fact of Sidney, to whom she returned in her thoughts constantly, obsessively, like a dog licking at a wound. She wanted to believe that her rejection of him was resolute, but the vision of his mournful face tugged agonizingly at her heart and she had to accept that her attempts to banish him from her thoughts were futile.

'Did you see the puppy, My Lady?' asked Alfred, handing her the ground comfrey root and offering the jar of grease so she could spoon in a measure.

'Puppy?' She took some of the mixture and gently began to rub a film of it over Dulcet's sores, feeling the mare flinch and then calm beneath her touch.

'One of your mother's spaniels whelped in the barn. She had two, but one was stillborn. The head groom told me to put the other in a sack of stones and throw it in the river.'

'You didn't, did you?' She looked at him, appalled, following him as he began to lead the horses inside.

'Of course not, My Lady. I was rather hoping you might take pity on him.' He threw her a beguiling smile.

'You know me too well, Alfred. You'd better show me.'

He pointed into a corner that had been partitioned off with a plank of wood. Penelope could see a pair of suspicious eyes trained on her. The bitch was on her side in the straw; beside her on his back, legs splayed, belly up, the sight of him tugging Penelope's heart, was the puppy. She gazed at the scene for some time, watching mesmerized as he made little squeaking sounds, his legs twitching as if he were dreaming of chasing mice.

'You knew I'd be a soft touch. Didn't you, Alfred?'

'My Lady, I would never suggest such a thing.' But his grin gave him away. 'He's ready to leave his ma; I've been weaning him. Will you take him?'

'You villain; you knew I'd not be able to resist.'

The puppy stirred, his eyes popping open, rolling over on to his front to get to his feet. He wobbled, drunk with sleep, and sniffed her hand, so she scooped him up, allowing him to chew on her fingers with sharp little fangs, thinking what a comfort it would be to have such a creature to love.

'Can I take him now?' She stood and the bitch glanced up at her once more, then closed her eyes, falling back to sleep.

'Of course, My Lady.' Alfred removed his cap, a gesture that seemed to indicate his discomfort at being asked permission for something by someone so far above him in the pecking order. 'Look how she is content to see her little fellow go with you.'

She made for the house, entering by the back door, pulling her hat from her head, allowing it to fall to the floor and flinging her cloak to the side. She then stopped a moment to bring the little dog close to her face, where he snickered and snuffled and she caught a whiff of his sour puppy smell. Hearing voices in the hall, she opened the door quietly to see what company was there. In a huddle about the hearth were her mother, her stepfather, Jeanne and Dorothy, but there was another amongst them. She felt choked, as if a stone had stuck in her gullet, and though her instincts were telling her to flee, she found herself rooted to the spot. Sidney, even turned away from her, was instantly recognizable – she must have scrutinized the contours of that back a thousand times.

It was the puppy that betrayed her presence. Seemingly sensitive to Penelope's heightened anxiety, he began to yap in urgent, high-pitched discharges. The company turned as one, Dorothy emitting a delighted squeal, forgetting all sense of propriety as she ran towards her sister and the little dog, who had stopped his barking and had begun to wriggle with excitement.

'Is he yours? Where did you get him?' Questions poured out of her sister but Penelope's mind churned on other things. 'What's his name?'

Penelope's annoyance flared at this invasion of her family, hiding deeper, sharper feelings – *how is it that I can be at once so glad to see him and so angry he is here?* She made every effort not to look at him but couldn't help a glance for he seemed to glow, as if he wore a halo, like Christ in a painting, and despite his plain black velvet clothes, he outshone everyone there, even her stepfather in his cloth of gold, even her mother, known for her astonishing beauty.

Eventually, Penelope emerged from her stupor to answer her sister. 'He doesn't have a name yet.'

'Well, we must give him one,' said Dorothy.

Penelope girded herself, moving into the chamber and passing the puppy into her sister's eager hands. She kissed her mother and stepfather then, bobbing in a curtsy, offered a hand to Sidney, as if he was nothing more than an ordinary guest, mustering all her willpower to avoid meeting his eyes.

'My Lady,' he said with a polite bow, holding her hand longer than was necessary. She turned to Jeanne and Dorothy, who were cooing over the dog, opening her arms to take him once more, scattering kisses over his face and head. Penelope was aware of her mother watching her closely, her eyes moving between her and Sidney, seeming curious as to what might have been going on beneath the formal coldness of her daughter's greeting. She wondered then if the silent conflict that was laying waste to her emotions was somehow visible on her surface.

'What about calling him Chevalier?' proposed Jeanne, stroking the puppy.

'Too much of a mouthful,' said Penelope.

'Why don't you suggest a name, Sidney?' said Leicester, patting his nephew on the back, 'since you are the wordsmith amongst us.'

Her mother was still looking at her intently. 'Are you quite well, Penelope? You look pale.'

'I am well enough, Mother.' She supposed her mother was wondering if she was with child. She half turned her shoulder to Sidney and tucked the little animal under her chin, folding him into the top of her gown, cooing, 'I love him already.'

'What *would* you name him, Sidney?' asked Dorothy.

'I need to know him a little first. Here!'

He held out his hands to take the puppy but Penelope shook her head. 'He is falling asleep. It would not do to over-excite him.' She couldn't bear the idea of those hands on him.

'Indeed he does look most content where he is,' said

Sidney, ignoring the rebuff, taking the opportunity to turn out a courtly compliment. 'Surely any young fellow would be rapturous to be in such proximity to Lady Rich.'

She felt herself blanch inwardly on hearing her married name in his mouth – the mouth she could remember, so clearly, too clearly, pressed against her own.

'What think you of Spero as a name?' he added.

'"Hope", how charming. Yes, Spero is perfect. And a Latin name will show we are not all ignoramuses,' quipped Lettice. 'Or is it ignorami?'

'The first is correct, I believe,' said Sidney.

'I think it is a perfect choice, don't you, Penelope?' said Leicester.

'I will think about it.' No matter how hard she tried to disguise her inner state, her voice betrayed her, sounding clipped and prim, and she couldn't help thinking of Sidney's motto at the recent joust, ~~SPERAVI~~: *I have hoped*, scored through to emphasize the loss. Her own sense of lost hope welled. She took a breath to steady her voice and turned to her sister to change the subject. 'When must you return to the Huntingdons?'

'I leave the day after tomorrow,' said Dorothy, looking suddenly downcast. Penelope was reminded of the dull routines of their guardians' household and realized that if she keenly felt her sister's absence, how much worse it must be for Dorothy in such a grim place.

'Never mind' – she squeezed her sister's hand – 'you will soon be at court with me, won't she, Mother?' She spoke with false levity for the benefit of Sidney, whose gaze she could feel on her, like an itch that insisted on being scratched.

'If the Queen wishes it,' said Lettice bitterly.

'Will you excuse me?' Penelope had the urge to flee. 'I must go to the kitchens and find this little fellow some meat scraps.' Making for the door, she added, 'Jeanne, are you coming with me?'

Once out of the room she grabbed hold of her companion's arm and dragged her away down the corridor in haste, waiting until they were out of earshot before asking, 'What on earth is *he* doing here?'

'I wanted to warn you but didn't have the chance.' She stopped, turning to face her friend, putting a hand on each of her shoulders, suddenly grave.

'What is it?' asked Penelope, feeling a rising alarm.

'Your stepfather is trying to broker a match between Sidney and Dorothy.'

'My own sister! No!' Light-headed, she put a hand out to the wall to steady herself. 'That can't be right. Sidney hasn't the wealth for us impoverished Devereux girls.' She collapsed on to a window seat, plopping the puppy into her lap.

Jeanne sat too, wrapping an arm around her friend, smoothing a palm over her tense shoulders.

'I thought Leicester had hopes she would wed the Scottish King,' Penelope muttered. 'What happened to *that* idea? Now I have brought Rich to the family, my sister is free to wed –'

'I don't think it is like that. I don't think your sister is willing. I don't even think she was aware of it. Not judging by the look on her face when it was mentioned.' Jeanne began to stroke Penelope's hair. They both knew, well enough, that if it was Leicester's wish then Dorothy would wed Sidney whether anyone wanted it or not.

'You are lucky not to have anyone telling you who you must wed –' She stopped herself, bringing a hand to cover her mouth, remembering the terrible circumstances in which Jeanne lost her parents. 'I am so sorry. I didn't mean it.'

'I know you do not mean it and anyway I have no wish to wed just yet.'

'You have a good heart, not vindictive and spoiled like mine.' Penelope was thinking how lucky she was to have a person such as Jeanne to trust with her secrets.

The sound of footsteps nearing silenced them and,

looking up, they saw the black shape of Sidney approaching down the passage. He stopped in front of them, giving a tight smile.

'I apologize for interrupting, ladies, but I wonder if I might have a word with Lady Rich alone?' Behind that clipped sentence he seemed to be making an attempt to contain something. Penelope wondered if it was rage or misery.

'I shall take the puppy to the kitchens and find him something to eat,' said Jeanne with false brightness, picking up the sleeping dog and leaving them alone.

Sidney sat beside her, close but not quite touching, and she edged away slightly, fearing his nearness. 'I wonder what it is that makes you so merry.' His voice, so full of bitterness, sent a wave of wretchedness over her.

'I am not particularly merry,' she said, allowing her guard to lower minutely and looking over at him sitting shuffling his hands together in his lap as if about to deal a round of cards. Her heart began to bloat inside her breast, until she felt she might not be able to breathe. 'Not merry to hear that you plan to wed my sister.'

'Oh Lord!' He wiped the back of a hand over his forehead. 'I have no intention of marrying Dorothy. I was merely humouring my uncle. Surely you know that.'

'And how can I trust you? You certainly have not given me reason.'

He looked cowed and small, not his elegant, splendid, usual self, and it was all she could do to resist reaching out and touching him. It dawned on her that all those years of yearning for some silly romantic ideal had nothing to do with this man at all. But it was this man, this Sidney, slumped beside her, with his blemished skin and slightly thinning hair, with his brooding demeanour and (she noticed for the first time) bitten fingernails, that had caught her heart and caged it like a bird.

'I should not be talking to you, here alone like this,' she

said. 'I am a married woman.' He seemed to flinch as she said it. 'And you *will* be promised to my sister. Even *you* are not in a position to disobey Leicester.'

His expression matched her sense of desolation. 'I have something for you.' He pulled a fold of paper from his doublet and all his self-assurance seemed to fall away.

She took it, opened it. 'A sonnet.' She stated the obvious to fill the silence.

'One of many. Will you read it? If you cared even a jot for me once' – he stopped, seeming lost for words, continuing without looking at her – 'then let me hear you recite my lines.'

Her voice was barely more than a whisper as she read: '*When Nature made her chief work, Stella's eyes . . .*' She read to the end, then let her hands drop heavily and, taking a deep inhalation, gathered herself together. '*I* am Stella?'

He nodded and his pale eyes looked so deeply mournful she could hardly bear to look at them, but neither could she bear to tear herself away.

'The distant star – and who are you?'

'I am Astrophil.' Something seemed to change in him as if he were unfolding.

'The star lover.' She whispered. 'So you *do* love me?'

He nodded again, this time with a flicker of a smile.

'What happened to force this change of heart?'

'I don't know. I was confused, felt blighted at losing the Leicester inheritance and ostracized by the Queen. I thought I had nothing to offer you . . . compared to Rich.' He spat her husband's name as if he had sucked poison from a snakebite. 'And I did not think my feelings ran so deep until it was too late. Love can surprise in its suddenness. Besides, you know as well as I the folly of being led into matrimony by passion.' The words spilled out of him urgently as if time was running out. His usual veneer of self-assurance had abandoned him entirely; she could never have imagined this vulnerable creature beneath that surface.

'Is it folly, or the path to happiness?' Her voice was bristling with cynicism.

'I thought my feelings would pass. I was a fool.'

'And when you realized they would not pass, you still thought me not worth fighting for.'

'No!'

She wanted, desperately, to take his hand, with its ink-smudged index finger, lean her body into his, to allow herself to be subsumed by him.

'I *did* fight for you. I begged the Queen to allow me to court you. I reminded her of your father's wish.'

'You petitioned the Queen?' It began to dawn on her that she had gravely misunderstood the situation.

'She laughed in my face, asked why I thought "a disappointment" like me – yes, that is what she called me, "a disappointment" – should have permission to court her favourite maid. Then she sent me packing. "You are not a man I fully trust, Sidney," she said.' He let go of her hand and cupped his palms, dropping his face into them as if ashamed, his speech barely audible. 'She thinks me too outspoken and dislikes my Catholic friends. But I am a person who speaks my mind and loyalty is a matter of honour for me, even when it comes to those who have differing beliefs.'

'So it is *her* fault.' Penelope felt clogged with loathing for the woman who had visited a catalogue of disasters on her family. 'And I am stuck for all eternity with that man.' *Those whom God hath joined together, let no man put asunder.*

'It is consummated, then,' he muttered, seeming to think aloud, still unable to look at her.

'Of course,' she whispered.

'I had hoped, beyond reason, that there would be some way the union would not . . .' – he stammered, seeming unable to put his thoughts into words – 'could – could be annulled, and that in time we might have convinced the world to . . .' He stopped again. 'What a fool I have been with my hopeless dreams.'

He looked up at her then, his face stricken, opening his arms, and she allowed herself to be enveloped in his embrace. They held each other tight, eyes closed, as if to shut out the entire world until the sound of someone nearing caused them to snap apart. They inspected their hands as one of Leicester's clerks passed carrying a sheaf of papers, sitting in silence until he had disappeared through the far door. 'Let me come to your chamber tonight.'

'No, I cannot.'

'I beg of you.'

'No, no! Anyway I will not be alone. Jeanne and my sister will be with me.'

'Then somewhere else . . . please.'

'No!' She could not look at him any longer for fear that she would lose her resolve. 'And what of *Dorothy*? You are promised to my sister.'

'I am not promised.'

'Not yet,' she said. 'You must go.' They sat in silence for what seemed like an age. 'You must go,' she repeated.

Eventually he stood, walking slowly away, and she thought her heart would burst with longing.

'I will wait for you,' he said, looking back towards her, 'in the music room that overlooks the river . . . all night if I must.'

March 1582

Leighs, Essex

It was Penelope's first night at Leighs, though she had been married four months. She had been at court, mustering favour and trying to understand the complicated web of loyalties surrounding the Queen. There had been new rumours of a planned assassination and they had all been on tenterhooks, apart from the Queen herself, who always seemed cool as a November pond; so in truth Penelope was glad to get away. She was in her bedchamber alone, by the hearth, awaiting her husband and unsuccessfully trying to banish Sidney from her mind. It had been some three months since their encounter – three months of feigned happiness. She threw a log on the fire and yawned, wondering how much longer her husband would keep her waiting. She had left him in the chapel praying fervently.

Earlier she and Jeanne had wandered about the house with its labyrinthine corridors joining the old parts to the new. It had once been a religious establishment and the evidence of its earlier use could be found in the occasional carving of a saint or a cross, tucked away in a neglected corner. The place had the same solemn atmosphere of the Smithfield house, where she spent the occasional night when she was not required at court. It was a gloomy place that had the musty smell of a mausoleum and an oppressive silence pervaded. On each visit she had been required to perform her conjugal duties. Every occasion was as perplexing as her wedding night had been and Rich, who was civil enough, if distant, during the daylight hours, became charged with anger as night fell. He never harmed her again, but the threat of it loomed over their nocturnal dealings and she was always thankful to know that Jeanne was on the other side of the wall but worried too that she would overhear Rich's fervent biblical recitations punctuated by the breathless panting and moaning. When Rich was done and gone, Penelope would knock on the panelling and Jeanne, dozy with sleep, would come quietly and slide into bed beside her.

'This is all yours?' Jeanne had exclaimed on their arrival at Leighs, as they rushed about the great house like overwrought children, bursting into the great hall, holding hands and spinning in the vast space until they were gasping with laughter.

'Mine but yet not mine,' she'd replied, once their excitement had abated. 'It feels dead, as if no one has lived here for years.' She would so much rather have remained at Wanstead with Lettice, where they had stopped for a night on the way, her mother hungrily grabbing at any information she might have gleaned from the privy chamber.

Penelope always thought of Wanstead bathed in sunlight and filled with music, like a corner of earthly paradise, filled with joyful memories of the brief interludes spent with her family, rendered sweeter perhaps by the comparison with her life at the Huntingdons' in the north, where the miserable weather always seemed in league with the ambiance. An unsmiling servant showed them to Penelope's own suite of rooms, which faced to the north and were further shadowed by three towering elms, ancient and knotted and leaning towards each other at the top, like a huddle of elderly men sharing a secret. There were three large chambers leading one to the other.

Jeanne had helped her undress and they had combed each other's hair before retiring, singing a song they had heard at court very quietly so as not to be overheard, for Rich had made it quite clear that music was forbidden at Leighs. Once Jeanne had gone Penelope sat before the fire; it crackled, flaring blue on the dry bark of a new log, and her thoughts wandered back to that night at Leicester House.

In the aftermath of that last encounter with Sidney she had lain awake in bed, filled with anger and confusion towards the forces that had contributed to her situation. It was as if God was mocking her by making her love one man – for if it was not love then she knew not what it could be, that burning awareness that life could only make sense in proximity to him – yet be wed to another who cared nothing for her. Dorothy was sleeping soundly beside her, the soft rhythm of her breath punctuating the silence, a taunting reminder of the betrothal plans that had been concocted on her behalf. The idea of Sidney wed to her sister was unthinkable, akin to anticipating one's own passing. The knowledge that Sidney was waiting for her in the music room – his words whispered in her head, *all night if I must*, had drawn her as the moon pulls the oceans, and it felt inevitable when she finally slipped out of the bed into the night chill.

Fumbling in the dark for her gown, she began to be aware of her heart palpitating in her breast, as if it had taken on a separate life, as if something was growing in there, something planted by Sidney that would not be uprooted. The chamber was cold – cold enough, as her eyes became accustomed to the dark, for her to see little clouds of her own breath in the vague moonlight. She tied her gown tightly at her throat and found a shawl which she wrapped about her shoulders, then wondered if she should dress properly, couldn't imagine confronting Sidney in her nightclothes. Though of course her nightclothes would be exactly appropriate for such an assignation. Before she thought too much about it she picked up the puppy, shoved her feet into her slippers and slid out of the room like a spectre.

It was only as she felt her way, one hand on the wall, along the dark gallery that led to the music room and saw a sliver of light beneath the door that the reality of what she was about to do overcame her. She stopped, as if turned to stone, and the ugly word dropped into her head like a toad into a pond: *adulteress*. Remembering the bewilderment of her wedding night, how bereft of tenderness it had been, she began to question whether she truly wanted such an experience with Sidney. But another part of her was pulling her inexorably towards such an event. Surely, that part of her reasoned, the fact of love would render it different, making her aware of a fizzing sensation at her root.

As her thoughts began to do battle, the man waiting behind that door became ever more strange and distant. He was either the site of sin that would cast her soul into an infinite wilderness or something else, perhaps even more disturbing: a pleasure she would never be able to give up.

She stumbled against an object in the gloom, a chair that fell to the floor with a crash, and turned tail, running away back from where she came, a pulse drumming loud in her ears. She heard the door behind her open and felt a surge of fear, as if it was a monster coming for her.

'Come back,' he called, his voice pregnant with dismay. 'Stella, my love, come back.'

She sped down the long gallery and up the stairs, only stopping when she was safely in her bedchamber. Leaning back against the closed door, she tried to catch her breath and the thing where her heart should have been was protesting so loudly she feared it would jump right out of her.

'What's the matter?' It was Jeanne's sleep-dulled voice coming from the truckle.

'I took fright, that is all,' she replied, going to perch on the edge of the little bed, feeling the comfort of Jeanne's steady arms folding about her.

'Where were you?' she asked.

'The puppy needed to go out,' Penelope said, wondering at how easily the lie had formed, thinking of all the other lies she would have to tell if she allowed herself to be drawn into that looming temptation, and each one of them a further sin.

'You'll catch your death wandering about on a December night like that.' Jeanne pulled her down into the warmth of the blankets, still holding her, the puppy snuggled in and she must have fallen asleep for she woke in the morning squeezed up in the truckle, wondering for a moment how she came to be there.

Sidney disappeared from court after that, but not from Penelope's thoughts, where he circulated like a dirge that had become trapped in her head, and not from the gossip, which was filled with speculation upon his whereabouts. 'He is at his sister's at Wilton'; 'He has gone to Ireland to fight with his father'; 'He has gone to the Low Countries.' She didn't dare join in the discussions for fear that a slip of the tongue might reveal her black secret, and her thoughts pondered constantly on the way love could distort a person beyond all recognition.

As she waited by the spitting fire for Rich to finish his prayers she wondered what it was he felt he must pray for so vehemently, what sins he harboured that needed forgiving. She thought of Sidney's poem, carefully folded and cached away in her casket of sentimental treasures, asking herself what kind of sin *she* was guilty of in regards to *that*. You can sin in thought as much as in deed; the countess had said it often enough. Penelope had never given it much analysis, for if you think about pilfering a few plums from the kitchens or consider telling a little inconsequential lie, then the sin is hardly worth the bother of worry. But this was different. She couldn't help wondering if *thinking* about adultery was as wicked as the deed itself, because she *had* thought of it – many times. The state of her soul frightened her, she imagined it shrivelled and dry; it seemed impossible to live a life free of sin.

She heard Rich's footsteps on the stairs. They were precise, as if carefully measured out. A knot of trepidation tied itself in her belly. He entered, lit ghoulishly from the candle he carried; she turned to look at him; he touched her lightly on the shoulder. 'You are still up.' The kindness in his voice was unexpected, confusing her for a moment, allowing her to feel a fragment of hope. 'I need your help, Penelope.'

'My help?' She could not imagine, for the life of her, in what way she might help him.

'We have to do this thing.' His voice was heavy with something akin to dread, as if he had been threatened with the thumbscrews.

She nodded, not really understanding what he meant.

'It *must* be done. Perhaps you would . . .' He stopped and looked about the chamber, seeming unable to meet her gaze. 'Could I ask you to wear these?'

She hadn't noticed until then that he was carrying a carefully folded pile of clothes, which he placed on her lap.

'Is it a gift?'

'In a manner of speaking . . . It is more a gift I wish you would give to me.'

She took the item on top. It was a black velvet cap, in the plain style of the hoods that students liked to wear to make them appear more serious, and was lined in black cony fur, which elevated it from something ordinary into a thing of discreet luxury. Beneath it was a doublet of black damask, soft as a peach to the touch, beautifully tailored and backed with fine, inky quilted silk. She took each item, unfolding it, spreading it over her knees: a pair of hose to match the doublet; silk stockings, as delicate as those worn by the Queen; a shirt of white, gauzy linen; a starched ruff, its modest diameter belying its acres of starched fabric. None of those garments appeared to have ever been worn.

'These are a boy's clothes,' she said, supposing there had been some mistake. 'They are too small for you.'

He said nothing, just put his arms up, a gesture a nurse makes when undressing a small child. Penelope mimicked him, without questioning, and he slipped her nightdress over her head, replacing it swiftly with the fine linen shirt. Then he handed her the silk stockings, which she rolled up her legs.

'A masquerade,' she said, thinking of carnival, when everything is upside down and sometimes, though she had never seen such a thing herself, loose women go about for the day dressed as men, with woollen moustaches and wadded codpieces. She wanted to ask him what he meant by this but didn't know how to form her question, realizing how very little she knew her husband, feeling all of a sudden lost in this unfamiliar house with this strange man, wishing she could call for Jeanne in the adjoining room. She thought then of what she had promised – to be obedient, chaste, to honour her husband. *Those whom God hath joined together, let no man put asunder.* She allowed herself to be helped into the hose and then the doublet, which he laced all the way up, before attaching the small, stiff ruff about its collar. He then plucked her coif from her head and smoothed her hair back into its ties, fitting the velvet cap on, its silken fur caressing her ears.

'Stand and let me look at you,' he said gently. She did as he asked and he handed her a New Testament, which was marked at a page. She opened it, finding Paul's letter to the Corinthians.

'Please would you recite the passage I have indicated?' The smallest of smiles appeared on his lips fleetingly and he placed a candle into the sconce beside her so she could see to read.

Do you not know that the wicked will not inherit the kingdom of God? He reached out, touching the edge of the doublet, rubbing it between his thumb and forefinger, seeming entirely absorbed in the fabric, as if it held the secrets of the heavens. *Be not deceived: neither fornicators, nor idolaters, nor adulterers, nor wantons, nor buggerers, nor thieves, nor covetous, nor drunkards, nor railers, nor extortioners shall inherit the kingdom of God.* He seemed to have fallen into a trance, his eyes at half-mast, mouth slightly open. *And such were some of you. But ye are washed, ye are sanctified, ye are justified in the name of the Lord Jesus and by the Spirit of our God.*

He took the book from her, wordlessly, closing it, placing it to one side, leading her to the bed and taking her shoulders, turned her away from him, pushing her forward until her face was pressed into the plummet and she was immersed in the dusty scent of plucked feathers.

Afterwards, when he had gone, she removed the clothes, stowing them under the bed guiltily as if they might tell of her shame. She had noticed the blood on the fine linen shirt, a dark circle against the white, wondering how it was she could have been so blind as to not realize that her marriage had been unconsummated for months, inwardly cursing the countess for keeping her so strictly. Had she been at court from a younger age, with those maids-of-the-chamber seasoned to romance, she might have been less naive. She had thought they told stories when they talked of the pain, the member swelling to several times its right size and becoming hard as a stick, and the emissions, but they had been telling the truth.

The recent memory of Rich's urgent pounding brought bile to her throat and the animal groan, loud and sudden and ecstatic, making her realize that his moans on the previous occasions had been the sounds of frustration. And if she didn't know it already by then, the hot wet trickle between her legs hammered home the fact that her marriage was sealed. Only then did the realization skewer itself into her that had she known she was still a virgin, even after her vows were said, she might have found a way to escape her ties. She could have announced that Rich was incapable and the marriage might have been annulled. She tortured herself with what might have been, until a knock at the door distracted her.

'It is Jeanne; can I come in?'

'Of course.'

Jeanne slipped under the covers beside her. 'I heard Rich going to his chamber and thought you might like the company.'

'Thank heavens for you, Jeanne.' Penelope found she couldn't explain the ritual of the boy's clothes; the shameful episode defied description, but she did confide the belated consummation, glad to share her woes.

'Well, it is done now,' Jeanne said. 'For better or worse.'

For all eternity, thought Penelope. 'Let us hope he has planted an infant in me.'

'If only I had realized,' said Jeanne.

'How could you have possibly known?'

'Even so . . .'

'Rich asked that I read to him' – Penelope paused, unsure about sharing such a fact, saying it quickly before she changed her mind – 'from St Paul to the Corinthians.'

'What, during?'

She nodded.

'Do you think that is a Puritan habit?'

Penelope began to consider the strangeness of it all and the depth of her own ignorance, wondering if the evangelical countess had deliberately kept her in such a state in order to make her more pliable in the marriage bed.

She woke early to find Jeanne already up, calling for someone to come and stoke the fire. Through the fug of sleep she remembered the boy's clothes hastily shoved beneath the bed, imagining them being discovered, her thoughts racing. What would she say? That they were Rich's weeds? But they were too small by far. She would never be believed. And how would she explain away the bloodstain? She quietly gathered the offending items together when Jeanne's back was turned, screwing them into a ball and tugging a sheet from the bed to wrap them in.

'What are you doing?' asked Jeanne.

'I suppose I ought to do something with this.' She held up a corner of the sheet. 'Blood.'

Jeanne made a grimace. 'I'll deal with it.'

'No, let me.'

Penelope was afraid her insistence would arouse suspicion but Jeanne didn't seem to think anything of it. 'It is for me to do such things, but if you insist.'

Penelope tucked the incriminating bundle under an arm and made her way to her husband's rooms in the far wing of the house, unsure of the way, having to stop one of the pages to ask for directions. His door was vast and hewn from a single piece of oak. She didn't think to knock; it was morning and the household was up and about, though if she'd thought about it, she'd have noticed it was still quiet as a morgue outside Rich's rooms.

She lifted the latch and the door swung open silently. The hangings were drawn tight about the bed. She had planned to leave the bundle beside him so when he woke he would see them before anything else, and tiptoed across the chamber, aware of a loud rhythmic snore. She peeped round the edge of the bed-curtains. It was dark within so she stood silently a moment for her eyes to become accustomed to the gloom and began to realize that what she had thought was snoring was more like some kind of panting sound. She thought that one of the dogs had become overheated in the airless space. Pulling back the curtain further a square of light fell over a face, not her husband's face, a face she had never seen before. It belonged to a startled boy, a naked boy, who was supine beside her naked husband, whose face was buried, eyes tightly scrunched, in the pillow.

Penelope stood stock-still, her eyes locked on to the stranger's.

'Don't stop,' Rich was moaning. 'For God's sake, don't stop.' His hand moved round, finding the boy's mouth, slipping two fingers into it. But the boy twisted away and Rich seemed only then to understand that something was wrong, heaving himself up, seeing Penelope, who was standing immobile like that wife in the Bible turned to salt.

'Get out!' he shouted. 'Get out of here you . . . you . . . *bitch*!'

His words sprung her from her paralysis. She spun round and ran from the room, through the winding passages, turning here and there in the maze of corridors until she was completely lost. Eventually she happened upon a small staircase, descending it round and round, clinging on to the rope handle for fear of falling. At the bottom in complete darkness she could feel the outline of a locked door and banged desperately at the wood until her hands hurt.

'Who's that making such a bleeding racket?' came a voice beyond the door, which then opened to reveal the kitchens. A man stood before her whom she supposed to be the cook or the butcher; he wore an apron covered in blood and brandished a knife. 'My Lady, please excuse me.' He swiped the cap from his head and the others in the kitchen all turned from their stations and, realizing who she was, did likewise.

A big-bosomed woman stepped forward. 'You do not look well, My Lady, are you sickening for something?'

Penelope couldn't find her voice but she shook her head.

'Then you must have seen the ghost. There is one that wanders the top corridor. That is why we keep this door locked, not that a door provides much of a barrier to a ghost. Was it the ghost you saw, My Lady?'

Penelope made a small cough and at last found she was able to stumble out a reply. 'It was, I think. A ghost, yes.'

'Come, My Lady.' The woman held out a hand, which Penelope took. 'Heavens, you are cold as death. Come and sit by the hearth; I will mix you a posset and send for your maid. Here.' She clicked her fingers at one of the lads who stared gormlessly at the mistress of the house, in her nightclothes, sitting there on a stool by the kitchen hearth like a lost infant. 'Go and fetch the maid-of-the-chamber, the French one.' Then, turning back to Penelope, she said, 'Let me take those things off you. I can't imagine how you came to be wandering the top corridor with a pile of laundry, when there are more servants in this place than there are rats in London.'

Only then did Penelope remember she was still clutching the guilty bundle. 'Oh, no,' she said, holding it close to her body.

Seeming to understand that something was amiss, the woman said, 'Come with me to the laundry, it is warm and clean in there and you will be away from all the foul kitchen smells.'

Penelope allowed herself to be led across a small cobbled yard and into an outhouse. Inside, the air was thick with heat and the acrid tang of lye. There was a vast bubbling vat hanging over the fire and above it, on a rack that had been winched high up to the ceiling, hung rows of linens that wafted and billowed in the rising heat. She collapsed on to a bench and let the bundle fall to the floor, the boy's clothes spilling out on to the flags.

The woman picked them up, folding, not really looking, certainly not surprised by the boy's garments, only inspecting them for dirt, throwing the bloodied shirt into a basket of other linens with the crumpled sheet and placing the ruff, which had been crushed beyond recognition, on a stand. The rest she put to one side then sat next to Penelope, heaving out a sigh.

'I have known Lord Rich since he was an infant. Indeed I wet-nursed him when I was still a girl. So I probably know him better than even his mother. I know all about his little foibles.'

'His foibles . . .' echoed Penelope.

'The lads! With some men it is just the way. They have that preference.'

'But . . .' The tears came then, in great sobs, and the woman enfolded her in her arms, holding her head against the soft pillow of her breast. She had heard of it, of course, but could not even allow herself to say the word, not even silently, for even the thought of it seemed so very profane.

'It is more common than you think, my little lady. And the ways of the flesh cannot always be explained.'

'But he is a God-fearing man, a Puritan,' was all she could think to say.

'Perhaps that is why.' There was a strange logic to the woman's reasoning. 'Now, I want you to know that I am here for you. You just call for me – Mistress Shilling – if ever you get yourself in a muddle. And remember, your husband is a good enough man at heart, just plagued by his own personal demons. And soon, I feel sure of it, you will be childing and all will be well. Nothing will matter when you have your own infant in your arms.'

Her tears dried up. Mistress Shilling handed her a square of linen to wipe her face and blow her nose, then found a crisp coif, which she slipped over her head.

'There. Good as new.'

It wasn't until the afternoon that Rich summoned her, after she came back from riding out. She had taken comfort in Dulcet's familiar gait as they galloped across the heath, with Alfred calling out for her to take care as she spurred the horse on. She imagined the wind, whistling about her, was blowing away all traces of the morning's events. It caught in her cape, causing it to fly out behind her like wings, and her ears filled with the thunder of hooves. Dulcet came to a halt eventually, at the edge of a wood where they spooked a small herd of deer that took cover amongst the trees. Dulcet dropped her head to tear at a tussock of grass and a young stag took a step forward to stand proud and immobile save for the slight heave of breath moving through his flanks. He regarded Penelope with a pair of dewy eyes that showed nothing of his fear. She was reminded, instantly, of the hart she had once shot, regret welling with the memory of killing something so full of life, and predictably her thoughts returned to Sidney.

She couldn't help but think of what might have been if she'd had the courage to go to him that night, if she had given *him* her maidenhead – what then? But, as she made her way through the house to Rich's rooms, a new thought insinuated itself into her mind: that perhaps the situation with her husband could be turned to her advantage.

Something got hold of her with inexplicable force; a refusal to become a victim to circumstance. If she were to be the one to play power games at court on behalf of the Devereuxs, then what better time to start learning how to turn disadvantage on its head. She saw with clarity then that power could be gained, not necessarily by brute strength, nor by political sophistication, but by holding others' secrets. She thought of that young stag and its fearless gaze, sensing a change taking hold in her as if steel was threading itself through her veins.

She knocked at Rich's study; he opened the door himself, looking pale, quite distraught, and was rubbing his hands together as if trying to warm them, though the chamber was stuffy. They sat and eventually he spoke. 'Can you forgive me?'

She reached out for one of his hands, prising it from its partner. 'Forgiveness is something between you and God, but if you mean, "Do I understand?", then I do . . .' She paused and looked at him but he couldn't meet her eye. 'Though many wouldn't.'

'My shame would be yours by proxy were people to discover my . . . my . . .'

'Your transgressions?'

He looked at her then, with a nod.

'We do not know each other very well yet,' she continued. 'And something you will learn about me in time is that I care not for people's opinions.' This was something she only realized about herself as she was saying it. She had seen her mother ostracized and condemned, diminished by shame. She, Penelope, would not be the casualty of others' judgements. 'The Devereuxs are not so easily uprooted.'

'I beg that you remain silent on this matter,' he pleaded, clutching the edge of her sleeve, seeming debased. There was nothing left of the vile bully of her wedding night. She was filled with a new sense of puissance, as if she had grown out of girlhood in the space of a few hours.

'There is no need to beg. It is simply a question of striking a bargain.' She stood and began to pace, as she had seen Leicester do on many an occasion, surprised by herself, finding she was enjoying holding the upper hand, feeling she might get used to it.

'A bargain? I don't know what you mean by that.' He stopped, wiping a hand slowly over his mouth. 'Do you mean there are conditions for your silence?'

'Exactly that,' she replied, only then beginning to list in her mind what her conditions would be.

'You cannot ask me to give up my Puritan faith, it is all I have that gives me hope – the slenderest possibility for redemption.'

'Your faith is your business but I will practise mine as I wish. In this house I will respect your strictures on certain pastimes but within my own chambers I shall do as I wish.'

'Yes, as you wish.'

'You will give me the freedom to live under my mother's roof, if I so desire it, and you have my word that I will spend enough time under yours to fulfil the obligations of our marriage. I shall be faithful until I have given you a pair of sons. Then I will be free to live as I choose, with discretion, of course.' She felt she had the wind behind her as she paced;

his eyes followed her. 'Our children will be raised here but under the auspices of nursery staff of my choosing, and none of them Puritans.'

'But . . .' he began.

'I do not think you are really in a position to barter. Do you?'

He slumped back.

'And as for the business of last night – the outfit.'

He hid his face in cupped palms. 'Please, no.'

'If that is what is necessary to get me with child then so be it.' She was thinking of Mistress Shilling's pragmatism. It was not such a great hardship to play pretend in the dark, and if it was a sin, it was his sin not hers.

He looked up, his face awash with relief. She had forgotten how striking he could look when he was not twisted with anger. 'You would do that, for me?'

'Not for you, no; for me – so that I can bear children. I too have made vows before God. And the rest – your proclivities – I want to know nothing of it. Is that clear?'

'Clear. You want to know nothing of it,' he repeated. 'That is the price for your silence?'

'Yes. It is not so much to ask, I think, for me to keep the secret of your sodomy.' He flinched.

She felt further empowered in speaking the word she had not even dared think of only hours before, understanding in that moment that words held a power all of their own. And she felt a little pity for him, gripped by his urges, quite eaten away by them, deciding then and there that she would never allow herself to be subject to her own animal instincts, understanding too how the Queen managed her power so effectively by at least giving the appearance of curbing her base desires.

'You will not tell even your nearest?'

'Do you mean my mother, my sister, my brother? Well.' She made the pretence of being unsure, to watch him squirm a little more. 'I think it best they are kept in the dark too.'

'I thank the Lord that he has sent me such an understanding wife.'

He looked cowed and desperate and grateful, and even squeezed a little sympathy from her, but her prevailing feeling towards him was of indifference and she would not allow for her newly discovered authority to be tainted by sentiment.

July 1582

Chartley, Staffordshire

Essex appeared over the crest of the hill in silhouette, with the afternoon sun low at his back. Penelope felt her heart jolt at the thought of being reunited with her brother whom she hadn't seen since her wedding the better part of a year ago. She was travelling with her mother and Jeanne in the carriage, for she had missed her courses that month and Lettice had advised her not to ride at such an early stage. 'Particularly with a first pregnancy,' she had said. 'My first grandson.' None of them considered the possibility of the infant not being male. Penelope wondered often about the theatrical complications of the baby's conception, to what extent it mired her in sin, and had woken from a nightmare the previous night, in which she had birthed a monster.

Despite the ballast of cushions and bolsters, she had been jolted and jostled for the entire journey; the motion and the cloying summer heat had induced waves of nausea, making her think she would have been far better off astride Dulcet, who was reliable as the days of the week. She had said nothing yet to Rich of the invisible ministrations of her body, somehow hadn't wanted to share her secret joy with him, wanted to keep it close for a while longer. She was developing a talent for keeping secrets. She imagined the bud of her boy growing inside her – the first step to her freedom.

'Is that Robin?' said her mother, grabbing Penelope's hand. She too must have been feeling the excitement of a reunion.

'Of course. I would know his shape anywhere. Isn't he on Dancer?'

'I believe he is.'

They watched as Wat, who was riding alongside the carriage, girded his horse into a gallop to join Essex. The brothers leaned out of their saddles to get their arms about each other, holding their embrace.

'Is that not a heart-warming sight?' said Lettice. 'My two boys – time and distance has not broken their bond – and I have a third in the nursery.'

'How is the Noble Imp?' asked Penelope.

'Robust as ever. I should like to give Leicester another, though. One is never enough.'

'And you cannot?'

'I am nearly forty – it becomes less likely.' She paused, pursing her lips. 'And if the Queen refuses to let my husband leave her side for more than five minutes it will *never* happen.'

The bitterness of her mother's tone made an adequate response impossible, so Penelope looked out at her brothers once more. They had turned and were riding back towards the carriage, which had begun to make the slow climb up from the valley. Though Penelope hadn't been to Chartley for some years, each bump and bend of this route was etched into her mind, remembered from childhood rides. They were close enough to sniff the Chartley air. Soon they would be over the hill and past the great oak from where there was a view of the moated house, the sun making its golden stone brilliant against the lush green of the surrounding hills, like a coin dropped in a bed of grass. She could see it in her mind's eye, and the ruins of the castle beside it, surrounded by ancient fortified walls, where they had played as children. She and Dorothy used to climb the scuffed steps up to the turret, pretending to be in distress – chased by a dragon or a shape-shifting demon – and Essex, so small then, would scale the walls, a stick serving as a sword, and save them from that imagined malign force.

The carriage pulled to a halt as the brothers cantered back

towards them, dismounting on the run, in a clatter of hooves, bridles chinking, horses puffing. Penelope jumped out to greet Essex, who flung himself into her arms like a lover. He had filled out, felt like a man beneath her touch, not the boy he used to be, and he had grown so she had to stretch up on the tips of her toes to reach him, but his skin was still smooth as a peach, though she could see a scattering of bristles on his chin where he must have begun to shave. She had a sense, in that moment, of time passing too swiftly – Essex nearly seventeen already, she nineteen and with child, even little Wat was twelve – wishing she could turn back the pages of their lives, flicking past those years of separation and back to the chapter when they used to play together in the ruined turret.

'Ride to the house with us,' said Essex.

'I shouldn't –' she began, but on seeing the rejection in his face she whispered. 'I am with child.' Instead of the jubilant smile she expected, he looked inexplicably devastated and refused to meet her eyes – perhaps he too was musing on the passing of time.

'Be happy for me,' she said.

'I am.' But his scrunched brow told another story, which made Penelope wonder if the unfathomable gloom that sometimes plagued him had returned.

He greeted their mother with, at last, a glimpse of the smile that dimpled his right cheek so charmingly, before climbing back up on to Dancer and heading off, calling to Wat to catch him up.

'He seems perturbed,' Penelope said, once back inside the coach beside Lettice.

'He has been melancholic of late. I am counting on you to pull him out of it.' But Penelope knew well enough that there was little she could do to alleviate his black moods.

The carriage began to trundle on once more, shuddering over stones and potholes, and Penelope couldn't shake off the sense of her lost past. The intense awareness of time passing was causing a buzz of panic at the core of her, as if she were speeding towards her own end faster than she could bear. Even the thought of the baby taking shape inside her, that minuscule seed sprouting in the dark, offered little comfort, serving only to remind her that the best of her had been given to a man who couldn't muster a scrap of love to throw her way.

By the time they had passed the old castle gates and drawn up by the doors she had been shaken to the bones. The servants, presumably alerted by her brothers, had formed a line of greeting but as she was helped out of the carriage she realized that she barely recognized a soul amongst them, another stark reminder of the flight of time. Even the house had changed; it seemed smaller, the vast double doors to the great hall rendered modest, the hall itself diminished, and, when she looked closely, a little dilapidated, though perhaps, she reasoned, that was because she had become more used to the cavernous royal palaces and Leighs where everything was so very sumptuous and carefully tended.

Penelope crossed the room to look at the old portrait of her father, seeing it as if for the first time. He, clad in his inky armour with its intricately gilded panels and crimson velvet edging, looked out of the picture directly at her as if the past had come back to life. He had a smile hidden beneath his moustache reminding her of how he used to be, his stern front always compromised by an irrepressible sense of joy, and she had a sudden memory – surprised at the way the past could strike from nowhere – of him being fitted for this very same suit and how he had put the helmet on over her head and played peek-a-boo with the visor.

Her father's image inevitably turned Penelope's thoughts to his wish for her, making her wonder what he would have thought of the man she'd ended up with, whether he would even have allowed such a match. Her mind conjured an image of Sidney begging for her hand, on his knees before the

Queen, and she felt the now familiar hatred well up for that woman. Her father had always thought chivalry more important than wealth and Sidney was the epitome of chivalry.

Sidney had returned to court in the spring, wringing out her heart with his presence. She had done all she could to avoid him, taking strength from her victory over her husband, focused on keeping abreast of the labyrinthine allegiances in the privy chamber; on keeping one eye on Burghley and Cecil; on keeping informed of any plots afoot; amassing information to pass on to her mother. But Sidney's presence was almost too much to bear.

She had feigned sleep late one evening in a corner of the privy chamber, making as if she had drifted off but in fact watching an exchange between Cecil and a young man she didn't recognize. She remembered wondering what it must be like to be born with a body that was so misshapen, feeling sympathy for Cecil, but there was something about him that unsettled her nonetheless. She watched, through half-shut eyes, a purse pass from Cecil to the other man, absorbed by the surreptitious nature of the action and the way Cecil looked about shiftily. But she must have truly dropped into sleep at some point, for she had woken, disorientated, to find Sidney gazing at her as if she were a constellation of stars and he an astronomer. As she woke properly, realizing that the room had cleared and she was alone with him, she felt her long-suppressed desire ignite, but with it came the sense that she had been violated by his secret scrutiny, as if her pockets had been gone through without her permission.

She must have appeared horrified for he said, 'Forgive me, Stella. I couldn't help myself,' and was full to drooping with shame, as though he had done something truly wicked.

She wanted to ask what it was exactly he asked forgiveness for, fearing that perhaps he may have stolen a kiss when she was defenceless with sleep, but instead admonished him for compromising her in such a way. 'If someone should happen upon us alone together . . .' She didn't finish, turning to face the panelling where some long-ago lovers had carved their initials. He went without a word, leaving her feeling as if she had been visited by an apparition.

She forced her attention back on to her father's portrait, only then noticing the film of dust over the surface of it and the awkwardly painted hand, not like any human hand she had ever seen, and the old-fashioned ruff, open at the front and high up about his ears. 'Why did you have to die?' she whispered. 'Was it the Queen's doing, or God's will?' She thought she saw his eyes shift but told herself not to be so fanciful and read the faded gold lettering at the side of the portrait, the Devereux motto: *Virtutis comes invidia*. She had never questioned its meaning until then: *Envy is the companion of virtue*; to be virtuous, then, is to be envied, so why strive for virtue if it turns others into sinners? A shiver moved through her despite the warm weather. Virtue by whose measure? Looking away, she saw that Spero was about to cock his leg on the wainscoting and clapped her hands loudly, shouting to divert him, chasing him out of the door, glad of the distraction.

Outside the light had begun to fade and everything had taken on a magical luminous quality. Spero scampered towards Essex, jumping up at him, marking his white stockings. Essex pushed him off, irritated, and Penelope suggested they walk a little before dark.

'I could do with stretching my legs after the journey,' she said.

They ambled side by side in silence with the dog running ahead, finding themselves at the foot of the old tower. She led the way up the tight spiral stairs, the stone steps worn to a shine by generations of ancestors' feet, to a small room now open to the elements and overgrown with ivy. They sat on a ledge, which must have served once as a window sill, though the window was long gone, and took in the view to the west, the house a dark shape against a marmalade sky and the blushing hills beyond rolling towards the mountains of Wales.

'You do not seem yourself,' Penelope said, trying to break through her brother's silence. He had got hold of a lock of his hair and was tugging at it as if to pull it right out of his scalp. She gently wrested his hand away. 'You will hurt yourself.'

He looked at her then, his eyes were flat and unlit. 'All this,' he said finally, sweeping his arm about, taking in the landscape. 'And all the rest. It will all be mine on my majority . . .' He stopped and she tightened her grip on his hand as if to squeeze the words from him. 'And yet I am left with debts that I will never be able to pay off. The burden is so great, Sis. I fear I am not up to it. Leicester advises me to court the Queen's favour. He says if she likes me enough she will undo my debts.' He sank his chin on to his upturned palm with a sigh. 'Mother never stops reminding me that the family's honour lies in my hands. She fusses about me. You know how she is.'

'Her expectations are so high,' said Penelope. 'I know.' She prised the strand of hair out of his fingers, smoothing it away.

'I fear I can never live up to it all. She says I must secure the future for us. I must make us formidable . . . bring glory to the Devereuxs. Oh God, Sis, how can I ever manage it?'

'She is ambitious for us, that is all. She asked the same of me. You are young still, Robin.'

'Boys my age have been knighted on the battlefield.' His voice was filled with despair.

'But you will find your strength – give it a year or two. You are still a sapling, and you shall become a –'

'A Sidney,' he interrupted.

Hearing that name caused her heart to flounder. 'Is that who you would model yourself on? He is not so well favoured by the Queen.'

'That may be, but he has . . . he has something others don't . . . I can't say what it is.' He stopped, seeming to think about what it was he wanted to say. Penelope had often heard people struggle to articulate just what it was that set Sidney apart. 'He is truly good.'

Penelope could not help but think that the 'truly good' man they were talking of had done his best to incite her into adultery, but he was also the man who loathed cruelty of any kind, even to beasts, and was that rare thing too: a person prepared to admit he had been wrong. 'He is a man of honour,' she added, aware of the inadequacy of such an expression.

'I don't have it in me to be as he is. I am beset with resentments and petty dislikes. I am hot headed, weak willed, quick to judge, vain. I want to be admired by all.' His shoulders slumped as he expelled a great gust of air.

'Do not think Sidney, or any of the great knights for that matter, are not human beneath the surface. You are only describing what it is to be a man. Knowing one's failings is a quality few have.' She stopped, before adding as an afterthought, 'Sidney has feet of clay like us all.'

'I may be good in the lists and at the sword, but I am not sure I have the strength up here.' He tapped the side of his head twice, hard, with the heel of his hand.

'I will always be beside you. Never forget that.'

'Do you promise?' His face was utterly desolate but his skin was touched with roseate light making him, with his raven curls and even with his eyes flat as slate flags, unbearably beautiful. She wondered if that beauty would be his triumph or his downfall. It was true that the Queen liked to surround herself with beautiful things. And beauty has its currency, just as there is a value in nobility, as she had learned to her cost, but there is no achievement in it.

'You have my word.' She placed a kiss on her brother's cheek. 'Always.' She thought then of how she had stood up to her husband, driven a deal with him. She had achieved what she wanted through guile rather than fluttering her lashes, and it was a feeling she liked, a sense of unshakeable potency in the understanding that Rich was weakened by his secrets. She would never be brought low by the fear of others' judgements – never. 'I am stronger than I appear.'

'I have never doubted it.' And that dimpled smile crossed his face fleetingly once more. But then, inexplicably, he crumpled into tears – heaving, moaning sobs as if gripped by some inner agony. 'Oh, Sis, I am nothing, less than nothing . . .' Then he began to knock his head repeatedly on the rough stone of the wall.

She stood, grabbing him about the shoulders, pulling him away, remembering how he used to do the same thing as a child, beating his head against the nursery walls, and how his nurse would call for her as she was the only one who could make him stop. She had assumed he would grow out of it, they all said he would, and it cut her to the core to see that he still suffered so. She took him in her arms, kissing the swelling on his head, humming a childhood tune to soothe him. 'Little Robin, you are safe with me, I will protect you – I promise.' As the words left her mouth she felt the burden of that promise settle itself heavily about her shoulders.

She was assigned the chamber that she had shared with Dorothy as a child but, rather than feeling comforted by this, she was beset by a sense of unease in the aftermath of her brother's outburst, and lay awake for hours. It was a still summer night, close, without a whisper of breeze, and as she listened to the quiet rhythm of Jeanne's steady breath she began to hear other sounds: the crack of a beam as the wood shrank back a little in the heat; the scratch and scurry of mice behind the skirtings; the gentle fluff of the swallows shifting in their nests in the eaves; the faint call of an owl far down in the woods and then the unmistakable dry crunch of footsteps below the window. She at first supposed it must have been the steward making his final rounds, but then realized it was too late for that; the house had been locked up hours ago. Perhaps it was one of the grooms seeing to a lame horse, but no, the stables were on the other side.

She got out of bed and went over to the window, pressing her forehead against the cool glass. The moon was almost full and touched the edges of everything with its pale light, casting inky shadows in the places it couldn't reach. The footsteps continued, pacing back and forth, but she couldn't see to whom they belonged. Her breath clouded the panes. A figure, diaphanous and insubstantial, appeared from the gloom below, a man's shape, floating across the courtyard, disappearing into the gatehouse arch. Her heart beat frantically like a dog scratching at a flea. She ran to the bed, shaking Jeanne awake.

'What's the matter?' Her voice was drunk with sleep.

'A ghost!'

'What do you mean?'

'In the courtyard.' A pulse thrummed at her temple.

'You must have dreamt it. Get into bed.' Jeanne patted the place beside her.

'No, it was really there. I heard the footsteps. It drifted over the yard.'

'Shhh, it is just your imagination. It is easy to mistake things in the moonlight. If it were a ghost you would not have heard its footfall.'

'No, of course.'

'It was probably one of the servants slipping off for a lovers' tryst.'

'Yes, yes,' said Penelope, feeling silly in the face of Jeanne's pragmatism.

'You are unsettled. No wonder, in your condition.' Jeanne brought her small hand to Penelope's belly. 'Just think, you have a new life growing in there. It is bound to put you off kilter until you are used to it. Turn your mind to happy things. Dorothy will be arriving tomorrow, she will cheer you.'

The following day was sultry, so hot that Penelope and Jeanne wore their bodices only loosely laced and left off their sleeves and farthingales altogether. Essex and Wat had their doublets open to the waist and even Lettice, who liked to be dressed correctly whether or not visitors were expected – for the sake of the servants, she always said – had abandoned her ruff. They sprawled in the great chamber with all the windows and doors open wide in an attempt to encourage the sticky air to shift a little, but it refused and lassitude settled over them. Penelope thought of Dorothy travelling in such heat, hoping their party had broken the journey at an inn. Jeanne passed round cups of small beer but it was lukewarm and unappetizing. Even shuffling a pack of cards seemed like a Herculean task, so they chatted about nothing much and swapped riddles.

'I am tall when I am young. I am short when I am old,' said Wat, his voice squeaking and cracking as he spoke, making him redden and clear his throat, reminding Penelope that even the baby of the family was becoming a man. She remembered, with a jolt of love, rocking him as an infant. 'I live long when I am fat, and short when I am thin. What am I?'

'A candle,' they replied in unison.

'That is an old one,' said Essex. She scrutinized him but he seemed relaxed and content, with just the bruise flowering beneath his curls as a reminder of the previous day's distress. When she looked closely though she could see that his eyes remained flat as flint. 'Your turn, Mother.'

Lettice waved her fan in the general direction of her face. 'If I have it, I share it not. If I share it, I have it not. It is what?'

'Love?' said Jeanne.

'You answer "love" to them all,' teased Penelope. 'I think it is a secret.'

'It is, indeed,' answered Lettice. 'Your turn.'

'Let me think.' Penelope shut her eyes, allowing her head to sink back into a cushion, and found those familiar words circulating in her mind: *When Nature made her chief work, Stella's eyes.* She had thought it a great compliment to be named a star, burning brightly, a heavenly body, but it came to her then in a wave of sadness that a star is a distant thing offering nothing but an ephemeral spark in the night sky. The sun offers warmth and light and life, even the moon lights the darkness, but a star is cold and impotent – just a pretty speck. 'I can fall but never am hurt. I can shoot but never do harm. I can burn but never do scald. I can be seen but never be touched. What am I?'

'This one is love, surely,' said Jeanne, which caused everyone to laugh as Penelope shook her head and rolled her eyes.

'Is it water?' asked Wat.

'Water can scald,' said Lettice. 'Is it pride? No it can't be that.' She took a sip from her cup, scowling. 'Is there not a chip of ice to be had in this house?'

'I don't know. What are you?' asked Essex.

Penelope felt a vortex of nausea pass down into her belly, and, suddenly desperate to move, pulled herself up to her feet, taking in a series of deep breaths. 'I am a star.'

'Oh, of course,' said Jeanne, 'a falling star.'

Penelope looked out of the window, remembering the stream that ran through the bottom of the orchard, suddenly girded by a desire to sit on its bank in the shade of the trees and dangle her feet in the cool water. 'Who will join me on a walk?' No one replied. 'In that case I shall go on my own.'

Once out of the house and in the orchard where the grass grew soft, she kicked off her shoes, pulled off her coif and unpinned her hair, picking up her pace to feel, at long last, the movement of air on her exposed skin. The grasses and wild flowers grew tall, harebells and poppies, bright patches of colour, haloed in clouds of baby's breath and cow parsley. She followed the path, stepping carefully over the brambles where it was overgrown, occasionally stopping to unhook her dress when it became tangled. The bushes were thick with vivid green berries, promising an abundant late-summer harvest. A vague memory came to her of picking blackberries in that very place once, years before, cramming them into her mouth as if she were starving. Someone was stung by a bee that day, but she couldn't think who, could just see an image of adult fingers trying to prise out the sting, and recalled learning that a bee dies once it has stung. She tried to make sense of it, wondered why God would make a creature whose only defence had such grave consequence. She walked on, drawn by the thought of the cool water. But as she arrived she saw that the stream had dried to little more than a trickle. She walked beside it, seeming to remember that somewhere along that stretch the water gathered into a natural pool.

A twig cracked, she stopped, suddenly feeling watched; a little chill moved through her and with it all the fear from the previous night returned. She stayed silent for a moment, hearing only birdsong and the hum of crickets, but then came the sound of something rushing through the orchard grass and she only understood what it was when Spero let out a yelp, jumping up at her in an excited frenzy. She stooped to stroke him, laughing at herself for her misplaced unease, supposing it must have been the past crowding about her that was having that effect. Spero tore off ahead in pursuit of a scent and she ran after him, feeling simple happiness rise up in her as if she were a girl once more and free of cares.

Her foot suddenly caught on a root and the ground came hurtling up to meet her. She broke her fall with an outstretched palm, bending it right back at the wrist as she crashed heavily to earth, knocking the breath right out of her. She lay on her side, cradling her painful hand, and was besieged by a creeping fear that somehow she had dislodged her baby in the fall, feeling swept up in regret for her recklessness.

'Are you hurt?'

Looking up, she saw a man looming above. The sun was behind him so she couldn't make out his features. Her mouth opened to scream but, as in a nightmare, no sound came and she felt her mind separate off from her fear, offering up the idea that she must have hit her head and lost consciousness, for this man she imagined before her was Sidney.

'Stella, are you hurt?'

He squatted beside her, seeming so very real, with that black smudge of ink and the male tang of his sweat. She stretched out a hand to his sleeve, then took it back, fearing the illusion might vaporize under her touch.

'Sidney?' she whispered. She could see the faint embroidery of scarring on his face, as if someone had stitched a word there that she was unable to read.

'You are hurt.' He took her hand. She could feel him; he was solid, fleshy, warm, as if real. 'Look.' There was a cut across the ball of her thumb where she'd broken her fall and the blood had seeped on to the white cuff of her shift; but she felt no pain and wondered momentarily if she were dead, finding herself slipping into a maelstrom of panic, thinking she might have been caught up in some kind of witchery.

'I have frightened you.'

'What are you?'

'Stella! I did not mean to alarm you.' She lifted herself up on to an elbow, only then feeling the sharp pain of the cut and the throb in her wrist. It began to dawn on her that this was no spectre, or figment of her imagination, or malign, conjured-up ghoul. 'What a fool I was. I wanted to surprise you and I scared you half to death. I should never have come.' He had taken out a handkerchief and was wrapping it around her hand to quench the blood flow and then, without a word, she allowed him to help her up and convey her to the shade of a nearby tree where they both sat leaning against the trunk. Spero appeared once more, bounding out of the undergrowth, stopping a few feet away from them, curling his lip in a silent growl.

'Here, boy,' she called, patting her thigh to beckon him, but he sat at a distance in the path, stiff, like a sentry. She turned to look at Sidney properly; he was dishevelled, his clothes creased and covered in burrs, his eyes ringed with dark shadows. 'I think you need to explain yourself. What are you doing here?'

'I was with my father in Ludlow. It is but a day's ride. I arrived late last night. Too late – I slept in the woods.'

'It was you.' A wave of tenderness broke over her. 'I heard your footsteps. I thought you were a ghost.'

'I terrified you twice, then! What a fool I am to come upon you in such a way. I had thought to see you without all the others . . .'

'No.' She took his hand – 'Not a fool' – bringing it up to her lips, seeing the dirt trapped beneath his bitten nails, opening his fingers, closing her eyes and planting a kiss at the centre of his palm. 'Though perhaps an inn might have been a more sensible choice of resting place.'

'I wanted to be close to you.'

'Now that is a little foolish.' She was trying to dilute the atmosphere with humour, fearing she might be entirely overcome.

'I have tried to forget you but you draw me like a lodestar.'

'You think of me as a star,' she said quietly, 'as if I have no feelings. Yet I am a woman – flesh and blood.' She pinched the thin skin of her inner arm, as if to prove the fact. 'It is painful for me too, to be apart from you.'

He expelled a deep breath, as if releasing a century's worth of air. She held his gaze as he inched closer. When their mouths finally met, tongues slip-sliding, she teetered on the precipice of lust, on the brink of losing herself irretrievably. But with sudden clarity she remembered the life growing in her belly and pulled away abruptly. 'I cannot.'

He groaned, like a dying animal, as she prised herself out of his grip.

'If you love me truly, you must let me go,' she said.

'What, for your honour? Because you belong to that man . . . *Rich*?' He was billowing with anger then, as if all the love in him had transformed into rage. 'You will not make a cuckold of *Rich*? What do you owe *him*?'

'Oh, my love,' she murmured, placing a hand over his, which he snatched away like a sulking child. 'I do not love him.' She took his hand again, holding it tight that time, refusing to be denied. 'It is you I love, with every fibre of myself, and no other. But . . .'

'But, what?' He looked at her then, his eyes teeming with anguish.

'I am with child.'

He brought a hand up to each side of his head and shut his eyes. '*His* child; you carry *his* child.'

'Yes,' she said, 'my husband's child.' It was only the thought of the seed germinating inside her, which she hoped to heaven had not been dislodged by her fall, that was holding her in check. 'I have made an agreement with Rich. It is not he whom I must honour, but the pact I made.'

'Pact?'

'I will give him two boys and then I will be free.'

'But –'

'No,' she interrupted. 'Do not ask me why, for I will not tell you, nor anyone.'

'Stella,' he said, pulling her back into his embrace. 'I am lost without you. I have never wanted anything as I want you.'

'And I you.' The words seemed woefully inadequate but as she said it, at last, she fully understood the true meaning of desire, the invisible hand that will push a grown man, who should know better, into a day's hard riding in the hope of a glimpse of his love at the end of it; the torture described in poetry; the force that will make a person drop every principle they ever had to quench the thirst of it. She collected together all her resistance, finding somewhere the strength to hold her ground in the face of him, to put her head before her heart. 'But I cannot. I have promised to remain faithful until I have birthed both boys.'

'Oh God.' His face was the image of despair.

'If I keep my side of the bargain, he will keep his, and once I have fulfilled my duties I will be at liberty.' She paused, picking a long grass stem and pinching the seeds away from its head. 'Then I will be yours.'

'But he will never know.'

'*I* will know,' she replied. 'If I cannot adhere to my own moral code then I am not worth the flesh and blood I am made of. I do not care about what others might think of me. I do not even care if I make my husband a cuckold or myself a whore. But I care to keep my promises – or I am not me.'

'You . . .' He took both her hands in his, faltering, seeming to search for words. 'You are remarkable. There is no one like you.'

'Not so remarkable,' she said, thinking about the extent to which she would lose the power she had got a taste for if she compromised herself with a dark secret of her own.

'I will wait,' he said, then repeated it: 'I will wait.'

They sat in silence for some time, she tucked into the crook of his arm, he stroking her hair. She dared a moment's wondering about how it would be, until finally she said, 'I must go. They will be worried about me – in my condition.' She extricated herself from his arms, suddenly deflated by the thought of separation. 'What will you do? Will you present yourself at the house, say you were passing?'

'I don't know,' he said, shredding blades of grass with

his fingers, then grabbing her arm again and pulling her back to him – 'Don't leave' – then releasing her once more – 'No, you must go. I don't think I could bear to spend a night under the same roof, knowing you were only a few yards away.' He picked a poppy and handed it to her without another word.

She stood, gathering all her strength, and whistled for Spero, who skirted round Sidney with a sideways look before falling into her wake. She turned, briefly, and blew him a kiss, then reprised her path back through the orchard, twisting the stem of the poppy between her fingers. At the gate she retrieved her shoes and her coif, replacing them, as if to put everything back to normal, but her entire world had shifted off its axis and she knew that nothing could ever again be normal. She looked at the poppy; a scarlet splash in her hand, but under her scrutiny its veined petals seemed so very fragile and insubstantial, translucent like the papers of a bible, wilting already, as if all its life had been spent in that moment of vivid display.

She heard the horses before she saw them, and rushed to the stables.

'Dorothy,' she cried, running to where her sister was dismounting. Dorothy turned, her face smudged with tears, her eyes rimmed in red. 'What is it?'

She flung the reins to the groom and took Penelope by the elbow to a quiet corner of the yard. 'Leicester will have me wed Sidney. It is sure this time. He is gaining the Queen's permission and has offered a dowry of two thousand pounds for me.'

Penelope felt unsteady and sank on to the edge of the mounting block. She couldn't think of what to say, just repeated, 'Two thousand pounds.'

'I love another,' said Dorothy, 'and I need your help to wed him quietly.'

So they both had their secrets. It was as if a shaft of light had fallen across her path. 'Then you will not be free to wed Sidney.'

'Clearly!' Dorothy seemed impatient at her sister's statement of the obvious. 'You will help me, won't you?'

'But you will be disgraced, Dot – ostracized from court. You know what that means? Look at Mother.' Her conscience pricked at her, would not allow her to encourage such an elopement lightly.

'Look at *you*! I couldn't bear a loveless union like *yours*.' Dorothy's words stung, despite the fact she spoke the truth. 'And Sidney – when we met he barely looked my way; there was not a sympathetic gesture in the man. He was haughty, cold, arrogant, distant – not even the flicker of a smile.'

Penelope's prevailing thought was that, given her sister resembled her so greatly, this was proof that Sidney loved what lay beneath. She wanted desperately to confide in Dorothy but something held her back, the fear that perhaps her sister might see it as a means to escape this marriage by lifting the lid from her secret. She had always trusted Dorothy and felt a twinge of resentment that the circumstances of love and secrecy could so easily come between them in such a way.

'You risk too much, Dot. My conscience will not allow –'

Dorothy cut in sharply, locking on to her with black eyes, twins of her own: 'You think you understand everything, but you do not. What do *you* know of love, in your loveless union?'

Penelope took a breath to prevent the truth from spilling out, saying quietly, 'You do not know everything about me.'

'I'm sorry.' Dorothy looked chastened. 'This whole business has driven me quite out of my mind. You must help me. I don't care if I am banished from court for all time, as long as I am with my Thomas.'

'Thomas who?'

'Perrot.' Dorothy, embarrassed, dropped her eyes as a flush marched over her breast.

'I see.' Penelope knew well enough that Thomas Perrot, though a childhood friend of theirs, was nowhere near sufficiently noble to make a match with the daughter of one of England's foremost earls. She couldn't help but admire Dorothy's spirited defiance. How easily she would escape the responsibility of being a Devereux at court, with this marriage. 'He is a fine lad, but no one will support the match.'

'Do you think I don't know that? That is why I beg of your help. You are the only soul I trust. Please, Penelope. I understand the consequences. Please . . .'

'I suppose that now you are one of the Queen's maids you need me to provide an excuse for your absence?'

'So you *will* do it?'

'You know what might happen to you? The Queen has put maids under lock and key for less.'

'That is a risk I am prepared to take.' Dorothy's conviction was infectious and Penelope found herself caught up in it.

'I don't suppose there is any sense in us both having marriages entirely bereft of affection. I would not want that fate for you.' Penelope felt a smile open over her face. 'But Mother will be furious.'

September 1583

Whitehall

'Was it as painful as they say?' asked Martha. The Queen's maids had gathered round to greet Penelope on her return to court.

'Excruciating,' she replied. Martha's eyes popped, round as pennies. 'I bellowed like a heifer, didn't I, Jeanne?'

'I've never heard such a sound,' agreed Jeanne with a laugh.

'But they say you forget the pain the instant you set eyes on your infant,' said someone. 'Is it true?'

Penelope looked at their expectant faces. They all wanted it to be true but it was not. She wanted it to be true too. Her baby had not been the panacea of all ills she had hoped for. What she had felt when she held Lucy for the first time was a profound dread, as if she were on the brink of an abyss.

'Mother told me you fall in love with your baby on sight,' sighed another girl. '"An indescribable feeling," she said it was. What is it like – tell us?'

'Yes.' Penelope pretended to adjust her skirts so as to avoid meeting their eyes. 'An indescribable feeling.' She was afraid that they would see, etched on to her, the mark of a bad mother, a mother who didn't love her infant.

'Were you not disappointed that your firstborn was a girl? Your husband cannot have been pleased.' This came from Peg, who hovered at the edge of the group. She looked thin, as if her own bitterness was eating away at her.

'A healthy child could never be a disappointment.' Penelope looked Peg in the eye then, maintaining a steady gaze and a painted smile, willing herself not to reveal her true feelings. She said nothing of how her baby had not thrived – the

141

struggle for breath, the tiny ribcage heaving with each wheez-
ing inhalation – and that she blamed herself for her lack of
love. The midwife said she had seen cases such as that before,
declared the baby would not live. Lucy had been hastily bap-
tized but Penelope could not accept that her infant, even one
she could not find a way to love, would be taken by God
before her life had begun. She had called for the Queen's
physician, Doctor Lopez, who rode to Leighs from London
in haste. He palpated Lucy's tiny chest; as if by magic she
coughed up a gob of matter and her life was saved.

'Becoming a mother for the first time can be daunting,'
Lopez had said to her, indicating that somehow he understood Penelope's turmoil. 'You will take to it, just you wait.'
Those few kind words had caused a change in her and almost
instantly she felt a splinter of love for her daughter.

'You will understand how it is,' continued Penelope to a
sneering Peg, 'when you have an infant of your own.'

Peg looked away tight-mouthed. Penelope knew well
enough that there was no sign of a match on the horizon for
Peg and that her words had hit their mark. She'd forgotten,
in her months away, how sharp one's aim needed to be at
court.

'You must miss her terribly,' said Martha.

Penelope nodded, remembering how glad she had been to
hand over her infant into the capable hands of Mistress Shilling. A thick cloud of despair had settled over her, making
even the simplest task seem quite beyond her reach, as if all
the joy had been siphoned out of her. She tried to pray, to
ask forgiveness for whatever it was she had done to lose
God's favour – she had resisted Sidney, was that not enough,
she had done her husband's bidding – but she felt her faith
worn thin as parchment. It was only the kind care of dear
Jeanne that kept her going through those dark days. Rich,
contrary to Peg's belief, was delighted with his daughter,
which pleased Penelope, though that pleasure was felt at a

distance as if she were watching someone else's experience, not her own.

Eventually Jeanne had got her up and dressed and to the chapel to be churched and then forced her to leave the house, to feel the warmth of the sun, to walk, to ride. Little by little she unfolded, as if she had been left forgotten in a chest for years and was being shaken out and aired. But the residue, when her mood had lifted enough to feel herself again, was guilt, and she suspected that no amount of Jeanne's tender care would shake that out of her. What kind of mother cannot love her child? she asked herself silently over and over again. There was no answer to that.

'Dorothy is gone,' said Peg, running her fingers over her feather fan.

Penelope did not reply, just smiled as if nothing was wrong. But Dorothy, like their mother, was not to be mentioned in earshot of the Queen. Penelope hadn't witnessed Leicester's fury at the secret wedding, nor the Queen's. Perrot had festered a few weeks in the Fleet prison and it was only through her stepfather's influence that Dorothy wasn't also incarcerated, though she was banished from court. But Penelope had received a letter from her sister with a rapturous description of her country idyll. She explored herself for envy, but found none, understanding her taste for power meant there was little allure in a quiet existence.

'She is *persona non grata*.' Peg was failing to aggravate her but nonetheless Penelope was glad of the distraction when a group of men strode by, stopping before the women, removing their hats and stooping into polite bows. She hadn't seen Sidney initially, only realizing he was there when Spero began to growl on her lap. She followed the dog's gaze and there he was, trying to catch her eye. Her stomach lurched and she wanted to hate him for being the reason she could not love her baby, for existing, for stealing her heart.

'Lady Rich's spaniel appears to have an aversion to you,' quipped one of the men.

Sidney's expression was pained, even perhaps rueful, but she turned sharply away and kissed the smooth dome of the dog's head. Sidney had written letters, reams of them, beautiful secret words that wrung her out. She burned them all, in the grip of her misery, instantly regretting it. Jeanne had found her before the dead hearth, covered in soot, searching desperately for fragments. She had helped her to her feet and begun to undress her as if she were a child or an invalid incapable of even removing her own clothes, quietly saying, 'arms up', 'turn round', 'step out of it'. Penelope obeyed like a puppet, as if she had lost her soul. Jeanne wiped away the soot with a cloth and combed it carefully out of her hair, but even so the following morning there was a dark shadow on the white linen pillow, a manifestation of her state of mind.

'I thought you had lost your grip on things altogether,' Jeanne had said of that time. 'I worried I would never get you back.'

'The Queen has asked for you,' said Peg, jolting her into the present. 'You'd better not keep her waiting.'

Penelope was glad of the excuse to remove herself from Sidney's doleful gaze. There were six armed guards at the door to the privy chamber, which made her wonder if there had been a further plot uncovered. She found the Queen deep in conversation with Burghley and Cecil but as Penelope entered they all looked up and watched her walk the length of the chamber. Burghley wore a smile that seemed counterfeit and the son was expressionless, making Penelope ask herself what he was hiding, what it was they had been discussing. She prepared herself for a volley of questions from the Queen, as she dropped her dog to the floor and sank into her curtsy, anxious she might have to bear the brunt of her sister's misdemeanour.

But all the Queen said was, 'You were missed. Come and

play a game of cards. I'm tired of listening to this company of old wives fretting over my safety.'

Penelope was, as ever, impressed by the Queen's nerve but felt the familiar confusion of feelings, admiration tainted with something infinitely darker, flooded back as she sat on the stool that was procured.

'They are convinced I am about to be murdered.' The Queen flicked her eyes in the general direction of Burghley and his boy, who shrank back like dismissed children. 'I'll play you for that trinket on your gown.' She rubbed her hands together like a miser, as Penelope fumbled at the jewel, unhooking it and placing it on the table. It was one of her mother's brooches; Penelope knew that the Queen would recognize it as such, and think it a small victory. Penelope had thought often about her mother's treatment at the hands of the Queen and the misery her ostracism had wrought. She had long realized the Queen's favouring of her was a revenge of sorts; to take ownership of her enemy's daughter, to make a pawn of her, was indeed a for-midable gesture but one that fuelled Penelope to play her own game.

It would take more than a little royal favour to break the bond between a mother and daughter; and the Queen had no daughter, nor did she ever really know her mother, so couldn't comprehend the depth of such a bond. Favour brought its own advantages and even a pawn, if it is placed well on the board, can hold more power than it might seem.

'And *my* wager is this.' The Queen untied a coin purse from her girdle and put it on the table. 'But I don't intend to lose.' The purse was fashioned in the form of a frog and, even exquisitely embroidered as it was, looked like a dead creature, lying there with its legs dangling over the table's edge.

'Nor do I,' said Penelope.

'Watch and learn, Pygmy. Watch and learn,' said the Queen, turning briefly to Cecil.

Penelope had not heard her call Cecil that before. She knew the Queen was fond of pet names but 'Pygmy' seemed so cruel. If he was offended he didn't show it, just smiled the Queen's way, his lips peeling back to reveal a row of surprisingly neat, sharp little teeth. She remembered the incident when his book was snatched from his hands and thrown about, how the savage jeers had slipped off him, and wondered if his resilience was learned young. She had seen the runt in a litter of puppies grow up to become the most savage in the pack.

'This girl could teach you a thing or two about playing cards.'

There it was again, that smile that could so easily have been mistaken for a snarl, and he said, 'I have heard Lady Rich is most proficient,' but the Queen had already returned her attention to Penelope.

'I don't like it when my favourite ladies go off like that.'

'I shall try not to make a habit of it, Your Majesty.' The Queen laughed at that and made a passing comment about how different she was from her 'disobedient dolt of a sister'. Penelope kept her smile intact as the Queen shuffled the cards, snapping them out on to the table one by one, then picking hers up and spending several minutes ordering them and reordering them in a fan.

They played in silence; Penelope could sense Cecil's scrutiny and the thought came to her that perhaps he had been advised to watch her, just as she had been to keep an eye on him.

'I am most displeased with that sister of yours,' continued the Queen. 'I would have thought she'd have had more sense.'

'Love can make people do silly things,' said Penelope.

'Yes,' she replied with a sigh, then murmuring, 'like mother, like daughter.'

Penelope clenched her jaw, refusing to be riled.

'I cannot fathom why all my courtiers insist on being so disobedient when it comes to marriage. It reflects badly on me.' She played on a while before adding, '*You* would not seek to betray me, would you?' casting a look Penelope's way that was so icy it took all the self-control she could muster not to show her apprehension.

'Never,' was all she replied, fearing, had she said more, her words might have been judged insincere.

They played on silently once more; it was Burghley who spoke next: 'What think you to the Sidney wedding, My Lady?'

Penelope's breath caught in her chest a moment until she understood it must have been the younger brother he was talking of. 'Robert Sidney is to wed? Who is the bride?'

'No, not Robert,' said the Queen, 'the older one – Philip – the poet.'

'Philip Sidney . . .' She was hollow, emptied out of everything, and it took all her strength of will to remain seated with that uninterested smile spread over her face, feeling Burghley and his boy observing her.

'With Frances Walsingham. She's a rather bland girl, very young. Do you know her?' continued the Queen. Penelope slowly shook her head, trying to assimilate the news. 'It pleases her father. Walsingham has served me well. What do you think?'

Penelope shrugged. She was afraid to open her mouth for fear of what might emerge from it. It made sense then, that rueful look Sidney had worn in the long gallery earlier. The Queen seemed to approve of her apparent indifference and Penelope noticed Cecil exchange a look with his father, wondering what it meant.

'He has matured lately – used to have ideas above his station,' the Queen went on. 'Took it upon himself to try and dissuade me from my match with Anjou once.' She huffed, rearranging her fan of cards. 'Came to nothing anyway,' she murmured under her breath as she placed a trio of clubs face up on the table: a nine, ten and knave.

Penelope managed somehow to make her play as if all was normal, as if a seed of jealousy had not sprouted in her and sent out shoots into the far reaches of her being, twisting about her vital organs, suckering themselves to her heart, woody fingers gripping tightly, staunching her blood flow.

'Sidney once asked me for *your* hand. Tried to resuscitate that old betrothal your father arranged. Did you know? Don't know what he expected; you were already promised to Rich, and Sidney had nothing much to offer you.'

Penelope cleared her throat and uttered, 'Is that so?' as if she had barely ever given Sidney a thought, but the suckers continued pushing and winding, ever deeper.

'I've rather warmed to him lately though,' continued the Queen. 'I believe Sidney may be destined for great things. He is certainly much loved, isn't he, Pygmy?'

'Indeed,' replied Cecil, oozing indifference and straightening his cuffs, which were bright and stiff with starch, before throwing her a look that suggested he knew more than he should. Penelope only then realized that, while she had been away birthing her infant, Cecil, who had once barely been able to meet her eye, had become someone who knew things. Here was an example of knowledge as power – these two men, father and son, bristling with the confidence that comes from having looked into every dark cranny, from knowing that nothing occurred without their knowledge. Burghley's espionage network was renowned, spreading secretly out through Walsingham, into the royal courts of Europe. She attempted levity, placing her cards on the table with the words, 'Beaten again! I am out of practice, madam.'

Penelope compared herself, a woman with no inkling even of her beloved's marriage, entirely disempowered by ignorance, to this man Burghley who had eyes everywhere, who held the reins of England behind its Queen because of all he knew. Was Sidney's marriage to Walsingham's daughter a power play – was Sidney shoring up his position with connections? Whatever the reason, it felt as if a knife were being skewered into her heart. But something hardened in her and with it came the realization that she too could have eyes everywhere, make a web of connections, if she put her mind to it, and she resolved to never be the victim of ignorance again.

A man approached Burghley, quietly whispering something to him, upon which he turned to the Queen. 'There is pressing business, Your Majesty, with the Scottish woman.'

Penelope's curiosity was pricked by this. It was Mary of Scotland they spoke of, surely – the Queen's cousin who had lost her crown to her infant son and languished for years as England's prisoner. Penelope wondered if she truly was a threat to the throne as they said, or if it was more complicated than it appeared.

'We shall continue our game later, my dear. I am required,' said the Queen, nudging her head in Burghley's direction.

Penelope sensed Cecil's eyes slip over her as she walked from the chamber. She picked up Spero, and took the door to the long gallery, forcing her thoughts away from the Sidney marriage, refusing to give voice to her inner devastation as she made her way to her rooms.

'I have been searching for you,' said Jeanne as Penelope entered. Something of her hidden distress must have shown on her surface, for Jeanne said, 'What is it?' All she could do was shake her head, clutching at Spero for comfort. Jeanne guided her to the bed and, sitting beside her, placed an arm about her shoulders and passed her a package. 'This came for you.'

'What is it?'

'I have no idea. Come, let me untie you, make you more comfortable.' Jeanne peeled away her layers of clothing and loosened the laces of her bodice. She lay down on the bed, numb to the core. Jeanne must have sensed her need for solitude for she began to gather up some linens and announced she was going to the laundry. When Jeanne had left the room

Penelope picked up the packet. Recognizing the hand instantly as Sidney's, she flung it back on to the bed but then took it up again, tearing away the wrapping.

It was a loosely bound ream of papers. She flicked through it; each page was filled tightly with Sidney's precise writing, divided into verses, the front page saying only *Astrophil and Stella*, no note, no explanation, nothing. She pulled a chair to the window where the early-evening sun flooded in, alive with floating motes of dust, dipping and swirling in the agitated air as she moved.

She began to read. The words took hold in her, catching on to the dry kindling of her sadness as she began to understand that this – marks in ink on a sheaf of pages – was the intimate articulation of Sidney's love, a true likeness of his heart. Entranced by the rhythm of his words she read on, unable to recognize herself in that distant Stella, black-eyed, alabaster-skinned, pearl-toothed tyrant – thief of his heart, in one moment cold stone, in another a heavenly nymph and elsewhere a deliverer of delightful pain. His love was monstrous, terrifying, filled with jealous rage and desperate longing, sweetness, sadness – an endless battle between ecstasy and pain.

She barely looked up when Jeanne returned. 'What is it?' she asked.

'Poems.'

'From *him*?'

Penelope nodded, unable to drag herself away from the words, reading as if her life depended upon it; as if she were lost and the marks on the paper were the map that could either guide her to safety or its opposite – she could not know which.

To you alone I sing this mournful Verse,
The mournful'st Verse that ever Man heard tell;
To you whose softned Hearts it may empierce,
With Dolour's Dart, for Death of Astrophel.

Edmund Spenser, *Astrophel*
(his eulogy to Sir Philip Sidney)

News of Mary Stuart's execution had begun to seep out on the day Sidney was laid to rest, but such was the outpouring of grief for the poet soldier that the death of a deposed queen did not resonate as it might have done on a different day. It had been a full three years and more since Penelope had begun to understand the intrigue surrounding Mary of Scotland, and how Burghley had invisibly orchestrated her circuitous route to the scaffold. Penelope had watched and listened, allowing information to accumulate in her, knowledge to shore up her future, as she observed the business of state take place beside the fickle amusements of court. She had grown to understand that the Queen had to sacrifice her Scottish cousin for the sake of England, that politics are ruthless and sometimes death, even if it is cruel, makes perfect sense.

But there was no sense to Sidney's death – injured, fighting far from home. It was not even a fatal wound, yet it had been the death of him. If Mary's death symbolized Elizabeth's supremacy, Sidney's was its opposite: it achieved nothing and stood for nothing, unless it marked the end of chivalry. The Queen had chosen him for greatness but none could have predicted how short his time in the sun would be. And Penelope's heart was shattered.

She had been asked by Leicester to accompany Sidney's wife to the funeral and they stood together in the gallery on Cheapside to watch the cortège go by. Penelope was thankful for her sister's reassuring presence right behind her, one firm hand on her shoulder. She had been conveyed to Cheapside in a trance, was too riddled with desolation to be aware of anything around her. Jeanne had helped her dress – there had been a fuss, her black velvet would not fit, for she was with child again, and she had had to borrow a gown of her mother's; she couldn't have cared less what she wore.

She could feel Frances's slight presence beside her, barely there, as if she were a figure in a dream. She glanced at her wan profile and was surprised by the force of feeling that surged in her. What was it: a brooding envy of the girl for being the one who held Sidney's hand as he died; for being the one who had lain with him and been his wife near on four years; for being the one to bear his child; for being the one who would spend eternity alongside him. It was an ugly emotion, but undeniable. She couldn't find a way to truly hate the girl, though she had tried. But Penelope was strangely glad of Frances's presence that day, for it meant she had to hold the disparate parts of herself together, on the surface at least – beneath she felt herself crumbling like plasterwork in an abandoned building.

The cortège seemed endless, seven hundred mourners, and thousands more turned out into the streets to watch in silence – it was like a royal funeral. She wondered what he would have thought of that – he would have liked it. For all his chivalry he was not immune to vanity.

The press of the crowds in the street directly below was so great that the procession struggled to pass. They watched without a word as the high-hatted men went by in twos, their long gowns dragging in the dirt. Behind a pair of guards, with halberds held pointing to the ground, walked two drummers beating out a mournful rhythm. On and on they passed, his men-at-arms, his household, his friends, his distant kin, and all heralded by the beat of those infernal drums, until the horses came into sight – Sidney's field horse, followed by his beloved Barbary, both rattling with finery and mounted by his preferred pages. On seeing the broken lance carried by one, Penelope felt a lump, hard as a stone, in her throat and lines of his poems began to float through her mind.

> *While no night is more dark than is my day,*
> *Nor no day hath less quiet than my night.*

She knew what was to come, could hardly bear to look and yet could not help herself, as the bier came into view, draped in black, swaying like an ancient barge, the bearers struggling under its weight. Frances made a small gasp and Penelope felt a storm of tears gather in her. Without thinking, she took the girl's hand, squeezed it.

> *What sobs can give words grace my grief to show?*
> *What ink is black enough to paint my woe?*

Frances leaned in against her, light as a cloud, and Penelope put an arm about her shoulders. There was his brother, Robert Sidney, face half hidden beneath his cowl, leading the chief mourners, and then came Leicester and Huntingdon with Essex and all the great noblemen – mounted, jangling, magnificent.

It was Essex who first brought her the news. They had all been on tenterhooks at court, for they knew Sidney had been injured fighting the Spaniards in the Low Countries, protecting England from the Catholic threat. Everyone talked of his heroism, of how he had removed his leg armour in an act of solidarity with his captain who had left his back at camp; how he had bravely gone in to rescue a comrade; how a shot had caught his thigh, shattered the bone; how he had offered his drinking cup to a dying man, deeming his need greater. Penelope wondered which stories were true – they all sounded like gestures he might have made. She never for a moment imagined he would not survive. She thought perhaps he might walk with a limp, or a stick, or even lose the leg altogether, but never was he going to die. He was always going to return and continue loving her.

But Essex burst into her chambers unannounced, filthy from the road, wild-eyed like a man who has seen unspeakable things.

'Sidney is dead.' He said it bluntly. There is no way to cushion such news.

'No. You are wrong.' The chamber began to swim and she thought she might fall, but he grabbed her arm and led her to a seat.

'I was there,' he said. 'He gave me his best sword, asked that I take care of his wife.'

'His best sword . . . His wife.' She was like a parrot, with no words of her own to speak.

'He gave me this . . . for you.' He pressed a fold of paper into her hand.

'For me . . .'

Rich walked in then. Greeted Essex, seeming delighted to see him, appearing to be completely unaware that his wife was in a trance of shock, her hand gripping at a scrap of parchment. He began to question Essex about the conflict and then said, 'I hear Sidney met his end,' flippantly, as if he were talking about someone he didn't know. But then he *didn't* know Sidney. She wanted to ask him why he, who so loathed papism, had not been there fighting for the cause. 'Are you ailing?' He turned finally to Penelope, who feared her face was creased with distress. 'Not losing the baby, are you?'

She brought her hands to her belly and taking a sharp inhalation of breath said, 'I am quite well, thank you, husband,' and slipped the letter out of sight.

Essex was striding back and forth on the oak boards, agitated. He had been changed by battle and she knew she had not only lost Sidney, but she had also lost the brazen boy who grinned at her from the deck of the ship, departing to war. She excused herself, pleading exhaustion caused by her condition, and finally, in the privacy of her bedchamber, read the paper, just a scrawled line in a wobbly hand: *Yours 'til the end.*

Essex looked up from the procession now, seeking her in the gallery. Their eyes met; his jaw was rigid as it had been when, as a child, he held back tears. Frances cupped her hand and spoke close to her ear. 'It was you he loved. I always knew. He said it to me when we agreed to wed, that his heart belonged to another. I knew it was you, for I read his poems, even the ones he hid from me. He asked if I could accept that.'

Penelope wanted to inquire how she had answered, but couldn't bring herself and just held the girl more tightly, as they watched the Dutch consignment go by and then the soldiers, weapons down, and another pair of drummers, a lone piper – on and on.

'I did accept it,' Frances added eventually.

'He was never mine in . . .' Penelope couldn't say it.

'In body.' It was Frances who finished her sentence. The girl suddenly seemed so substantial, so calm and stoic beside her, not a feather-light wisp at all. 'I know.' It was Penelope who felt as brittle as a dead leaf.

Her mind drifted back to their final farewell. Sidney was so proud to at last have a meaningful commission from the Queen; she had made him Governor of Flushing. He had sought Penelope out to tell her. She hadn't seen him for months – she had been lying-in with Essie, her second girl – but all the old desire gushed to the surface. He was different, more cheerful, and she'd considered that it might have been marriage, or fatherhood, that had done that to him; but it was more likely to have been the long-awaited royal favour. He was knighted at last – she teased him, called him 'Sir Philip' with an exaggerated curtsy; he had laughed it off, said it meant nothing, but couldn't quite hide the fact that he was pleased. 'The Queen is to stand godmother to my daughter,' he had told her. She wished he hadn't said that, had wanted to pretend he wasn't married with an infant daughter, that he was still entirely hers.

He had tried to see her alone many times since his marriage, had sought to explain himself in letters (he had been obliged to wed, something to do with a promise to the girl's father, she understood; that was the way of things) but she had made an art of repudiating him. After all, neither of them was free. Though she held a possibility in her heart that one day . . . Thinking of it, there at his funeral, shot her through with sorrow. She had relented, just that once, and seen him for that final farewell. Had Jeanne not interrupted them she might have found herself breaking her promise to her husband – was on the very brink of it.

She had never imagined it would take so long for her two boys to arrive. Watching the gloomy parade continue, she wished from the depths of her being that she *had* given herself to Sidney, and she turned her rage inward for wasting all that love. She felt the dregs of her faith in God slipping away. She had often wondered what He was punishing her for by giving her a husband such as Rich and then to deny her a son. She had decided that her daughters signified God's displeasure at her intention to commit adultery, that God was protecting her from sin.

But to cut Sidney down in his prime – it was a ruthless

God who would choose to kill Sidney and let Rich live; the idea shocked her, it was a sin too great to contemplate that she might have wished her husband dead. But there it was, a devil clinging on to her with sharpened claws. She could not help thinking that, had she had the courage to defy her own misplaced loyalty to Rich – her own faith in God's plan – that the baby, her third infant, who was shifting in her belly as she watched the mourners from the window, might well have been Sidney's.

If it was God's plan, He was a callous God indeed because that baby was to be her first boy. She may not have borne his child but part of her crumbling self was buried with Sidney and from that fragment sprouted an understanding that it was she – not God, or her husband, or the Queen, or her misplaced moral code – who would be the agent of her own happiness; she alone who could secure her future. She would forge powerful alliances, secret lines of favour, to ensure that whatever should occur the Devereuxs would be at the sharp end of power. As the final mourners passed and the drumbeat faded she felt herself solidify as if a great force was gathering in her; never again would she leave her fate to God alone.

PART II
The Oyster

My mistress' eyes are nothing like the sun;
Coral is far more red than her lips' red;
If snow be white, why then her breasts are dun;
If hairs be wires, black wires grow on her head;
I have seen roses damasked, red and white,
But no such roses see I in her cheeks;
And in some perfumes is there more delight
Than in the breath that from my mistress reeks.
I love to hear her speak, yet well I know
That music hath a far more pleasing sound;
I grant I never saw a goddess go;
My mistress when she walks treads on the ground.
And yet, by heaven, I think my love as rare
As any she belied with false compare.

William Shakespeare, Sonnet 130

November 1589

Theobalds, Hertfordshire

Cecil stands for a moment at the window. A gardener is sweeping leaves and another is high up in a tree, coppicing. A branch falls to the ground with a crash. A mizzle starts up and Cecil shivers. The damp at this time of year makes his crooked back ache horribly and once it has set in it will not leave him until spring. But he is not thinking about the damp and cold; he is thinking, with a frisson of excitement, about Lady Rich and her letter to King James. He has had his eye on Lady Rich and she has been quietly forming allegiances, shoring up her family with powerful friends, for some years now. But with the Scottish King, secret letters of friendship to a foreign monarch and one who has a strong claim to the English throne, has she reached too high? There is room for only a single nexus of power about the Queen. A vista has opened up before him in which he can see the downfall of Essex and that family of his. If only he could have got his hands on one of those letters — hard evidence.

He seeks out his father, finding him in the library. Burghley has nodded off by the fire with his mouth drooping open; a hefty volume must have slid off his lap for it lies spread-eagled on the floor. His cheeks are hollow and his eyes sunken; were it not for the loud snores emanating from him, he might appear dead.

'Father,' he gently strokes Burghley's arm, causing the old man to start out of his sleep, his eyes popping open, his head swivelling in confusion before alighting on his son.

'You startled me. Had I dropped off?'

'You had, Father. Can I bring you something? A little wine?'

'I fancy I *would* like a sip of sweet wine. There is a jug of it on the table.'

Cecil pours out a measure for each of them and pulls up a stool to sit close. They touch cups, their eyes meeting, and simultaneously say, 'To we Cecils.' It is a small ritual they have performed for years. The wine is thick and its sweetness comforting.

'You know the Queen intends to award that pup the licence for sweet wines when it comes up next year,' says Burghley. They both know exactly whom he means by 'that pup'. It has been their private name for Essex ever since he arrived in Burghley's household as a boy, filled to the brim with swagger.

'Sweet wines, that is worth a fortune,' Cecil says.

'Yes, no more "poorest earl in all of England".'

'A wealthy Essex might prove too great a threat to us.'

Burghley looks at his son's slumped shoulders. 'Don't brood on it.' Cecil may have mastered the art of hiding his feelings but his father can see right through him. 'With a little fortune she will give him enough rope to hang himself one of these days.'

'I have some news of Essex's sister,' Cecil says.

'What sort of news?'

'From the man I have informing on the Scottish court. Lady Rich has made overtures to King James. Letters of friendship.'

'So the Essex faction are playing their hand early. Rather too early, I fear.' Burghley smiles. 'Our beloved Queen has some years in her yet.' Cecil wonders how his father can be so certain, when there have been so many attempts on her life. In the fifteen months since the Spaniards and their Armada were crushed, he has felt their desire for revenge in his bones; his network of informants whispers constantly of it.

'But all the Catholic world wishes her dead.'

'Well then it is up to us to ensure the papists do not achieve their aim.' Burghley taps the side of his nose. 'King James will not be warming her seat just yet. Perhaps never – the fact remains he was not born on English soil . . . and there are others . . .'

'I could have Lady Rich in for questioning.' The thought sends a thrill through him. 'Essex must be behind those letters. I can make her implicate him. It is clear they are lining themselves up beside James as successor. That rings of treason. They are building connections.' He is speaking fast, his excitement fizzing in him.

'Of course they are building connections; and they will say it is all for the good of the Queen and England. Don't be so quick to jump. They may have played their hand but this game is a long one. Do not underestimate Lady Rich. You have watched her at court; you have seen how her beauty clouds the fact of her intelligence – *she* will not be so easily manipulated.'

'But we have them.'

'You are letting your personal feelings get away with you. Don't think this is a vendetta; vendettas only end in devastation and we must make sure we Cecils survive – survive and thrive. You have not lived twenty-six years on this earth to be ignorant of that.'

Cecil nods. His father is right – his father is always right.

Burghley continues as if thinking aloud: 'Our long-term survival, just as theirs, means putting a wager on the winning cock in the succession: James of Scotland's suit may appear to be the strongest but it may not be the best for *us*,' he begins to count the others on his fingers – 'Lord Beauchamp, or his brother; the Stuart girl; even the Spanish Infanta. They all have a claim and, you never know, Essex himself might throw his hat into the ring if his popularity burgeons further.'

'Surely not, Father. Essex is too long a shot.'

'England loves a soldier and Essex has martial skill, teamed with an abundance of charm and a dribble of royal blood. A potent mix indeed, my boy.' Cecil feels his envy poke at him. 'Yes, it's a long shot but don't underestimate him. The English want to think there is someone to lead the armies. The Spanish may have been humiliated but they will be back; all are aware of that. Essex's popularity is founded on his desire to go out and meet the enemy. Makes the English sleep easy in their beds. If only they realized that more can be achieved through intelligence and quiet dealings than bravado, blades and gunpowder.' Burghley smiles and rubs his hands slowly together.

'Besides, war is expensive.' If Cecil has learned anything in the years he has sat beside his father in council meetings taking notes, it is that the Queen is loath to spend money on anything with an uncertain outcome.

'Watch and wait,' says Burghley. 'You have a valuable nugget of information, but that is all it is at this stage. Watch the lady; watch and wait.' Cecil is reminded of being fleeced by a card trickster once, who had said the very same thing – *watch the lady*. He lost all the gold buttons from his doublet. That was a lesson learned. 'Essex is young and foolish and may yet be the author of his own downfall and he'll drag his family down with him.' Burghley pauses, rubbing the back of his neck with his palm. 'Water hollows a stone, not by force but by falling often.'

Cecil's excitement recedes, leaving him feeling flat. He finds that whatever he does he cannot quite gain his father's full approval. His impatience niggles at him.

'I made Leicester my nemesis,' continues Burghley. 'It was one of my greatest mistakes. Oh, how I tried to bring him down. At one time he was a whisker's breadth away from marrying the Queen. Imagine; he would have been as good as King. I nearly lost myself in my desire for his downfall. There was a moment when I came to understand that the Queen would never have wed the man. Once I saw that clearly, my animosity for Leicester petered out. Then he fell foul of his desire, anyway, and married that woman.'

'Essex's mother.'

'She will never be forgiven for marrying the favourite. Besides,' he reaches his hands forward to warm them by the flames, 'Leicester is no more and the pup has taken his place as the chosen one. It is best not to make enemies, for you never know how things will end up. Cecils are diplomats – that is our strength – peaceful negotiation rather than war.' He pauses. 'And of course keeping abreast of things. That attitude has set us in good stead.'

'She treats him – and the sister – as if they are her own children.' Cecil can't help sounding sullen. Why is it that his father reduces him to a sulking boy? He laughs inwardly at the irony, for he, Robert Cecil, is greatly feared, indeed he has worked hard at being greatly feared, and yet in his father's eyes he is – he seeks the word to describe the feeling he always has with regards to his father – *inadequate*. Yes, it is inadequate that he feels.

'But they are *not* her children.' Burghley smiles, the firelight catching in his rheumy eyes. 'To we Cecils,' he says once more, lifting his cup and draining the dregs of his sweet wine.

May 1590

Leicester House, the Strand

Penelope can feel the little palpitations of her baby deep inside. A bird trills in the tree above, a chaffinch she thinks; she sees a flitting movement in the leaves, but can't catch sight of the bird itself. She makes a silent prayer that this baby will be another boy and thinks of her first son, little Hoby, in the nursery at Leighs with his sisters, feeling the familiar maternal heart tug – her mother thinks her over-indulgent with her offspring, but she cannot help this overflowing of love. And it is true, particularly with Lucy. Perhaps she indulges her eldest as compensation for that initial rejection. Doctor Lopez had been right when he'd said she would grow to love her daughter, but the residue of guilt still resides in her even after eight years. If this one is a boy she will have done her duty to Rich and she will be freed from the marriage bed. She thinks of the deal she struck with her husband, the moment of her transforma-tion from girl to . . . to what? Someone had called her a virago recently. It was meant as a criticism but Penelope had rather liked the term, with its heroic implications. She had never imagined back then that God would make her wait so long for a son.

She can hear her brother and mother bickering as they approach, arm-in-arm, with Spero trotting behind. Lettice must have arrived from Drayton Bassett last night after Penelope had retired. This infant she is incubating is draining her force and she has found herself lately unable to stay up long after supper, when usually she is the last to bed and the first to instigate the evening's entertainments.

Spero grapples at her skirts as she stands to embrace her

mother, enjoying the familiar musky scent that catapults her back to childhood. She remembers her mother then, more beautiful than anything she had ever seen, in her finery as she left for court, sparkling with brilliants and decked with pearls. As she leaned in to kiss her daughter those jewels would tumble forward with a soft clatter, like rain on a window, and Penelope would be engulfed in that scent. That was when Lettice had the Queen's favour. How things have changed. That lustrous beauty is faded almost right away now, robbed by the death of her beloved Leicester. She notices a look of concern on her mother's face, her brow ruffled.

'What is it?' Penelope asks.

'Your brother has promised himself to Frances Walsingham.'

'Not her,' Penelope says before she has time to consider how it might sound. 'I mean . . .' Her mind is cast back to that day three years since, when she stood with Frances watching Sidney's funeral cortège. The thought twists her heart out of shape. On his deathbed Sidney had asked her brother to look after his wife – she doubts *this* was quite what he meant.

'You mean you do not want me wed to Sidney's widow?' says Essex pointedly.

'No, I mean, yes, in a way. You must wed who you will, Robin, but . . .' She couldn't hate Frances, though she tried. The girl was too sweet, too meek, to merit such a force of feeling. 'You could do so much better. She is not from a noble family.'

'*And* he does not have the Queen's permission,' says Lettice, her lips pursed tightly. 'God knows, don't you think this family has suffered enough from the Queen's disfavour. First my disgrace, then Dorothy's, now this. Me . . . I . . .' – she punches her breast with a fisted hand – '. . . now Leicester is gone she even threatens to take this house from me. I have had letters to that effect for some months. I am hanging on here by a thread.'

'Why did you not say something, Mother?' asks Penelope.

'Oh, I don't know. I am so tired of it all.'

Penelope admonishes herself inwardly for thinking first of herself: the loss of Leicester House will mean having to use her husband's gloomy Smithfield property when she is in London and not at court.

'I shall see what can be done about it, Mother,' says Essex. 'And vex not about my marriage; the Queen loves me like a son.' Only on seeing his mother wince does he seem to realize how hurtful his words are.

'The Queen is in your thrall, now,' she says sharply. 'Think of the power that brings to us, to your family. Would you throw that away for a wench?'

'Frances brings wealth and her father's network. That is the way to gain power – to know what is going on, to keep a step ahead of Cecil.'

Penelope smiles inwardly – it is true; to prise Walsingham's web of agents from the clutches of the Cecils would be a triumph indeed.

'The network, the network,' says Lettice, unable to hide her impatience. 'We already have people well placed.'

Penelope is thinking of her most recent correspondence with the Scottish court and the discreet lines of information she has set up lately. 'But this *is* an opportunity. We could do with good European connections if we are to keep abreast of things.'

'Did I not wed my new husband for the very reason that he was at the heart of Walsingham's network of spies? I might have enjoyed a few years of widowhood instead. A few years of freedom, rather than a third husband . . .' Her voice trails off.

Penelope knows, as they all do, that Lettice could no more be without a man at her side than a fish can be out of water, but it is true she might have looked elsewhere than Sir Christopher, a man twelve years her junior who brought neither wealth nor status.

'Our new stepfather is a good man,' says Penelope. Her

mother gives her a look, as if to accuse her of taking the wrong part. 'Even with that vast bird's nest of a beard,' she adds, in an attempt to add some levity to the atmosphere.

But Essex has the bit between his teeth: 'Walsingham's fingers reach further . . . all over Europe, and if I am wed to his daughter –'

'Fool!' blurts Lettice. 'The Queen will oust you. You mark my words. There is no network that can make up for losing *her* favour.'

'You have no idea what it is like, Mother, having to dance around that woman all the time' – Essex is almost shouting – 'with everyone speculating if I have bedded her or not. You think you have suffered humiliation at her hands, how humiliating do you think it is that all those fawning courtiers imagine I have swived that . . . that aged *hag*?' He is purple with rage. 'I have my dignity.' Essex will not listen and has a wild, feverish glaze to his eyes, which Penelope recognizes only too well, wondering which is worse, this crazed ebullience or the leaden misery she had to coax him out of a few months ago. With him there is no middle ground.

'Stop that!' Lettice slaps the back of his hand. 'Should the servants hear and spread it round that you speak of the Queen thus, you will lose more than your dignity.'

'She forgave Leicester when he wed you. *He* was back in the fold within months.'

'But not me! I am *still* not back in the fold. I am still pointed at in the street as the she-wolf who defied the Queen.'

'But Frances Walsingham has no royal blood. No child of ours could be any kind of threat.'

'Nor any child of mine,' snaps Lettice. '*You* are the ones with royal blood. It is from your father not me.'

'That is disingenuous, Mother. We all know where our Tudor blood comes from.'

'Out of wedlock,' says Lettice with a scowl. 'It counts for nothing.'

They continue to squabble like hot-headed children. Penelope is glad she inherited her measured temperament from her father. Though some called him a ruthless soldier, she never saw that side of him. Perhaps she too has a hidden ruthless streak. A flock of starlings is pecking about the yew bush in their speckled iridescent jackets, whistling and stuttering. She watches their darting movements. Her baby shifts again and she makes a renewed prayer that it is a boy she carries.

'Penelope!' Her brother pokes her upper arm. 'Are you daydreaming? I was asking you a question.'

'I'm sorry, I drifted off.' She circles a palm over her belly.

'Have you heard from Scotland?'

'There has been no direct response yet, though I have sent a number of letters. A scribe close to him has implied the King is not averse to our allegiance but is not prepared to risk putting it in writing.'

'Yes, it would certainly give the wrong impression if the Queen were to find out her Scottish cousin was presuming to line himself up to succeed her,' says Lettice. 'Look what became of his mother.' She makes a chopping action at the side of her neck with a grimace. 'What is important is that our intentions have been declared.'

'And that *I* have not been arrested for treason.' Penelope's response sounds flippant, but she has had months of worry that her letters may have fallen into the wrong hands. They are silent for a while and Penelope continues to watch the starlings. In truth she is discovering that risk holds a dark allure; there is something about the danger that makes her feel alive. Perhaps, she reasons, that is why men return to the battlefield time after time, despite the horror.

'I *will* marry Frances Walsingham,' says Essex, all of a sudden reprising the quarrel with his mother. '*I* am the head of this family and I shall do as I please.'

'You would do well to curb that arrogance of yours, my boy, before it gets the better of you. Obtain the Queen's permission and I will bless the match.'

'She is carrying my child. The Essex heir.'

'For goodness' sake.' Lettice wipes her forearm across her brow. 'As if things were not already complicated enough,' she huffs before turning to make her way back to the house.

'You are too much, Robin,' says Penelope. 'Try and be nice to her.'

He smiles. It is an irresistible smile, like the sun appearing between clouds, reminding Penelope why so many women have fallen under her brother's spell – including the Queen. She wonders how timid Frances Walsingham will fare wed to him, given Penelope is almost certain he is conducting a secret dalliance with one of the Queen's maids.

'She is worried about the debts Leicester left her,' Penelope reminds him.

'I know, I know, I have tried to approach the Queen on that front but . . .' He doesn't finish. They are both sharply aware that they cannot expect the Queen to show even the smallest glimmer of favour regarding Lettice, despite most of Leicester's debts having been accrued in the Queen's service. 'I intend to buy Wanstead from her.'

'Really? How will you pay for it? I don't want you taking advantage of Mother's straitened circumstances.' She looks at him sternly.

'What do you take me for?' He appears slighted. 'Family first, always.'

'I suppose it *is* a way to keep Wanstead in the family.' Wanstead is her favourite house, a place of happy respite with her mother, full of fond memories, a refuge from her husband. If she were ever able to, she would choose to end her days at that house.

'It will be taken from her otherwise,' he points out.

'Has the Queen talked of that?' Penelope can imagine the conversation, the Queen winding Essex round her little finger.

'She thinks it would be a suitable place for me to entertain foreign visitors.'

'Oh, does she?' Penelope is imagining herself wandering through the light-filled rooms of Wanstead. 'But you still cannot afford it.'

'She taketh away and she giveth,' is all Essex replies with another of his disarming smiles. She is glad to see him so content, yet still finds herself scrutinizing him for signs of that lurking melancholia.

They get up and walk a little, stopping at the river. It is a still day, barely a breath of breeze; she can hear the cheer of the crowd in the bear pits and men on a building site calling out to each other on the south bank. She gazes into the water, allowing her thoughts to drift, and an image of Charles Blount pops into her mind. This has happened with increasing regularity of late. Beyond his obvious qualities there is something about the man's forthright steadiness, a reassuring thoughtfulness to him, as if he thinks carefully before speaking, which reminds her, undeniably, of Sidney. 'I am glad you took my advice and befriended Blount.'

'I was wrong about him. He's a good man.' Essex turns to his sister, inspecting her face, finding there the flicker of a smile that she is unable to suppress. 'You *like* him.'

'I like any man with good manners. Besides, I am a married woman – *and* with child.' She turns her face away, bending to throw a stick for Spero, but she is thinking of a moment the other evening, when Blount had paid a visit. They had talked of the importance of loyalty. 'There are sometimes occasions,' he had said, in that grave way he has, 'when loyalty asks us to betray our moral codes.' It had touched her, allowed her to see something of his profundity. She can feel the effect he is having on her in a physical sensation, a pull in her depths, over which she has no control. It is something she has felt only once before. Thoughts of her younger self tap at her, and she can't help remembering how preoccupied she was with love then, as if there were nothing more important in the world. How different she is now from the green girl that fell for Sidney.

Cecil hears the sound of horses entering the yard and makes for the privy chamber, from where there is a view of the stable arch. Urgent business agitates in his head and he has waited an age for the Queen's return from the hunt, that he may take his leave and join his father at Whitehall. Trouble is brewing in France, where King Henri has managed to alienate both Catholics and Protestants alike, meaning the Spaniards could gain an easy foothold in Normandy. There is a multitude of pressing matters to discuss with Burghley. Cecil has been ruminating on ways to stop Essex from persuading the Queen he should take an army across the Channel to aid the Protestant cause. He can't help imagining the earl's glorious return, parading through London at the head of his triumphant legion, banners flying, cheering crowds thronging the streets. It is a thought that rankles.

Cecil still waits to be made Secretary of State. Though he has performed the duties of the office for more than a year, he is treated like a glorified scribe. He may give the outward impression of success, but Cecil's insides churn with a sense of failure born of his father's disappointment; it is there in the sideways looks and the little deflating comments that seem innocuous but are not. How he longs to impress his father. He stops outside the privy-chamber door to straighten his clothes. His ruff is starched stiff and scratches the skin of his throat but the idea of loosening it and risking it sitting crookedly is unthinkable. He can hear women's voices as he enters the privy chamber, stopping, unseen, shifting into the shadows. There is something conspiratorial about the tone of their conversation that makes him want to listen.

'It is showing,' says one of them in an urgent whisper. 'You *must* find a way to retire from court.'

'She will not let me out of her sight. You would not believe the lies I had to tell her so as to be excused from the hunting party.' Cecil recognizes the voice of Frances Walsingham; the other woman is Lady Rich – her forthright manner and musical tone are unmistakable.

His curiosity is provoked, for he has never noticed a particular friendship between these two women, certainly nothing to suggest that they would be in each other's confidence.

'You must say to her that you remain distressed by the death of your father and that you need a little solitude to mourn him. Ask leave to go to your mother's house,' says Lady Rich. 'She cannot refuse you that, not with your father so recently dead.'

'But it would be a lie,' says Frances. 'And I could not use Father's death for deceitful ends.'

'For goodness' sake, is it not a greater lie by far to have wed in secret?'

Cecil feels the hair on his neck prick up as he waits for the conversation to unfold and reveal itself fully.

'If you go to your mother at Barn Elms you can have the baby quietly. We can put it about that you have contracted something, an imbalance of the humours. Within a few weeks you will be back at court and the Queen will be none the wiser.'

Cecil finds himself, not for the first time, envying his adversary for having such a formidable sister. Cecil thinks of the wife he wed a year ago, a serviceable woman inhabiting the background of his life, and well connected – she brings her father, Lord Cobham's, favour – an ally on the Queen's council. But she cannot quite hide the disgust she has for his deformities, nor the pleasure in the luxuries he brings. He doesn't care, as long as she bears him a son; but how he could do with a woman like Lady Rich at his side.

'I am afraid,' says Frances. Her voice is waterlogged, as if she might cry, and Cecil feels a drop of sympathy for the poor meek girl – the Queen will eat her alive for this misdemeanour. He is remembering how Anne Vavasour fared all that time ago when she got herself with child to Oxford, they both ended up in the Tower, and Anne was a far more stalwart type than this fragile creature.

'This is no time for fear, Frances.' There it is again, that unemotional response, Lady Rich's formidable expediency. His admiration flourishes. 'My brother is on a path to glory and this must not get in his way.'

So Essex is the husband! He'd thought he was stalking a rabbit but this is no rabbit, it is so much more, it is a lion at the very least. This could be the means to bring down his adversary – Oxford was out of favour a full five years after his slip-up with the Vavasour woman. He finds himself wondering what on earth Essex sees in such a girl, wondering if there is more to it, making a mental note to look into some of his informers and where their loyalties lie; particularly those once affiliated to Frances's father. Since Walsingham died his network has become notably less reliable, agents have fallen from the map.

'Ladies,' he says, stepping fully into the chamber. 'I did not think to find anyone here.'

Lady Rich turns, calmly, with a half-smile. 'Good day to you, Cecil. We did not join the hunt. You will no doubt come to understand, when your dear wife has an infant, that it takes a month or so to get back in the saddle after the childbed.'

Lady Rich's beauty always takes him by surprise, as if he is seeing her for the first time. She has cast off her coif and seems not to care that her bright hair is falling in tangles over her shoulders; nor that her ruff is undone, exposing her pale undulating breast; nor that the dark fabric of her skirt is scattered with white dog hairs. Her hands, though, are perfect; they might have been stolen from a marble statue, and her black eyes fix on him with an unsettling steadiness of gaze.

'Felicitations on the birth of your baby, My Lady,' he says. 'A son, was it?' Cecil wonders if her comment – 'when your dear wife has an infant' – was a veiled criticism of the fact that his wife is not yet in whelp. He has thought of Lady Rich more than once during his desultory marital duties. He wrenches his eyes away to glance at poor Frances, who, though quite comely enough, with translucent skin and striking round grey eyes, is like a mouse beside her companion. She shifts uncomfortably in her chair and picks at the hem of her handkerchief, fraying it right away so little fragments of thread lie over her lap.

'A boy, yes,' says Lady Rich with a triumphant tilt of the head. 'We called him Henry.'

'Two boys; Lord Rich must be delighted after such a time.'

'Indeed,' she replies, with that victor's tilt of the head again, not acknowledging his comment about the years it took to produce a brace of boys for her husband. 'Will you take a little ale with us?' She pats the seat beside her. He is fascinated by her coolness; there is not an inkling of concern to suggest she fears he might have heard the conversation that came to an abrupt halt on his arrival.

He sits, turning to Frances: 'You stayed to keep Lady Rich company, I suppose?'

Frances's eyes are startled as she tries to form a response.

'She is unwell,' says Lady Rich, pouring out a measure of ale and handing him the cup. 'Frances, why don't you go and lie down? Go to my chambers, they are more private than yours.'

'What ails you, my dear?' The endearment sounds false on Cecil's lips.

Lady Rich looks towards him making a minute shake of the head, as if to say *don't question her*, and helps the girl to the door, smoothing a palm over her forehead as a mother might and whispering something. Cecil saw clearly, as Frances stood and her gown pulled open a little, the evidence of her state. Lady Rich is right; she will not be able to hide that much longer. Seeing her fragility occasions a moment of conscience as he turns over thoughts of what he will do with this precious knowledge – but only a moment. If it is not he who reveals the news it will be someone else.

Lady Rich returns to her seat. 'They will be coming up. I heard the hunt return some time ago.'

'Yes.' Cecil's mind is machinating on Lady Rich's plan to get the girl to her mother's house – if anyone can pull off such a ruse it is she – and he is girded by a sense of urgency.

A clatter of footsteps in the outer chamber announces the Queen's imminent arrival. When she enters, she does so on Essex's arm. They are laughing loudly together, heads tossed back, mouths wide. A group a dozen strong follows on, amongst whom is Blount; Cecil spots the man exchange a look with Lady Rich and wonders what it signifies, stores it in his inner memorandum. He'd thought Blount was *his* man, or at least he'd gone out of his way to court him a few months back, aware that Essex wouldn't want competition for the Queen's attentions from a comely upstart such as he. But he's not so sure which way the wind blows with Blount now – he is a man who doesn't reveal himself readily.

They are all still in their hunting habits; the Queen's skirts are muddy at the hem, tendrils of her hair have sprung free, and her hat dangles from her hand like a warrior's shield. She wears her fifty-seven years lightly, seems more full of life than all the hangers-on put together, save for Essex, who is bursting with verve and self-importance. Cecil reminds himself of his father's words of advice from years ago – 'Never approach her with fear in your heart. You must love her and do everything for love of her.' It became an interior refrain, but he is not afraid now, he is buoyed up with his secret knowledge and relishing the thought of five years in the wilderness for Essex.

'Ah, Pygmy,' says the Queen on seeing Cecil. 'Do you know why Essex here is so happy?'

Cecil loathes the Queen's pet name for him, feels it casts him amongst the beasts and curiosities of court, makes him a figure of fun, though ironically others are envious of the intimacy it signifies. 'I am sure, madam, that the earl delights in the proximity of Your Most Esteemed Highness.'

'You are a paragon of sycophancy, Pygmy, but that is not it. I fear you will disapprove, as will your dear father. I have given Essex the sweet wines' licence.' She pinches Essex's cheek as if he is her beloved son.

Cecil had thought she'd changed her mind over the sweet wines. It hadn't been mentioned for months. Essex wears his coup draped over him like a toga and Cecil feels his hatred tie itself in a painful knot: hatred of those abundant inky curls, those fine limbs, endlessly long – making Cecil feel squat and monstrous – the sculpted shape of him, as if he belongs on a plinth. He remembers Essex as a boy at Theobalds; he was just the same, and though he never joined in with the cruel games of some of the household lads – the daily humiliations – he gave off the air that he was above such things and watched on, doing nothing. What Essex did was worse than all that overt cruelty – Essex ignored him completely; it was as if he didn't exist in his own father's house.

'Congratulations, My Lord.' Cecil's smile is a tight rictus.

Lady Rich has gone over to greet them and they stand together, informally, like a family group. Cecil ponders on the notion that the Queen has stolen these two perfect specimens from their own mother and appropriated them for herself. He has often thought this, from that moment he first saw Penelope Devereux presented some nine years ago; the Queen may as well have set her in a ring like a jewel and worn her on her finger. He recognizes an act of revenge, however

181

subtle it may be, and this was surely revenge on the woman who stole her love. But Cecil knows what the Queen refuses to acknowledge; that those Devereuxs are tight as a suit of cards and they will always remain unassailably attached to their mother.

'The funds will be most useful, I'm sure, My Lord' – Cecil's voice is light, as if uttering mere ordinary politesse, and he feels the frisson already before the words have left his mouth – 'now you are wed.'

The Queen's face falls momentarily, loses its shape as if the stuffing is gone from her, but in an instant she is back and has turned to her favourite, who has his own venom-filled gaze resting on Cecil.

'Perhaps you could enlighten me, Essex,' she says, enunciating each syllable slowly and clearly, as if to rein in her rage. 'Is Cecil here mistaken?' The chamber falls into a tomb-like hush.

Lady Rich appears entirely unperturbed. 'I think it best, madam, if my brother explains himself in private.' Cecil is astonished by her courage. He has never heard anyone – perhaps only his father once or twice – speak out of turn when the Queen is enraged.

'Yes,' the Queen answers, nodding towards her guards, who begin hustling people out.

'I beg your leave too,' says Lady Rich, dropping into a curtsy. 'This is between Your Majesty and my brother.'

Clever, thinks Cecil, she will go and warn the mouse, I suppose – magic her away to Barn Elms. His admiration expands despite himself, but he knows if it came to it he would sacrifice Lady Rich to bring her brother down – he would have to, for she would be far too great an adversary. He turns to follow Lady Rich to the door.

'Not you, Pygmy. Come sit, sit by me.' She moves towards the upholstered chair under its canopy of state, indicating that Cecil should take the seat nearest to her. Essex is marooned in the centre of the chamber with a hangdog face, awaiting her order, looking like a child of four rather than the man of twenty-four he is.

Cecil takes his place next to the Queen, feeling somehow taller, more finely wrought. She points a long finger to the floor before her and Essex moves slowly forward to kneel there.

'Tell me, Pygmy, who is the bride?'

Essex is fumbling with his gloves.

'It is Frances Walsingham, madam, and she is with child.'

The Queen's nostrils flare as if she has smelled something rotten.

'That whey-faced girl! Is it true?' She stretches out a foot and pokes Essex with it right at the centre of his doublet, leaving a mark.

He looks up at her with a small nod; Cecil is astonished to see the gleam of a tear in the corner of his left eye.

She sighs, as a nurse might, in response to an infant who has committed some minor misdemeanour. Cecil feels bereft – he had wanted her to show the earl the full force of her anger and watch him abase himself pleading for mercy, but her expression is overflowing with sympathy.

'You do know what this means?'

He nods once more.

'You will have to go. The girl too. How far gone is she?'

'Six months.'

Her mouth draws together like the lips of a purse. 'I will *not* see her. You are to tell her she is no longer welcome in my presence . . . in perpetuity. As for you – well, we shall see. Understood?'

Her anger is still too muted to provide real satisfaction for Cecil.

Essex nods yet again and then emits a strangled murmur: 'Please tell me I have not lost your love. My adoration of you is so great I cannot find a way to express it. My tongue is entirely tied with love . . . I would rather die . . .'

He is a better actor, thinks Cecil, than Mister Shakespeare himself.

The Queen does not answer, just says softly, 'Go now.'

Cecil can barely believe she has been touched by that display of hyperbole and yet feels his envy brewing, for he would like to have such a gift of expression. But words like that do not match a misshapen creature such as he.

Essex rises and, head stooped, slowly backs out of the room. Cecil's triumph feels small. After the door has closed the Queen drops her face into her hands and sits like that, motionless, for some time.

When she lifts her head, she says, 'Pygmy, be a dear and pour me a cup of wine.' As he moves towards the table she adds, 'Watered as I like it. You know how I like it, don't you?'

'I do, madam – three parts water.'

He hands her the cup; she sips it carefully and mutters under her breath, 'Of all the girls, my splendid boy has chosen that dull little thing.'

Then she sits up, shunting her shoulders back. 'Now, Pygmy, we have business to attend to, England will not run herself.'

It is as if it never happened.

Whitehall

Penelope is seated next to Cecil in the Queen's party, looking down on the tiltyard. She can feel his sideways look on her. He folds his handkerchief carefully, squaring up its edges, before inserting it into his cuff, and then brushes some invisible dust from his doublet. She has a letter from Scotland concealed beneath her gown and it gives her a little thrill that Cecil, who thinks he knows everything, knows nothing of it. The viewing stands are filled to the gunnels. Twelve thousand souls, come from miles around, have each paid their fee to watch England's finest horsemen battle it out in the lists. Each year the Accession Day Tilt seems to have become a greater affair; Penelope thinks back to all the times she has sat up here listening to the drums and trumpets, the roar of the crowd, the thunder of hooves and the great applause, as some earl or other enters to recite his piece to the Queen. She listens to the babble as people repeat the jousters' mottoes, speculating on their hidden meanings and whose favours they might be wearing tucked in their breastplates.

She has heard of little else for weeks in Leicester House, where her brother has been dreaming up ever more far-fetched schemes to ensure that his performance is the one on everyone's lips. There have already been signs that the Queen is ready to forgive him for his marriage; she had sent word stating that she expected him to participate in the tilt, and there had been other good indications. Essex had said he wouldn't be in the wilderness for long, and it seems he was right, but it is the women for whom the Queen holds the deepest antipathy. Indeed, Penelope now has a mother, a sister and a sister-in-law in exile. She will not allow herself to imagine her own fall, though its possibility lurks constantly at the edge of things. It would only take a single mistake, a slip of the tongue, an intercepted letter. The thought sends a shiver through her.

'Are you warm enough, My Lady?' asks Cecil, looking as if he would like to take a bite out of her.

Her brother's bid to regain the Queen's favour means the house has been a hive of activity in preparation for this day: reams of poetry have been written, learned, picked through, rewritten and relearned; the armourer has been welding and shaping a new jousting suit; Essex has spent hours in the paddock putting his new black mare through her paces. Lettice enlisted all the women of the household to stitch banners and embroider sashes and they sat in the great chamber for weeks with their needles.

A collective gasp goes up from the crowd as one of Penelope's Knollys uncles is almost unseated by his brother. He trots away disconsolately, throwing his broken lance to the ground, causing the crowd to boo and chant 'Bad loser', while his brother makes a lap of honour to enthusiastic handclapping.

'The lists are full of your kin today, My Lady,' says Cecil. 'I have counted four uncles and a brace of cousins already.'

'And my brother is next.'

'Indeed.' His tone is clipped.

'The Queen requested his attendance personally.' She draws out this last word, well aware that Cecil must already know that, but enjoys reminding him all the same.

He changes the subject abruptly: 'Sidney is never far from my mind at the tilt.'

'I think you speak for everybody.' She wonders if Cecil is playing a similar game to her: deliberately talking of Sidney to rile her or to make her think he knows more than he lets on, but she offers him a bland smile.

'No one has quite managed since to embody the chivalric values of our warrior poet.'

Penelope is thankful for the blast of fanfare that silences the crowd, for she does not want to enter into a discussion about Sidney with Cecil, of all people. Sidney inhabits her far reaches, like a spectre – always there. She would like to ask Cecil what a man such as he, a man of politics and shady negotiating, could possibly care about chivalry.

'Ah look, my brother!' she says, as Essex enters upright in a chariot, like an emperor of Rome. The crowd burst into applause, cheering and stamping their feet until the stands shake. His new armour is blackened and shaped to show off his athletic form, the chariot is painted black; the horses at its prow are dark as coal with sooty ostrich feathers billowing up from their bridles like plumes of smoke. His men come in behind him wearing black sashes, their mounts caparisoned as if for a funeral. With them is Wat; it is his first proper tilt. As he passes close by the stand Penelope blows a kiss to him; he does his best not to smile and ruin the warrior air he aims for. Her heart dilates with pride to see her baby brother, a young man now, nineteen and betrothed already, riding before the Queen. She had offered him Dulcet for the occasion, knowing he would cut a dash on her, and that she wouldn't easily spook and give him trouble.

Essex swells with the applause. Even the weather plays its part, as glowering November clouds have gathered above, seemingly from nowhere. The sound of a single mournful trumpet quiets the crowd as Essex comes to a halt before the Queen. Behind him two of his men unfurl a banner on which is embroidered the word DOLEO. Penelope had helped stitch it herself.

'*Doleo*, I grieve. He mourns Sidney,' calls someone behind.

'As do we all,' says another in response.

'You are wrong,' says the Queen, turning to the speaker. 'Essex mourns *my favour*.'

'He will have to go on mourning,' says Cecil under his breath.

Penelope can see clearly that the Queen is amused by the episode and hides a smile behind a feathered fan, which gives Penelope further hope that Essex will be back in the privy chamber before long. What is the use of her continuing to quietly seek allies if there is no Devereux figurehead to attach them to?

Essex bows deeply, pulling his helmet away from his head, allowing his dark curls to fall forward and then bounce back as he uprights himself. Penelope is thinking that if he loses the Queen's favour again he can always find employment on the stage. The stand creaks as the crowd leans in to listen to Essex recite his lines.

'We are all delighted by Her Majesty's bountiful generosity,' Penelope says to Cecil quietly. She had been waiting for this; indeed she had sat herself beside Cecil specifically for the purpose of delivering this piece of news.

'Generosity?' Cecil said. 'What generosity?'

Several people shush him angrily.

'You do not know?' she whispers, savouring the moment, watching him squeeze his hands together in his lap, as if wringing water from them.

'I am all ears,' he hisses.

'Has the Queen not told you yet that she means to bestow Leicester House on him?'

'Of course I knew.'

She would wager he is feigning.

'"Essex House" has a nice ring to it, don't you think? And we will all be neighbours. Your London house is nearby, I believe?'

'It is.' His jaw is rigid, his knuckles white.

'But of course you are not on the river, are you? That is a

shame, for the views are delightful.' She is twisting the blade now, and cannot quite stop herself.

'It was *my* suggestion that the earl retain Leicester House.' His eyes flick up to one side, not meeting hers.

'For someone who is so well known for espionage you are not very good at lying.' She says this with a smile.

It is rare that Cecil is the last to know something and it was quite possible that the Queen kept it from him deliberately, to make some kind of point about him getting above himself. It is the sort of tactic she employs to keep her acolytes in their place.

'I suggest you upbraid your informers for their ignorance of this matter. Do you not pay them to keep you in the know?' She can see the tips of his ears turning red.

'I know more than you think, My Lady.'

She presses her lips together to stifle her smirk. He is floundering and she is enjoying this moment more even than she had imagined she would, and more so when she hears the Queen mention something about the 'return of the prodigal son'. It couldn't have been better if Penelope had scripted it herself.

'Prodigal son,' echoes someone in the row behind. Cecil turns and gives them the full force of his venomous glare. The words are passed from mouth to ear, until someone in the public stands gets to his feet, throwing his cap in the air and cries out, 'The prodigal son!' causing a great cheer to go up like an explosion.

Cecil rises from his seat and, moving sideways awkwardly like a crab, negotiates his way down the row of spectators muttering, 'Urgent business to attend to.'

But the Queen calls out. 'Cecil, where are you sneaking off to? Do you not want to watch Essex break some lances? For goodness' sake sit down.' And then, catching Penelope's eye, says, 'Isn't your brother marvellous?'

Cecil sidles back along the row, collapsing into his seat

defeated, and watches sullenly as Essex demolishes each of his opponents, charging recklessly as if he thinks himself immortal. Penelope is quite relieved when he leaves the field in one piece. A final pair of riders enters at the far end and her heart stops, for there he is, mounted on a silver grey, its head tossing in eagerness, armour polished to a gleam, his colours blue and gold.

'Sidney,' she says under her breath as time collapses and she is back in the past, remembering the day Sidney had ridden in the lists in those same colours. He bore the motto SPERAVI scored through to signify his thwarted hope. How that had set the tongues wagging as to what it might have referred: his lost inheritance; a knighthood not offered; the Queen's favour always out of reach. But only Penelope knew what he had really meant by that motto and her heart feels hollow at being reminded of it.

'Spare us another Sidney homage.' This is Cecil, still spitting bile.

Penelope is jolted back to the present. The riders have made their circuit and have halted in front of the royal stand but her view is blocked and she cannot see who it is in Sidney's colours, though the banner his men carry slung between them on poles is clear enough: DUM SPIRO, SPERO.

'While I breathe, I hope,' she says, not realizing until it is out of her mouth that she spoke aloud.

'If Blount is hoping for preferment of some kind, then I'd say he needs to be more subtle,' says Cecil. 'A Sidney tribute. Not particularly original. It was always anathema to me – Sidney's excessive popularity. Of course, death on the battlefield is a nice chivalric flourish.'

It is all Penelope can do to prevent herself from slapping Cecil squarely about the face. She takes several deep breaths and focuses her attention on the field and the appreciative roar of the crowd. And as she watches Blount the realization dawns on her sweetly and slowly, like honey running down the throat. *Dum spiro, spero*: this is for her. She has carried young men's favours many a time; it is all part of the ritual. But this is different, more personal.

Her head is suddenly filled with a moment, two days ago, a kiss that had come from nowhere. It had happened in the narrow corridor at her brother's house that joined the old part with the new. She had become used to seeing Blount about the place, as his friendship with Essex was blossoming and he often made displays of courtly adulation to her, which she assumed had more to do with his public affiliation than personal desire. She had certainly, in private moments, imagined – even possibly hoped for – such a personal desire. There was no denying that Blount had increasingly begun to occupy her thoughts, in the easy way any comely fellow will infiltrate a woman's mind from time to time. But it was only coming upon him then in that tight corridor that something shifted from the imaginary to the tangible.

What exactly happened defies explanation. It was a moment of sudden intimacy – they had stood about a foot apart, neither one moving, looking at each other with an intensity that grabbed her by the gut. Without understanding how it came about, she found herself in his arms, the rough stubble of his chin scraping hers, her lips pressed to his, her tongue exploring his mouth, her body melting away. They were interrupted by the chaplain and Blount had hidden behind a tapestry while Penelope, still burning from the surprise of their embrace, had stifled her sudden laughter enough to stoop and pretend she was looking for a dropped trinket, which had the chaplain on his hands and knees searching with her.

When she was alone with Blount once more they had kissed again, slowly this time.

'I am falling,' he said.

'From grace?' she teased.

'For you.'

She felt like a long-desiccated plant that had been watered at last and was unfurling, sprouting hopeful shoots, vivid green and new.

She sighs, then becomes aware of herself, sitting up straight in her seat, saying to Cecil, 'Blount, is it? I didn't recognize him. After a title, is he, or a seat on the Privy Council?' She makes an adequate impression of sarcasm.

Cecil continues talking scathingly about all the shallow courtiers blessed with good looks who curry favour with the Queen, but Penelope isn't listening because she has suddenly become aware of the shape of her life, as if a light has been shone on it, exposing its contours. As she watches Blount gallop towards his opponent in the lists, it is as if time is folding back on itself, and she is watching Sidney on his quicksilver steed, the two men becoming inextricably intertwined in her mind. Understanding alights: fate is offering her a second chance at happiness.

Once the tilt is done she makes her way to the stables. Her brother is there, still in his armour, with Meyrick and a group of other men, emitting gales of laughter and making animated toasts, passing round a flagon.

'Ah! My beautiful sister,' he says. 'What brings you down from your gilded tower?' He is bursting with elation and it is infectious.

'I came to congratulate you on your performance, Robin. You were spellbinding.'

'The Queen was pleased, wasn't she?'

She remembers the small boy he used to be, forever seeking approval.

'There is no doubt of that. She was delighted.'

'Here,' says Meyrick, holding out the flagon. 'Will you join us in a toast, My Lady?' With his bulk he seems such a

brute but when he smiles, as he does now, he is transformed. She is glad her brother has such loyal men about
him.

They are all watching her, assuming she will give him
short shrift for expecting her to lower herself to drink
from an earthenware ewer with a crowd of rowdy men, so
she takes the jug. 'What am I drinking to? The death of
disgrace!'

'The death of disgrace!' The men echo her words in unison and with both hands she lifts the flagon to her mouth,
gulping down a measure. A cheer goes up. The liquid burns
her throat, making her splutter and cough and then laugh.

'What on earth is it?' she asks, once her composure is
regained.

'I'm sure you had worse in the maids' chamber,' says Essex.

'And *you* would know what goes on amongst the maids,'
she replies, 'given you spend so much time in their company.'
This provokes a new wave of laughter.

A cart trundles by. It is piled high with butchered car-
casses. They have been wrapped in linen but the blood
has seeped through, making it look like an executioner's
barrow.

'For the feast,' says Meyrick. 'We will eat well tonight.'

'If you do not drink too much of that poison.' Penelope
points to the ewer. 'Or you will be sleeping under the table
and wake with a sore head. Now, gentlemen, I must take my
leave of you.' She smiles and turns to go.

'Where are you going? The privy chamber is in the other
direction,' says Essex.

'I must fetch Spero. I left him with one of the grooms.'
The fib slides smoothly out of her mouth and goes unques-
tioned.

Her head is swimming pleasantly from the drink as she
enters the western stable block beside the orchard and is
reminded of her encounter there with Sidney all that time

ago – that blasted ferret – on the day she learned of her betrothal. That was after a joust too and she remarks on the strange symmetry of life and how events repeat differently in its pattern. It had been spring then and the blossom was out in the orchard; now the ground is covered in a mulch of forgotten apples, giving rise to the heady stench of rotting fruit. The building is not the same either and it takes her a moment to remember that the old block had been demolished some five years ago and this one built in its stead. Inside it has the same engulfing odour of dung though, which takes her back to that moment. 'I have to see you again,' is what he had said. She was green as a new shoot then – but not now.

A groom walks by.

'Could you tell me where I might find Sir Charles Blount?' she says.

When she finds him he is brushing down his horse with his back to her. She stands in the doorway watching the way the muscles move in his shoulders, and the way his dark hair twists into whorls at his nape. He is whistling and occasionally breaks off to whisper something to his horse, which responds with a quiet wicker.

'Should your groom not be doing that?' she says eventually.

He turns, eyes wide with surprise – and delight, she hopes. Putting a finger to her lips, she enters, bolting the door behind her, before unpinning her cap and allowing it to slide to the straw-strewn floor.

She approaches him, reaching out for the fabric of his shirt, lifting it over his head and pressing her face to his chest, breathing him in. He has the earthy tang of sage rubbed between finger and thumb. She twists round so he can unlace her.

Her stiff layers of clothing come away piece by piece until she is in nothing but her shift. They explore the terrain of each other's bodies with their hands, like sightless people.

She has imagined, many times, touching a man like this, but is unprepared for the intensity of feeling, sweetened by sin, that is aroused in her. Their breath deepens, each taking the other's rhythm. Time has slowed and the world outside has disappeared.

May 1591

Theobalds, Hertfordshire

Cecil feels foolish in his hermit's garb; the thick cassock is too heavy for the early summer heat and drags on the ground. Despite Cecil's protestations Burghley had insisted upon the outfit. Cecil feels it signifies his father's disappointment in him. The ridiculous costume is part of Burghley's planned garden entertainments for the Queen's visit – the hermit in his cave representing humility and making light of the fact that Burghley is spending too much time away from court, hidden away here at Theobalds; something the Queen complains about often. She had laughed when she saw Cecil – laughed *at* him, not with him – as he appeared in the cave's mouth, reciting a poem, stumbling slightly over the lines.

'Oh, Pygmy. You are not accustomed to performance, are you?' she'd said, wiping her eyes as if she'd just watched Lord Strange's men perform one of their best comedies. All he could think of, as he tittered in agreement, was that Essex would never stoop so low as to play a hermit, and a comedy hermit at that. 'Walk with me, show me your father's garden.'

This had been the artifice: Cecil would wander the gardens with the Queen, the hope being that as each horticultural symbol revealed itself he would impress his faithfulness upon her and his fitness for high office, a recognition that continues to evade him. How he loathes the courtly games. They stop before a maze planted with flowers and the gardener points out that each of the nine blooms represents one of the muses, indicating an effigy of the Queen at the maze's centre, where the plants have woven themselves about a hidden wired structure creating a floral statue that seems to have grown thus of its own accord.

'All this for me?' she says, as if no one had ever planted so much as a daisy for her.

Cecil thinks he might faint in the heat of his cloak and puts a hand up to the slim trunk of a cherry tree to steady himself, before they walk on to the arbour. The gardener there proudly shows off the different strains of eglantine that have grown through the trees, pointing out the bright blooms, some white, some palest pink and others deeply blushed, almost crimson. He picks one with outer petals that are scarlet and a heart of white.

'It is a Tudor rose,' she says, twirling it in her fingers.

'They say the roots of eglantine run so deep into the ground that even the ferocious heat of the Spanish sun cannot scorch it,' says Cecil, as his father had told him to.

'You are referring to our great triumph over the Spanish Armada, I think.'

'That is so, madam.'

'I like it very much,' she smiles at him and thanks the gardener, who melts away, leaving them to walk on towards the lake, where a miniature fleet of galleons bobs on the surface.

'I am sending Essex to Normandy,' says the Queen, absently pulling the petals off the eglantine and letting them drop.

This irks him, for it feels like preferment: Essex has been manoeuvring to lead an army to France for months. But Cecil wonders if it might be a good thing to have Essex out of the way for a time. Though if he gains martial glory his popularity will spread beyond comprehension. He is already more popular than Cecil had thought possible – it is quite unfathomable to him the extent to which Essex is loved by the people – and the Queen makes a pretence of refusing him but always relents. She had done so with the sweet wines, with Leicester House and now with France. Essex had begged to be sent there; he had described the threat of Catholic Spain to a divided France. His speech was laced with the usual fanciful embellishments.

'Your great and glorious defeat of the Armada, madam,' Essex had said on his knees like a supplicant whilst gesticulating with his arms, 'has made the Spaniards like angry wasps. They must be curtailed for if they gain a foothold in France it is only a step before they are here on our shores.' And he had dragged out all the old horror stories that circulated in anticipation of the Spanish invasion, about what the enemy would do to our English maids were they ever to step on our soil.

'I have already sent a force to help Henri of France.'

'But the Catholics are gaining ground. I beg you let me go –'

She interrupted the pleading earl. 'I haven't the funds to support a full-blown war in France. My answer is no.'

Cecil was there, he heard it with his own ears, and that was not the only time. Essex's response was to storm off into self-imposed rustication at Wanstead until she changed her mind. What is incomprehensible to Cecil is the effectiveness of such infantile behaviour in a grown man – all that mooning and sulking.

'It will be his first command,' says the Queen, stopping beside a row of foxgloves. There are bees buzzing in and out of the purple bells.

Perhaps he will get himself killed, thinks Cecil. He had known this was coming; he has a boy in Essex's kitchens who gives him snippets of information for a shilling. Essex's wife is with child again – one shilling; Lady Rich is carrying on with the Blount fellow – two shillings; Lord Rich is aware of it and says nothing – three shillings; Essex has sent out word to muster men and horses to take to France – four shillings. The lad will soon be rich enough to buy himself a knighthood. Cecil had begun to wonder if the boy wasn't making it all up and thought perhaps he should devise some kind of test to verify his honesty, but now the Queen has confirmed this last piece of news, everything else seems, all of a sudden, quite plausible.

'I hope no harm comes to him, madam. For that wife of his is in foal again.'

'Do not try and rile me, Pygmy. I already know Frances is with child. Essex himself told me.'

She walks ahead, coming upon a stone fountain set into a wall, and, picking up one of the cups that are stacked beside it, fills it. From nowhere a pair of guards appears, one taking the cup from her hand and sipping tentatively at the contents. They all wait, as if time has been suspended, watching the man for signs of poison taking hold. Cecil is thankful he was not called upon to perform that task. It is the sort of thing Essex might do, snatch the cup and drink it back, slapping his lips, provoking some kind of comment from her like: *You would lay down your life for me?* Eventually the guard nods and fills a new cup for her, before he slides away with his companion. She takes a sip. 'Wine? Ha! What an invention.'

Cecil is wondering how Essex told her about the pregnancy when he has not been at court. There must have been a letter that missed his eyes. His shilling-hungry boy is not doing his job properly. He remembers his father's words: *Water hollows a stone, not by force but by falling often*, repeating the phrase in his head to calm himself. He thinks of his own son in the cradle at home, his longed-for son, born after the string of miscarriages that had made him develop a distaste for his wife. Essex's first baby had been a boy, just like that, and now he has another on the way. How easy everything is for him. Sometimes Cecil wonders if a demon hasn't got inside him, so great is his hatred of Essex. He hears his father's voice: *Do not make him your enemy*.

He must be wearing that thought on his face, for the Queen asks, 'Are you dispirited, Pygmy?' She hands him a cup, seeming amused at adopting the role of server. He drinks it back in one to slake his thirst, instantly regretting it, as the wine is sharp and causes his head to spin slightly. He draws a hand over his brow to wipe away the sweat.

'No, madam, I could never be despondent when I have you here at my side.'

'I hope not, because if you are going to be petulant I shall change my mind about having you sworn on to the Privy Council.'

'The Privy Council, madam?' He can feel a fluttering in his chest.

'You must have been expecting it.'

'I never expect anything, madam. I serve you for love alone.'

'Your father is not getting any younger and I need sharp minds to advise me. Sharp young minds and people I trust. There is no one I trust more than your father and I expect you to be his equal.'

Cecil thinks of that drop of water eroding slowly the barriers to his success and imagines telling his father the news – his disappointment ebbing away. No man of fewer years than he, at twenty-eight, has ever achieved the office – Cecil has done his research. 'It is and always shall be my life's work to serve you, madam, as it has been my father's. We Cecils pride ourselves on our loyal service to the crown.'

'And you have not been ill rewarded.' She waves an arm to indicate the magnificence of the gardens and the house in the distance, its windows winking in the sun.

'Indeed, madam, your generosity has been bountiful.'

'You will be knighted, of course. Fancy styling yourself Sir Robert Cecil?'

'Madam, I hardly know what to say.' A warmth radiates out from his chest, making him feel in that moment tall and beautifully formed. She smiles warmly and pats the back of his hand, an affectionate gesture that makes him dare to press his issue once more. 'I was wondering, madam, if I may be so bold as to make a suggestion about France?'

'Go on.' Her expression is one of indulgence, as someone might look when they allow a favourite pet to sit on their lap.

'We might put out some feelers to see if the Spaniards are open to some kind of agreement – a treaty.'

'I know you favour diplomacy over warfare, but on this occasion I think you are wrong. What would the Spaniards want with us? They think me a heretic with no right to my own throne. They have sent assassins to my shores since I can remember – you know all this, Cecil – and they suffered a crushing defeat at my hands just three years past. Essex is right; they are vengeful wasps and will sting us rather than parley. It is imperative for our safety that Henri holds France. We *must* make a show of force.'

They walk on in silence, Cecil putting away his thoughts of Essex and imagining once more how his father will receive the news of his appointment to the Privy Council, feeling a bubble of pride swell in his chest.

Penelope is running. Laughter puffs out of her. She stops at the edge of the woods, leaning against a tree to catch her breath, shoulders heaving, picking strands of hay from her clothes. Standing absolutely still, she can hear the gentle scurry of something alive in the undergrowth and the rustle of the breeze worrying at the leaves, nature's own particular music; a woodpecker thrums above, she follows the sound, running her eyes up the trunk, gazing through the canopy at the sky above, the vivid blue of a painted ceiling. The leaves are on the turn, though, and there is already a slight chill in the air. She imagines merging with the tree, her roots burrowing deep to the earth, branches soaring, becoming light-headed with the idea of her own smallness.

This sense of freedom has evaded her since she was a girl at Chartley, before her father died, when everything was turned on its head. But a thought rises to the surface of her mind – freedom is an illusion; even the tree is trapped, its wooden body silent and immobile, its movements dependent on exterior forces, even its music originates with the wind. A russet and white hound sidles up to her, panting, pressing its wet muzzle on to the back of her hand. It is Leicester's old dog that still wanders listlessly about the Wanstead grounds seeking its dead master. As she bends to stroke the animal, it turns to her with a mournful expression that pricks her with a moment's sadness, that familiar, acute awareness of time passing, people passing. It is more than three years already since her stepfather died and fifteen since her father went. The thought creeps up on her: she will be thirty in less than two years' time. Picking a dandelion clock, she blows, watching the wisps fly off, whirling up into the air, and fragments of memory float back to her of games with her siblings, Essex reckless to the point of danger, loyal Dorothy and little Wat, always desperate to keep up and too young really to join in their play. All of them looked to her to lead them, to stop them before things went too far.

Her thoughts are interrupted by a clump of hay landing smack on the side of her head. 'Got you!' cries Blount, with a burst of laughter.

She scoops it up, bunching it together, and launches it in his direction with the words: 'It's war.' And they grapple, shoving itchy fistfuls down each other's clothes until they are so breathless with laughter they lose their footing and collapse to the ground.

'So much for your reputation for quiet contemplation,' she says.

'*You* are a bad influence.'

'So tell me,' she laughs, 'does it not bring you happiness to be bad occasionally?'

'"Happiness" seems an inadequate word.'

'If God had wanted us never to be happy he would not have put us in the way of each other. I do not care if it is wrong.' She has the sense of grasping this love with both hands, no matter what, and wanting to stop time, never to go beyond this perfect moment, but there is something dragging at the depths of her, something she must tell him but can't quite bear to.

'You are wicked to the core, Lady Rich,' he teases.

'Don't call me that. I don't want to be reminded of him.' She feels heavy with the facts of her life and is struck by a sudden fear of what the consequences might be were the Queen to learn of this, trying not to think of it, yet feeling the imaginary walls of the Tower pressing close. 'Not now; I want to pretend for a while more that I am free.'

He takes her in his arms. 'I know, I know.'

She feels the crunch of paper inside his doublet. 'What is this?' Slipping her hand inside, she pulls out a folded sheet dense with text and is glad of something to distract her from her darkening thoughts. 'Has someone been sending you love letters?' She is teasing. She has never felt so sure of a man's love; with Sidney it was different, she was only sure of his love when it was too late.

'Some scribblings from that Bacon fellow – interesting stuff.'

'Bacon; he who seems so taken with my brother.' She is remembering Francis Bacon here at Wanstead in the spring when the French ambassador visited. Bacon, fresh-faced, sitting at the dinner table, gesticulating with a pair of elegant hands, as if playing a harp, arguing the finer points of French foreign policy with an astuteness that belied his boyish looks. But all the while he flicked glances towards Essex. Penelope recognized desire in those brief looks and felt sorry for the young man. Knowing Essex, he would find a way to keep the clever Francis Bacon in his thrall, as he did with all who fell for him, including the Queen.

'The very same. I believe he might be a good ally to your brother – to us – but he is Burghley's nephew and I wonder if he is entirely trustworthy.'

'I have heard he sought preferment through Burghley and it wasn't forthcoming,' she says. 'He is an interesting type. You're right, he might be useful to us.'

'Yes, I suppose Burghley feared he would be competition for his own son. But Bacon has a far finer mind than Cecil, a greater subtlety of thought.'

'He has an older brother, Anthony,' she says. 'I am told he is an expert gatherer of intelligence.'

'Yes, crippled with gout these days they say. Do you suppose the pair of them come as a single lot?'

'We shall see. Perhaps I will extend an invitation to them

both to visit us at Essex House. My brother is in need of good advisors.'

'Even with you to guide him?'

'Don't be silly.' She nudges him. 'I am only his sister. So what does Francis Bacon write about in these papers?'

'The Church, primarily. He thinks that of Catholics and Puritans, Puritans are the lesser evil.'

'I am not sure I entirely agree.' Penelope is thinking of the time she spent in the Huntingdon household, how severe life was, so lacking in joy, so divested of pleasure. Her husband likewise. 'Puritans have a way of taking all that is good in life and crushing it, in the name of God. There is a cruel streak in that branch of faith.'

'But politically speaking –'

'Ah, but I am not speaking politically,' she says.

'For once,' he replies.

She meets his eyes, allowing herself to be swallowed up into their depths, not wanting to think of her Puritan husband, changing the subject. 'I am so very glad the Queen forbade you to go to France.'

His lips brush hers in a kiss as light as a butterfly. 'Do you not want me to cover myself in glory?' He smiles.

'Not particularly – or at least not now. I would rather have you here than fighting skirmishes in Normandy.' That thought floods her with an old loss and for a moment she allows herself to imagine that butterfly kiss was Sidney's.

'I'm afraid things do not seem to be going to plan for your brother over there.'

'What have you heard?' She had been so wrapped up in Blount that she had not even thought to ask him if there was news from Normandy.

'Henri rode off and left him stranded at Rouen with the Catholics breathing down his neck and the bloody flux running wild through his men.'

'And the Queen is furious, I suppose.' She sighs, wishing she were in a position to advise her brother.

'And blames him, though it is not his fault.'

'Poor Robin. I would throttle that Henri myself . . .'

They lie in silence for a time, her worries for her brother and his thwarted campaign for glory circling about her head, thinking of how Cecil must be revelling in his adversary's failure. She has seen, etched all over him, the extent to which Cecil loathes her brother. But that other thing presses at her – something closer, more tender, more deeply secret and potentially more dangerous – that she hasn't yet found a way to articulate.

She sits up, looking away into the undergrowth, and takes a deep inhalation, girding herself. 'I think I shall soon be confined again.' Still looking away, she waits for his reaction.

'A child?' He sits up too, abruptly. 'Of mine?'

'Of course yours.' Her head snaps round to him.

'My darling one.' He touches his palm to her belly. 'A baby. Our baby.' His face seems filled with wonder, an expression so far from the matter-of-fact nod Rich had given when she'd announced to him she was first expecting.

'Our bastard,' she says bitterly, finding a memory slipping itself into her head, of Anne Vavasour birthing her baby in the maids' chamber and it never being spoken of again.

'Don't say that. This infant is the product of true love.'

'Then you do not mean to save your favour with the Queen and send me back to Rich's bed in shame?' She cannot help the weight of pessimism in her voice.

'If you think that, then you do not know me.' It is his turn to be prickly now. He stands and begins to walk away, back towards the house.

'You will not leave me, then?' She clambers to her feet, running to catch up.

He stops, turning towards her, taking both her hands. 'In my world you are first, above everything.'

'Above God?'

'I said "in my world", and God is not of the world.'

Her elation is punctured with the reality of her situation. 'The Queen will want rid of me. Look what happened to Dorothy, Frances, Mother, poor Anne Vavasour . . . there are so many.' She can feel herself falling into a spiral of despond but silently says: *Head over heart, Penelope, head over heart.*

'Anne Vavasour was one of the Queen's maids – Oxford deflowered her. Frances Walsingham was a young widow. Your sister . . . This is quite different – you are a married woman. If we behave with discretion . . . We are not two fools rushing headfirst into an unsanctioned marriage.' He seems to be thinking out loud, sifting through the possible outcomes.

'People will assume it is my husband's baby,' she says. 'But Rich will not take kindly to wearing horns.'

Blount seems to tense and opens his mouth to speak, then, changing his mind, looks away into the distance. 'Is it . . . Is it possible that Rich will think . . .'

'It is his?' She understands what he is really asking. 'No . . . He has kept to his bargain; we are no longer intimate.'

He takes her shoulders firmly, his tension dissolving, replaced now with concern. 'What do you think he will do? Will he divorce you?'

'No,' she responds, now fully in control of her feelings once more. 'He may not like the idea of being made a cuckold but he is entirely invested in his alliance with my brother. He is no one if he is not part of the Essex tribe and my brother will make an enemy of him if he slights me in public – he has always known that.' She stops and looks up, taking in a gulp of chilled air, remembering that her hold over her husband can save her from the Queen's wrath, as long as the gossips don't sharpen their tongues. 'And he harbours a secret that could destroy his reputation entirely, were it to emerge.'

'What is it?' Blount's curiosity is palpable.

'I cannot say.' She wraps her arms about herself, shivering.

'You are cold. There will be a fire lit in the house.'

She loves him all the more for not pressing the matter.

They walk back hand-in-hand, silently, until he says, 'I will never leave you. My life means nothing if you are not part of it.'

'But one day you will want a wife, children you can acknowledge . . .' The words stick in her throat painfully like something too hot swallowed in haste.

'No. It is only you I want.' There is a graveness in his tone and his expression makes her choose to ignore the fact that all men want an heir. She rests her head on his shoulder without replying, allowing herself a moment to wallow in his love, not thinking about returning to Leighs and confronting her husband.

Before they reach the house she sees the welcoming flicker of the hearth through the window. 'I love this place. More than anywhere it feels like home.' She can't help counting down the hours they still have together here, before life will impinge once more on their bliss.

'It is our paradise.'

'Not paradise,' she says. 'That implies we will lose it and it will be my sin that causes that loss.'

'You are no Eve.'

'Some would not agree.'

As they get to the steps a horse clatters into the yard; the rider, on seeing them, leaps from the saddle, flinging the reins to one of the stable lads.

'Who knows we are here?' asks Blount.

'No one – only the servants; they can be trusted. And my brother.' She reaches up to tuck her hair into her coif, finding a stray frond of hay, wondering if she looks as dishevelled as she feels.

'I bring news from the Earl of Essex, My Lady,' says the rider, proffering a letter.

'News from the French war,' she says as if thinking out loud, taking it, feeling a knot of worry tighten in her throat, imagining it can only be bad news. She reaches for her purse, realizing she has nothing with her. 'Do you have a penny?' she asks Blount, hoping this man will not spread the word that Lady Rich is alone at Wanstead with hay in her hair and a gentleman who is not her husband.

Blount gives the messenger two pennies and takes control, suggesting he go to the kitchens where he will find something to eat, asking if he needs a bed for the night.

Penelope looks at the letter, relieved to see her brother's own script, meaning he at least had a steady hand at the time of writing, calculating how long it might have taken this letter to arrive from Normandy. She walks up the steps and into the library, finding there are no candles lit and evening has appeared suddenly like an unwanted guest. She fumbles in the box for a taper, which she touches to a flame in the hearth. Sitting at her brother's desk she lights the candles, waiting a moment to gather her courage, running a finger over the familiar Devereux seal. She hears Blount enter the room quietly, not speaking or pressing her. She can hear the dog turning in circles before settling himself by the fire. Finally, she gathers her mettle to rip the seal and unfolds the paper, reading, unable to take in the words fully, so reading again. She feels tears begin to accumulate as if the root of her is being slowly squeezed out.

'Wat is dead, a bullet to the head. It was quick, he didn't suffer.' She sits slumped, still with her back to Blount, remembering Lettice and Essex fighting over whether her youngest brother should join him in France. The thought is too much for Penelope to bear and she finds herself heaving with sorrow.

Blount pulls her to her feet, as if she is a doll, and holds her in a tight embrace, whispering, 'I'm so, so sorry. So very sorry. I know how you loved your little brother.'

'I rocked him as a baby. I nursed him through the measles.'
It is some minutes until she has cried herself out.

'Poor Robin is in a desperate state out there. Rambling, beside himself with grief. Here – read for yourself.' She gives Blount the letter, scrumpled and sodden with her tears. She fears her brother has sunk into one of his black moods.

Blount scans the text. 'He is not in his right mind. I will petition the Queen to have him recalled.'

'No,' she places a firm hand on his arm, pulling herself together. 'It would be worse for him to return having achieved nothing. I know Robin – he will need to feel that Wat has not died in vain. At least if he stays there is a chance he will turn matters to the good.'

They sit and watch the fire for some time and Penelope finds herself thinking, as she often has, of the first hart she shot on the hunt – her first blood. It was in the woods at Kenilworth; everybody congratulated her on the sharpness of her eye, her quick reflex, her deftness with a bow at such a tender age, but all she could think of was that magnificent creature felled by her own hand: the destruction of something beautiful.

January 1592

Whitehall

'Congratulations on your elevation to the Privy Council,' Essex says. He wears a slick smile and his voice is smooth as goose fat, betraying none of the envy he is surely feeling at his adversary's elevation. The treacle-dark curls spill around his face and some trick of the light makes his eyes, with their intensity of gaze, spellbinding. He has shrugged off his boy-ishness too. He left for France a youth and has returned a man. Cecil had watched him walk the length of the long gal-lery and seen the effect his passing had on the milling courtiers, like the wind on long grass, who bowed and bent and whispered in his wake. He is magnificent and Cecil feels himself – despite his high office, despite his influence, despite his clear favour with the Queen – a nonentity in comparison. How is it, he asks himself, that Essex returns from a French campaign that was, if not quite an unmitigated disaster, at best inconsequential, and yet he is filled with the swagger of a conquering hero, a Caesar?

'Yes,' Cecil forces a smile on to his face and looks up to meet those gleaming eyes. 'It is a great honour.' Beneath his surface Cecil is seething at having been denied the oppor-tunity of being the first to impart news of his preferment. He would have enjoyed observing Essex's reaction, the fleeting moment of unconcealed disappointment. But someone has usurped him and the earl's face is now an unreadable mask. Cecil wonders who told him. The sister, he supposes, imagining Lady Rich schooling him to hide his feelings. Someone must be shaping him, for he is a man greatly given to impetuosity.

Cecil can hear that musical voice of hers: *Do not show so*

much as a twitch, Brother. Smile, but not too broadly, and appear to have your mind on pressing things of import. He can feel himself stirring at the thought of Lady Rich. She has left court now to birth an infant. His boy informer has said she is lying-in at her brother's house, not her husband's. The husband either knows nothing or says nothing, for Cecil has a strong suspicion that the baby is Blount's, but he has found no proof. Oh, how he would like that proof, but Lady Rich's women are tight as a fisted hand. What would he do with the information anyway, for the Queen seems determined to think Lady Rich, like her brother, can do no wrong?

Essex has a cluster of allies with him, the young Earl of Southampton is one, gaudily got-up and winding a long strand of hair absently about his finger. Francis Bacon also hovers at Essex's side, clutching a ledger with a hand that is slender as a girl's. 'I see you have found employment, Cousin Francis,' Cecil says to him, acknowledging inwardly that he and his father had misjudged Bacon's usefulness when they refused him a place – and now he has given his fine legal mind to Essex. His brother, Anthony, has joined the Essex camp too. Cecil's mind is whirring: Anthony may be half crippled these days but he was a cog in Walsingham's European espionage machine and will be feeding the earl with information gleaned from his contacts on the Continent. Cecil, having felt he had gained ground with his preferment, now feels outfoxed.

Essex talks loudly over Bacon's reply: 'How sad that Her Majesty has not also made you Secretary of State, since you seem to perform the function of the role without recognition. The post has been vacant for some time now. When was it Walsingham passed away?'

Cecil does not bother answering; they all know the post has been open for almost two years. Is that a sneer or a smile, Cecil asks himself. Essex turns briefly to Bacon and

Southampton. Did he wink at them? Southampton brings a hand to his mouth and coughs as if to disguise a laugh.

'The role on the Privy Council is enough – I merely seek to serve my Queen and country in the best way possible.' Cecil wishes he could think of a light and witty riposte but he is not given to verbal acrobatics.

'I have an audience. Mustn't keep Her Majesty waiting. Will you join us, Pyg–' Essex stops himself before uttering the name. No one but the Queen has ever called Cecil 'Pygmy'. 'Will you join us, Councillor?'

Cecil wonders what the ulterior motive might be. 'With pleasure!' He ought to feign nonchalance and refuse but he wants to see this, wants to see what happens when he reminds the Queen that Essex knighted no fewer than twenty-four of his army captains. The Queen is not wont to spread honours too thinly. When the dispatch had arrived informing her of the knighthoods, she had lost her temper in the council meeting and thrown her pomander across the room. He joins the earl's party, walking with them into the privy chamber, aware of Bacon's scrutiny.

Cecil makes an appraisal of the company: the Queen is seated talking quietly with her physician, Lopez. He is one of the few she trusts and it shows in her manner, relaxed and light-hearted, like an ordinary woman conversing with a dear friend. Ralegh is across the chamber lit by cool winter sunlight from the window, regarding Essex with a disdainful sneer. Now there is a man, thinks Cecil, who would like to see the earl brought down a peg or two; after all, it was Essex who usurped him in the Queen's affections. His mind begins to work up a plan of collaboration with Ralegh to recompense his loss of the Bacon brothers. Ralegh is a man of influence – he could do with that – but he is unpredictable and there is a rumour afoot that he has got one of the Queen's maids in the family way and wed her in secret. The maid in question is sitting at the Queen's feet, sewing, as if she wouldn't be fuzzled by wine. The pair of them might be travelling downriver to the Tower before long.

Cecil scans the chamber to see what other secrets it might reveal while Essex, seeming to forget himself, flings his person at the Queen, grabbing her hand and scattering it with kisses. The room falls silent, awaiting her response to this assault. But her face fills with delight at the earl's unrestrained outpouring.

'My dear boy,' she says. 'I am glad to have you back. It is beneath you to have to play puppet to that faithless French popinjay. Isn't it good to have him back, Pygmy?'

'The pleasure is indescribable, madam.' Cecil wonders if perhaps he has overdone it, as the Queen expels a sharp snort of breath and rolls her eyes slightly.

Doctor Lopez has stepped to one side and is mixing some kind of tonic. Cecil notices another of the maids-of-the-chamber gazing at Essex with a look of undisguised longing. She had been a conquest of his before he left for France – one of the many – if Cecil's informers are correct. The girl has run to fat and is looking quite plain these days, causing Cecil to wonder if she might not be calving with Essex's bastard. It is no wonder the Queen's women are gaining a reputation for their loose morals. Cecil's mind is shuffling all the fragments of information he is gathering, trying to make an entire picture of them.

'Now tell me, Essex, what have you gleaned abroad that might serve us here in England?'

Cecil watches on as they converse, Essex talking of the Spanish threat, how well fortified their coastal towns are, how many ships in their fleet, and which of those English Catholic exiles might be preparing to make an attempt on the Queen's life. This information must be coming from Anthony Bacon's Continental network. Cecil can see Francis nodding in agreement and scribbling notes into his ledger. They are talking of Ireland now, and how Essex fears the Spaniards will seek a foothold there. Ralegh taps his foot impatiently as he watches.

'Will the Irish be a problem?' the Queen asks Cecil, taking the tonic from Doctor Lopez, sniffing it and swigging it back with a grimace. 'Whatever do you put in this, Lopez? It is foul!' She smiles at the doctor, taking his hand. 'I know you only seek my good health.'

'That could not be more true, Your Majesty,' the physician replies.

Cecil has a sudden realization about this Portuguese doctor. He thinks he once heard of Lopez having important contacts at the Spanish court that Walsingham had sought to exploit. He doubts his own memory – surely this genial old man was never a spy – but the thought twitches beneath his skin and he makes a mental note to look into the matter before the Essex camp get their claws into Lopez and his Spanish connections.

Putting his mind back to the conversation, Cecil says, 'I think Ireland is a little close for comfort, but I see no evidence of the Spaniards seeking an allegiance with Tyrone.'

'Essex?' the Queen turns back to the earl.

'If we attack the Spanish fleet in the harbour at Cadiz, we eliminate all possible risk.'

'I think it is a little premature for that.' She sweeps her arm in Essex's direction as if to dismiss him as one would an irritating child. 'What does your father think, Pygmy?' She turns back to Cecil, whose confidence begins to swell.

'He thinks we should watch the situation carefully.'

'Burghley is always right about these things.'

'Yes, my father has the species of wisdom that comes only with age.'

'Watch and wait, watch and wait,' the Queen says, echoing Burghley's oft-used expression.

There is a pocket of silence until Cecil speaks. 'Her

Majesty was most interested to hear of the knights you made in France, My Lord.'

'Those men fought bravely,' says Essex. He is on the defensive at last, thinks Cecil. 'They were greatly deserving of recognition.'

That maid is mooning at Essex; Cecil would like to knock some sense into the silly girl.

'And you decided to knight them all despite my express command that you do not bestow honours at your whim.' The Queen is looking at her favourite gravely and he appears cowed, seeming to lose a little of his lustre. Cecil feels a puff of satisfaction in his breast.

'I beg your pardon for my audacity in the matter, Highness.' Essex is looking at the Queen with his infernally beautiful eyes. Cecil wills the earl to answer back, to try to justify his actions, a sure way to raise the Queen's ire. But he adds nothing, just drops his eyes to the floor in obeisance.

Instead of the angry outburst Cecil has quietly been hoping for, the Queen sighs theatrically, saying, 'What shall we do with you, Essex?'

'If you wish to punish me, Most Gracious Majesty, then I beg you do not force me out of your presence, I could not bear it. It would be as if the sun were extinguished from my world. I would wither and die.'

Cecil is glancing towards the window and catches Ralegh's eye; judging by the look on his face, he is thinking the same thing. Perhaps now the Queen will at least dismiss the earl's nonsense with a harsh word or two.

But all she does is smile and say, 'No, Essex, I will not banish you. You are my brightest bloom. I would not see you wither.'

As the Queen dismisses them Cecil has the feeling that a cutpurse has spirited something precious from him and left him bewildered, patting his empty pockets. He bows and makes to leave but the Queen bids him stay, says she would 'like a private word', and shoos off the girls at her feet, indicating that Cecil should take their place.

'Pygmy, you wear your envy outwardly. It is not becoming.'

'Highness, I –'

'No,' she holds up a hand to stop him. 'I can see that you are not fond of Essex and it irks you when I favour him. But consider this: you have grown up under the wing of your magnificent father, the man I have trusted more than any other – I see evidence of him in you.' Cecil begins to tingle with pride but if he was looking at her expression rather than her hands he would see the slight sneer she wears, as if he is something distasteful she must tolerate for her own good, like Doctor Lopez's remedy. 'And your mother – God rest her soul – was a wise and honourable woman, who was there to guide you until your twenty-fifth year. Essex can barely remember his own father, and as for his mother.' She spits out the last word as if she cannot bear her mouth to be adulterated by it. Her eyes narrow. 'That woman couldn't mother a litter of pigs.' She lowers her voice and drops her gaze. 'She stole my most precious treasure.' She must surely be talking of Leicester. 'Essex even lost his stepfather at a tender age.' Cecil is thinking that twenty-two is not *such* a tender age. 'You see, Pygmy, you may be lacking what Essex has in beauty but I see your loyalty. It shines from you.' For Cecil it is like a purification to hear such words from her. 'Essex is in desperate need of guidance and who better than I to act as both mother and father to him, but do not think that because I value him so greatly I value you any the less.' He feels a surge of emotion like a man remembering he is loved by God.

'I hardly know how to describe my gratitude,' he says. 'I live only to serve you. You and England.' He understands now what his father has been trying to make him see, that just to serve her is enough – all else is distraction.

217

'Overcome your envy, though, for it is an ugly trait.' She holds out her hand. It is his cue to leave and as he kisses her ring he feels all his wickedness, the envy, the covetousness, the jealousy, drop away as if he is reborn.

March 1592

Essex House, the Strand

'I still don't understand why you are here and not at your husband's house,' says Lettice, who sits beside the bed with Dorothy.

Penelope does not want to think of her husband now but cannot help remembering his reaction when she had announced to him that she was carrying another's child.

'One day you will have to atone for your behaviour,' he had said. She resisted pointing out that he was hardly free from sin either. He looked deflated, resigned, too burdened to be angry with her. They sat in a hollow silence for some time. Rich didn't inquire who the father was; perhaps he knew. It is hard to know where gossip has spread when you are the subject of it. She has watched the Queen closely for signs that it has reached her ear but has discerned no change in her behaviour. Either she knows nothing of Penelope's adultery, or she chooses to pretend so. Rich looked so desolate that she reached out to touch his hand, but he snatched it away, as if he might be defiled by her. 'You kept your side of the bargain,' he said. 'Despite myself, I admire that.'

'Thank you.' She was aware that he must have had to muster all his magnanimity to pass the compliment.

'And I must give the bastard my name, for the sake of appearances.'

'Yes.'

'Well, so be it.' His expression pained her. 'We are both burdened by a secret now.'

She wanted to tell him to try to wear his own more lightly, to point out that no one is entirely free of sin, that

219

the opinions of others are not so important. But to him they are, as is his opinion of himself. It is he who chooses to live his life shrouded in shame.

Her mother is still talking but she is not listening. She closes her eyes, pushing all thoughts of Rich to the back of her mind and, grabbing Jeanne's small hand, takes a deep breath to fend off the next wave of pain – they are coming thick and fast now. Her mother's voice is grating. She squeezes Jeanne's hand tighter still and imagines Blount pacing the chamber below.

Jeanne whispers, 'Nearly there.'

'And where is Rich, why is he not downstairs awaiting the birth of his baby?' It is Lettice again.

'Shhhh,' whispers Jeanne, smoothing a cool damp cloth over her forehead.

She begins to pant as another wave engulfs her.

'Rich really should be –'

'RICH IS NOT THE FATHER!' The shout bursts out of Penelope with the force of cannon fire.

The midwife gasps and Lettice stares at her daughter in open-mouthed shock. Dorothy takes their mother's hand: a gesture that says, *leave it be.*

As the pain abates Penelope wonders if her mother is more horrified in the deed itself or the fact that it is spoken out loud. The tension falls from her body and she sinks back into the bed, taking a sip of caudle from Jeanne. It is likely Lettice, whose expression has settled into pinch-lipped indignation, is wondering how she could have spawned children so lacking in morals: Essex has an infant on the way with one of the Queen's maids – though no one else is yet aware of it – Dorothy eloped and wed in secret and now *she* is birthing a bastard. Penelope can feel her annoyance building at her mother's outrage.

'For God's sake,' says Dorothy. 'She wouldn't be the first woman to birth another man's baby.'

'What will people think?'

'You must know by now,' says Penelope, 'that I couldn't give a fig about people's petty judgements and hypocrisies.' She can see her sister smiling behind her hand.

Lettice expels an exasperated sigh but Penelope can feel another contraction accumulating in the small of her back and sending spiked fingers round her belly. She heaves herself on to all fours, moaning like a cow, surprised by the sounds emanating from her, and Dorothy begins to rub her back with firm fingers, while Jeanne wipes the cooling cloth over her brow again, but there is no relief. She rocks back and forth until the pain recedes once more.

'Not long now,' repeats Jeanne.

Lettice is having words with the midwife: 'Nothing goes beyond this chamber, understood?'

'My lips are fastened, My Lady. Women say things in the heat of labour that they do not mean. Your daughter is confused by the pain.'

Penelope hears this exchange as if from under water. Jeanne is holding her with her eyes and emitting short sharp puffs of breath for her to mimic.

'Here he comes,' says the midwife. 'Push, My Lady, push and pant.'

A sound gathers in the deepest part of her, a terrible savage noise, and with it a new kind of pain sears through her body. She keeps her eyes locked on to Jeanne's. Puff, puff, puff, and then comes the irresistible need to push this baby out. She is being torn in two. Another ghoulish howl escapes from her. And it is out.

'A girl,' says Dorothy.

'Never mind, you have two boys already,' says her mother.

Penelope lifts her head away from the pillow, straining to catch a glimpse of her infant, but she cannot see properly. 'Let me have her.'

'But we must clean her,' says the midwife, 'and let her begin suckling to bring down Nurse's milk.'

'Give her to me,' Penelope's voice is firm.

'Darling,' says Lettice, 'I don't think –'

'I want to hold my baby.'

It is Jeanne who takes the infant, still bloody, from the midwife and places her on Penelope's breast, covering her with the blanket for warmth. And it is as if the whole chamber falls away, everything falls away – the worries about her brother, his erratic moods, that niggle at her constantly; concerns about Rich, that delicate balancing act that is her marriage; the seam of dread that runs through everything, of her correspondence with Scotland being uncovered. Slowly, slowly, she is making inroads, gaining King James's trust, letters moving up and down the Great North Road, but it is a most delicate matter; then there are the Catholic plots; the Spanish threat; the plague, which they say is running rife in parts of the capital; a thousand fears that habitually haunt her – all dissolved and she is left in a state of complete contentment with her daughter – Blount's daughter – drifting in space.

A great flood of love surges in her, inundating them both, and she takes in the sight of her infant: the miniature hands waving as if under water, the mop of sticky black hair, the pink scrunched face. Penelope is mesmerized by this perfect creature made inside her own body, astonished by the miracle of it. The infant's eyes pop open suddenly, meeting those of her mother, and Penelope is shot through with a fear-tinged euphoria at this confrontation, as if those eyes hold secrets within them so great they can never be uttered. They are black and deep, a place to become entirely lost. A voice insinuates itself into her mind, a faint recitation, fragments of poetry, an incantation from the dead, forming, shaping, becoming whole:

. . . in beamy black, like painter wise,
Frame daintiest lustre mixed of shades and light?

She has the overwhelming sense as she gazes at her baby, of looking into her own eyes, feeling that God has made in this infant a mirror to the past. She can hear Blount saying, 'If it is a girl we shall name her after you.'

'Little Pea,' she breathes.

Lest if no veil those brave gleams did disguise,
They sun-like should more dazzle than delight?

Sidney is there with them; she feels him in a shiver that runs up through her being. 'You are made in love,' she murmurs to her infant.

She e'en in black doth make all beauties flow?

And slowly, like a leaf twirling and drifting to the ground, Penelope returns to the birthing chamber to see the smiling faces of her mother, her sister and the midwife at the foot of the bed, and Jeanne, dear, dear Jeanne, beside her, head cocked, enchanted. 'She has the look of her father,' Jeanne says very quietly, so the others cannot hear.

Penelope smiles. 'He will want to see his firstborn.' She can feel the strings of her heart attached to the pulsating core of Little Pea and her others in the nursery at Leighs and also flying out like a fishing line to draw Blount in, right in, to the fulcrum of her world.

April 1593

Theobalds, Hertfordshire

Cecil sits beside the lake remembering the Queen's visit almost two years earlier and the miniature galleons enacting a sea battle for her delight. He has been on the Privy Council for some time now but still feels ineffectual, as if his function is merely to be his father's proxy. He is a man of almost thirty, should be at the height of his powers, but he can see no way out from Burghley's shadow. Whatever heights Cecil rises to there is always the sense of Burghley's bitter dissatisfaction in his son's failure to achieve the appointment of Secretary of State. How he would love to create something brilliant, some kind of extraordinary policy, something to make the Cecils' legacy indelible. Peace with Spain: he imagines his father's delight – his ancient face opening into a rare smile – as the papers are signed, the Queen's name beside King Felipe's. Then his father will recognize his worth. But as he is thinking it, the pragmatic side of him simultaneously recognizes the impossibility of such a thing – but great things are achieved by those who dream, are they not?

The lake is covered in flotsam, a scum of debris; a swan has made herself a nest on a platform that had once been the stage for a magnificent display of fireworks. He walks towards the water's edge, carefully picking his way around the weeds and mud, where he remembers a bank of fragrant wild flowers artfully designed to appear as if they had seeded there by chance.

It upsets him to see the place in disorder; he finds it almost unbearable to sit amongst such chaos, and he tries to cheer himself by thinking of his son and heir, William, back in the nursery at Pymmes. He conjures up an image of the child in his mind's eye, sensing the blossoming of feelings – love and pride – deep within. He makes the nurse strip William naked from time to time, just so he can marvel at his boy's straight spine, imagining the little mobile shoulder blades are the nubs of wings that will one day sprout and allow him to fly. Thinking of his boy, so unlike him, with his perfect proportions, gives him hope.

He can see the chimneys of Pymmes from where he stands, emitting strings of grey smoke. Another wave of inadequacy washes over him; to live in a house, however magnificent it may be, that is built on land carved out from his father's estate, funded by monies gained by his father's clever dealings, is not the sign of a successful man. If he had been of a different disposition, a different shape, he might have earned martial glory and had his own honours bestowed on him.

He walks through the arbour towards the house, ankle-deep in dropped blossom, refusing to see the wild beauty of the unkempt gardens, only irritated by the lack of order. Essex had stolen away his father's gardener. The earl had wanted something spectacular to impress the Queen and had achieved it by covering his cherry trees with sacking to hold off their fruit. A week before her arrival they had been exposed to the sun and, by the day of her visit, they were groaning with cherries a month after the harvest was over. It was on everyone's lips at court, how Essex's trees had borne fruit magically in the glow of the Queen's splendour. Cecil would have chopped those blasted trees down, given half a chance.

And now Essex is sworn on to the Privy Council. He had taken his place beside the Queen with a look of supreme self-satisfaction and proceeded to blather about various incidents. She listened intently as he told her of disturbances in Ireland, insisting that the council take the Irish problem seriously. Then the discussion turned to Spain and the threat of a new Armada. One of Cecil's chief informants on Spanish affairs had been found dead in Deptford – a murder, he suspected, made to look like a brawl – so Cecil wasn't able to add anything. Essex seemed to know the exact numbers of the Spanish fleet, who was lined up to captain each ship, even the names of the vessels. Cecil supposed this all came through Anthony Bacon's lines of information, but he couldn't be entirely sure for the boy in his pay at Essex House had died of the plague.

Now Cecil understands why Essex was so determined to wed that insipid daughter of Walsingham's, for the entire network has shifted his way. They are all backing the earl – they know Burghley is fading and they see the influence Essex has with the Queen. The Queen looked like a proud parent as her favourite offered up his news. It was Burghley who eventually turned the discussion to the succession. Elizabeth's annoyance smouldered – his father is the only one who can get away with raising the matter.

'I know I have been unwell of late, Burghley, but I am quite recovered now so there is no need to ready my replacement just yet.'

She *had* been ill and had the court scurrying about in fear, trying to ascertain which way they would jump when the time came. At three score years a serious malady can carry a person away with ease, even a queen. While she was being ministered to by Doctor Lopez, there were huddled conversations in corners; letters declaring allegiances, to be read then burnt, were sent about; new friendships were struck from nowhere.

There is no doubt that the earl has gained advantage since he installed those clever Bacon brothers at Essex House, and also through Blount's and Lady Rich's influence reaching out quietly through court like a miasma. Cecil longs to get to the bottom of *that* relationship; if he could only discover something against Lady Rich, he might turn her. What a coup that would be, but the likelihood of turning sister against brother is a remote dream and Lady Rich is apparently impervious to scandal. He suspects that correspondence continues to pass from Essex House to the Scottish court, but it is nothing more than intuition and a few unreliable whispers.

He can sense the earl's power base burgeoning while his own dwindles. It seems that wherever he turns at court, he is surrounded by relatives of the Devereuxs, all those Knollys uncles, the Careys, the Huntingdons; not to mention Lady Rich still at the heart of the Queen's rooms, despite her adultery; the list is endless and all linked by blood to Elizabeth. He imagines his own blood as thin and slightly sour, like young red wine, unsatisfactory, the sort that leaves your head thumping in the morning, while the Devereux blood is concentrated with history, viscous and dark.

A magpie carks above, making an awful racket. Cecil would like to shoot it but he never was a proficient archer. He had made an attempt to recruit Doctor Lopez but the old man was unresponsive – perhaps he should be less subtle. Cecil kicks at a pile of apple blossom, watching it fly up and drift back down to the ground like snow. He makes an attempt to shake off his dispirited mood, reminding himself of his friends in high places: his father-in-law, Lord Cobham; Lord Grey; and not to forget Ralegh, who may be unpredictable in his loyalty, and in and out of royal favour, but whose hatred of the earl equals his own.

He stops at the fountain. It is dry now and tangled with ivy. While the Queen was abed with sickness at Greenwich the Spanish were planning what they would do in the event of her death, readying the Infanta, whose lineage can be traced directly to Edward III. It is common knowledge there are many secret English Catholics who would rise up to support such a scheme. Perhaps he might persuade Doctor

Lopez to find out more about the Infanta. The problems hadn't disappeared with the Queen's recovery. There had been rumours of another assassination plot – this time it was to have been a poisoned sword – but nothing came of it beyond rumour. Nevertheless, the question of the succession is as pressing as it ever was, but the Queen remains infuriatingly intransigent on the matter.

As he leaves the arbour Cecil is confronted by the full splendour of Theobalds – the house always surprises him with its beauty, the shimmering windows, the artful stonework, the appealing symmetry of proportions.

Once inside, he seeks out his father, finding him with his physician.

'Ah, my boy, I am glad to see you,' he says. 'My gout is troubling me. Doctor Henderson seems to think he can ease the pain.' He gives his physician an affectionate pat on the arm. Cecil cannot remember a time when Henderson was not in his father's pay and wishes he could inspire such loyalty himself, but his own staff come and go and he trusts none of them. 'I think I am past mending.'

'Now, now, My Lord. Nothing ventured, nothing gained,' says Henderson as he shakes a tincture bottle and pours out a measure.

Burghley leans back with a sigh. 'To court in a fortnight. If only Her Majesty would allow me to retire. I have become too old for all this.' He massages his hands together. They are warped and knotted with painfully swollen knuckles. 'I am exhausted.'

It jars Cecil to see his father thus, overcome by decrepitude, and he can't help dreading his inevitable demise, wondering if he, Cecil, will survive such an event. He imagines all the power and wealth his father has accumulated coming to nothing under his watch, then admonishes himself for his lack of mettle, resolving to be more of a man. Once Henderson has departed, despite his misgivings about appearing weak in his father's eyes, Cecil finds himself confiding his worries.

'What has occasioned all this?' asks Burghley.

'I don't know, I feel things slipping through my fingers. My informers are becoming unreliable. Essex is gaining on us. His followers are tightening their hold on the Queen.'

'Loyalties ebb and flow, my son. And never forget we Cecils have wealth on our side and it is wealth gained from true loyalty.' He pauses, looking at his son through glazed eyes. 'All those ancient nobles are scrabbling for favours, begging to raise wars in the hope of scraping a little more land together. Their coffers are empty and yet they must still strut about in the finest of everything. There is no true loyalty in those men. It is men like us that are the future – quiet men. Don't you forget it.'

His father's words are like a tonic and Cecil feels his misgivings begin to fall away.

'But remember. Essex is not your enemy. You are *both* on the side of England. I warned you of this – you risk losing control.' His tone betrays his impatience, as if explaining something to a recalcitrant child. 'It's just a question of setting up some new lines of information.'

'I am hopeful of making a connection with Doctor Lopez,' says Cecil, not mentioning his recent failure with Lopez and resolving to renew his efforts. 'I believe he has a line to the heart of the Spanish court.'

'Yes, yes,' says his father. 'Walsingham set that up, if I remember rightly. Never came to anything. I'm not entirely sure Lopez had the stomach for espionage. Agreeable fellow, I seem to recall.'

'Perhaps I can persuade him to reignite those connections.'

Burghley nods, as if to say: that's more like it. 'Never forget this,' he adds. 'The Queen has always needed me to perform the necessary evils of the state. I can be demonized while she remains beloved, and all in the best interests of

England and peace. Take the case of Mary of Scotland. Elizabeth could not be seen to be the one generating the demise of an anointed Queen, much as she understood its necessity. I could absorb all the horror and hatred – take the blame.' Cecil remembers well the determination with which his father hounded Mary Stuart and wondered at the time if he was using entirely honest methods. He laughs inwardly at this, for after all there are no truly honest methods when it comes to statecraft. Burghley looks directly at him. 'If you learn only a single lesson from me, then let it be that people need someone to hate; it is part of the mechanics of power. If you can learn to be that hated person, you will be indispensable. Essex – the moody pup, cares too much about being loved, seeks popularity; he cannot bear to be reviled. You and I, my boy, we are essential as long as we remain happy to be vilified.'

It is as if a spark has fired up in Cecil's head – all that time seeking approval, when to truly serve the Queen required something else, something he knew he had a talent for – a talent for being loathed.

'Just keep watching the sister,' continues Burghley. 'That one cares not a jot for the opinions of others and that lends her formidable power. You would not want her playing her brother's dark twin – she would be a formidable adversary.'

'Lady Rich?'

'The very same – my advice would be to win the lady over.'

July 1593

Wanstead, Essex

The players are scattered about the room, still in their costumes. One is dressed as an ancient king with black eye-paint ghoulishly smeared into a chalk-white face and a crown sitting crookedly on his pate. Another lolls beside him in a partly unbuckled soldier's breastplate, daubed with some kind of red matter. Beside him is a pretty boy with rouged lips; he is laced into a set of bodices, above which wisps of fine golden chest hair sprout. He swigs at his cup then burps loudly.

'Desist that,' says the pretend king, cuffing him on the shoulder. 'Have you forgotten we are in polite company?'

Penelope laughs. She has not enjoyed an evening such as this for a long time and plans to make the most of it. The plague is raging in the city and the theatres have been shut to prevent the spread of infection, leaving this troupe of players in need of employment. It was she who suggested to her brother that they invite them to Wanstead. Rich had gone to his chamber, muttering, 'Your ungodly pastimes will lead you to hell.' She is glad he has retired, for Blount is here, at a discreet distance across the room, and she is always a little uncomfortable when her husband and lover are breathing the same air.

Essex is sprawled in the chair beside her, sucking on his pipe, making the occasional comment to Southampton on his other side, who, with his voluminous shirt billowing from an open doublet and hair as long and carefully arranged as Lady Godiva's, looks as if he better belongs with the players than the family. The Earl of Southampton has become an almost permanent fixture at her brother's side. Essex seems to have taken a shine to the younger man's flamboyance. She watches Southampton draw deeply at his own pipe then, like a magician, puff out a ring of smoke.

'I put young Robert on a pony the other day, Sis,' he says. 'My boy is a natural in the saddle.'

'He is only two and a half,' she says, aware that her brother is prone to exaggeration.

'But he showed no fear.'

It pleases her to see this unperturbed version of her brother and no sign of the blank gaze of melancholia.

'I will ask Frances to bring him to Leighs, when you return to court,' she says. 'He will enjoy spending time with his cousins.'

'Excellent idea, Sis!' He seems so normal, untroubled, which invests her with a sense of optimism.

'And what do you plan to do with the Wandering Spaniard?' She is talking of Antonio Pérez, a Spanish exile who has inveigled himself into the Essex circle. He arrived with a French delegation in the spring and is now in her brother's pay.

'He will stay here. Or come with me. I am in need of a good secretary.'

Pérez, who is seated across the room, a pair of hooded eyes half hidden by a straggling curtain of oily dark hair, seems to have divined that they are talking about him, as he raises his cup in their direction with a knowing smile and whispers something to Francis Bacon beside him.

'You have Anthony Bacon as secretary,' she says.

'But Pérez has particular qualities.'

She wonders what those might be, imagining the worst. She is not so innocent as to be unaware that espionage requires foul practices on occasion. 'He unsettles me a little,' she says, smiling back at the man and nodding. 'He seems to know things he shouldn't.' Francis Bacon unsettles her too, though she would never say it, for Essex is so very close to him. She can't put her finger on what it is but there is something infinitely shifty about him – that baby face belying an intimidating depth of intellect. He seems not to like women. Perhaps that is it. Perhaps he is too clever for his own good. She prefers his brother, poor Anthony, beset with gout and always in pain, who gives off a more authentic air of loyalty – or that is her instinct anyway.

'I would say that knowing things one shouldn't is a fine quality in someone of Pérez's profession. He has brought some information to my attention' – her brother is whispering now – 'about Doctor Lopez.'

'What sort of information? Don't tell me Lopez is up to no good, for I would never believe it. He has seen us both through many a crisis.'

'Appearances can be deceptive, Sis.'

'I refuse to believe that. He saved Lucy's life – she could have choked to death in her cradle.' Her whisper has become a hiss.

'Your daughter is nearly ten. I have it on good authority that the old fox is now in the pay of the Spanish King – England's enemy.' His excitement is unmistakable. 'There is a poisoning plot afoot and Doctor Lopez lies at its heart. I just need to gather the proof and –'

'I hardly believe that,' she cuts him off. 'Doctor Lopez is no fox, he is benign as a kitten.'

'Even a kitten has claws that could scratch an eye out,' murmurs Essex. 'I need to look further into it and Pérez will be useful in that. He seems to be on terms with all the Spanish and Portuguese in London.'

'You are imagining things, Robin. Don't draw Doctor Lopez into your intrigues. He has been a loyal friend to our family for years, and served the Queen even longer.' Penelope can see his suspicion swelling like a tumour. 'Do not make this a personal affair. I refuse to believe Doctor Lopez is planning to poison the Queen – it is absurd.' She pictures the man's neatly clipped silver hair framing those kind eyes. But a shard of doubt has burrowed beneath her skin. In this dissembling world, it is impossible to know with complete certainty who the enemy might be.

She knows enough men who go about pertaining to be poets but are spies beneath the surface, Henry Constable for one, who is now on the Continent gathering information. And she herself, with her secret correspondence, is not entirely innocent. The lines of communication had reached a frenzied crescendo as the Queen lay in her sickbed lately. They were no longer the friendly missives of before. These were letters that spoke of the succession, that would send their author to the block in a breath, written in orange juice, only visible with a flame passed over it. All awaited to see which way the die would fall. With each letter thrown on the fire, she imagined those flames licking about her own body, whispering the word *treachery*.

But since the Queen's recovery Scotland has fallen silent. All her careful secret diplomacy seems to be achieving little towards the cause of the Devereuxs. She wonders if the danger is worth it, if perhaps she would be better emulating her sister and opting for a quiet life. She laughs inwardly at herself for that thought but a feeling of dread creeps over her, as if she is teetering on the edge of something and that the consequences of an unsure tread might be grave. Beneath the dread though, buried deep within her, is a prickle of excitement, an exhilaration that can only be found when the stakes are at their highest.

'Don't you see,' Essex says, 'I can make political capital of this. To prevent an assassination . . .' That spark has ignited in him once more, a flicker of madness, which makes her forget what she was about to say.

One of the players stands, clapping his hands to attract everyone's attention, and manages to spill ale down his robes, which provokes some ribbing.

'There is one amongst us who fancies himself a poet.'

'Just one?' cries Southampton. 'I think there is hardly a

soul in the whole of England who is not trying their hand at rhyming verses these days.' Everyone laughs, for there is some truth in this.

'My husband is not,' says Penelope to another gale of laughter. 'He abhors such ungodly pleasures.'

'Then I fear My Lady is wasted on such a man,' says the player.

She swaps a brief smile with Blount. 'Why do you say that, sir?'

'Because someone such as you was put on this earth to inspire great poetry.' The laughter builds. It is common knowledge these days that she is the Stella of Sidney's sonnets. Though when she thinks of it she is so far removed from that girl she hardly believes herself the same person.

'Come on, Will,' says the player, tugging on the injured soldier's sleeve to pull him to his feet. 'Why don't you try and come up with something worthy of Lady Rich.'

The player takes the floor and people shuffle back to make space for him.

'I have been working on something. It is but half formed.' He takes a bow and silence falls while the player concentrates all his attention on his shoes. Eventually, lifting his face to look directly at Penelope, he begins to speak: 'My mistress' eyes are nothing like the sun . . .'

'Sidney did that a decade ago,' calls out Essex, teasing the actor, who seems in his own world and entirely unperturbed. '"In colour black why wrapped she beams so bright?" Did Sidney not already turn Petrarch's fair lady on her head with his black-eyed beauty?' He nudges his sister with a laugh. 'Give us something we have not heard before.'

The player turns to his corseted friend, wipes his thumb over the boy's mouth and holds it up so the room can see the crimson stain: 'Coral is far more red than her lips' red.' This provokes more laughter as the player circles the space, seeming to seek inspiration. He stops in front of a dark-skinned girl who is the mistress of one of their party, lightly touching the smooth skin of her throat with the words: 'If snow be white, why then her breasts are dun.'

The girl laughs too, taking a hank of her thick black hair, twisting it about a finger, and adding: 'If horses have hair, then horse hair sprouts from her head.' This rouses a burst of applause. And the player is pacing again, seeking for words, then returns to the dark girl. 'I have seen roses broidered –' he stops. 'No. I have seen roses damasked, red and white, / But no such roses see I in her cheeks.' He moves towards the boy once more, calling out to the room, 'A rhyme for "cheeks".'

'Peaks,' says someone.

'Squeaks,' says another.

'My mistress is not a mouse,' answers the player. 'I have it!' He holds up a hand to quiet the laughter and leans in to the boy, sniffing with a grimace. 'And in some perfumes is there more delight / Than in the breath that from my mistress reeks.'

This incites more mirth, but the poet doesn't wait for it to die down before continuing: 'I love to hear her speak, yet well I know / That music hath a far more pleasing sound; / I grant I never saw a goddess go; / My mistress when she walks treads on the ground.'

'Which one is your mistress, then?' calls out Southampton.

'Why, my Lady Rich, of course. Is she not the muse of *all* poets?' And he steps forward to Penelope, dropping on to one knee with a flourish and a slight smirk, hesitating, seeming to cast about inside himself for his rhyme, before speaking: 'And yet, by heaven, I think my love as rare / As any she belied with false compare.'

There is no applause now, only a thick hush. Perhaps they are all wondering, as Penelope is, if they have not just witnessed something completely new, as rare as a seam of diamonds in an Indian mine. But beneath her delight churns unease for Doctor Lopez, as she wonders what her brother meant by 'making political capital'.

'Yours is an uncommon talent,' she says. 'You make the object of love human, invest her with flesh and blood. It is refreshing, indeed, to have something other than the nymphs that inhabit the lines of most verse.'

'You take Sidney and shake him up,' says Southampton, leaning forward in his seat, his voice breathy with barely suppressed excitement. Penelope had not thought him such a lover of poetry. 'Have you more like that?' he asks.

'A hundred thousand,' replies the player.

'They must be published.'

'But they only exist in here.' He taps the side of his head. 'And besides they are' – he hesitates – 'not for the world.'

January 1594

Burghley House, the Strand

'You should not have come to me here,' says Cecil, carefully lining up the items on his desk, bringing the inkwell exactly level with his container of quills and picking up a sheaf of papers, standing it on its side, tapping it against the surface of the desk to ensure its leaves are all even. 'It makes you look guilty.'

Doctor Lopez appears terrified. He tucks his quivering hands away beneath his arms. 'But I am *not* guilty. You well know that. You must do something to help me.' His diction is perfect but his accent is thick with Portuguese, even after thirty years in England.

'Fret not.' Cecil sounds calm but he isn't, for he is struggling with his conscience. It would be better if there were at least some ambiguity, at least the possibility of Doctor Lopez's guilt. But this man is clean as a new-starched ruff. He gets up and moves to the window, leaving Doctor Lopez stranded beside the desk without a view of his face. 'I will ensure nothing befalls you.'

This is a guarantee he knows he cannot deliver. He watches the traffic on the Strand below, hearing the shouts of the carters and hawkers and the bleating complaint of a herd of sheep being driven by. London is coming back to life again, now the worst of the plague is over. Watching the scene, he can feel his annoyance that Burghley House, however plush and new it may be – with its tennis court, bowling alley and gardens filled with exotic blooms – is on the wrong side of the Strand and not on the river, as Essex House is. He should be looking out on pretty boats with all their pennants flying and watching the royal barge glide by, not some farmer driving his sheep up the Strand, leaving a trail of droppings. A cluster of pigeons is perched on the sill below, squabbling. They have fouled the stonework. He can imagine their necks snapping under his fingers.

'But Essex has convinced the Queen of my guilt.'

'I doubt that. Her Majesty is not so easily swayed.' He turns and smiles at the man. It was a good plan, but it went awry. The Spaniards had taken the bait. How could they resist an approach from one of Queen Elizabeth's trusted physicians? Who was better placed to slip Her Majesty a phial of something or other? Cecil could sense that their tongues were about to loosen; he could feel all the Spanish state secrets finding their way into his hands. His fingers had itched at the very thought of it. He had imagined his resulting rise, the effect of Elizabeth's gratitude.

But in the end Doctor Lopez wasn't cut out for the job, he didn't have that seam of steel necessary for espionage. He hadn't held his nerve when it mattered most; he panicked unnecessarily and allowed a poorly encoded letter to fall into the wrong hands – the man had trusted Antonio Pérez; that was a mistake, for it seems Pérez is now in Essex's pay. Essex is calling it treason, but it is best Lopez is not aware of that fact. It would not do to have him falling to pieces and blabbing everything. Essex has fortune on his side. Cecil thinks of the drop of water slowly eroding the stone and, taking a deep breath, reminds himself to be patient.

'But you will set them straight, won't you, Cecil?' Doctor Lopez twitches, flicking his hand up repeatedly, seeming to swipe away an imaginary fly from his face. Give the man his dues; he *had* stuck to his story and not mentioned whose pay he was in – not yet, anyway. And it must stay that way, for if the Queen were to get wind of the fact that Cecil has endangered her dear and faithful old physician, it is unimaginable how she might retaliate. All he can do now is limit the damage.

'Yes, I will set them right,' he says. 'But don't you try and explain my role in it all. They will only assume it an attempt to shift the blame. And it will cast you in a bad light if they think you did it for money.' Cecil reassures himself that the man hasn't been *entirely* innocent in all this. He was paid a generous sum for his services. He must have known that much money comes only with great risk. 'Tell them that you saw an opportunity to serve the Queen and acted on your own. Tell them that the Spaniards approached *you*.' He pauses, allowing an idea to alight that might turn some small advantage out of this mess. 'You could say they approached you through Pérez.' Getting rid of Pérez would be a bonus.

'But that would be a lie. I couldn't incriminate an innocent man.'

Cecil can feel his annoyance building – this man's naivety is astonishing. 'Innocent? The man has fled from Spain a convicted murderer, leaving his wife and children hostage. I'm sure he would have no qualms about doing *you* an injustice.'

'I have to be able to reconcile myself with God.' As he says this, Doctor Lopez draws himself up in his chair, seeming invested with new life.

'If you are serving the Queen then you serve Our Lord.' This is what Cecil has been telling himself vehemently, though he has lately begun to wonder to what lengths his morals will be stretched in serving Her Majesty. He comforts himself by thinking of what his father had said about someone having to take the immoral load from the Queen's shoulders, that it is a crucial function of statesmanship: taking the blame.

'But if they . . .' Lopez stops, drooping once more, and takes a deep, trembling breath. 'If they torture me?'

'I will make sure they do not.'

The man's eyes now look wild with fear, as if he is an animal at bay. Cecil can't look at him. 'Can you not help me out of the country?'

'That won't be necessary. Listen.' He takes the doctor's shoulders, finally meeting his eye, feeling like Judas. 'Hold your nerve, man.'

He calls in his servant, telling him to convey the doctor back to his dwelling discreetly. 'No one is to know he has been here,' he says. 'It is for your safety, Doctor Lopez.' Cecil smiles but wonders when they will send a guard to arrest the poor fellow, stopping those thoughts in their tracks. He can't have a crisis of integrity now. Lopez makes an attempt at a smile in return but does not quite achieve it.

'I can trust you?' he asks, as he is bundled out of the door.

Cecil nods. It is beyond even him to say the words themselves.

Back at the window he cranes his head in the direction of Essex House, a little to the east, though he knows he can't see it, for St Mary-Le-Strand lies in his line of sight. He imagines what is going on in there and has to give the earl due credit: he has built an effective ring of informers. Inevitably, Lady Rich springs to mind with the familiar quiver of admiration, which is only increased when he remembers his father's warning: *That one cares not a jot for the opinions of others.* Cecil wonders if that is truly the case, for doesn't everyone care in some small way about the opinions of others? He allows himself to entertain the idea of bringing Lady Rich down, imagining the whole of Essex's faction falling with her.

He looks down into the Strand and sees a man loitering, fancies he had his eyes trained on the window and looked away as Cecil turned to face him. He is sure that this same man was there earlier, when the sheep were being driven by. Unease takes hold in him as he wonders what might have been seen, glad that he insisted on Lopez leaving by the back entrance. It is inevitable, he supposes, that people will watch him. He feels his resolve strengthen.

June 1594

Essex House, the Strand

'My brother thinks it a victory,' says Penelope quietly as she picks up a pack of playing cards, handing it to Blount. She casts her eye about the room and asks the usher who is standing by the door to leave. She believes him to be trustworthy but the fewer people who listen in, the less likely things are to get out. When the door has shut she continues, 'I fear Essex went too far to gain ground over Cecil.'

'Even now, do you doubt Doctor Lopez's guilt?'

'Oh, I don't know, Charles. It is all so opaque . . . You think you know someone. He was a gentle soul . . . and honest, or so I thought. An honest man stands out amongst all that duplicity and . . . well, Lopez seemed honest to me.' Blount shuffles the cards and deals. 'It is possible, I suppose, that he became unwittingly embroiled in something; but I feel sure he was not as guilty as my brother believed.'

Essex had been like a dog with a dead rabbit, his teeth firmly gripped about its throat. Penelope feels sick at the thought of Lopez meeting his end on the scaffold – a traitor's death, the worst kind; a horrific spectacle of suffering. She thinks in the distance she can hear the roar of the crowd baying for blood but knows it is in her imagination; Doctor Lopez died over an hour ago.

Blount must see her distress for he leans towards her across the table, taking her upper arms in his hands. 'I know he was dear to you.'

'He saved Lucy's life.'

'I know, but the evidence against him *was* convincing,' says Blount, leaning back but keeping a hand on her forearm. Their game is forgotten.

'Well it would have been, wouldn't it? Evidence is meaningless.' Penelope cannot prevent her voice from cracking.

'There were rumours years ago that he was concocting poisons. It is *possible* he truly intended to do away with the Queen.'

'What, the very man who cared for her health for years?' She stops. 'I know, I know, people are complex creatures and what they do doesn't always make sense.'

'Your brother was entirely convinced of his guilt,' says Blount. 'Though I did try to make him look further into it. I felt sure there was a way to deal with the situation without it ending in . . .' He doesn't say the word 'execution' but it is an axe suspended silently in the air.

'I know you did what you could, as did I.' But she wonders if she might have done more. She had tried to speak to the Queen and at least persuade her to delay the execution, but Elizabeth refused to have anything spoken of it, said justice must run its course. 'Sometimes people see what they want to see.'

She has been worried about Essex lately; there is a disconcerting zeal about him. The Queen's favour knows no bounds as far as he is concerned, and it is going to his head. And the uncovering of this plot, if that is what it was, has thrust him further into the ascendency. He has become over-inflated and his bubble will burst. Penelope has gathered the broken fragments of her brother many times over the years and she recognizes the signs.

'I'm puzzled by Cecil,' says Blount. 'If Doctor Lopez had been working as a double agent, as he claimed, then surely Cecil would have been *au courante*. But he pleaded ignorance of the entire affair.'

'Cecil can't be trusted,' she says, wondering if it could be possible that it was Cecil who threw Lopez to the wolves, trying to understand what advantage it would have gained him, unable to find a reason. 'But my brother's fervour was excessive.' She shakes her head and feels all of a sudden as if

244

everything is too fragile, as if she too could find herself inside the Tower having information extracted from her like Lopez. It would only take a small slip; for the wrong person to whisper in the wrong ear. Panic rises in her from nowhere.

'Penelope?' The sound of Blount's voice soothes her and the panic recedes.

'Will you keep an eye on my brother?' she asks.

'Of course I will. For your sake.' He leans across the table once more, this time kissing her on the lips and stroking her cheek. 'For *our* sake.'

'Sometimes I imagine us living together as man and wife.' She is not quite able to articulate what she means by that: a life that is not lived on the edge of a precipice and weighed down by secrets.

'I think of nothing else.'

'Now you exaggerate. Your mind is always turned to politics.'

'And yours is not?'

He is right. She could not give up the feeling of power her secrets give her and the sense of herself as a cog in the machine of government. She is party to the covert information gathered by Anthony Bacon, secrets that could have great bearing on the state. She imagines Essex House as the root of a vine that spreads out, down through Europe, over to Ireland in the west, up to Scotland in the north. 'I have had correspondence lately, from Scotland.' The thought assaults her, not for the first time, that this correspondence could quite well be used as evidence one day should *she* be tried for treason, if someone wanted rid of her. That particular long-awaited letter had fallen from her sleeve in the privy chamber before she'd had the chance to burn it. Peg Carey had plucked it up, quick as a magpie.

'What is this? A love letter?' she had held it to her nose and sniffed, as if she might have smelled its contents. 'What are you hiding from us?' She was pretending to tease but

Penelope feared she knew something and she could see Cecil watching the exchange from the corner of her eye. It was little consolation that Peg Carey was a kinswoman.

'Don't be silly,' said Penelope, trying to sound unperturbed, though her heart was throbbing, and holding her hand out for the letter, marvelling that it didn't tremble.

After what seemed an infinite pause Peg relented and handed the letter back with an indecipherable smile.

'Thank you,' she said as she slipped it into the fire, watching it burn right away, resolving never to read such things at court in future. 'Just another petition.'

She inhales sharply to erase the memory.

'From King James?' asks Blount.

'Not the King himself, but from one close to him, suggesting he might welcome our allegiance. It is discreetly written but the implication is undeniable.' She looks at her lover and sees that his face is filled with concern. 'What is it?'

'Nothing.'

'I have been doing this a long time. It is five years since I first put feelers out in that direction so I know how to cover my tracks.' The look of concern is still there. It is only lately that she has felt sufficient trust to discuss such things with Blount. It is one thing to trust a lover with your heart, quite another to share confidences that could take them both to the scaffold. 'Sometimes I wonder if patience is not the most important quality in statecraft. I wish my brother would come to understand that. He is so very impetuous.' A shiver runs through her, as if someone is walking over her grave, and with it a thought: that she might one day have to distance herself from her rash brother – there are so many stories of those who have striven to reach too high and none end well.

She pushes the thought aside, reminding herself that the ties of family are unbreakable and that the love she has for her brother is immutable, despite his imprudent ways. Besides, she is there to curb him. It was ever thus: as the eldest, it was her duty to stop him climbing to the highest branches of the orchard trees at Chartley or mounting the unbroken ponies in the paddock or running the river rapids on a homemade raft tied together with twine, all just to demonstrate his courage. But she had failed to curb him on this occasion.

It is a burden indeed to carry the weight of an entire family's hopes and dreams. She has a picture of those eyes, flat and dead with gloom. When her mother announced their father's death she said to him, 'You are the Earl of Essex now.' He had looked forlorn and small, much smaller than his ten years. 'You have the responsibility of the Devereuxs. You are the head of the family.' It was as if his childhood was stolen from him in an instant and it was soon after that she saw the empty, stone-eyed look for the first time.

'If you had been a boy you would have made a fine statesman,' Blount says playfully. He is trying to cheer her up and she loves him all the more for it.

'And if you had been a woman, you would have made a terrible wife with your nose always in a book. Your husband would fear you getting above yourself with learning.' He laughs at this and flutters his eyelashes like a maid. She is glad of the levity, even if it is a little forced.

'Think,' she says, serious now. 'If we were to live at Wanstead together, imagine how our life would be.'

'I fear you could not bear such a quiet life.'

'Not now, perhaps, but one day.'

'One day,' he echoes. 'Why do you love Wanstead so?'

'I don't know exactly what it is; there is an atmosphere of contentment about the place. It was a refuge too, when I was first married.' What she doesn't say is that it is a place that is untouched for her by memories of Sidney, who haunts every other place. Blount takes her hand, weaving his fingers through hers.

The door opens and they snatch back their hands, picking up their cards once more. 'Your turn,' says Penelope, as Essex invades the room with an entourage that includes her husband. Rich glances her way briefly. They had argued recently about Blount, when Rich had reminded her about her promise of discretion. 'Do you think I want to wear a cuckold's horns for all to laugh at behind their hands at court? Is it not enough that I let you raise his daughter with my own children?' She had not mentioned that she thought she might be with child once more. Neither has she told Blount, for the last time she'd miscarried and he had been brought so low by it.

'I have kept my side of the bargain,' she'd replied to Rich. 'I have served as your foil and turned a blind eye to your . . .' She didn't know quite how to describe his affairs, never had found a satisfactory term. 'You have two sons in the nursery,' she reminded him. 'And fine boys they are too.'

Penelope's heart is always squeezed when she thinks of her children. Her mother never fails to tell her she is over-indulgent with them, but she cannot help herself. On her last visit to Leighs she had brought them a pair of guinea pigs, a rarity procured at great expense from a merchant, and feels a flush of warmth remembering their delight on being introduced to the odd creatures with their bead-like eyes and twitching whiskery noses.

There is a disturbing air of suppressed excitement about her brother and his crowd, as if they have been carousing or fighting.

'Is it still raining?' she asks, noticing that Essex's hair is slick. It has hardly stopped raining all summer, which will likely ruin the harvest.

'You must have heard it. It was torrential,' says Essex, shaking his head like a dog. Rich flinches as a wave of droplets catches his face, causing Essex to laugh. Rich laughs too, ingratiatingly. Essex cannot ever do wrong in Rich's book and Penelope has often wondered if there was an unrequited longing there.

'You have a letter,' says Essex, proffering a damp fold of

paper towards Blount. 'Your man was searching everywhere for you.' This causes a venomous glare from Rich, who must have supposed them cached away together, up to no good.

'We were in here all the time,' she says. 'Playing cards.'

Blount has opened the letter and scanned it and is now sitting, wearing an expression of shock.

'What is it?' Penelope asks.

'My brother is dead.' He looks utterly deflated. 'Suddenly.'

'I am so very sorry, Charles,' she says, wanting desperately to comfort him but unable to – not in public and in the company of her husband.

'It is God's will,' says Essex, patting him on the back in that awkward way men have when grief is concerned. 'I suppose it means you are Lord Mountjoy now.'

Penelope kicks her brother sharply on the ankle, annoyed at his tactlessness.

'Would you kindly excuse me?' Blount says, rising and leaving the room. Penelope wants to follow him out but feels Rich's eyes on her. It would not be seemly. She begins to clear away the cards, gathering them together and tying them with a frayed length of ribbon. Essex peels off his wet doublet and flings it to his man. Rich watches him. Sudden understanding alights in her and with it a heavy feeling; of course, they have come from Doctor Lopez's execution. That is the reason for her brother's callous mood. Anger buzzes about her and she stands, taking her brother's arm, pulling him to one side.

'You went too far with the Lopez business,' she whispers. 'Much too far. You should have listened to me. I am horrified –'

'For God's sake, Sis,' he interrupts. 'You do not know the truth of it. The man was guilty, he planned to poison the Queen. He was a traitor. I have saved Her Majesty from assassination.'

'Or you have convinced yourself so.'

'He was guilty, I heard his confession with my own ears, so don't patronize me, Penelope. I am not your infant brother any more. And look how my star is in the ascendant while Cecil – he wears boots of lead.' He takes her chin, turning her face to his. 'Don't you understand, I do this for *us*.'

'I know,' she says, repeating, 'I know.' He is drawn tight as a bowstring.

'You don't know what it is like. So many would see me brought down: Cecil, Ralegh and all their minions.' He is hissing out his words with livid vehemence now. 'Just because it doesn't appear as such, does not mean it is not a war. People die in wars.'

Her brother's world is painted black and white: it is either war or peace, kill or be killed, high or low, there is nothing in between.

'It would serve you to be more measured . . . and do not go about celebrating the poor man's death. Show some decency.' She is thinking of Doctor Lopez's widow. She will set up an anonymous stipend for her; that will in some small way make amends.

'You are right. I will be more measured. Good as gold.' He kisses her cheek, looking at her with puppy eyes. 'Don't be angry with me, Sis, I cannot bear it. It makes me feel I have lost your love.'

Her rage towards him subsides, turning inward, and she feels suddenly filled with shame, as if she had put the noose around the man's neck with her own hands. She cannot deny that her ambition to secure the Devereuxs' future is as great as her brother's; it is like a demon that inhabits them both. Without it they could live in contentment. She could have run away and wed beneath her station as Dorothy had, set-tling for a life in obscurity. But the truth is that even for Dorothy there is no such thing as obscurity, for she is a widow now and Essex is making an attempt to broker an illustrious match for her. Escape is only ever temporary if you are born into a family like theirs, even for dear reckless Dorothy, who hasn't a political hair on her head.

Besides, Penelope knows well enough that she could no more stay away from the heart of things than her brother. He has never had the choice, wouldn't have two pennies to rub together otherwise – the poorest earl in England, that was what they used to say. Families like theirs, if they don't move upwards they die. So Essex must rub around the Queen's ankles like a cat, batting his paws engagingly at the trifles she dangles over him, constantly seeking patronage to keep the Devereux name alive. And she must help him.

'You have not lost my love, Robin.'

Was there a moment, she wonders, looking back into her own past, in which she turned from the simple girl she was, when the egg became the oyster? It began with Rich. She remembers the delicious feeling of power when she struck her deal with him. If it began with Rich, then it crystallized when she came to understand that even if you do your duty and keep your word, circumstances will not always do your bidding. It was Sidney's death that changed her; she does not feel sadness any longer but there is a quiet well of rage at the root of her that must always be kept in check. But rage has a formidable potency, and one day she may want to draw on it.

There is a loud crash and a shattering of glass, followed by a *thwump* as a heavy object comes into contact with the side of his coach. His immediate thought is that the exterior has only just been repainted, at great expense, but a panicked shout from one of the coachmen – 'We are done for if we remain here. To the river! To the river!' – makes Cecil realize that this is no accident. 'Hold hard. Turn the horses.'

The coach lists on the turn and there are more battering sounds. A cold sweat takes hold of Cecil's body as the vehicle begins to rock violently.

'Get your filthy hands off!' cries another coachman. A whip whistles and cracks. Scraping together a ration of courage, Cecil opens the curtain an inch, afraid of what he will find beyond the sanctuary of the cabin. There is a man with his face pressed up to the glass, fingers gripping the lip of the door. His mouth opens in a gap-toothed howl as the knotted tail of the coachman's whip meets his back. Cecil flinches. The man has hold of him with a look of unadulterated loathing. He is saying something – 'See the likes of us go hungry, would you, in your fancy coach, while all of London starves?' – then spits on the glass.

Cecil shrinks back, dumb with horror, and becomes aware of a distant chanting: *Honest day for honest pay; honest day for honest pay; honest day for honest pay*, and another: *Come all workers, with us stand, England for the Englishman*. The gob of spittle trails in a fat drip down the pane and the man, still with his eyes locked on to Cecil's, begins to fumble with the latch. There is a scuffling to the other side of the coach; there must be more than one of them. Cecil's hands are quivering like a drunkard's and he cannot help but imagine being dragged out and having the life beaten out of him, seeing himself, as if from outside his body, cowering in the mud as men kick at his crouched form.

The sudden ear-splitting crack of a pistol being fired takes his breath away. His ears hollow out, ringing painfully. The man turns tail, leaving only the imprint of his loathing on Cecil's mind. The coach moves off fast in the direction of the river, flinging Cecil hard back into the upholstery, cricking his neck. It seems only moments until they are at the pier. The door is flung open and one of his men is helping him out, explaining that he fired into the air. 'No one was harmed, sir.' The thought had not crossed Cecil's mind as to the fate of their assailants. 'It was close. I feared we might have been –'

'Yes,' interrupts Cecil, at last coming to his senses as he is hustled down the pier to the waiting barge.

'Bad trouble, sir,' says the boatman, as he helps him into the boat. 'They're rioting all over the city. Word is they've ransacked a gun-maker's shop and torn down the Cheapside pillories. Apprentices, too young to know better – think they can change the world. Headed for Tower Hill.'

'Take me there.' Now in the relative safety of the barge Cecil feels emboldened, as if their narrow escape has invested him with new courage and even an appetite for danger – it is not a familiar feeling but he is in its grip and is quite lightheaded with it.

'I do not think it a good idea, sir.'

'It is not I who is afraid.' Cecil can hardly believe himself; it is the kind of thing Essex might say to goad a man into committing folly. 'Downriver to the Tower, I said.'

'But the tide is turning. We will have to run the rapids at the bridge.'

'So be it!' Cecil can feel the admiring looks of the oarsmen, impressed by his mettle. A swell of pride catches him.

As the rowers settle into a rhythm, Cecil remains girded by his unfamiliar sense of pluck. When he thinks about, it he should have seen these riots coming. Prices have been rising out of control and a failed harvest has meant an influx of country dwellers into the city, all wanting work. But London is already filled to bursting with foreigners seeking refuge from the wars in the Low Countries and *they* need work too. He saw a gang of youths set upon a Dutchman outside the Mermaid the other day. They had him on the ground, were kicking him; one of the assailants undid his hose and pissed on the poor fellow, who was begging for mercy. Cecil sent in a couple of his men to deal with it, but curbing a single incident is futile.

He can see, from the safety of the water, a group of about fifty men running along the north bank of the river, shouting. The boat glides by the skeleton of the half-built Swan Theatre to the south, a rickety structure reaching up to the sky, higher than all the surrounding buildings except for the church. There is no stopping the playhouses, it would seem. Cecil had made a half-hearted attempt to prevent the building of this one but had abandoned his line for fear of aggravating the Queen, who is fond of the theatre.

For Cecil there is something innately sinister in this burgeoning form of entertainment and its power to influence the masses; he has observed how bloodthirsty a crowd can become when they see a political injustice on the stage and fears the insidious way drama has the potential to incite a crowd to rebellion. There has been a particular play of late enacting the usurpation of King Richard II. Cecil cannot fathom why the Queen should approve such an entertainment, though scenes most likely to cause offence *had* been removed. But even so, he is convinced such things cannot fail to put ideas of dissent into men's heads. This is what happens, he thinks, when the uneducated masses are exposed to such things.

A small vessel draws up with the boatman standing, shouting, 'There's a mob a thousand strong at Tower Hill!'

All of a sudden Cecil is caught up with the sense that all the fragile structures of the state are collapsing, and not only here in London. The Spanish cannot be contained in Europe, it is only a matter of time before they will be pressing at the south coast of England. But the most alarming development, news of which has lately been whispered along Cecil's lines of intelligence, is that the Spanish do intend to join forces with Tyrone in Ireland, against the English, just as Essex had feared, a sobering thought indeed. Essex is rattling his sword as usual, raring to cover himself in glory; Cecil fears the depleted coffers will have to fund a war on two fronts. His mind has been turning over it all constantly, seeking a diplomatic solution. There must be a deal that can be done without the bloodshed and the crippling expense of war. Cecil imagines achieving this, thinking of the Cecil legacy stretching gloriously out into the future.

Looking up, he is jolted out of his thoughts by the vast structure of the bridge looming above and he feels his newly discovered courage begin to seep away. What kind of madness led him to this? He has already narrowly escaped destruction today and the rapids are easily as perilous as the mob. That cold sweat returns, blossoming beneath his clothes, and his breath is shallow and trembling.

But it is too late to go back, for the water has them in its grasp. The rowers bring in their oars and cling on tight as the force of the current begins to push the barge through the narrow arch at a pace. The men whoop and cheer, taken up by the thrill of it. With the roar of the angry water in his ears, Cecil closes his eyes, too petrified to look as they enter the shadows beneath the bridge. He grips the edge of his seat and holds his breath, trying to focus his mind on staying afloat, as if he can prevent them from capsizing by sheer willpower. The crick in his neck intensifies but he dares not let go to rub it. In his mind he is tossed from the boat, into the raging torrent, and pulled under, twisting and turning down into the depths until his lungs burst.

The barge lurches, sending Cecil's stomach into his throat, and then hangs in the air before smacking back down on to the water, listing heavily so that a wave washes over the lip. Cecil smashes his shoulder against an upright. 'Lean in!' cries one of the men and they all shift across their benches, causing the craft to right itself. Cecil's feet are wallowing ankle-deep in water – his best shoes, Italian leather, tooled by an expert artisan.

Then they are through; the men cheer loudly in unison and laugh, teasing each other for being lily-livered. Cecil emits a deep sigh, sending up a silent prayer of thanks, fixes a look of nonchalance on his face and hides his shaking hands. It wouldn't do for them to see his weakness, though he finds it hard to understand how anyone could derive pleasure from such a terrifying experience, except perhaps the pleasure of finding oneself still alive when it is over.

One of the lads begins to bail out the bilge and Cecil inspects his wet shoes. He can see throngs of men filling the narrow lanes leading up from the river. They are all bearing some kind of makeshift weapon or other and moving in a mass towards Tower Hill. The barge stops in view of the battlements, dipping and tossing in the water. Refusing help from the boy, he manages to heave himself up on to the roof of the cabin to gain a better view.

There is a man on the scaffold shouting to the crowd and waving a gun above his head. Cecil is remembering the last person he saw meet his death at that place – Doctor Lopez, a year since – feeling a heaviness in his gut, which he supposes must be shame, and wonders how he will reconcile himself with God when the time comes. He could have saved Doctor Lopez but he would have lost favour for it.

He has watched an innocent man die and as a result seen his enemy rise to impossible heights. It riles him to see Essex puffed up with self-importance but it is the lesser of the two evils – to lose the Queen's trust would have been the end of it for the Cecils. Sometimes he is sickened by the things he does. But *I do it for the sake of England,* he reminds himself – *for the Queen.* And he consoles himself with the thought that, with Essex rising so high, if he falls the parts of him may be scattered too far to be recombined.

The man on the scaffold fires his gun into the air and the crowd roars. Some are throwing stones at windows; a mob near the dock has kicked in the doors of a storehouse and is making away with barrels of fish. Cecil is thinking hard about which of the men in his pay he can ask for names of the ringleaders. There is one who has contacts amongst the apprentices, he will know. A public punishment should curb the worst of it. That man posturing on the scaffold, firing his gun, will find himself back up there before long, asking forgiveness from God and watching in agony as his guts are spilled before his eyes. Cecil will recommend that the Queen impose a curfew. He wonders now why he came. It is not as if he can do anything from his floating refuge.

'Get me back to the palace,' he says to the boatman.

At Whitehall Cecil finds his father watching as the Queen and Essex play chess. Essex now sports a voluminous beard, lustrous and masculine like the mane of a lion. The Queen gazes at the earl as if he is a creature of her own making and she is delighted with her handiwork. Cecil feels his old envy bubbling up.

'Pygmy!' she says, turning to him. 'I hear you have been at the battle front.' He wants her to make more of it, to congratulate him on his bravery, but she seems quite light-hearted

257

and he knows that to describe his ordeal would make it look as if he were fishing for accolades.

'I did witness the events.'

'From the safety of your barge,' says Essex. He is smirking as if to say, had it been him, he would have been in the midst of it all, dispersing the crowd single-handedly.

Cecil looks down at his ruined shoes; there is a white tide-mark on his black stockings. He supposes Essex is the sort who would whoop and cheer running the rapids. How does *he* know, anyway, that Cecil was on his barge? He feels watched as much as he watches; it is not a comfortable feeling. Cecil runs through those he employs as oarsmen, wondering which of them cannot be trusted – or perhaps it was someone on another boat.

'Essex thinks . . .' The Queen pauses to move her knight.

'I see what you are trying to do, madam,' says the earl playfully. 'You have a mind to snatch my castle.'

What *does* Essex think, wonders Cecil, exchanging a brief look with his father. He approached the earl's one-time mistress not long ago, to see if she might be stupid enough to share unwittingly a few of the Essex secrets, to no avail. It would seem, for all his bad-tempered bluster and arrogance, he inspires great loyalty even in his discarded slatterns.

'Perhaps it is not your castle I am after, but something else.'

'No!' cries Essex, slapping a palm to his forehead. 'You have my queen in sight. How could I have not seen that? You are too crafty for me. I do not stand a chance against you.'

The Queen smiles, emitting a gleeful huff of laughter, and Cecil wonders if Essex is allowing her to win. If so he is making a damn good show of it.

'Essex thinks I should impose martial law,' says the Queen, 'but your father is of the mind that it would stir things up further, aren't you, Burghley?'

'I am, madam. I feel it would be prudent to try other methods before resorting to force. We wouldn't want the Catholics jumping on the back of this, or we might have a full-blown rebellion before we know where we are.'

'What do you think, Pygmy?'

'I agree with my father. Take a prudent approach, round up the ringleaders, make an example of them . . . keep a close eye –'

'And allow others to take their place. We must make a show of strength,' argues Essex. 'I've a mind to get down there myself.'

Cecil imagines him astride his horse, breastplate gleaming, wielding a sword, with that beard – all man. How London would love that, their warrior hero down amongst them – for all his noble blood he has the common touch. Cecil has an image of that man with his ghoulish face pressed up to the door of his coach. The knot in his gut tightens with the memory, making him glad to be safely sealed within the sturdy walls of Whitehall.

'As it happens, I have already had the guard instructed,' says the Queen.

Cecil seethes inwardly. Essex conceals a smile with a hand.

'But,' she continues, 'I want names. You are right, Pygmy, we must make an example of the ringleaders. You don't mind getting your hands dirty, do you?'

He looks at his father who nods minutely. 'I am happy to do what is necessary, madam.' It rankles that she considers *his* approach the dirtier of the two, feels that he has lost ground in this exchange.

'I have you in check, Essex.' The Queen holds up her hands gleefully.

'You have me always in check.' Essex bats his lashes in her direction and it is all Cecil can do to prevent himself from groaning as the Queen stretches out to take her favourite's hand.

'My dear boy,' she says, then turns to Burghley. 'Are you not proud of the way he has turned out?'

'Indeed I am,' he replies. 'All the young men raised under my roof are –'

'Oxford has not turned out so well, scandal sticks to him like raw egg.' The Queen's expression is unreadable.

'Southampton. He is a good fellow,' says Essex.

Your lapdog, Cecil barely prevents himself saying.

'Southampton has yet to prove himself. He's hardly out of boyhood, but I like him.' She swaps a smile with the earl – it is a smile that excludes all but the two of them.

And *me*, what about *me*, Cecil wants to say, upbraiding himself internally for allowing his envy to get the better of him. But this is an insurmountable wall of intimacy that Essex has constructed about the Queen. His father shows no sign of annoyance. *Not by force but by falling often.* I am indispensable, he reminds himself, indispensable.

'I have given permission for Essex's sister to wed,' says the Queen.

An image of Penelope flashes through Cecil's mind but of course it is the other sister, Dorothy – the one who eloped and was widowed last year. This is a sign of favour – it isn't so long ago that the Queen wouldn't sit under the same roof as Dorothy Devereux, so far was she in disgrace, and now she has the royal blessing to wed.

'Ah, a wedding, how delightful,' says Burghley, though Cecil knows his father will be as concerned as he is about the meaning of this favour. 'May I ask the fortunate suitor's identity?'

'I cannot save myself,' says Essex, hovering his rook above the board. 'There is no move I can make that will avoid my destruction.'

'Northumberland,' announces the Queen.

'Ah,' says Burghley. He is putting on a good show but Cecil keeps his eyes on the chessboard for fear of revealing his excessive displeasure. Northumberland is one of the country's leading earls. Essex's influence over the Queen has become impregnable. This is a tactical match; Northumberland and Ralegh are in each other's pockets and Cecil had believed them generally to lean towards *his* side of things. Even if Ralegh is a little hard to pin down, they had always been useful to each other, had an understanding – they both loathed Essex. His mind is whirring. Perhaps there is a way to turn this to his advantage.

'Pygmy, whatever happened to your shoes?' says the Queen, pointing to his feet. Even the women on the other side of the chamber look over.

'We ran the rapids in order to get to Tower Hill. I thought I should come to you with news as soon as I could. I should have changed but I thought . . .' He is rambling. The Queen is wearing a wry smile. Is she enjoying his discomfort?

'You ran the rapids?' she says. 'Goodness!'

He wishes he'd made some other excuse because he cannot bear feeling patronized, like a small boy who has sat atop a pony for the first time.

'Those rapids are quite the lark, aren't they?' says Essex.

'A lark, yes,' Cecil echoes, trying to keep the smouldering resentment from his voice.

October 1595

Leighs, Essex

Penelope bursts into the nursery before she has removed her mud-spattered travelling clothes, greeting Mistress Shilling, who has Little Pea on her lap and rocks a cradle with her foot. The children crowd round, all talking at once, apart from Lucy, her oldest, who hangs back by the window, shrouded in the shyness that comes at the brink of adulthood. Penelope scoops the three-year-old up into her arms, whispering, 'My sweet pea,' delighting in her lisp as she says 'Mama' with a dimpled grin. Penelope presses a finger on to her little snub nose, raising a chuckle. She wonders if Rich has remarked that Little Pea has her father's upturned nose. She lifts the linen cap, breathing in her scent, and looks into the cradle to see her newest child, swaddled tight as a joint of meat, fast asleep.

'Baby,' says Little Pea, pointing a fat finger at the infant.

'Look at you all,' she says, taking in the sight of her offspring dressed in their best clothes for her arrival, bursting with excitement to see their mother. Her heart swells. Some women she knows complain that their children cling to their nurses for dear life when they visit. The circumstances of her life may keep her distant from her offspring but she has always made sure that the precious time she does spend with them is devoted entirely to their pleasure.

Her youngest son holds up his guinea pig. 'See how well I have taken care of him.'

'He is thriving in your care, Henry. You have grown, young man.' Penelope strokes the little proffered creature, sitting down cross-legged on the floor, plopping Little Pea on to her lap, with all but Lucy coming to sit beside her. A thought keeps niggling – something she heard about on the journey. A Catholic dragged out of a priest hole at a neighbour's house. He had hidden there for four days without food or water and was half dead by the time he was found. She shivers, turning back to her children, hoping the world will be a safer place for them when they are grown.

Little Pea wraps a hand around her mother's necklace, lisping, 'Pretty.'

'Do you have gifts for us?' asks her oldest boy.

'Hoby!' admonishes Essie. 'That is not the way to greet our mother when you have not seen her in a month.'

She strokes Essie's irresistible, top-of-the-milk skin. 'As it so happens,' she turns to Hoby, who looks more and more like his uncle Essex as the months pass, 'I do have something for you.' She looks at him, her acquisitive child, her magpie, watching the excitement flash in his eyes. 'Outside.'

He jumps to his feet. 'May I see?'

'Not until I have had a kiss and a hug.' She opens her arms wide and draws them to her, smiling over their shoulders at Lucy, who remains beside the window, pretending to be interested in something outside, but glancing over periodically at the family huddle. She returns the smile with a half-hearted one of her own. Penelope supposes Lucy must feel too grown-up for all this – she is thirteen, after all – and remembers herself at that age arriving at the countess's house, feeling too old for childish things and yet secretly wanting them nonetheless.

Henry plants a sticky kiss on her cheek.

'Off you go, down to the stables, and ask Alfred to show you. Essie, you are in charge of your brothers.'

The three of them rush out, Henry holding tight to his guinea pig with one hand and his sister with the other. Penelope can't quite put out of her mind the priest, imagines he must be at the Tower now, having information extracted from him. The thought makes her feel sick and she wonders about all those nameless men gathering information on the Continent and what they are risking. And this poor man, apprehended just a few miles away, makes this place, which she'd always regarded as a refuge, seem flimsy as paper.

She pulls herself to her feet and hands Little Pea back to the nurse. 'I am so grateful to you for the care you give them.' She cannot help but remember how Mistress Shilling had scooped her up that day, years ago, when she thought she would go quite mad with distress. The comforting fug of the laundry wafts back to her through time, as if it was yesterday and not nearly fourteen years ago. She finds herself wondering how old Mistress Shilling is; if she wet-nursed Rich she must be well past fifty by now. She is listing all the children's accomplishments, telling Penelope how the new tutor has settled in and what the music master has been teaching them. She has the sudden thought that either of these men might be secret Catholics, but admonishes herself for being dramatic. She interviewed them herself and they came with watertight recommendations.

Penelope goes to sit beside Lucy in the window. 'What are you reading?' She touches a finger to the book her daughter has in her hand, but Lucy pulls it out of reach.

'I'm sorry. I found it in your private things.' Lucy has her head down, will not meet her eye, but allows her mother to prise the volume from her hands.

Now she can see it properly she recognizes the book; it is *Astrophil and Stella.*

'What is this?' Lucy pulls out a leaf of paper – *My love for you is eternal as the stars, my own heavenly body.* A note signed by Sidney that she had used to mark the pages.

'Let me explain.' Penelope looks over to Mistress Shilling, who instantly understands, gathering Little Pea up and leaving the room.

Lucy challenges her with a hard look. 'You loved Sir Philip Sidney?'

'Yes, I did.' Penelope is not about to weave herself into a web of lies and excuses; she is already freighted with enough untruths to last through this life and the next. Even if she had wanted to she couldn't have put into words what it was she had with Sidney, the way she had been caught inextricably in his web, and he in hers. She has often wondered if it was separation that fuelled their feelings. She knew so little of love then and the way first love can shape a person. Not a day passes when she doesn't think of Sidney in some small way. She might hear a phrase that he once used, or see his brother at a distance and think it him, or dream vividly of him, or a line from one of his poems will pop into her head unexpectedly.

'And what about Father?'

'It had nothing to do with your father, Lucy.'

'But if you loved another, then you betrayed him.'

'It was an entirely chaste love.'

'What is that supposed to mean?'

'It means exactly that, my darling.' She stretches out to take her daughter's hand but Lucy does not return the gesture, letting her hand sit stiffly beneath her mother's. 'There is much you do not yet understand about love. It is not always straightforward.'

'I have read the romances,' says Lucy, as if to suggest she is being patronized. 'I know about courtly love. Are you saying it was that?' She taps the cover of the book with an insistent knuckle.

'Not exactly.' She could smooth it over easily by saying it was just this, but it wasn't, it was more than that and she can't bring herself to dismiss it in that way, as just some kind of formal distant adoration. 'One day you will be entranced by someone and it will more than likely not be the husband your father and I choose for you.'

'I don't want to wed, ever.' The stiffness suddenly drops away from her and she wraps both her arms around her mother, clinging on tightly, suddenly a child again.

'Marriage means children, and having children is truly one of the most wonderful pleasures God has given us.'

'Father has been talking of a match.'

This is the first Penelope has heard of it, and she seethes inwardly that he hasn't discussed it first with her. 'I will not allow it, Lucy. You are only thirteen. There is no rush.' She makes a mental note to confront Rich about this. She rarely sees him alone these days, only in public when they have to put on a good show of things at court, or when Rich attaches himself to her brother's crowd, which is too often. He has an annoying habit of popping up at Essex House when he is not wanted.

'I wish I could stay a child for ever,' Lucy says in a small voice.

She holds her daughter; feeling a surge of love and remembering the disappointment she had felt when this child was born. But it was not the usual ordinary disappointment parents have at the birth of firstborn girls. It was a backward shift in the path of her agreement with Rich. Sidney's ghost looms. She is reminded then of Doctor Lopez, his kind words, his extraordinary empathy; a sense of desolation sweeps through her and with it a twist of anxiety at the thought of the truth being so far beyond reach. She still refuses to believe in his guilt – though there was incontrovertible evidence of his dealings with Spain. He will always be the man who saved Lucy's life.

'You will never stop being my child,' she murmurs, peeling away Lucy's coif and smoothing a palm over her molasses-dark hair.

'I am afraid, Mother. The servants were talking the other day . . .' Oh God, thinks Penelope, girding herself, hoping desperately that Lucy hasn't got wind of her father's sexual proclivities. She is a girl who struggles to control her curiosity, listening at doors, sifting through things, reading letters, as if she has a need to make sense of the world to make it seem safer. Penelope has always carried a burden of guilt for her daughter's insecurities, as if that initial rejection imprinted itself on the child indelibly.

'What is it, my love?'

'Will the Spaniards come?'

Penelope is momentarily confused. 'Spaniards?'

'They burned four Cornish towns to the ground – I heard them say so.'

'There is no reason to fret over that, Lucy. It was just a raid, not a proper army . . . they were opportunists . . . not even towns, barely villages . . . it was nipped in the bud. And besides, Cornwall is just about as far as you can get from Essex and still be in England.' She rocks her daughter gently. Lucy is not the only one vexed over the Cornish raids; the whole of the south of England is on tenterhooks. The Spanish are calling it a triumph – the first step in their invasion – and they were aided by English Catholics. Thoughts surge into her unbidden of that French massacre, the way Jeanne's eyes seemed to contain all the horror of that night when she talked of it, only ever in fragments, as if to describe its entirety might be to enter hell itself.

'But it is what they did to –' She stops, as if she is unable to say the words, and Penelope is wondering about what she might have overheard the servants talking of – lurid stories of pitched battles and burning houses, no doubt. 'The womenfolk,' blurts Lucy, eventually. 'They did terrible things to the women – had their way with them and tore them limb from limb.'

'It is only stories, exaggerated each time they pass from tongue to ear, my love.' But they are not stories. War is brutal, as much for the women as for the men, and if Penelope allows herself to ponder on such things she risks losing her grip. The raid originated in Brittany, where the Spaniards had overcome the French. It is too close for comfort.

'Fire must be fought with fire,' she had said to Essex when

they were discussing it with the Bacon brothers. 'Burghley's diplomacy is an ineffective tool for dealing with the Spanish. Take a force to Spain, Robin. Burn their fleet.'

'You will earn glory that way,' said Anthony Bacon, rubbing at his thigh to ease his gout.

'The Queen will take some persuading,' said Francis with a graceful wave of his hand and a little sniff. She has noticed he often punctuates his discourse with such sniffs and wonders if it means anything, like a 'tell' in cards. 'Cecil will not like it.'

'All the more reason,' chipped in Anthony.

'I will quietly work on the Queen,' Penelope said. 'And you must too, Robin. But subtlety is what's needed. She must think it is her own idea.'

Her brother had flashed his beguiling grin at her then. 'I think I can manage that.'

'But don't –' She stopped herself from telling him not to get too full of himself.

The Queen's regard is a powerful force, and her brother seems to rise and rise in her favour, whilst all the other favourites pale beside him. She fears it has caused him to think himself invincible. It makes her uneasy, for when you are elevated to the very pinnacle of things there is only one way to go. There are many who would like to see Essex topple and Penelope feels the pressure of needing to protect him, ensuring he remains measured in his actions, keeping his mind on what will happen next; Elizabeth cannot last for ever and they *must* ensure that it is James who succeeds, for the Devereuxs' prospects are now linked inextricably with the Stuarts. She has worked hard to win the Scottish King's confidence. All that secret correspondence, and all the fear that it will visit trouble on them one day, is a weight perpetually about her neck.

'I wish I were a boy,' Lucy says with some force, turning Penelope's thoughts back to her daughter. She unfolds herself from her mother's arms and looks at her directly. 'I should like to learn to fight like Uncle Essex.'

'It is your wits, not brute force, that make you strong, my sweet.'

'What use will my wits be against a marauding army?' Lucy spits out an acid laugh as she says this.

'You'd be surprised,' says Penelope, glad to see some of her daughter's spirit return. 'Think of the old Duchess of York.' She has told them many times the story of the woman they called the Rose of Raby, who, a century and a half ago, reasoned with a bloodthirsty army to spare her life, and her children's. 'Here, pass me the comb.' She unravels Lucy's plaits and begins to run the comb carefully through her hair, remarking on the beauty of it, glossy like treacle. She imagines how, were Lucy called to court, she would see the other maids and want it hidden beneath a wig of coloured frizz dripping with pearls, real or false, just like them – what a shame that would be. She remembers how she had felt so very out of place on her first day there, in her dark velvet, yearning for those gossamer wings – how quickly she had bored of them, the discomfort of the wires that poked into the flesh at the back of her neck.

'What was he like, your Sir Philip?' Lucy holds up the book of poems. 'I have read them. They made me cry.'

Penelope wants to compare him to Blount but Lucy doesn't know Blount and it saddens her to think of her life so harshly divided into its separate parts, like preserves bottled and sealed and stored on a shelf. One day perhaps it will not be so – she entertains the idea of living with Blount and her children at Wanstead. It is always Wanstead she thinks of – the house of happiness. But it is a daft dream, in truth. 'He was someone who was not afraid of his own . . .' She seeks the word, not finding one that fits exactly. 'Of his own softness.' As she says it – softness – it sounds silly, inappropriate, but the truth about Sidney is impossible to articulate:

269

his brooding nature; his absolute conviction of love; his hatred of senseless violence; his pursuit of truth. That was what she had meant.

But Lucy doesn't ask for an explanation. 'I have read it in the poems. He was battered by his emotions.'

Penelope buries her face in her daughter's hair, breathing it in. It smells of wild flowers, as if she has been rolling about in the fields, a gloriously unadulterated scent, and she thinks she too would like Lucy to remain a child always. The things she cannot confide, the truth about her father, her love for Blount, silt her up, make her feel dishonest. 'We are all battered by our emotions,' she says. 'Sometimes love is hard to resist.'

'Are they all about you, really?'

'The poems? Yes, that *was* me – another me.'

'What do you mean?'

'Time and circumstance can change people beyond recognition.' She is thinking of the egg and the oyster.

'How old are you, Mother?'

'I am thirty-two – goodness, how the years pass, without one realizing.'

Lucy flashes a glittering, open smile and they fall into silence once more with just the soft scrape of the comb passing through Lucy's hair, until they are interrupted by the clatter of feet on the stairs. The children rush in, jabbering excitedly, with Spero, who had travelled down in the luggage cart, scampering after. They throw themselves at their mother, smothering her with kisses and thanks for the two piebald ponies she brought them from Essex's stables.

'Can we take them out?' asks Hoby.

'The groom said they were too tired from the journey,' says Essie.

'He's right. It's quite a hike from Wanstead.' Penelope cannot help thinking of the previous night spent at Wanstead with Blount, and the wretchedness of their parting, assuaged only by the thought of being reunited with her children. 'You can put them through their paces tomorrow.'

'Mother, why has Spero got a grey muzzle, when it used to be black?' asks Henry, who is holding tight to the dog's collar to prevent him from getting at the guinea pig.

'He is an old boy. Dogs go grey as we do,' she replies, placing an arm around her smallest son's shoulders.

'Like Grandmother! I saw her without her wig once,' says Hoby.

'You should never look in at a lady when she is not dressed, Hoby,' says Lucy primly.

'I didn't mean to, she was just –'

'I don't want Spero to be old,' interrupts Henry, and Penelope can see the manoeuvrings of her son's mind, as he ponders on the finite nature of things. She feels clogged up then, thinking of all the years she wished for time to pass more quickly so she could have her freedom, and yet also wanted time to stand still. Her agreement with her husband, it strikes her only then in such a way, has been a little like Doctor Faustus's pact with the devil in Kit Marlowe's play. Not that Rich is a devil, just a man who is not well designed for this world. He is a benign soul really, unlike some others who are too close for comfort.

November 1595

Burghley House, the Strand

Cecil's man places the carton on the floor of his study. 'Shall I open it for you, sir?' He brandishes an iron prise-bar.

'No need,' says Cecil.

'It will only take a moment.'

'I said, "No need."' Cecil is finding it hard to keep the vehemence from his voice, knows he mustn't attract attention to the package. He has been waiting for this delivery. 'It can be done later. It is nothing more than some Spanish volumes on garden design and I have important papers that need my attention.'

'As you wish, sir.' The man turns to go.

'Leave the tool,' says Cecil.

The man places the prise-bar carefully on the carton before exiting.

Cecil sits for a moment, looking at his long-awaited consignment of books. A letter had been delivered a few weeks ago, from a trusted contact in Spain, informing him of the imminent arrival of this crate. The letter, though in cipher, seemed clear enough. The gist was that the package would contain the means to bring down his 'greatest adversary'. There was only one person that adversary could be. Now the awaited shipment is here before him, his anticipation has reached a crescendo. The intensity of the feeling twists in his gut; it is almost painful, like colic.

He opens the door, casting his eyes about to ensure he will not be disturbed, and takes up the prise-bar, hooking it under the join where the lid has been nailed down. The wood makes a satisfying crack as the cover comes away. He gets down on his knees, pulling out fistfuls of the straw packing, scattering them over the floor, not caring about the mess he is making. He lifts out the books, one after the other – several large tomes – flicking through one or two to see what is inside them. He finds the expected drawings of plants and plans of gardens, a fountain here and there, some ornamental ironwork, but nothing else.

A few more books come out, still nothing, and he wonders if perhaps there is something coded and buried within the pages of one of them, beginning to seek clues, burrowing simultaneously with his hands in the straw. He takes out another book; it is smaller than the rest and rather beautifully bound in red stained leather. He opens it, reading the frontispiece: *Conference on the Next Succession to the Crown of England*. This is it! The mere existence of such a tome is treachery; all such discussion is forbidden within the shores of England.

There is a tremor in his breath as he reads on: *Directed to the Right Honourable the Earl of Essex*. Treachery in the name of Essex, then! The author is one Doleman, doubtless a pseudonym, but it is the dedication that is making anticipation flutter through his body. A leaf of paper slides to the floor. On it are written a few numbers. He shuffles through, searching for the indicated pages, skimming the dense text, finding, with a thrill that runs all the way up his spine – somehow making him feel that it is straighter, its kink ironed out – a passage so deeply drenched in treason that he has to read it twice to believe his eyes. It argues the validity of the Spanish Infanta's claim on the English throne, tracing her line back to the third Edward. This stinks of Catholic treason and Catholic treason dedicated to Essex. Cecil can barely catch his breath.

He sits back on his heels, running his fingers over the soft leather, and has a momentary gruesome fantasy that the book is bound in the earl's skin. He has heard stories from the New World about savage men who keep the scalps of their slain enemies as trophies. He continues to fondle the smooth surface, his thoughts turning unavoidably to the sister – her pale smooth skin, the hidden skin of her body that he has only ever imagined. How had Sidney described her in those poems of his: *of alabaster pure*? He finds himself wondering, not for the first time, if the love between Lady Rich and Sir Philip Sidney had been chaste – if he had passed his fingers over those secret parts of her. It is certainly possible, given her brazen behaviour with Blount. The idea partly ignites his disgust but also that other feeling, the one he does his best to suppress.

He turns his mind back to the earl now, picturing him mounting the scaffold. There he would be in his finery, for the last time. He would make his speech, asking God and the Queen for forgiveness in the usual way. His man would remove his outer clothing, leaving him in his fine linen shirt, the shape of his body visible beneath: a perfect specimen of manhood. The gathering would be silent until a lone voice will shout 'Traitor!' and the crowd will erupt, jeering and screeching, baying for blood.

The blindfold will be tied then and he will kneel. The executioner will make the signal and with a steely flash it will be done. His head will drop, with a dead thud, to the boards, blood spurting from the stump, blood everywhere, all over that snowy linen shirt, all over the faces of those at the front of the crowd. Cecil can feel it – a warm splat against his own cheek. Then the executioner will grab a fistful of those gorgeous raven curls, hold the head up to a raucous cheer and those star-bright eyes will be extinguished.

PART III
Icarus

The setting sun, and music at the close,
As the last taste of sweets, is sweetest last,
Writ in remembrance more than things long past.

William Shakespeare, *Richard II*, Act II, Scene 1

June 1598

Greenwich Palace

Cecil screws up a pamphlet, tossing it towards the corner with force, emitting a groan of frustration. It is another panegyric to Essex.

'England's great hope,' he mutters, quoting the pamphlet as he leaves his rooms, making his way to the council chamber. His ire simmers. He had been angry when it was decided that Essex would lead the army to Cadiz and angrier still when the man covered himself with glory, destroyed the Spanish fleet, occupied the city. Cecil had to listen to everyone, down to the boy who lays his fires, talk of 'Essex's finest hour'. From his window at Burghley House he had watched the swarms come out into the streets to cheer the return of the conquering hero – hadn't seen a crowd such as that since Sidney's funeral nearly a decade before. The chant of *Ess-ex*, *Ess-ex*, *Ess-ex* rings on in his head. The alehouses are still full of stories about the earl's great triumph, how a second Armada had been dispersed and England saved from Spanish jaws. That was two years ago, though the pamphlets continue to appear with regularity and Essex's popularity burgeons unimpeded.

Cecil had believed the book would bring the earl down, had been entirely convinced of it, had imagined the charge of treason, the death warrant that the Queen was going to sign with a pen handed to her by him, Cecil – then that perfect head struck from its shoulders and left on a pike for the seagulls to peck at. But it was a mere matter of months before the Queen relented. He got on his knees as usual, tilted that pretty face up to hers and convinced her of his innocence. 'Someone seeks to blacken my name, Dearest

Majesty. I had no knowledge of this' – he thwacked the book hard with his fingers – 'this monstrous treason, this filthy Catholic plot.' He was probably telling the truth, Cecil begrudgingly supposed.

Cecil had been charged with hunting down the author and the earl had been sent away for a spell in charge of the Northern Council, which seemed more privilege than punishment, though Essex railed at 'being sent away from my Queen's glorious person' and had to be teased from a sulk of monstrous proportions. He had been forgiven, as he always was. Cecil's disappointment was eating away at him, hollowing him out. He had thought he would see Essex go in a torrent of blood. His father had, as ever, been right: patience, patience, drip, drip, drip.

For Cecil has noticed, over recent months, that the Queen's infatuation with her favourite is beginning to erode. The effect is subtle but nonetheless apparent. Things have never been quite as they were before that book came to light and, besides, the Queen is tiring of the earl's warmongering with Spain now the immediate threat has receded. War is expensive and she has the mind for peace. But something else quite unanticipated is afoot: instead of his popular esteem working in Essex's favour, Cecil can sense that the Queen doesn't like it; they are *her* people, after all, and it doesn't do if they cheer more loudly for the earl than for their Queen. The man's popularity is poisoning his favour with her, like a corpse in a well.

Cecil has come to understand that the Queen likes *him* all the more for the fact that he is generally loathed – drip, drip, drip – and his long-awaited appointment as Secretary of State is testimony to that.

'You are late, Secretary,' the Queen says as he scurries into the council chamber. 'I trust you have a good excuse.'

'I do, Your Majesty.' He is on his knee, looking at the floor. It has not been properly swept and there is dust collecting in the corners. He has to resist brushing off the edges of his gown where it might have gathered as he knelt.

'Well?' she says.

'I think it is a matter Your Majesty would prefer to hear in confidence.'

Essex, who is sitting slouched back in his chair beside her, huffs loudly. There is an air of louche dishevelment about him that lacks respect, as if the usual formalities do not include him. Cecil takes his seat amongst the privy councillors between his father and George Carew, who nods and smiles at him – Carew is proving a useful ally.

'At least let us know to what it pertains,' drawls Essex.

'Indeed,' agrees the Queen.

'It is regarding My Lord of Southampton.' He looks at her now. The paint on her face, rather than hide her age, increases it and he has a memory of how she used to be, so vibrant, filled with verve and resilience, which has faded to a disarming frailty. He calculates her years, coming to the number sixty-four, and a sense of urgency grips him with the thought of what might happen when she passes. There will be bloodshed in the scramble for her throne; of that there is no doubt. He wonders if he is sufficiently shored up yet with supporters to survive such events.

'I sent him away,' says the Queen. 'He's not been so tiresome as to get himself killed, has he? I should not like that; despite his misdemeanours, I liked the boy.' Essex is looking uncomfortable, thrumming his fingers on the table. Something seems to dawn on the Queen's face. 'I sincerely hope he hasn't married my maid,' she flicks a vicious look towards Essex, 'your cousin, Lizzie Vernon. Now that *would* be foolish.'

Cecil nods. 'I am afraid so, Your Majesty.' He does not add that the couple wed at Essex House with the help of the earl and his sister, nor that the bride was already great with child when she made her vows. The Queen will discover all this soon enough, but he is enjoying watching Essex's discomfort. Essex is not stupid enough to jump to his friend's defence, however.

'Shame you seem always to be the bearer of bad news, Pygmy.' Cecil flinches inwardly at the reprised pet name. She had not used it since he was made Secretary of State and he feels it renders him a figure of fun rather than a statesman. 'Have it dealt with.' Not a flicker of emotion registers on her face. 'There are more pressing things afoot,' she continues, sweeping a hand from left to right, as if to indicate that the topic is dismissed for the time being. 'Ireland! There is the question of whom we shall appoint as Lord Deputy. We were thinking of our nephew, Sir William Knollys.'

Cecil watches Essex swap a brief look and a minute shake of the head with Knollys, whose expression is unreadable. Cecil had planted this idea in the Queen's head a few weeks ago and is glad to see it coming to fruition. Essex's influential uncle far from court: drip, drip, drip. He glances at Burghley, seeing rather than the usual half-smile he wears when things are going the preferred way, that his forehead is clammy with sweat and his breathing is laboured. He indicates to one of the pages to pour a drink and places it carefully in his father's hand. Burghley swallows it back with a grimace as if in agony and the Queen stretches out her long fingers, placing them on his sleeve – a gesture of fondness. She cannot be unaware of the cruelty in insisting on his continued presence at court, though he is approaching eighty and ought to be enjoying his dotage. She strokes his arm as one might a beloved pet.

Essex seems oblivious to this subtle, silent communication. 'Knollys would be better used here, Highness,' he says loudly.

'We think him well suited to the Irish position.' The

Queen's reply is firm and Cecil notes that she is not using the usual 'I' for her sometime favourite. Her hand lingers still on Burghley's arm.

'Spain is fast encroaching on Ireland and we need a firm rule there. Knollys is of a more diplomatic than martial disposition,' says Essex.

'I do not believe the Spanish threat on the Irish front to be as great a threat as the esteemed earl deems it,' says Cecil, trying to keep his tone even and absent of sarcasm. He is encouraged when the Queen looks towards him for reassurance. 'It is likely based on rumour, madam. None of my own sources has come up with anything tangible.' He notices the Queen relax a little, her shoulders lowering beneath her ruff.

'Perhaps your sources are not earning their keep, Secretary,' sneers the earl.

'You think too much of blood and slaughter, My Lord,' says Burghley, looking calmly towards Essex. Cecil can hear the wheeze in his chest. 'You are familiar, I suppose, with the fifty-fifth psalm: *The bloody and deceitful men shall not live half their days.*'

'You mean what exactly by that, My Lord?' snaps Essex.

The councillors look back and forth as if watching a game of tennis.

'My father means,' says Cecil, 'that life is short for he who would fight first and speak later.'

Essex's eyes flash cold and he opens his mouth but then seems to quash his retort, waiting a moment before speaking. 'That sounds like a threat.'

'Enough!' barks the Queen.

But Essex seems to have his blood up. 'I nominate George Carew for the Irish position. Who stands with me?' The Queen's mouth is tightening into an angry knot. Cecil feels Carew shift nervously beside him.

'We were not aware that we asked for your opinion, Essex.' The Queen's voice is magnificent, imperious, would stop any man in its tracks – any man but Essex, apparently.

'Carew has martial experience. You served me well in Cadiz, didn't you?' Carew makes a vague awkward nod in the earl's direction. 'Well enough for me to knight him.' Essex has turned back to the Queen, who is rigid-faced.

It is probably not wise of the earl, thinks Cecil, to remind her of his liberal bestowal of knighthoods. But Essex is losing his reason. Cecil looks round the table to see whom he can count on to take his part in this – his father-in-law, Lord Cobham, is one; he assesses the others, making a tally in his head, wondering about Ralegh, sitting opposite, stroking his beard – the man is infuriatingly opaque.

'Carew is *your* man, now, is he, Essex?' The Queen's sarcasm is sharp; the entire council are aware that Carew is Cecil's man.

'Carew is trustworthy,' says Essex, thrusting his chin in the air.

'Are you saying Knollys is not?' The Queen is playing with him now, like a cat with a ball of wool, and Essex is becoming unravelled.

'They both have many fine qualities.' This is Nottingham, the Lord High Admiral, with one foot in each stall as usual.

'Knollys is better suited to the Irish job.' The Queen slaps her palm to the table as if to indicate that the issue is decided.

Ralegh is smirking.

'You are *wrong*,' the earl blurts, almost at a shout.

There is a collective sharp intake of breath and the whole company is suspended, awaiting the Queen's response.

'You need some of that insolence knocked out of you.' She has turned to Essex and pulled back a fisted hand. A rosy stain moves over her pale skin, visible even beneath the white paint, betraying her fury.

He looks her straight in the eye. 'I am not some small boy

to have his ears boxed by his mother,' he says before standing, his chair scraping loudly against the floor, and turning his back to her.

The Queen is out of her seat in an instant, her fist flying to meet the side of Essex's head, spitting the words, 'Brazen varlet!'

With the quick reflex of a soldier, Essex brings his hand to the hilt of his sword. The company gasps as one. The Lord High Admiral jumps up and grabs the earl from behind, pulling him away, and the Queen settles back in her seat quite calmly, as if nothing has happened. 'Get rid of him!'

They all wait a moment; expecting her to add, 'Lock him up!' For if threatening to draw your sword on the Queen is not high treason, then Cecil doesn't know what is. But she says nothing and the Admiral sets about unbuckling Essex's sword belt.

The earl struggles, complaining angrily about the affront to his dignity, how he will not put up with such a thing. The offending sword is flung aside, landing near to Cecil, close enough for him to see the Sidney insignia on its pommel. He had forgotten that Sidney bequeathed Essex his best sword, as if to hand him the role of chivalric knight to England – so much for that. The Admiral manages to hustle the earl to the door. 'For God's sake, man, pull yourself together.'

Cecil shuffles his papers, not daring to look up for fear that his triumph is smeared over his face. As the earl is pushed over the threshold, he turns back and shouts at the Queen, 'You are as crooked in your disposition as you are in your carcass,' before the door is slammed behind him. The council look round at each other. The Queen is God's envoy on earth and it clearly shocks them profoundly to a man, seeing her treated like some kind of quarrelsome fishwife. Cecil dares a glance in his father's direction and can see the faint suggestion of a smile on him. Drip, drip, drip.

Silence echoes through the council chamber as they wait for the Queen's reaction. The Admiral takes his seat, clearing his throat.

All she says is, 'Now, what other matters are arising?'

July 1598

Drayton Bassett, Derbyshire

'Can you not make him see sense, Brother?' Lettice says to Uncle Knollys. They are sitting at the far end of the chamber with Dorothy, whom Penelope hasn't seen for months. 'I asked my husband to go to Wanstead and talk some sense into him, but it was to no avail. He simply refuses to apologize.'

Penelope is not really listening; she has things nagging at her. Her cousin Lizzie Vernon is in the Fleet prison for her unsanctioned marriage to Southampton. The Fleet is a rat-infested hellhole and is no place for a young woman with child; a fact she had attempted to press upon the Queen, to no avail. Penelope has grown fond of her spirited cousin Lizzie, imagining the brightness knocked right out of her in that squalid place. 'What if she should meet her end there?' Penelope had said. 'The little whore has what's coming to her,' was the Queen's answer. Penelope had helped arrange that wedding and wondered if the Queen knew, if she was compiling a list of Lady Rich's misdemeanours to use at a later date. The Queen seems to have no pity left in her and that doesn't bode well for Essex. He is a constant source of worry, with his refusal to apologize, his vast debts, his frame of mind, his dead eyes.

'He thinks *the Queen* should apologize *to him*.' Lettice expels a huff of breath, shaking her head. 'However did I manage to breed such misplaced arrogance?'

It rained not long ago, a sudden storm that came as swiftly as it went, leaving the gutters running and the eaves dripping. Penelope can still hear the faint trickle of water. Another fear burrows beneath her surface: a messenger, carrying her latest missive to King James, has disappeared. She tries to dismiss it with mundane explanations of sickness and delay but the spectre of Cecil lurks constantly – him passing the paper over a flame to reveal the text, his eyes sparking up, him handing that letter to the Queen, him drawing up a warrant for her arrest. It is as if a noose tightens gradually about her throat. If only Blount were with her in Derbyshire and not at court.

'I will write to him,' says Uncle Knollys. 'He is flying close to the wind. The Queen has had enough of his pique. He is too old for such antics, a man in his thirties . . . It may have seemed charming once, but not now.' Penelope doesn't attempt to explain that her brother's so-called fits of pique are something so much darker and entirely out of his control. She is tired of endlessly discussing her brother's offences, would rather be lying in bed at Wanstead discussing philosophy and drinking good French wine with Blount. Their letters move back and forth across the countryside, fond words exchanged, but she wants to witness the joy on his face when she tells him that their baby, St John, has sprouted a tooth, and that his older brother, little Mountjoy, spoke his first proper word the other day.

Her mother had baulked at that choice of name. 'For goodness' sake, everyone will know whose boy he is if you call him Mountjoy,' she had said.

'What people think is no concern of mine,' was Penelope's reply.

'That attitude will be your downfall,' her mother had said, not for the first time, before adding, 'I still cannot fathom why your husband allows himself to be made a cuckold.'

Penelope couldn't answer that. The burden of her husband's secret has become increasingly heavy over the sixteen years she has carried it. She daren't share it, even with her beloved Blount – the man who has filled her life with joy.

Rich has tolerated her affair for his own reasons, and she

has played the obedient wife. They have managed to carve out a mutual respect, in a manner of speaking. She has sometimes questioned why none of the boys he beds has exposed him, but she supposes he pays them well. He has never spoken of it to her. She has come to understand that a secret is like a lie; it blights everything it touches.

'How can he be such a fool as to make an enemy of *her*?' With a desolate sigh, Lettice brings her hands up to cover her face. 'Was it not enough for him to see *me* cast out? The same fate awaits him and he brings it upon himself.'

The trickle in the gutter has now become a drip. Penelope is remembering how her mother's humiliation had been compounded a few months ago, before all this, when the Queen could still refuse Essex nothing. He had at last persuaded her to receive Lettice at court. It felt like a triumph, as if all the ills of the past were to be laid to rest. The air of optimism over Essex House was tangible, like the sun reappearing after a storm, making all the world's surfaces glisten. Lettice had sparkled with anticipation, had the seamstress fashion a new wardrobe for all the court appearances she expected, had three new wigs made, a dozen strings of pearls, had commissioned a jewel to offer the Queen.

'It must be a splendid creation,' Lettice had said to the goldsmith. 'Something more beautiful by far than the vulgar gewgaws she is given by the foreign ambassadors.'

The goldsmith had barely been able to help rubbing his hands as he spoke. 'I have lately acquired a ruby in the shape of a heart, a rare beauty, and big – big as a rosehip.'

He charged three hundred pounds, which Lettice could ill afford. Essex had taken the bill with a flourish, saying, 'This is mine.' But later he had confessed to Penelope that he owed thirty thousand pounds. She was shocked at the figure, hadn't realized the extent of her brother's debt, and she had convinced Rich to settle the bill, in the end. 'I will persuade the Queen to bestow another licence on me,' Essex had said when she asked what he was going to do about his financial liability. The whole business weighed heavily on her but her concern had been counterbalanced by the excitement of Lettice's proposed audience and the hope it brought.

Even to Penelope, who was not given to such flights of optimism, it had seemed that her mother's years in the wilderness might finally be over and when the day came it felt like a wedding. She helped Lettice dress in a satin gown the colour of lemons, all stitched about with pearls, one of the new wigs, russet curls scattered with jewels, perched upon her head. She looked like a young woman, not fifty-four with most of her years used up, and Penelope could imagine the figure she cut at court as a girl, had a glimpse of the fateful allure that had turned Leicester's head away from the Queen.

Penelope couldn't accompany her, for it was not long since she had birthed St John and she hadn't yet been churched. She awaited her mother's return with a sense of well-being, as if all the old scores had been finally settled. But Lettice returned late, exhausted, having pulled her wig off in the coach, her hair awry, giving her the look of a lunatic. 'It pinched terribly,' she said in response to Penelope's bewildered look.

'So, what happened?' she asked.

Her mother simply shook her head, saying, 'Perhaps tomorrow. Your brother said I should come back tomorrow.'

Lettice had flicked her head away but not before Penelope saw the tears. She had never seen her cry before, had always thought her incapable. As she held her mother's heaving body she felt a new rage gather in her that was unfamiliar in its intensity. It made her think of a play she had seen in which a tragedy, one that might have been waylaid by a simple act of forgiveness, had played itself out relentlessly to its inevitable conclusion. The sensation was physical, gripping her body almost to the point of pain, and Penelope knew that just as the Queen would not forgive Lettice, so *she* would not forgive the Queen.

Her mother waited three days in the public rooms to be seen, and eventually the Queen passed her in the gallery, took the jewel, offered her cheek for a kiss and passed on with barely a word. The invitation to court was not extended again. Every time Penelope sees that heart-shaped ruby pinned to the Queen's breast, she feels the same tightening in her and is reminded of the other events: her father's death; her mother's banishment and her sister's; her own thwarted marriage to Sidney; all with the Queen's imprint on them.

'He thinks himself immortal.' Lettice is still talking about Essex.

'I will deal with it, Sister,' says Knollys. 'He's making things difficult for himself by staying away such a time. There are others ready to jump into his place. Two months is an age at court.'

'I have seen him in this temper many times,' says Penelope. 'It takes him to a sinister place.' The light drains from the room and spots of rain appear once more on the window panes as if her words have an effect on the weather. She absently puts a hand down to stroke Spero's domed head, but finds only emptiness and is jolted by the memory of discovering his lifeless little body at the foot of her bed a few weeks previously. Despite his long life and the quiet manner of his demise, she mourned him desperately, the dog named by Sidney. The sense of time passing catches up with her suddenly, the sense of all those she cared for gone. Even Jeanne has gone now – to France with her new husband.

'Dark place or not, he needs to pull himself together,' says Lettice. Penelope wonders if Lettice has found out about the vast debt Essex has amassed. If he isn't able to dance to the Queen's tune, he has no chance of diminishing it.

'Don't vex yourself, Lettice, dear.' Knollys pats her hand.

'I shall make him see sense.' He stops and then seems to remember something. 'As long as I am not sent to Ireland.'

'And will you be?' asks Dorothy. 'If you are, it will not be immediate. Surely funds must be raised, men mustered.'

'No, it will take time and, besides, she is dithering.' By 'she', he clearly means the Queen. 'There are others being considered.'

'Who might they be?' asks Lettice.

'Lord Mountjoy is the favourite.'

'Blount?' Penelope's distress catches in her throat and her sister meets her eye with a look of sympathy. 'She can't send Blount.'

'Such a position, Lord Deputy of Ireland, would *make* him. It's an opportunity to prove himself in high office.' Knollys pauses and turns to speak directly to Penelope. 'Since he seems to not want to hoist himself up by marriage.' He glares at his niece pointedly, as if to ask what kind of a hold could she possibly have over him that would make him cast off his right to a wealthy wife and legitimate children to pass his title on to. 'I'd say Ireland was the ideal appointment.'

Penelope can hardly bear to listen as her uncle speaks. 'I know, I know,' she murmurs, 'but . . .' She can't say it; Uncle Knollys is right, Blount must take all the opportunities that come his way. She can't help remembering, though, the fate that befell her father in that dreadful place. An unexpected trickle of bitterness spills from her: 'I wish she would send Rich.'

Uncle Knollys laughs. 'What, he who was so overcome with seasickness on the last campaign he had to be put to port barely before they were out of the harbour?' Dorothy emits a snort of laughter too but Penelope is not amused.

'Yes, your husband is not exactly the epitome of courage,' Lettice says, joining the wave of laughter. Penelope hasn't seen her mother laugh since her foiled return to court, but it doesn't bring her a splinter of joy, for all she can think of is that she might have been married all those years ago to Sidney, a hero, instead of a man who makes her family fall about laughing. As their mirth dies they become aware of a hubbub of voices coming from the courtyard below.

'What's that racket?' asks Knollys, moving towards the window. 'Goodness, there is a crowd of folk down there.'

'They come every day,' says Lettice. 'They are after kitchen scraps.'

'Such a number?'

'They are starving, poor souls,' says Lettice. 'The land is completely barren. After four years of failed harvests they are reduced to making bread from crushed acorns. I do what I can.'

'It is such as these that turn into an angry mob,' says Knollys. 'If people like Burghley and his boy weren't siphoning so much from the public purse there might be more to go round.'

Penelope is beside her uncle and sister at the window, looking down at a tattered mob. The rain has stopped again and the cobbles are slick with mud. The people below seem to be held together by their sodden clothes alone, bundles of sticks tied with rags. Penelope has seen the farm workers coming in their droves into London, seeking work, until the city is bursting at the seams. But this is different; these people seem barely alive. A woman with a pinched baby in her arms looks up, catching her eye, and she feels ashamed by her healthy plumpness, her fine gown strung with seed pearls, her fingers heavy with rings. She thinks of her own fat babies. She imagines what the woman must see at the window: two ladies draped in fine silks, no sign of hardship on their smooth faces. There is something in that woman's unstinting gaze that cuts her down to size.

August 1598

Burghley House, the Strand

Cecil is thinking about his father. He has only a month or so left, the doctors say. When Cecil's wife died two years ago there was some sadness – more for the sake of his son losing a mother. His wife had tolerated him at best, and he her, if he is honest. He cannot forget her look of disgust whenever he sought his conjugal rites and remembers thinking he would never have to see that look again. He loved her for giving him a son, though. When he looks at little William's face he can see something of Burghley printed there.

As Burghley fades the urgency builds in Cecil finally to make him proud. He has built a fantasy in his mind of the moment he will tell his father that he has succeeded in making peace with Spain. He can see the smile that will spread over his face, can hear his words, 'This is a true legacy for we Cecils – a Spanish alliance made in peace, such as England has not seen for forty years.' Cecil closes his eyes, allowing the dream of his father's delight to take hold, now imagining the Queen congratulating him too, on his great triumph.

His resolve is renewed by his imaginings. He recently had a meeting with the Spanish ambassador at which they had danced around the issue, until Cecil came to understand what it was that would make the deal palatable for the Spanish King. There is a high price for peace with an enemy of such long standing. He pulls out a piece of paper, girded by the image of his dying father. He dips his quill and a little glut of fear collects in his chest. He is writing without thinking: *I feel sure some kind of accommodation can be arrived at in respect of the Infanta's claim.* He can hardly believe he is thinking such a thing, let alone recklessly committing it to paper. But that is the condition for peace and once he has them at the table he can always find a way to slide out of it. It is not a promise, after all.

His servant appears in the doorway and he slips the paper between the pages of a ledger, out of sight. He will seal it and send it later. His fingers are prickling; is it fear or something else? He doesn't know, but his heart is knocking urgently at his chest.

'Lord Mountjoy is here, Mister Secretary,' says his man.

'Send him in.' His voice sounds odd, high-pitched – guilty.

'I am most perturbed to hear about your father,' says Blount as he enters.

Cecil replaces the lid on the ink pot, stands and moves towards him, noticing how tidily the man is put together, how discreetly dressed, his hair a neat black halo beneath a fashionably high-crowned hat, his moustache trim, everything in its place; just a single pearl in his ear nods to a restrained flamboyance. 'Lord Burghley is an old man. But one can never be prepared.'

Cecil doesn't want to think of his father's failing health now; fears it will make him drop his guard. A page takes Blount's cape and hat.

'Let's sit.' Cecil, careful not to glance at the ledger and invite suspicion, waves an arm towards the window seat, which is flooded with August sun, making a grid of shadows over the cushions. He forces himself to focus on the matter in hand, wants Blount to feel at his ease, as if this is a gesture of friendship, rather than business alone. Blount sits with a smile, giving nothing away of the curiosity he must be feeling at being invited to visit Cecil, who is, after all, if not quite an enemy, then an inhabitant of the other camp.

'Is he at Theobalds?' asks Blount, declining the page's offer of wine.

'No, he is here. We have positioned his bed so he has a view of the gardens, which are splendid at this time of year.'

'I am told they are marvellous. I hope one day to have the

chance to see them.' Blount folds his hands together in his lap and Cecil notices that his nails are perfectly clipped and clean, like his own, which pleases him, makes him feel optimistic. There is nothing of the decadent dishevelment of his friend Essex on this man. 'I hope one day to cultivate a fine garden myself.'

Cecil is surprised by Blount's continued small talk, his seeming lack of desire to move on to the reason he is here. 'I was lucky enough to see a row of sunflowers recently – a most unusual sight.' Cecil knows that Essex has acquired some of those rare blooms for his garden and wonders if Blount is subtly advertising his allegiance by mentioning them. 'Quite monstrously large and vividly coloured.' He makes a circle in the air, describing the shape, and Cecil can't help thinking of those clean fingers caressing the body of Lady Rich. 'I couldn't decide if I liked them.'

'I myself am not particularly fond of the things. Find them rather vulgar.' Cecil hopes he will not be drawn into a discussion about the aesthetic virtues, or otherwise, of the sunflower, for it may become apparent that he has never actually seen one, only a drawing. 'I will take you on a tour of our gardens, if it would please you.'

'It would, indeed. I believe you have some very pretty fish ponds.' Cecil considers taking him outside now, but hesitates. He cannot be sure they will not be overheard in the gardens with all the casual weeders they take on at this time of year. It would be impossible to verify each one of the army employed to keep the place as it should be.

The two men lock eyes, Cecil noting the attractive dark velvety brown of Blount's, quite able to see what it is about this man the Queen likes so much. Aside from the air of efficiency, those eyes are warm, trustworthy – intelligent but without apparent guile. He tries to soften his own expression in return, wondering if the years of scheming are carved into his face. 'You are the kind of man I should like to see on the council.' He doesn't elaborate, waits for Blount's response. But Blount says nothing, simply nods and waits for Cecil to continue, seeming not in the least uncomfortable with the silence that ensues. Cecil is thinking increasingly that this is a man he would like to have on his side. He imagines it – dividing the Essex faction by getting his claws into Lady Rich's lover. The thought excites him.

It is Cecil who eventually breaks the silence. 'I could make such a suggestion to Her Majesty.'

'I was under the impression that I was being considered for Ireland,' says Blount, smoothing his moustache with a finger, first one side, then the other. 'I wouldn't be much use to the council over there.' He smiles, widely and generously, as if he has just paid a compliment.

Cecil cannot tell if he welcomes the Irish position or not. 'Lord Deputy is a position of great honour but Ireland is a very distant place.'

'A great honour, yes,' says Blount. 'Very distant . . . and dangerous . . .' He hesitates before continuing. 'I am not entirely sure I have the required martial experience for such a task.'

At last, thinks Cecil, he is revealing something of himself. 'You were most effective in keeping the Spanish threat at bay on the coast last autumn.'

Blount offers up that congenial smile again. 'I was simply doing my duty.'

'And you have a reputation as an excellent scholar.'

'I have a modest interest in bookish pursuits; this is true.' He is choosing his words so very carefully.

'I will advise the Queen of your merits.'

'If you so wish it.' Cecil is finding him frustratingly abstruse. He had hoped at least that Blount would reveal some enthusiasm for the idea of getting his backside on to a council pew. But he is clearly too subtle for that. 'What I would be most keen to do is . . .' He pauses.

'Is what?' urges Cecil, losing his patience slightly, awaiting to hear exactly what it is Blount wants.

'To see your gardens.'

It is all Cecil can do to prevent himself from smashing a fist on to the window sill. 'Of course.' His smile must seem forced – this man will take some wooing but he is sure it will be worth the effort.

They rise and Cecil is calculating how to configure their exit so as to allow him time to cache the ledger, with its hidden letter, safely away from any prying eyes until it can be sealed – though his servants know he'd have their hands cut off if they were caught rifling through his private papers.

As they are at the door a messenger arrives. 'Not now,' Cecil barks, allowing his impatience free rein, now there is someone other than Blount to direct it at. 'Can't you see I am busy?'

'I believe you have need to hear this news urgently . . .' The man is talking nervously into his ruff.

'Would you be kind enough to excuse me, My Lord?' Cecil says to Blount, who tactfully moves into the outer chamber. Cecil closes the door and turns to the messenger, waiting for him to say something.

'There has been a most terrible defeat in Ulster.'

'Go on.' Cecil is trying to untie the muddled threads of knowledge he has of the Irish conflict.

'A massacre of Englishmen.' The man's face seems ghoulish.

'How many?'

'Something nearing two thousand.'

'Good Lord!'

'Our men were attempting to liberate the besieged garrison fort of Blackwater.'

Cecil is trying to picture a map of the region. 'That is on the boundary of Tyrone's territory, is it not?'

'It is. Tyrone joined forces with another of the rebel leaders, so they outnumbered us greatly. It was an ambush.'

'Two thousand dead – that is hardly an ordinary ambush.' Cecil feels a little out of his depth. He is unused to the language of war.

'The Irish methods are different.'

Cecil nods, 'Yes, different,' though he is unsure exactly what the man means.

'Their tactics are reliant on surprise.'

Surprise sounds like such an inappropriate word, more suited to a birthday gift than a massacre. Cecil is chilled to the bone at the thought that one day it might be his own precious son facing that Irish army with their 'different methods'. He puts a hand to the wall to steady himself. 'What intelligence has our man out there garnered?'

'Tyrone's broad plan, once the English are driven out, is to recognize Spain as their ruler.'

'What evidence have you of such a plot?' Cecil is trying to collect himself. This is exactly as Essex predicted. It has been whispered about for so long he thought it wouldn't happen; he chose to ignore it. He suddenly feels at a loss, as he used to, and wonders if Blount already knew of this. Perhaps they are all laughing at him for his ignorance.

'A letter from Spain was intercepted.'

'Get me that letter. I want it in my own hands.'

'I do not think that is possible, it was intercepted and read but not copied. There was not the time, I am told.'

'Did any other eyes see it?'

'That I cannot answer.'

When the messenger has gone Cecil stands alone a moment, his thoughts turning over, wondering if the man is trustworthy. He might also be working for Essex and feeding him titbits too, when the time suits. He, Cecil, might be on strings like a puppet and not even know it. He wishes he could consult his father. His father would calm him down; make him see sense. But he is barely conscious, will not last the month. That thought sends a gust of panic through him, real fear, as if it will blow his body inside out like a discarded doublet. Pull yourself together, man, he says silently, before taking the ledger from his desk and sliding it into a drawer out of sight.

As Cecil enters the outer chamber Blount looks up. He has a book in his lap, which he closes, placing a thumb between the pages so as not to lose his place. Cecil scrutinizes the bookcase to see which is missing. It seems to be Plato – benign enough.

Cecil expects Blount to ask what the urgent news is, but he taps the book in his hand, saying, 'Good actions inspire in their turn more good actions. Christian doctrine can be found in the ancients, wouldn't you say?'

'I . . . I . . .' Cecil does not know what he thinks about this for his mind is abuzz with other matters. 'There has been a massacre of our men in Ireland. Two thousand dead.' He watches the other man for signs that he knows this already.

'Oh my goodness,' Blount says, with a look of what appears to be genuine shock. 'I pity the mothers.'

'I'm afraid our garden visit will have to wait. I must get myself to Whitehall.'

'Indeed,' replies Blount, rising, replacing the book; lining it up with its fellows. 'Send word if I can be of any assistance.'

As he waits for his litter to be prepared, Cecil wonders what exactly Blount had meant by that, whether it was a gesture that implied a potential alliance, or simply a genuine offer of help. The man is utterly indecipherable. Time will tell, but for the moment a new idea is beginning to form that might put this situation to best use. He will impress upon the Queen that the only man capable of handling a situation such as has arisen in Ireland is the Earl of Essex himself.

How should he form his suggestion? *There is no greater commander in England,* he imagines saying. *The esteemed earl is the sole man with the skill to overcome the rebels effectively.*

No, he must allow her to believe it is her own idea: *It would take a great leader of men to quell such angry forces, Your Majesty. It is such a very important role and one that will cover its incumbent in glory – it needs a person of great courage.*

Who is such a man? she will ask.

But she will already have half the answer forming in her mind, as he shakes his head saying, *We must consider carefully; such men are rare.*

He might list some unsuitable possibilities, all his own allies, as if he is making an attempt to elevate one of his own; which she will dismiss with something like, *Pygmy, you have no understanding of martial matters.*

It will take time, months maybe, but Cecil is nothing if not patient these days. And when it comes it will be like a flare of flame in the Queen's head: *Our man is Essex. He is the only one.*

I am sure Your Majesty is right, but I was of the understanding he . . . – he will offer her a look that suggests his nose is a little out of joint – *that the earl was in disgrace.*

Now, now, I will not have you sulk, Pygmy, over Essex being preferred for such high office, she will say. *You will accept my decision on the matter, whether you agree or not.*

He is helped into his litter, thinking how fortunate it is that the earl remains at Wanstead and not at court to fight his corner.

Whitehall/Tower of London

As Penelope watches her daughters kneel before the Queen, she sees Elizabeth as they must see her: an intimidatingly stern old woman, her face smeared with a thick, chalky-white substance that has rubbed away in places to reveal the sallow skin beneath. Her mouth is stretched into a thin, tight smile that does not reveal her teeth, which Penelope know to be quite rotten and a source of consternation to her. Her wig is the colour of marmalade, curled and festooned with jewels; her dress is heavily embroidered, swathed with strings of fat pearls and cut girlishly low, exposing an expanse of breast also thickly spread with white, which has gathered in the pits and wrinkles, so, instead of disguising, rather accentuates them. She wears the heart-shaped ruby that was Lettice's gift. Penelope tries not to look at it.

'Come closer!' The Queen is squinting at the two girls as they shuffle forward on their knees. 'That's better; I can see you now.'

Penelope is reminded of when *she* was first presented, and an image of the Queen, as she was then, returns to her momentarily: that vibrant, haughty creature whose eyes flashed, whose long-fingered hands danced in the air as she spoke, whose voice had the tone of a well-tempered lyre in the hands of an expert. She was spellbinding at forty-seven, but at sixty-five the hands no longer dance and the eyes are granite; they have seen too much.

She had warned them that the Queen would seem menacing and that they were simply to answer her questions as if they were not afraid. But Lucy, particularly, looks terrified and caught in the grip of her crippling shyness; Essie, only just thirteen, is holding her own: answering her questions with aplomb.

'And what is your given name?' asks the Queen, picking out a sugar comfit from a dish beside her.

'Essex,' replies Essie, her eyes flitting back and forth between the Queen and the plate of sweets. 'I am named after my uncle.'

'Ah, your handsome uncle! You resemble him a little too.' She munches as she speaks.

'He is my favourite relative.' Essie has a disarming glimmer in her demeanour and Penelope can see the Queen falling a little for her charm. She is reminded once more of that first encounter, how it felt to have such illustrious approval alight on her and how desperately she wanted a position at court as a way out of the grim Huntingdon household. She is shunted back to that day; it was this very chamber she cast her eyes about for Sidney, hardly knowing then what he looked like. Now his image is branded on her memory and she wonders how he would have looked in middle age. It is twelve years since he was taken. Time has disappeared with sickening speed.

She is thankful there is no vacancy in the maids' rooms at present, for were the Queen to offer either of her daughters a place, there is not a circumstance under which such an honour could be refused. Penelope will not see her girls swallowed up into this court – the court of an elderly, pitiless Queen with everyone looking over her shoulder at who will follow.

'But *I* am your relative,' teases the Queen.

'You are without doubt my most esteemed relative,' says Essie. 'But as I have never known Your Majesty in person, it would not have been possible to call you my favourite. Now, though' – she offers a dimpled smile, just like the earl's – 'he shall be my favourite uncle and I hope Your Majesty will allow me the honour of thinking of you as my most favourite cousin.'

Penelope wants to cheer; this is exactly the kind of spirited response the Queen will love.

'You may resemble your uncle in looks but you have your mother's wit.' The Queen returns Essie's smile and offers the dish of comfits. Essie takes one, popping it into her mouth. 'And you.' The Queen turns to Lucy. Penelope can see that her hands are quivering. 'What is your given name? Lucy is a pet name, is it not?'

Penelope takes a deep breath. She had hoped to avoid this, had told the usher simply to announce them as 'Lady Rich and her two eldest daughters'. She had told Lucy to not mention her given name unless directly asked, and she can see the girl droop with fear.

'My name is . . .' Her voice is barely audible.

'Speak up, child,' says the Queen.

'Lettice.'

'Lettice?' The Queen directs a withering look at Penelope. The ruby gives her a mocking wink. 'I thought as much. Not really a name to be proud of, is it?' Lucy's face turns beetroot and she shakes her head. Penelope wants to pick her up and run from the chamber. 'Off you go, girls. Introduce yourselves to the maids over there.' The Queen waves an arm in the vague direction of a gaggle of young women on the window seat who are sewing. Penelope recognizes Bess Brydges, who has been the most recent object of her brother's clandestine attentions, or so he has told her. Bess smiles at her; she nods in return.

'Well,' the Queen says, 'at least they look sufficiently like Rich to avoid rumours. There were those who suspected Sidney.'

Penelope staunches an angry riposte, taking a breath to calm herself. 'My friendship with Sidney was entirely proper, madam.'

The Queen winks, an unappealing, lascivious gesture, which raises Penelope's ire further, but she stops herself from a defence that would only seem to underscore her guilt. The Queen takes another comfit, chewing it with closed eyes; then shuffles the cards deftly, like a conjurer, in spite of her swollen knuckles. Thankfully a boy comes to stoke the fire for the chamber is bitterly cold. He throws on several logs and pumps the bellows until the flames flare, spitting and crackling, sending a scent of applewood into the room.

'I suppose that wicked cousin of yours has birthed her baby,' says the Queen, once she has finished masticating. She is talking of Lizzie Vernon and Penelope is on high alert, for she is clearly in the mood for a game of cat and mouse.

'She has. A girl. I stood godmother.'

'Another little Penelope, then.' She continues shuffling the well-worn playing cards. Dividing the pack and using the table as a support, she flicks the two piles together, then taps them against the hard surface. 'I like Southampton, but I can't for the life of me understand what she sees in him. He is as fey as a girl . . . that abundance of hair, the way he carries himself.' She sits upright, one shoulder forward, chin down, looking up above her lashes, in imitation of Southampton.

'Attraction can alight in the most surprising of places, I suppose,' says Penelope.

'And he is not short of wealth.' The Queen laughs, a loud, brief burst like a trumpet salute. 'If I'm honest, I miss them about the place. He was decorative and Lizzie was a bright spark.' The humour drops from her face as she adds, 'But if I am seen to relent, they will all be disobeying me.' She casts her gaze in the direction of the maids across the chamber. They are talking in low voices, heads in a huddle.

Penelope pulls her shawl more tightly about her shoulders, glad she wore her fur-lined gown, but her shoes and stockings are still damp from the short walk through the snow to the stables this morning.

'It was an act of great kindness to grant Lizzie her liberty.' Penelope is thinking that the Queen's loss is her gain, for

Cousin Lizzie, banished from court, is now ensconced at Essex House, at Penelope's invitation, and has proved to be a delightful companion. She has gone some way to fill the yawning space left since Jeanne departed for France.

'I am not made entirely of stone, as most would have it,' retorts the Queen.

'There are few who could be more aware of that than I.' Conversing with the Queen is like a game of chess, words placed carefully to best advantage, but Penelope has become used to it over the years. Blount had asked her once what she truly thought of the Queen and she had not known how to answer but had eventually responded with another question. 'If you have respect, do you also have to have admiration?' There was another Catholic plot uncovered only a matter of weeks ago: some fanatic named Squire planned to smear poison on the pommel of her saddle. He thought to do away with Essex too, so it was said. The Queen scrutinizes Penelope's demeanour as if trying to read her thoughts. 'You have always been most tolerant with me,' she adds.

'I suppose you mean the blind eye I have turned to your' – the Queen pauses – 'your unconventional arrangement with your husband. It has been in place for some years, I believe?'

Penelope nods. 'I have often wondered why –'

'Why I have shown you such lenience,' interrupts the Queen, 'when I have been harsh with others? It is all a question of appearances. And you didn't wed without my permission. That is the thing I object to most strongly – that kind of direct disobedience makes it appear that I have no control over my ladies. It gives the wrong impression, and impression is paramount in my position.' The Queen deals the cards.

'I understand that.' Penelope picks up her hand. The cards are smooth with use. 'And I understand that trust is a precious commodity if you wear the crown.'

'Ah, trust!' The Queen emits a small sour laugh.

They play without speaking for a while, picking up and placing down cards, rearranging their hands, planning their strategies. They have played together so often each has learned to recognize the other's tics: the unwitting blink the Queen makes when she has picked up a winning card, or the way Penelope clenches her jaw slightly when she knows she has lost.

'Also,' says the Queen, breaking the silence, 'I find the idea rather appealing of a woman behaving like a man. There are enough men who go about sowing their seed with women other than their wives.' Penelope scrutinizes her for signs that this is a veiled criticism of her incorrigible brother. But the Queen doesn't seem to be thinking of Essex. 'Heaven knows how you have kept that husband of yours in line for such a time.'

A thought pops into Penelope's mind so wicked it makes her hot with shame: were she to reveal Rich's proclivity for sodomy he could well be hanged for it and she would be free. She may have sinful thoughts but she would never act upon them.

'I must say,' adds the Queen. 'I *have* had regrets in the past over your match with Rich. It seemed so advantageous at the time. I didn't want you impoverished. Your brother was never going to have enough to keep you. He is so indebted to me now it will take a hundred lifetimes for him to pay me back.'

Penelope nods. She can't think of an appropriate reply. The Queen could easily have erased his debt or given him a monopoly; but how will she control him if he isn't in her debt?

'I can see now,' continues the Queen, 'that yours hasn't been a particularly contented union. You might have been happier with Sidney.' She looks at her cards, pulling one out and replacing it. 'He begged for you once. I sent him packing.'

Penelope can barely believe what she is hearing. It is as

close an expression of regret as she has ever heard from the Queen, but it makes a tight knot of resentment tangle itself in her, to be reminded that her life has been lived on the wishes of others. She has no sympathy now if the Queen is feeling wistful about the things she has done in the past – she will not get the satisfaction of absolution from her. 'And Blount has something of Sidney; I have always thought so,' adds the Queen.

Penelope can feel the truth bubbling up, pressing to explode from her. *Blount was not some kind of consolation prize, for you to bestow on me to assuage your guilt; Blount was never yours to give. It was my own choice, nothing to do with you. I am not a player in your drama, speaking your lines, acting out the part you have given me.* She thinks it but doesn't say it. What she says is: 'You have been most indulgent with me, and for that I am truly grateful.' She picks up her cards, fanning them out, sorting them into suits.

'I have been most forgiving too, towards your brother.'

'You have.' Penelope notices the Queen's tone of curt resignation; she has clearly not entirely forgiven Essex.

'It is only fair to give him a last chance. He is the nearest thing I have to a son, after all.'

The Queen has said such things before and it predictably raises Penelope's hackles further; she would like to point out that her brother already has a mother, but of course she doesn't.

'Besides, I require him in Ireland. Since the massacre, it has become imperative I have a strong arm out there.'

'Ah!' says Penelope. She is trying to work out if this is a good thing. 'As Lord Deputy?'

The Queen nods and smiles, allowing her lips to part and reveal, briefly, her bad teeth. 'It is an opportunity for him to redeem himself.'

Penelope doesn't allow her conflicting feelings to show. Part of her is relieved, for this means Blount will not be sent to the wilds of Ireland, but she fears that the commission may well be as much a poisoned chalice for her brother as it was for her father. Though, she reasons silently, if he manages to quell the rebels it will put him in a strong position, more than lands and glory.

She has talked this over at length with Blount; whoever is in charge in Ireland will have a vast company of men-at-arms at their disposal, which might outweigh the disadvantages of being away from court. The Queen is not getting any younger, she still hasn't named her successor, and it is quite possible someone may try to force the issue before long. 'I feel sure he will excel in such a role. He is a fine leader of men.' She cannot swallow away the lump of disloyalty in her throat.

Then the Queen latches her eyes on to Penelope's. 'I may have been tolerant with you and your brother, but don't imagine my lenience is infinite.' Her voice is cold and hard like a diamond, and sends a frisson of terror through Penelope, who is remembering that this is the woman who signed the death warrant of her own cousin, Mary of Scotland.

Penelope waves her girls off and watches as they exit the gates with the groom, looking away only when they have turned the corner out of sight. A great panel of snow slides from the stable roof, falling to the ground with a *thwump*, which startles her horse. She walks him slowly round the yard, humming a tune to calm him, while she waits for Blount. Gambit is a young gelding with a nervous disposition and she can feel his fear flicker beneath her with each unfamiliar sound. She continues her humming, leaning forward, stroking the soft mound beneath his ear. 'There, there, boy.' She wonders if he is unsettled by the feeling of trepidation that has set in her since her card game with the Queen.

Blount appears, his cheeks ruddy from the cold. Even after eight years the sight of him ignites a spark of excitement in her. He waves, approaching, and she wants to shout out the news to him that he will not be sent to Ireland, that it is her brother who will go, but she resists the urge. It would not do for it to be common knowledge just yet. She has learned the power of silence over the years.

'I think I have found you a puppy,' he says, grinning. 'A spaniel bitch whelped yesterday at the Inns of Court.' She is reminded of the time when she first encountered Spero, and inevitably recollections of Sidney drift through her mind. Sidney's spectral presence makes her appreciate all the more the solidity of Blount.

The road from Whitehall is bustling: women shuffle through the filthy slush under the weight of baskets piled high with wares. Carts trundle past, flicking up frozen splashes, men in pairs heave cartons between them, all delivering goods to the palace kitchens for the Christmas feasting. After the long fast of advent it will be good to eat meat once more and drink undiluted wine and dance. She can already hear the music in her mind. Once they are beyond the melee and on to the open land behind the Strand, they break into a canter, profiting from the sense of freedom before they reach the tight clog of the city.

Slowing as they pass the back gates of Burghley House, they notice the windows are still shuttered in mourning. It has been four months since Lord Burghley died, and his son has slipped seamlessly into the space he left behind. They decide to loop round, give themselves time to talk alone. 'I have news,' he says. 'Excellent news.'

'Tell me, then.'

'Essex received a letter from King James, in his own hand, acknowledging our support for his claim. And . . .'

'And what?' Penelope's gut is fluttering as if she awaits news from a lover, remembering how this was set in motion nearly a decade ago and how even then there had been a sense of urgency, as if the Queen's days might have been numbered.

'He has said that in return he will support your brother, "should he ever need it". Those were the exact words.'

'What do you think he means by that?' She is suddenly suspicious of this. It sounds invested with a drama that might prove tragic. 'Does it not smack of danger, Charles?'

'I think not. It seems to me he is saying that if things were to change . . .' He lowers his voice to a whisper, though there is not so much as a tree nearby for someone to hide behind, and besides if anyone were in the vicinity their footsteps in the snow would betray them. 'Were the Queen to pass away, he guarantees his preferment to Essex. James knows he will need powerful allies in England if he is to get to the throne without mishap.'

'Of course,' she says, but she cannot help but wonder if her brother has begun to stir up some other, more treacherous, business and implied a little of it to the Scottish King. Essex had felt so utterly disempowered after his latest disgrace it would make sense if he'd sought to shore himself up elsewhere. No, she concludes, he would have said something to me and, besides, he is back in favour now. 'Who else do you suppose will come forward with a serious claim when the time comes?'

'James's cousin, the Stuart girl, Arbella.' Blount begins to count on his fingers. 'It is said she might take up the Catholic cause.'

'She was raised in the New Faith, that I do know.'

'But there are Catholics in her family who may well be pulling her strings. There is the Seymour line: Lord Beauchamp. Their claim would be strong; Lady Katherine Grey was his mother, so there is an abundance of Tudor blood there. But there are problems of illegitimacy.'

'Katherine Grey was a dear friend of my own mother.'

Penelope remembers Lettice talking of Kitty Grey, the great-granddaughter of the seventh Henry, how she wed in secret and died a prisoner. Another woman to fall foul of the Queen's wrath.

'Then there is the Spanish Infanta,' Blount says.

'It would take a Catholic uprising of gargantuan proportions to achieve that,' she says.

'Or a Spanish invasion,' he adds. 'And if the rebels are not effectively suppressed in Ireland, that will be their gateway.'

Penelope shudders. 'And my brother is to see that it doesn't happen. It is Essex she is sending in your stead.'

'God help him!' says Blount. 'I cannot lie; I am glad it is not me.'

Penelope says nothing. She is glad too but cannot betray her brother by putting it into words. They ride on in silence for a while before she adds, 'We must ensure that King James is crowned, whether the Queen names him or not. Then we will all be safe. After all, his is the only uncomplicated claim.' They continue on, riding through the snow without speaking.

'Cecil approached me again,' says Blount eventually. 'I think he has a mind to recruit me.'

'What did he say?' she asks.

'Not very much. I'd say it was more of a gesture of friendship, than anything. Like before, he talked about how the Privy Council could do with someone like me.'

'And what did *you* say?'

'Oh, I was noncommittal. It might be useful if I go along with it.'

'Be careful.' She has a sense that things have become dangerously complicated, too elaborate to keep a firm grip on, and she is suddenly reminded of that hard, cold look of the Queen's earlier.

'You know me, I am the lord of all carefulness.' He reaches out to squeeze her arm and she is a little reassured. It is true he is the personification of caution.

'I am so thankful we have each other,' she says.

'Together we are a force to be reckoned with.'

'So where is it we are going?' she asks. He had sent word earlier saying there was something he wanted her to see.

'The Tower.'

'The Tower – do you mean to have me clapped in irons?' She smiles.

'I want to surprise you.'

'Why didn't we take the barge?'

'The river is almost frozen solid by the bridge. There were boys playing on it this morning. One fell through.'

'Oh no!' She is suddenly filled with misery at the thought of some poor boy meeting his end in the cold lonely world beneath the ice.

'They hauled him out. There was no great harm done to him.'

She cannot shake the idea of those chilled depths out of her head as they ride on, entering the city by Ludgate, and down Cheapside, where all the goldsmiths' signs have icicles dripping from them in long glassy shards. Soon they are at St Paul's, from where they have a view of the Tower: a sight which always shoots her through with apprehension.

'My brother says he may have to sell Wanstead to pay some of his debts,' Penelope says. 'I can't bear the idea of that house belonging to someone else – never being able to go there again.' She knows it is only a house, and not even hers, but somehow it has grown to represent all that is happy and good.

'I have discussed an offer for Wanstead with your brother.'

'You would buy Wanstead?'

'I am in need of a house suitable to my station. Since I have been going up in the world . . .' He throws his nose into the air with a haughty pout and then grins, laughing. It has been a joke of theirs these last few years, that he must have yeast in his blood, given the ease with which he is rising at court.

She can feel the joy welling in her. 'Like a loaf left to prove.' She stretches out a hand to take his. 'Maybe one day . . .' The rest of her words stick in her throat.

Their horses slide, struggling to get a grip on the icy planks of the bridge across the moat. It has frozen over entirely and its banks are thick with snow. The last time she was here was years ago when poor Lopez was in some miserable cell within these walls. She had tried to erase the memory of what happened between her brother and Lopez – it filled her with shame on Essex's behalf: the signifier of his hidden cruelty – but the incident found its way into her mind often, running round and round, like a tune that settles in and will not be expelled. She had brought the poor man victuals to ease his discomfort but they wouldn't let her see him. It was summer and the foul stench of the moat water then was almost unbearable. God only knows what lurks under that smooth white surface. A scarlet-liveried guard greets them and they dismount, handing their horses over to a groom.

She hooks her arm through Blount's as they follow the guard along a path cleared from snow that crosses the court-yard and runs around the White Tower. They stop at the far end, before a great door, and the guard takes the bunch of keys that hangs from his belt, inspecting them, finally select-ing one and opening the door with the words, 'The menagerie.'

She can hear a cacophony of strange sounds and, once through a further door, they find themselves confronted by an enclosure which is home to a colony of about a dozen large apes, swinging from the branches of a dead tree and howling in raucous glee at their visitors. A courageous fellow approaches the barred gate. He has a face that seems to be both dog-like and yet also curiously human, and when he yawns he reveals a pair of devilish eye teeth, that are long and pointed, capable of tearing a carcass to shreds. She gasps and the monkey cackles, proceeding to fondle his privates as a female sidles towards them with an infant astride her back.

The male turns away, displaying a purple behind, and Penelope reaches her hand out with the intention of stroking the soft fuzz of fur on the baby ape's head, but the guard grabs her, causing her to gasp, and says, 'That wouldn't be wise, My Lady. The mother'll have your arm off.'

She laughs to hide her alarm. 'It is like a scene at court. Look how that fellow resembles Cecil.' She points to one with a dark glossy coat who is carefully picking fleas from his head.

'And there is your brother and Bess Brydges.' He indicates a half-concealed couple mating behind the tree. She can't help giggling, wondering if the guard is shocked that she is not hiding her eyes in horror. 'And that one is . . .' Blount exchanges a look with Penelope and she follows his eyes to a vast female with pendulous breasts sitting alone, scrutinizing a leaf, as if it is a book of philosophy, and snarling if any of the others come too close.

'Shhh.' She puts a hand to her mouth to stop herself from saying it but he is surely thinking, as she is, that in this odd, upside-down court of apes, that cantankerous and solitary female baboon is the Queen.

'Once *more* unto the breach, dear friends . . .' One of the players stands stage-centre. He is bootless but wears a chain-mail vest over his shirt and waves a broadsword, thrusting it into the air.

'I think the emphasis ought be on "friends" rather than "more",' says the playwright, walking over, 'and repeat "once more" – "Once more unto the breach, dear friends, once more", then you thrust the sword upward.' He makes a stabbing motion into the air with his hand, 'and then into, "Or close the wall up", and so on.' They have an exchange of words, which Penelope cannot hear from where she sits in the balcony with her brother and friends.

'Do you suppose he is meant to be me?' asks Essex.

'Of course,' replies Meyrick, who cannot imagine a world without Essex at its heart. 'Otherwise I can't imagine why they were so keen for you to watch them rehearse.'

'It is because we will all be gone by the time the first performance is fit to be shown,' says Southampton. 'You think they are all you – the heroes, anyway!' He slaps his friend's shoulder with a laugh. 'Of course it is you! The great conqueror Henry V, victor at Agincourt.'

'We shall take our fight to the Irish,' says Essex. Meyrick and Southampton emit a muffled cheer that causes the rehearsing players to break out of their huddled conversation and turn their heads up towards the shadowed balcony. Penelope notices that her brother is jigging his leg nervously. She fears it will visit trouble on him to be so publicly compared to a king. Southampton brings his hand down firmly on Essex's jittery leg, letting it rest there. She is thinking about a rumour she has heard that some scholar or other has penned a treatise on Henry IV's usurpation of Richard II and dedicated it to her brother. She has tried to discover who the scholar is, had put Anthony Bacon on the paper trail, in order to suppress it, for she doesn't want a repetition of the business with that infernal book of a few years ago. To have her brother's name attached to a tract that lauds the deposition of a monarch – the consequences could be devastating.

The player has started his speech again: 'Once more unto the breach, dear friends, *once more*; Or close the wall up with our English dead . . .'

She is not watching the stage; she has her gaze fixed on her brother's profile and can see, in the faint glow of candlelight, the beads of perspiration on his forehead, gleaming like little jewels, and the slight movement of his jaw where he is grinding his teeth. His mouth is set in the scowl that, she recognizes from childhood, is designed to hide his apprehension.

When the players are done with their rehearsal Penelope leads the way down the narrow stairs, through the empty pit and on to the stage.

'May I try this?' She points to the chain-mail vest hanging discarded over a chair with the broadsword propped beside it. She unpins her ruff and a player helps her into the garment. It rings as it is lowered carefully over her head, the chime of a thousand tiny bells, but once it is settled on to her shoulders it is a dead weight, so heavy she can barely move. She is handed the sword and it takes both hands to hold it off the ground. It is vast, a battle broadsword, nothing like the fine things the gallants wear attached to their belts at court. She had imagined herself prancing about, wielding the weapon, raising a laugh out of the company but she finds she is weighted to the spot, paralysed. 'How on earth do they manage to fight?'

'This is nothing compared to the armour we wear these days – a full suit, you should try one of those,' laughs Southampton, who looks too delicately wrought, with his smooth skin and girlish features, to wear anything but the finest silk. He grabs the great sword from her hand and with a flourish of his wrist, makes a figure of eight in the air. She sees then the muscles in his forearms are sinewy and deceptively strong and remembers Lizzie describing his body the day after she first gave herself to him. She had commented on his strength, how he had pinned her down so she was unable to move, compared him to Samson. Penelope had thought her exaggerating but now – watching him play-fight with her brother, who has snatched up another weapon, a pike with a point that would have your eye out were you not careful – she can see that Southampton is more a man than she'd thought.

The chain mail is making it difficult to breathe and she is struck by the thought of all these men on the battlefield, knee-deep in Irish mud, fighting for their lives. A wave of nausea moves through her. She can hear the whoops and cries, a trumpet blast, the terrified whinnying of horses whose hooves thunder to the urgent rattle of a drummer's beat: rat, tat-tat-tat-tat; the whistle of arrows, the slick swoosh of steel, the slice and clash as it meets like; cannon fire, a sound so deep you fear falling into it and never being found; lead balls thud to the ground, cracking through bone – a crescendo of dissonance building and building until it drops, leaving only the quivering groans and final exhalations of men. She plucks at the edges of the chain mail, trying to lift it away from her body.

'Let me help you out of that.' It is Meyrick, whose brutish bearing belies a kind disposition. He lifts the jangling garment off her. 'I feared you would faint on us,' he says. 'Do you need a drink, My Lady?' In that moment she is deeply thankful that her brother will have loyal Meyrick at his side in Ireland.

'Will you keep him safe out there?'

He looks at her directly with those invisibly lashed eyes and says, 'Do not vex yourself. God will be on our side.'

'Yes,' she replies faintly, remembering when it was that she started doubting God's plan – when Sidney died.

Later at Essex House Penelope dismisses the company, begging a few minutes alone with her brother, and, sitting at the virginals in the great chamber, begins to play. She looks over at the puppy, Fides, curled up by the hearth. He is so like Spero, yet not Spero. She thinks of her old companion and, as if he can read her thoughts, Fides looks over, tilting his head, gazing at her, daring her to love him.

She shuffles through her sheets of music, barely able to see in the dim light, resorting to a familiar tune, one of her favourites. 'You danced to this on Twelfth Night,' she says, beginning to hum along, allowing the sounds to envelop her, the hammers meeting with the taut strings, sending out their precise reverberations.

'I danced with *her*!' He means the Queen, of course. He is stuffing his pipe with tobacco, pressing it down with his thumb.

'It was the first time she'd danced in months. Did you see Cecil?' Penelope says. Now he is sucking the flame into the pipe's bowl from the sole lit candle in the chamber, his face cast sharply in shadow.

'Mouth tight as a dog's sphincter.' He inhales and laughs, sending a stream of smoke into the room.

'Robin!' She pretends to be shocked but can't help her own laughter and she thinks of Cecil watching Essex shiftily, picking invisible dirt from his doublet, adjusting his ruff minutely, repositioning his chain of office. 'It was good to have a chance to show the world you are back in her favour.'

'They may all think I am, but I am not, Sis.' He sighs. The black leather pouch containing his recent correspondence with King James dangles over his lap, half visible in the gloom.

'What do you mean?' Penelope is remembering how the Queen seemed in bliss as she allowed him to lead her through the steps, basking in the delighted smiles of her ladies. Penelope stood at the side counting the sour faces, a row of gargoyles: Ralegh, Cobham, Carew, Cecil – those who would happily see the Devereuxs take a tumble. If one falls, they all do. That is how it works.

'It is not the same. She no longer trusts me. I asked her lately if she had made a decision on the Court of Wards. She knows if I had charge of the Wards it would set my money worries behind me. I told her I could serve her better that way, could repay my debt to her. She has dangled this over me since Burghley died and left the vacancy. The Court of Wards made *him* rich beyond his dreams.' Penelope's doubts must show in her expression, for he adds, 'I asked her nicely – not as if I'm entitled. Just as you have always told me I should, Sis: humble but not ingratiating.'

'And what did she say?'

'She changed the subject.' He slumps in his chair.

'But she was teasing, I'm sure. Did she not always play with you thus?'

'No, this was different. I can't describe in what way exactly, but . . .' He stops, covering his mouth with his hand, speaking through his fingers. 'I'm scared, Sis.'

'Scared of what, of fighting?'

'Of failure.'

She goes to sit beside him, allowing him to rest his head on her breast like a child. 'You have many friends. Take reassurance from that. You may have enemies at court but the people of England love you.' She runs her fingers through his dark curls. 'You shall see tomorrow when you leave. They will line the streets, dozens deep. I know they will. They have had nothing but hardship these last years, with the plague and the famine and the constant fear of invasion.' She presses a fist to his chest. 'They *need* you to bring them a victory – to bring them hope of a better future, of safety, of plenty. And you will. I know you will.' She can hear that dreadful battlefield cacophony at the back of her mind, but refuses to listen.

'A victory,' he echoes.

'And I will be here, with Blount, to ensure no one takes any liberties while you are gone. And there is this.' She holds up the black pouch. 'This ensures us,' she hesitates. 'This ensures *you* against failure.' Their eyes meet and she thinks she sees a faint fleck of brightness there. '*And* it is a chance to finish what Father started.' She regrets instantly bringing their father's squalid death into the room, for it hangs like a poisonous miasma in the silence.

'Do you think Father's death could have been prevented, had the Queen sent sufficient funds, as Mother always said?' he takes several insistent puffs on his pipe.

'I don't know.' She rubs her hand over his shoulders, feeling how knotted he is.

'Well, we do know Father spent every last penny of the Devereux fortune trying to keep the rebels at bay.' He stops, shifting his shoulders slightly beneath her hands. '*For England. He lost our fortune for England.*'

She says nothing, doesn't want to think of the consequences of that loss: her blighted marriage, his obligations to the Queen. She continues silently massaging at his tight muscles, her fingers alighting on a swelling at the edge of his shoulder blade. 'What is this?' She lifts his shirt to look. 'There is something –'

'What? What have you found?'

'I don't know, it is something sprouting here.' She angles herself to better capture the candlelight.

'Pull it out, whatever it is.' He sounds horrified, strung tighter than a viol. 'Get rid of it!'

It is like a small wisp of thread protruding from a mound of distended flesh. She pinches it between her fingernails, whatever it is, and pulls. It slides easily out of his skin. She drops it into her palm, bringing it close to the light. A smallish white feather, like that from the underside of a goose, sits curled in her hand.

'Proof you are an angel,' she says, smiling, planting a kiss on his forehead, but he looks appalled.

'Or Icarus!' He spits the name out as if it is bitter in his mouth.

A sharp scrape emanates from the darkness at the far end of the room, a chair shifting perhaps. Fides growls quietly, ears pricked.

'Who's there?' Penelope says, sensing the hairs lift at her nape. She had assumed they were alone but the chamber is large and the only light comes from the hearth and the candle beside them. Her mind sorts through their conversation: what exactly was said – they discussed the Court of Wards, her brother's private conversations with the Queen, his fears, the Devereux finances . . . Did either of them mention the Scottish King by name or, God forbid, the letters themselves?

'It is I.' A figure emerges from the gloom, Francis Bacon rubbing his eyes with the heels of his slender hands and sniffing. 'It's cold.' His face is ghostly white and he wraps his arms about himself.

'Bacon, what are you doing lurking in the dark like a thief?' Essex sounds bright, not freighted with the suspicion that Penelope feels creeping over her. But this is Francis Bacon, Essex's dear friend, who has proved his fidelity a thousand times over with all his secret information. She tries to set aside her personal dislike of him.

'I must have fallen asleep over my paperwork.' He sniffs once more.

'Come and sit here by the fire.' Essex pats the place beside him. 'Warm yourself.'

Bacon settles in next to her brother, taking the pipe wordlessly and drawing on it deeply; it is a gesture that surprises Penelope in its familiarity.

'What were you working on?' Penelope asks.

'Some fellow has written a treatise on Henry IV and the ousting of King Richard. He dedicated it to you.' He directs his response at Essex, as if it were he who had asked the question. 'I managed to get my hands on a copy. Thought I ought to go through it to see if it was nefarious.'

'Not another unwanted dedication,' says Essex. Penelope can see him tense up again and is annoyed with Bacon for giving him something new to worry about on the eve of his departure. She had deliberately kept her own knowledge of the tract quiet for that very reason.

'And is there anything in it that could do damage to Essex?' she says. She wants to interrogate him on where he came upon this treatise but doesn't want to make too much of it, for her brother's sake.

'I think it will rather visit trouble on the author.' He answers Essex, still ignoring Penelope. 'Much of it is plucked from Tacitus.'

'We will make sure it is dealt with, won't we, Bacon?'

Even now, having been addressed so directly and by name, he doesn't look at her. 'Yes, yes, nothing to fret over.' He has begun to massage Essex's shoulders, as *she* was only moments ago. She wants to push him away, tell him to leave them alone, and wonders if it is jealousy or suspicion that is prodding at her. She catches him staring at the black leather pouch that is tucked into the folds of Essex's shirt. 'What do you keep in there? Pictures of your mistresses?'

'Something like that,' Essex replies.

Looking down, Penelope notices that the curled white feather has fallen to the floor.

March 1599

Whitehall

Row upon row of orange-clad horsemen stand to attention in the great court. The earl has managed to muster a vast army and it is said this is only a fraction of it. Thousands more will join them en route to Holyhead. They set out from Seething Lane this morning and a great horde of people had gathered along the roadsides to wave and cheer. Cecil had had to negotiate his way through them to get to the palace and he can see them now pressing at the gates, climbing on each other's shoulders and up to perch on the walls, just for a glimpse of their hero.

But even Cecil is impressed by the neat lines, the horses brushed to a sheen, hooves oiled, bridles gleaming and the men, poker straight, lifting their weapons in unison as the Queen steps on to the balcony. Perhaps with this lot Essex will do what none have done yet and quell the rebels. He wonders if he has made an erroneous move in quietly negotiating the earl's promotion to Ireland. But then again perhaps Essex will fail, as his father did before him. Cecil has pondered on all this for some time: whether victory in Ireland is worth the price of putting Essex beyond his reach and he no longer has Burghley to go to when he loses the courage of his convictions.

Taking a sharp breath to pull himself up before memories of his father overwhelm him, he finds an image appearing unbidden in his mind, of the earl lying, bloody, on a battlefield, all his splendid finery smeared with mud and gore. He is feebly tugging at the stump of an arrow lodged in his breast. No, the picture shifts, he is standing alone in a bleak wilderness, abandoned by his men, divested of his armour, just his orange sash, filthy, flapping ragged in the wind. A shot comes from nowhere, exploding into his chest; he falls with a howl, clasping the mess that was once his heart. His hands ooze crimson. Cecil can feel the weight of the musket in his own hand, can smell the gunpowder. It is the scent of celebration, of firework displays. Feeling suddenly adulterated, sickened by his own thoughts, he wishes he could make contact with the good part of himself.

Essex vaults from his horse, flinging the reins to Southampton – another of Burghley's glittering protégés. He is too young to have been one of his boyhood tormentors but he is just like them. And Southampton is on that bleak heath beside the earl. Cecil stops that thought in its tracks. He must not blow the flames of his ugly side. Another brisk inhalation into his lungs, and he straightens himself to his full height, feeling his bent back crack satisfyingly as he does so. Do not compare yourself, he says silently, we are all God's creatures. He forces a smile on to his face and sends up a prayer for victory. But he is being disingenuous even with God.

Essex has climbed the steps and is kneeling before the Queen, kissing her hand, and she is telling him once more that he must not 'under any circumstances – any circumstances' – she repeats it looking directly into his eyes – 'Do not under any circumstances capitulate with the Earl of Tyrone. He is our enemy. He must be fully crushed.'

'I am commanded,' says the earl, getting to his feet as a cheer spreads through the crowd, from those who can hear, outwards, like ripples in a pond.

Cecil looks over to Blount, who is nearby, standing between Lady Rich and Francis Bacon. Blount is not cheering, neither is Lady Rich. On Bacon's boyish face there is something like a smile. But Cecil doesn't know what it means. Francis Bacon approached him this morning, asked for a private appointment, which has roused his curiosity. There has been little love lost between him and his cousin Francis since he was overlooked for the job of attorney general in favour of Cecil's candidate. But that was years ago and perhaps Cousin Francis is ready to re-enter the family fold, unless he intends on double-dealing. It remains to be seen.

Lady Rich has stepped forward to kiss her brother. She holds him in an embrace. Cecil momentarily substitutes himself for Essex, surprised by this, for he has not had lascivious thoughts about Lady Rich for some time, had believed them in remission. The Queen nods to her women, the signal that they may descend to wish farewell to their husbands and brothers below, and Cecil is reminded that neither Lady Southampton nor Lady Essex are there – ah, the invisible Lady Essex, with child it is said. Their disgrace is final, just as it was with the earl's mother. The Queen seems always to allow her disgraced men to inveigle themselves back into her heart, but never the women. Perhaps she is right to be suspicious of the women. Cecil makes a point of gathering information on the wives as well as the husbands, for they do so like to get their hands dirty with politics these days.

He smoothes the velvet of his cape, arranging it so it drapes correctly from his shoulders, before stepping forward, as Lady Rich detaches herself from her brother. He takes the earl's hand and wishes him well, noticing the Queen's look of satisfaction, like a mother surveying a reconciliation between her squabbling children.

'Go to it, My Lord,' Cecil says. 'If anyone can outfox Tyrone it is you.'

Essex surprises him with a genuine smile that sends a waft of guilt through him, makes him feel fraudulent. 'I shall do my best to serve England and our Queen.' The gaggle of ladies that has gathered about him clap at this, their white hands fluttering like butterflies.

'Don't go and get yourself killed. I want you back,' says the Queen loudly, over the applause.

The earl's eyes twist fleetingly like those of an unbroken horse, allowing Cecil a glimpse of his fear, which surprises him for he had thought Essex's courage impermeable. 'I shall be back, don't doubt it, Your Majesty,' he replies, appearing to exude nothing but confidence once more, turning, descending the steps and mounting his horse.

A trumpet sounds and Essex moves off with his men. As they leave the gates, a roar goes up from the crowds without: *Ess-ex, Ess-ex, Ess-ex.* The royal party watches as the earl stoops to speak to a few in the throng, taking the hand of a woman and kissing it, then, to another great cheer, he hauls a delighted child up to sit pillion behind him, allowing the boy to inspect his sword. The Queen scowls. He remembers his father telling him how she loved to stop and chat with her people on state occasions. 'It is they who put me here,' was what she always said. Cecil has never seen that, she has become far too closely guarded these days, too fearful of the assassin's knife.

'I've seen enough.' The Queen turns and offers Cecil an arm to escort her back inside the palace. 'They love him,' she says quietly, unable to conceal her resentment. 'People are drawn to youth and beauty, always.'

'But you are the picture of –'

'Don't belittle me with the usual nonsense. I have eyes in my head. You of all people must understand.'

'Indeed,' he replies. 'Beauty is a quality that has evaded me.'

'But you have other assets.' He wonders what she believes his assets to be – loyalty perhaps, constancy, ruthlessness. Then she leans in close and whispers, 'I intend to bestow the Court of Wards on you, but shhhh, tell no one.'

'Your Majesty, I am astounded; it is too great an honour.' In his mind he is already spending the money it will generate: he will remodel the gardens at Theobalds, can imagine yew bushes shaped meticulously as classical sculptures set on either side of the entrance.

'I promised your father. It was my final benefaction to him, but mind you hold your tongue about it.'

He is fashioning a fountain in his mind: a nymph as beauteous as Lady Rich, pouring water from an amphora. But he is also thinking of how the Queen dangled the Court of Wards like a sweetmeat before Essex for months and wonders, in a sudden epiphany, if his hatred, his gross rivalry with the earl, has been generated from without rather than within. Was it the Queen, having noticed that original seed of dislike sown in boyhood, who has watered and tended its germination and set them further against each other with her subtle ministrations of favour, a titbit here, a titbit there, in order that neither became unmanageable?

'Are you not pleased? You do not seem it.'

'I am merely taking pains to hide my joy, for I fear it might arouse curiosity, madam.' Essex looms in his mind, for this is as much a triumph over his adversary as a triumph of his political career, but the thought of the earl's defeat does not affect him as he might have expected – the feeling is one of deflation.

July 1599

Leighs, Essex

Henry is chasing butterflies with Essex's boy, young Robert, both brandishing their nets like weapons, laughing as they run with Fides bouncing excitedly alongside them. Penelope sits in silence next to Lizzie Vernon, who has dozed off at her needlework with her little white dog curled into the crook of her elbow. Closing her eyes and lying back in the long grass she listens to the sounds of summer: the trickle of a stream, the distant parping of a duck and, further away, the 'hoy' of a cowherd and the gentle hollow clink of cowbells. She has been in town so long she has almost forgotten the melodies of the countryside. Her sister-in-law, Frances, is at a distance, with Dorothy. They are reading aloud to each other. Frances occasionally calls out, 'Be careful, Robert,' or, 'Not so fast, you might fall.'

Penelope laughs inwardly at her sister-in-law's caution, for Robert is as robust and reckless as his father, always bruised at the knees and with cuts on his fingers, he seems utterly without fear. Even her Henry, who is a year older, finds it hard to keep up. But Frances always was a nervy creature, a quiet little thing so easily overlooked. Even now it is hard to imagine she was once wed to Sidney. She remembers Frances on the day of Sidney's funeral saying, 'It was you he loved.' The woman has her own subtle brand of courage.

In spite of the past, Penelope has grown to like her over time, though they have little in common. Frances hasn't an ear for music and can never be coerced to express an opinion on political matters, but she is loyal to the core. She has never made much of being the Countess of Essex – there are others who would have milked the role dry, but not Frances; she values her privacy too greatly. But Frances seems more fretful than usual, worrying constantly about the infant in her belly, afraid she will lose it with all the agonizing over her husband. She is not the only one concerned about Essex. Penelope too, if she allows herself to think of what it might be like in Ireland, falls prey to the dread; it drips into her until it fills her so full there is no space left for anything else. She is thankful Blount is in London at court, 'Keeping an eye on things,' as he puts it.

A rumour is spreading that another Spanish Armada is about to make its way to England's shores and, thanks to Anthony Bacon's intelligence, Blount will be in the know before anyone else has thought of it. *She has made me Deputy General of the army*, he wrote in a letter the other day. *You are rising well with all that yeast*, had been her reply. She is not ignorant of the irony that if Blount proves himself in such a role, he may well render her brother expendable, but that is a thought that must be cached away, for she cannot bear the idea of having, someday, to pin her allegiance to one or other of them.

Things have not been going well for Essex in Ireland. He had defied the Queen's command to march north and confront Tyrone, travelling south instead to acclimatize his men and wait for provisions. He told her of the desperate need for supplies if the mission was to be a success. Penelope herself had entreated the Queen to send funds, but judging by his letter of yesterday nothing has reached him:

I fear greatly I have lost her favour altogether. I have no support from Whitehall and I can barely feed my army. She is enraged that I defied her in appointing Southampton as my Master of Horse, but she has no sense of the paramount importance of trust in the field. The Spanish are arming the rebels and it's only a matter of time before they send an army themselves. You must continue to plead my case with her, for

I have word that Cecil is profiteering from this war and monies that should be funding supplies are being diverted his way.

PS You cannot imagine what it is like here. The rebels use ambush tactics, which leaves all my men in a constant state of jitters and wholly dispirited.

She had burned the letter for fear of Frances reading it and sinking further into a mire of anxiety. There had been a violent storm an hour after Essex's departure and Frances had been near hysterical, saying it was a sign that the campaign would fail.

'No, not up the tree!' cries Frances now, getting to her feet, her eyes wide.

Robert is balancing on the gnarled trunk of an old apple tree, feet perched on a woody swelling, one arm slung over a low bough, the other stretching out with his net. He looks so much like his father that Penelope's heart lists towards the past.

'Fret not, Frances,' says Dorothy, taking her hand.

'My children have been climbing that tree since they were tots,' calls out Penelope. 'And there has not once been an accident.'

Robert jumps down, scampering off in pursuit of his butterfly, seeming entirely ignorant of his mother's concerns, and Frances settles back to her book.

Lizzie wakes, stretching with a yawn. 'Did I drop off?'

'If Mother were here she would criticize us all for being so lazy. She would have us in the dairy churning butter or making cheese or overseeing the salting of meat, or grinding herbs and distilling tinctures.' Penelope laughs at the thought of her mother: '"You idle housewife," she would say. "How can you be sure your servants are not thieving if you do not oversee them?"'

'I dreamed of Southampton,' says Lizzie, who is stroking her dog absently.

'Not a bad dream, I hope.'

'No, not bad.' Lizzie sits up and looks at her older cousin. 'But there is something troubling me about my husband.' She picks a daisy and begins to pull its petals off.

'Are you worried that war will change him?'

'I hadn't even thought of it,' Lizzie replies. 'No.'

Penelope has seen her own brother return from war altered beyond recognition – the effect of exposure to horror. He was locked into his own thoughts, completely impenetrable as if he were wrought from stone; and then would suddenly lash out to reveal a monstrous cruel streak, like a boy who swings cats by their tails to measure their screams. She doesn't say it, doesn't want to upset Lizzie, who is clearly out of sorts already.

'Tell me what it is that vexes you.'

'I love Southampton, more perhaps than most wives love their husbands.'

'But that is a good thing, Lizzie.' Penelope smiles at her young cousin, wondering what nonsense her nurse must have fed her about love and marriage: that love is a madness, that there is no place for passion in matrimony.

'But,' she hesitates, seeming not to know how to form her words and casting her eyes towards Frances and Dorothy.

'They will not hear if we speak quietly,' Penelope reassures her.

'I saw him kissing someone.'

'Oh, Lizzie.' She reaches out to take her cousin's hand. 'I wouldn't read too much into it. He still has wild oats to sow. He will settle down, I'm sure of it. I know he is fond of you. He has told me so, many times.'

'No, you don't understand.'

'Explain to me. What happened?'

'It was a while ago, when I was still carrying the baby, so we could not . . .' She reddens a little. 'You know.' Penelope nods. 'And I came upon him at Essex House in the gardens . . . with one of the servants . . .'

'One of the servants?' Penelope says, reminded of her own brother's relentless infidelities. There is surely not a servant girl left untouched at Essex House.

'In a manner of speaking.' Her skirts are scattered with shredded petals. 'One of the kitchen lads.' She says this very quietly and a tear slides down her cheek. Penelope puts an arm around her, remembering how she had felt on discovering her own husband in a similar situation and Mistress Shilling's pragmatic words. She has had her suspicions about Southampton, he is strangely androgynous and she has seen the way he behaves with the players, how drawn he is to that world of men dressed as women. In a way it is all part of his allure.

'Men's desires are not like ours, Lizzie. It does not mean he loves you less.'

'But it is a mortal sin.'

'I don't believe that.' She wishes she could tell Lizzie of her own experience, how she became tangled inextricably in a thicket of notions about sin when she was trying to make sense of her husband's case. Now they have arrived at a mutual and distant tolerance, with him here at Leighs most of the time – when he is not on her brother's shirt-tails – while she is in London or at court. 'Just a kiss – it is simply part of what makes him his own unique self. It is *that* you love.' She watches the boys over her cousin's shoulder; they are examining something in the grass. 'Do not wish him different.'

Lizzie breaks out of Penelope's arms, wiping her eyes on her sleeve. 'I thought you would be shocked. I have been so afraid to tell anyone.'

'It would take a good deal more than that to shock me. I have seen more than you could imagine. But never suffer the burden of a secret. Secrets eat away at you . . .' Her voice fades.

'But I fear he will tire of me.'

'None of us can control the desires of another. Just know

this: he is devoted to you and you are his wife and the mother of his daughter. There is no lad in the world who can give him *that*.'

'I am so very relieved,' says Lizzie, lying back on the grass, 'to have shared my secret.'

'But don't go making it common knowledge. Discretion is the thing . . . and for goodness' sake don't mention it to Frances. She would die of shock.'

Lizzie stifles a laugh, her usual verve reinstated. 'Sweet Frances, straight as a die.'

Robert is running towards them. He has the same round brown doe-eyes as his mother, but where hers flicker with timidity, his are bright and direct. He holds what appears to be a snake in his hands, the head pinched between his thumb and index finger, the rest coiled about his opposite wrist. Penelope gasps, but doesn't call out for fear of Frances looking up from her book and panicking.

She stands and moves towards him, seeing as she approaches that it is reassuringly dull green and not the patterned adder she had feared it might be. A scream of terror sounds out behind her and Penelope turns to see Frances, white as chalk, running towards them with Dorothy in pursuit.

'It's just a grass snake. It's harmless,' she calls. Dorothy is trying to calm her but Frances seems terrified, her arms flailing.

'I know how to handle a snake, Aunt Penelope,' says the boy. 'The gardeners showed me. If you grip it by the head it cannot bite.'

'It is wise to leave snakes alone, Robert, you never know. Let the poor creature go; it must be petrified.' Penelope is thinking once more of how like his father he is, apparently fearless but also oblivious to the fears of others, and she can't help turning her mind again to Essex out in Ireland, facing God knows what kind of enemy. Her nephew looks at her with surprising defiance and seems about to insist upon keeping the creature but she meets him with an expression that gives him no choice. He drops the snake to the ground and watches it slither away into the undergrowth before stomping off in a sulk to find Henry.

Despite the bright day outside, Rich's study, in the old part of the house, is dark and cool. Rich looks drawn.

'Are you quite well?' she asks.

'Do you care?'

'I care, yes. You *are* my husband, for what it's worth. And the father of my children.'

'Not the father of *all* your children.' She is surprised at this, for it is something that is rarely spoken of between them.

'No.' His eyes are hollow. She notices for the first time that he has lost his looks; however unattractive she found him, he was handsome once. She finds herself wondering if it is harder for him to entice boys into his bed these days, if he is obliged to pay them for their flesh as well as their silence. 'I have never sought to deceive you. You have what you want and so do I.'

'But you have made me a laughing stock.'

He seems so pathetic when he says this. It doesn't even occur to her to remind him that he is as much responsible for their situation as she. But a man cannot wear cuckold's horns without being the butt of a few jests. 'To hell with the jokers – at least they do not know the truth. Then you would be more than a laughing stock amongst your Puritans.'

His head seems to sink down into his shoulders and she feels truly sorry for him. 'I envy you, Penelope. I envy your insouciance, the way you seem not to care how people judge you, the confidence you have that you will always smell of roses when the rest of us have the stench of the gutter. That comes from breeding. I thought by marrying you I would have some of it for myself, that it would rub off on me.' He laughs resentfully. 'But I realize now that you have to be born to it.'

336

'What is all this?'

'I need you,' he mumbles into his collar.

'You *need* me?'

'I have a dispute over a large tract of land. I risk losing the greater part of all I own.' He pauses, turning a ring on his finger. 'But if we are seen to be united, that I have the force of your family behind me. Well then . . .' He doesn't finish, just sighs deeply. 'I am not considered seriously.'

She can see what it has taken for him to come to her begging for help. The last of his pride is in tatters. 'Of course! I will do whatever it takes. Arrange a meeting. We are man and wife and if anyone chooses to overlook such a fact, then they will have the weight of the Devereuxs on their backs.'

There might have been a time when she would have been glad of this – the knowledge that he needed her. She might have appreciated the leverage. But not now, not now she has an approximation of what she wants. Besides, she wonders for how long the Devereux name will hold such sway if her brother loses royal favour permanently. She reaches out to take his hand but he snatches it away as if she is leprous, bringing it to his forehead, so his fingers weave through his steel-streaked hair.

'I suppose you have often wished me dead.'

'What do you mean?' She is shocked to hear him say this, not because it is untrue, but because it is true. There have been occasions, but hearing him articulate it makes the guilt wind about inside her like poison ivy.

'If I were you, I would have wished it.'

She realizes only now that their situation has been so heavily weighted in her favour, for he has been trapped by his own sense of hypocrisy. His faith has condemned him to the lower rung of life. 'Do you still believe as you did?'

'My faith has had extreme challenges, but yes, despite everything I have not lost sight of God.'

'I have never believed God would condemn you for . . .'

She doesn't know how to say it. 'For where your desires have alighted.'

He drops an acerbic laugh into the silence, before saying, 'Are you trying to tell me it is not a sin?'

'We are all sinners. What I am saying is, there are worse things. Perhaps if you –'

'I don't need your suggestions,' he snaps. 'How can you possibly know what it is like to be me?'

'I cannot know. But I do know that God will find a way to forgive you.' She feels silly saying this. What does she know of his God?

'It is men rather than God I fear.'

'Tell them to look to the planks in their own eyes.'

They sit for a while, with just the occasional creak of an ancient beam punctuating their silence, and she notices it has become quite dark; night has fallen without them realizing. She is wondering about Blount. They had been hoping for a few days alone at Wanstead to celebrate the transfer of ownership of the house. It seems, though, that this business of Rich's will keep her here longer than she'd hoped; then she will need to return to court and get on her knees before the Queen, to plead her brother's part once more.

'Will you read through these and I will arrange for the meeting.' Rich hands her a thick ream of papers.

'The sooner the better,' she says. 'I am needed at court.' He looks at her askance and she continues before he has a chance to speak. 'It is for the good of us all. You stand to benefit as much as I from my connections.' She doesn't elaborate on her brother's troubles with the Queen, his lack of funds for the army; there is nothing Rich can do by knowing.

The early-morning light wakes Cecil. His bed hangings are open and he is still dressed. He sits up, confused for an instant, feeling a sharp spasm that moves from his nape and down through his shoulders. He rubs his neck with the flat of his palm – it is an age since he was properly touched by another's hand. Even his wife, in their most intimate moments, kept her hands to herself. He has sometimes paid young women, and, like his wife, they could never quite hide their disgust. But despite those women seeming clean in appearance he suffered weeks of anxiety in the aftermath of those few episodes, convinced he had contracted something unspeakable from them, scrutinizing his bodily emissions and consulting his physician repeatedly.

His page knocks softly and enters to stoke the fire. Cecil notices the paper, slightly crumpled, on the bed and remembers what it was that kept him up last night. He re-reads it, deciphering the scrawl where he supposes his man must have copied it in haste. It is from Essex to the Queen:

> *But why do I talk of victory or success? Is it not known that from England I receive nothing but discomforts and soul's wounds? Is it not spoken in the army that Your Majesty's favour is diverted from me, and that already you do bode ill both to me and it? Is it not believed by the rebels that those whom you favour most do more hate me out of faction than them out of duty and conscience?*

He is ashamed of the truth, scrawled there in black ink: that he, Cecil, hates Essex more than he hates the enemy.

Dropping the paper to his lap he mutters, 'What have I

become?' only realizing he has spoken aloud when his page replies, asking if there is anything he can do to be of service. He sends the boy away. He cannot bear a witness to his guilt; it is enough to be aware of God's all-seeing eye. Since when, he wonders, did he stop serving the Queen and England altogether? Since when did he begin serving his hatred alone?

If Essex fails in Ireland, it will be entirely Cecil's responsibility. It is he who has ensured that half the council has lost faith in Essex; he who has ensured that supplies have not been sent; he who has kept back important intelligence that might have helped the earl's cause; he who has poisoned minds against Essex's closest allies. Some of Essex's stalwarts have been recalled, and he has a direct royal order to demote Southampton from his position as Master of Horse: all Cecil's doing, one way or another. And then there is Francis Bacon . . . He scratches at some spilt wax on the table beside his bed and lines up the objects there, a candlestick, a few books, a small timepiece, the complicated workings of which used to bring him great joy, but no longer. He has lit the touchpaper to his adversary's destruction, a destruction that may well lay England open to the Spanish, and now the flame will not be extinguished.

He thinks of his botched attempt at diplomacy last summer with the new Spanish King, how high his hopes had been to carve out a peace treaty. But the whole thing that started with several careful conversations and letters exchanged with the ambassador had become a debacle. A misinterpretation of intelligence or foul play had made him believe there was a Spanish fleet gathering off the coast of Brest and invasion was imminent. He had ordered an emergency mobilization of troops under Blount, and the whole of the country was on the brink of panic, expecting invasion at any moment. He feels such a fool remembering it.

'Ah, Pygmy!' the Queen had said as he entered the watching chamber with the intention of discreetly imparting the news that had just come to him. 'Your great Spanish Armada was nothing more than a fleet of fishing boats.' She expelled a howl of laughter that was taken up by those around her, a row of eyes mocking him, open mouths filled with mirth at his expense. It was all he could do to stop himself storming from the room. He forced a small self-deprecating laugh from his lips, but the Queen had the wind behind her. 'And I suppose you think this glass bead' – she plucked at a decoration on the hat of one of her pages – 'a diamond!' Untrammelled titters ensued. 'And this pet' – she waved a hand in the direction of one of her ladies' lapdogs – 'is a wolf, I assume!'

He saw Ralegh amongst the company, shoulders heaving, and Carew with a hand over his mouth, Knollys wiping his eyes with a handkerchief. Only Francis Bacon was not laughing. He stood watching the scene, those slender hands folded together, with an expression of inscrutable indifference on his face, as if undecided as to which way he might jump.

'And this' – it was one of the Queen's ladies joining in, pointing to a flower embroidered on her dress – 'is a rose-bush.'

Cecil was wishing that the floor would swallow him up, as a stage trapdoor makes players disappear in a puff of smoke. He was rendered small, like some kind of idiotic fool, there only for the cruel amusement of the court. I am Secretary of State, he reminded himself. I am untouchable. But nothing could cut through the humiliation he was feeling that catapulted him back to the ruthless ribbing of the boys in his father's household.

'And I suppose you think *me*,' said the dwarf Ippolyta, 'the Queen herself.'

'That's a good one,' cried Ralegh. It went on and on;

even days later courtiers were coming up with ever more ingenious examples of his supposed stupidity: pigeons mistaken for peacocks, squirrels for stallions, needles for knives.

And now Cecil's dreamed-of peace treaty with Spain lies in shreds. Perhaps God is punishing him for his loathing of Essex – he knows well enough that it is a sin to hate in the way he has done. He places his hands together in an attempt at prayer, but cannot think how to form his supplications and instead tries to imagine how his father would have advised him. He might have said: *Sometimes to achieve one's ends may require deeds that are not entirely moral, but if they are for the good of Queen and country then they are justified.* He expels a puff of defeat on imagining the depth of his father's disappointment.

The door flies open, dragging him out of his torpor, and his page enters once more, flushed and out of breath.

'I thought I told you to leave me be,' barks Cecil.

'No but . . .' The boy is nervously twisting his fingers together. 'There is someone to see you. He says it is urgent.'

'Well, who is it, boy?' At this moment a man steps into the doorway, a great brute of a fellow. Cecil can't quite place him and there is nothing on his clothing to identify who he is.

'Sir Thomas Grey,' the man says, removing his headgear and dipping into a bow.

Cecil tries to remember if Grey is important. 'I assume you have news for me.' He thinks Grey might be part of the guard that was sent to protect the south coast from Spanish attack.

'It is My Lord of Essex,' says Grey.

'What about him?' Cecil's mind is agitating, wondering why this man has come to him with news of Essex. Perhaps the earl is dead. He allows that thought to percolate, feeling the first sensations of rapture.

'He is on his way here with a group of men, Southampton amongst them. They may have arrived already, for they were hot on my heels.'

'Nonsense! The earl is in Ireland.' His elation is replaced with impatience.

'I came upon his party on the road and made haste to inform you before he arrived.'

'You must be mistaken. Even the earl hasn't the audacity to leave his post without Her Majesty's permission.' He is wondering how it is possible that such an event is un-folding without his knowledge, wondering how it is that he pays so many to inform him and yet he is still in the dark.

'I hear them,' says Grey, moving towards the window. 'They are in the yard below already.'

Cecil steps the few paces to the window. He can see a number of grooms scurrying about with saddles and tack in their arms and some horses drinking at the trough, striated with sweat; it is clear that a party has arrived recently but there is no sign of the earl. Cecil is about to turn and give Grey a piece of his mind for wasting his time, when he sees the unmistakable head of trailing auburn hair. It is South-ampton disappearing through the stable arch.

'You are certain you saw Essex himself and not just his men?'

'I did most certainly, sir, with my own eyes.'

He is thinking fast now, his conscience pushed to the side. If Essex has abandoned his post it is treason. A memory flashes through his mind, of his father counsel-ling patience; *The earl might yet be the author of his own downfall*, he had said more than once. But a blanket of dread drops over him with the realization that Essex might have been driven to threaten the Queen's person. He is remembering the incident in the council chamber, when he was on the brink of drawing his sword against her.

343

Cecil suppresses the notion that it is *he* who has driven the earl to this, *he* who is to blame, and stands a moment, his hands on the sill. The vast army in Ireland is in Essex's pocket to a man – he remembers the atmosphere as the earl had left London, as if he were some kind of god. He looks out at the hills in the distance, half expecting to see the dust of an approaching army churning up a murky cloud and a line of mounted men on the horizon. He is not ready for this.

He turns, barking at his page for his gown, which he fastens hastily over his rumpled clothing. The Queen will be in her bedchamber with her ladies; he must warn her. 'What time is it?'

'The sun is barely risen,' says Grey.

'Warn the guards. Tell them that the Earl of Essex has abandoned his duty to the Queen and *must* be apprehended at all cost.'

Cecil's thoughts are whirring as he makes his way through the palace to the Queen's rooms, remembering that his head is uncovered, smoothing his hair with his palms. He almost trips on the stairs, his hem becoming entangled on his foot, but recovers and runs along the corridor holding his cumbersome gown in his fists, speculating fretfully on whether Essex has finally lost his mind and there truly is an army on its way to lay siege to Nonsuch.

He arrives at the door panting, barely able to find enough breath to tell the guards to let him in.

'The Queen is not alone,' says one of them.

Of course she is not alone, she is never alone, he is thinking but says, 'Just admit me!'

'We have orders to admit no one, sir.'

He can hear a faint commotion from behind the door. 'Who is in there?'

'The Earl of Essex, sir.'

'Tell her it is I who wishes to see her.'

'Our orders were explicit. "No one, no exceptions." I am sorry, sir.'

Cecil leans against the wall, defeated.

'Is he armed?' he asks.

'He removed his weapon before entering.' The guard points to a bench by the window, where the earl's sword has been discarded. Relief washes over him but then he begins to consider other ways the earl might do her ill, imagining a sharp poniard hidden in the folds of his shirt, or a phial of poison. He looks out once more across the countryside for evidence of an approaching army. But there is no sign.

He looks back to the guards, thinking to insist upon being granted entry, but they refuse to meet his eye, standing stiff, jaws tight, and he thinks better of it; the Queen will be surrounded by her ladies anyway.

Eventually, Essex appears in the doorway. His clothes are filthy from the road and a film of dust sits on him, collecting into dark lines around his eyes – he must have rushed directly to the Queen without stopping even to sluice his face with water. He is smiling and says, 'Good morning, Cecil,' as if it is any ordinary day. 'You look unusually dishevelled.'

'Uh . . . uh,' Cecil has lost his tongue and stands stupidly, staring at the earl as if he is an apparition and attempting to straighten his clothing, riled that he, England's most important politician, is made to feel insignificant by this wayward earl.

'You are surprised to see me? Surely your spies have told you of my whereabouts. No? You're losing control.' He laughs, picks up his sword, slinging the belt over his shoulder and strides away, whistling. Just as he reaches the end of the corridor he turns, saying with a smirk, 'You won't be admitted. She's not dressed yet,' as if laying claim to the Queen's body.

Cecil feels the hatred well once more as he rushes back to his rooms, to dress himself properly and give orders for scouts to be sent out to assess whether the earl has support in the vicinity.

Once done, he sits as his page polishes his shoes to a sheen, awaiting the Queen's summons. By the time he is called he is spick and span in black velvet. He asks his boy to brush his shoulders one more time before making his way back to her rooms, glad to find the guard has been changed. The pair who had witnessed his agitated dithering and his demeaning exchange with Essex are nowhere to be seen.

The Queen is with three of her women, who are putting the finishing touches to her outfit: one pinning a large jewel on to her dress, another helping her into her over-gown and the third slinging about her neck a string of plump pearls, that hangs down lower than her belly.

'I am glad to see you,' she says with a taut smile, sending her women to the far reaches of the chamber with a brisk wave of the hand. 'Come closer.' He approaches and sits on the stool beside her. 'I suppose word has reached you that Essex has . . .' she pauses, clearing her throat, 'returned.'

Cecil nods. 'I have been made aware of the situation, madam, and took the liberty of ensuring that he came only with –'

'Without an army,' she interrupts. 'Yes. He told me himself that he was only accompanied by a trusted coterie. "Enough to protect his person" was, I think, how he put it. But I am glad you had the wherewithal to see to it that we are not about to be laid to siege. We wouldn't last long in this place, would we?' She makes a little snort of laughter. It is true Nonsuch was built for pleasure, not to resist an army. She seems astonishingly calm and Cecil can feel his old admiration burgeoning.

'What was his business?'

The Queen leans her elbow on the arm of her chair and rests her chin on the heel of her hand. 'He made a truce with Tyrone.' Her eyes darken, revealing her fury. 'My *enemy*, Tyrone.'

'The single thing you commanded him not to do.'

She nods slowly. 'I am betrayed, Pygmy. It looks like surrender.' He is strangely glad to hear the old pet name. It makes him feel closer to her. 'They will all think that the English have capitulated.' By 'they' Cecil supposes she means the whole of Europe. 'I've called the council,' she nods her head in the direction of the door to the inner chamber. 'But wanted to give you the full picture before we go in.'

'If I may be so bold, I would suggest that the earl be put under lock and key. You cannot be seen to be —'

'Yes, yes, my indulgence has been stretched to the limit. We will make a list of charges.' She sighs, closing her eyes, dispirited. 'I shall sign it myself.'

'I am most sorry for this, madam,' says Cecil. The swelling of his conscience is dampening the thrill of victory. 'It is doubly distressing when it is those you love who betray you.'

'I loved him as if he were my own son.' Cecil thinks he can see her resolve harden as she adds, 'But he is not my son. He is the son of my enemy.'

September 1599

Barn Elms/Nonsuch

The room is shuttered and silent, save for the soft bustle of the midwife folding linens in the corner and the trembling susurration of Frances's breath. Penelope had removed the clock as Frances said its tick made her anxious. Frances lies on the bed in the gloom, curled on her side, holding a pillow as if it is a lover. 'God save me,' she murmurs, reaching for Penelope's hand. 'I fear this infant will kill me.'

'You must not allow such thoughts. This baby will be born, as have all your others.' Penelope can't bear to look at her big sad eyes. She remembers the dread she herself felt in the days before her babies were birthed, each time wondering if God would take her. 'I will sing to soothe you.' Penelope hesitates a minute, her head suddenly infested with an inappropriate ballad about a woman of loose morals that she heard at the Curtain Theatre the other day. So she picks up her lute and strums without singing. The midwife begins to hum along. They have already been waiting a full day and a half since the first labour pains came.

'Promise you will not leave me,' says Frances, grabbing Penelope's wrist. Her face is screwed tightly as if she is trying hard to prevent herself from crying.

'As long as I am needed I shall remain.' Penelope does not relish the idea of a birth – the blood and the screaming and the hours and hours of fretful waiting and always the possibility of death, brightly denied, yet looming. 'I will be aunt to this little one. Of course I wish to welcome him into the world.' They had hung Frances's wedding ring on a length of her hair and dangled it like a pendulum over her belly, as they always do for amusement in the longs days waiting for a birth. The ring had swung cleanly back and forth, indicating a boy, and they had congratulated her, though they all know it is just as likely to be a girl.

Lizzie Vernon appears in the doorway, beckoning Penelope. She slips out into the corridor. There is alarm in Lizzie's expression and she is squeezing her hands together tightly so her knuckles are white. 'What is it?' Penelope is going through the possible sources of her cousin's vexation: a case of plague in the household, someone they know committed to the Tower, a death in Ireland. She swallows.

'Your brother is under arrest.'

'What do you mean? Has he been taken prisoner?' She tries not to think of the stories she has heard of the brutal way the Irish treat their captives, consoling herself with the thought that Essex would be political leverage for them; it would not be in their interests to harm such a jewel.

'No, I fear it is worse.'

'Worse, what could be worse if he is not dead? What is it you are not saying, Lizzie?'

'He is at Nonsuch.'

'I don't understand. Where did you dig up this fantasy?'

'I had word from Southampton. They are together. Essex made a truce with Tyrone, and they rode hard from Ireland' – Lizzie is speaking fast, barely drawing breath – 'so he could explain himself to the Queen, before his enemies at court got wind of it and poisoned her mind to him.'

The information settles into her like a large object sinking in a body of water. 'And the Queen –'

'She let him explain himself initially and he seemed to think he was understood. But then she called a council meeting and since has ordered him arrested. Now she' – Lizzie pulls a letter from her sleeve and reads from it – 'sees it as a betrayal. Says he has surrendered to the Irish against her specific command. He is being held in rooms at Nonsuch.' She pauses, still scanning the paper. 'They are calling it treason.'

349

Penelope sinks on to the bench beside the door, sensing cold fingers of panic reaching for her.

'He says you must go to him. Southampton will wait for you at the sign of the keys in Ewell. He will make sure you get to your brother unseen.'

Penelope rifles in the drawer of a nearby desk, finding paper, quills and ink, hurriedly scrawling a note to Alfred the groom at Essex House, instructing him to bring horses in haste. She seals the paper and calls to one of the pages to deliver it.

'I'm sure I can find a way out of this.' Her voice is brisk, revealing nothing of her chilling sense of foreboding. She fears that her brother has gone too far this time, fears that he has used up the last shreds of the Queen's good will and that all the Devereuxs' painstakingly laid plans are about to go up in flames. What was it the Queen said of her lenience? That it was not infinite. It is a sickening thought. 'Would you get word to Dorothy?' she says. 'Ask her to inform Mother, and can you stay with Frances? She's in a terrible state and I promised I wouldn't leave but . . .'

'Of course, anything you want.'

'Don't tell her what the real reason for my absence is. We mustn't give her another source of apprehension. Think of a white lie.'

When Alfred arrives he has a couple of Essex House guards with him carrying torches. He asks no questions, though he must wonder what this night dash to Nonsuch, with Penelope improperly dressed, wearing just a heavy cloak over her petticoats, is all about. As they set off into the night, Penelope tries not to think about the thieves and brigands they might encounter travelling in the dark. She girds herself with a swig from the flask that Alfred offers and the fact that she has three strapping men to protect her, though on second glance one of the guards looks to be barely out of boyhood.

'How long should it take?' she asks.

'It's under twenty miles. If we make haste once we're on to open land, we should be there well before dawn.'

They ride without speaking, glad of the clement weather and the moon, which is not far off full. Penelope allows herself to be lulled by the steady beat of the horses' hooves, the puff of her own exhalation adding to the rhythm and the murmur of the passing wind like a drone string beneath the melody. She follows in Alfred's wake, glad to be in his safe hands; he knows this route well enough, has ferried the family back and forth to Nonsuch many a time. He has served the Devereuxs longer than anyone and is loyal to the core. There have been some amongst the Essex House staff who she is sure have sold secrets and one long ago in the kitchens whom she discovered was on Cecil's payroll. She persuaded him to turn on his master but he died of the plague before he had a chance to be of any use.

She can see the dark shapes of buildings up ahead. 'Is that Ewell?'

'It is, My Lady.'

They walk along the grassy mound in the middle of the road so as to make less noise – the fewer who are aware of a party of riders arriving in the dead of night, the better. She sees the sign of the keys, its gilding glowing in the moonlight, and there beneath it are two figures. She is relieved to see the unmistakable silhouette of Southampton, his long hair and the fitted cut of his doublet, realizing only after that the man beside him is Blount. Her heart bloats and it is all she can do to stop herself from leaping from her horse and running into his arms. They dismount quietly; she feels Blount's hand take hers and is reassured by his presence, knowing his support will see her through whatever it is that awaits her. He whispers, close to her ear, 'My darling one.'

They leave the horses with Alfred and make their way on foot. The palace looms, a shadowy shape, above the village, its twisted turrets dark against the sky, which is beginning to take on the first blush of dawn. Southampton explains the situation as they walk, keeping tight into the hedgerows so as not to be seen. The birds have begun to sing, trilling out their incongruously pretty morning tunes. 'How is he?' she asks.

'It is hard to say,' replies Southampton.

'How will you get me in unseen?'

'The night guards have served under me,' says Blount. 'A full purse works wonders.'

'It will lift his spirits to see you,' says Southampton.

'His wife is in her childbed as we speak. I think it best he doesn't know – just one more thing to vex him.'

'How is she?' asks Blount.

'Nervous. You know what she's like.'

They enter the rear court silently, hugging the walls and slipping in the door to the servants' stairs. They hear footsteps and see the glow of a candle on the turn of the wall. Blount pushes her into the shadows, standing in front of her so she can't be seen. She pulls up her hood and gathers the dark fabric of her cloak tightly about her.

'Up early, My Lords.' It is one of the ushers, rubbing sleep from his eyes.

Her heart is thumping so loudly she fears they will hear it.

'Actually,' says Southampton, nudging the man conspiratorially, 'we have not yet been to bed.'

'There's not much carousing to be had round here, dead as a doornail,' says the usher.

'You'd be surprised what can be found in a rural village.' Southampton winks. The usher's eyes brighten, his curiosity clearly aroused.

'Better be getting to bed,' says Blount, feigning a yawn and stretching his arms out. The usher bids them good morning, moving on down the stairs.

'That one's in Cecil's pocket,' whispers Blount. 'But he seemed convinced by our tale of debauchery.'

'So convinced, one might think you were up to such things all the time,' she teases. Her anxieties have receded a little in his presence but as they arrive and see the two men at the door, their halberds propped up beside them against the panelling, her throat dries out. Blount produces a purse from his doublet, passing it to one of them. The man weighs it in the palm of his hand, and loosens its drawstring, holding up a candle and peering in to verify he is not being duped, as if these men before him are not two of the realm's greatest peers but common market hawkers. He nods eventually and lifts the latch on the door, allowing Penelope to pass through. She wonders if the guards recognize her, bundled up as she is with her face obscured by her hood and none of her usual finery, or if they believe her to be nothing but one of Essex's lowborn mistresses come to comfort him in his hour of misfortune.

Essex sits crouched on the floor in the corner of the chamber in the gloom and makes no move to stand as she enters. The vague glow of early dawn barely makes it beyond the window, and the fire is just an ashy pile. She takes the poker, prodding the hearth until a vivid glow appears, throwing on some kindling and then tips in the half-bucket of coal that sits nearby. It catches easily, the flames fluttering up in blue and orange ribbons. She wipes her black-smudged palms on her cloak and, taking a candle from the mantelpiece, lights it from the fire, then touches it to the others about the room. Their wicks fizz as they flare. 'Things cannot be so bad if she has allowed you coal and beeswax candles, Robin.' She tries to sound bright, to draw him out of his torpor.

His reply is a vinegary laugh. She goes to sit beside him. The cold of the stone flags cuts straight through her clothes and his hand beneath hers is icy and unresponsive to her touch. After a time in silence she coaxes him to shuffle reluctantly closer to the hearth, which is now fully ablaze, throwing light and warmth into the chamber. His face is pallid and gaunt, as if he hasn't eaten in days, and his haunted expression tugs painfully at her heart.

'It would have been better I'd died a hero's death in Ireland,' he mutters, looking at her at last with those empty eyes.

'No, no!' she says, drawing him to her. He allows himself to be enveloped in his sister's embrace. 'Where's that fighting spirit, Robin?'

'She says I made an alliance with England's enemy. It's not true.' His voice is plaintive. 'It was nothing but a temporary truce. All those carpet knights round the council table send commands to do this or do that, but they have no idea what it is like out there. It's brutal, Sis, and I risked too much. My men would have been slaughtered. I truly believed I had done the thing that was best for England, and now it is called treason.' He looks directly at her, and she is glad to see his eyes are now wild with anger. Anger is better than torpor. 'I'd like to see Cecil handle himself under an Irish onslaught, the ambushes, never knowing when or where we might be attacked, the mud, the wet, the fear, the sickness, the hunger, the lack of supplies. Our supplies never came. I can only think that crookbacked rodent was behind that.'

'My poor, poor boy,' she says, stroking his hair.

He breaks away, sitting upright. 'I discovered things out there, Sis, things about Father that I wish I didn't know. He committed terrible acts, inhumane, so far removed from any code of chivalry . . .' He stops, holding his head in his hands. 'That place drives you to brutality. But I wouldn't . . .' He seems unable to articulate what it is he wants to say. 'I wouldn't . . .'

'I know.'

'But you don't know. I wouldn't be driven to such savagery. That is why I made the truce. I did not inherit Sidney's sword to fall into barbarity.'

'You have right on your side, Robin. God will recognize that.'

354

'I would sooner not make my case to Him just yet.'

'We shall get you out of this. You are not alone.' She can sense his spirit stir a little. 'I am here with you and there are many who will be prepared to stand at your side – the whole army, I wouldn't doubt. And we have the Scottish King behind us, remember.' She is chilled by her own words, for the end point of the army's involvement, Scotland's involvement, means . . . what does it mean? She cannot even think it. There must be another way to secure her brother's freedom.

'You must take this.' He fumbles inside his shirt, pulling out the black leather purse containing James's letters, lifting it over his head and handing it to her. 'I am to be taken into the Lord Keeper's care under guard at York House and I can't risk it being found.'

'Has he written recently?'

Her brother nods. 'We are all in accord.'

'So if the worst comes to the worst we can put *him* on the English throne a little earlier than expected.' She slaps her hand over her mouth, barely able to believe she has said this out loud, but they have all thought it: her, Essex, their mother, Blount, Southampton . . . the list goes on. This is about survival. 'But we are *not* at that stage. If she would just name King James the entire country could breathe a sigh of relief. It is the uncertainty that does the damage.'

'We are not at that stage *yet*,' he echoes.

'You have to muster all your charm with her and I will do everything in my power to secure your release.' She looks straight at him, attempting a smile. 'Once you are out we can think about our alternatives. I wouldn't put it beyond her to forgive you – stranger things have happened – but it depends on who is whispering in her ear.' She doesn't need to mention Cecil by name. 'Look, I must leave before the palace is up. But trust me, Robin.' She stands, pulling him to his feet.

'I'm frightened,' he says, his voice small. He has said this before and she supposes herself to be the only soul he can confess such weakness to. She is reminded of Frances birthing his baby back at Barn Elms, swathed in dread, and wonders how it is that she became the one to contain all the fears of the family – the one who can never be afraid.

She kisses him on both cheeks. 'I am by your side.' And she slips out of the chamber where Blount is waiting to take her back to Ewell.

Once they are beyond the palace gates, she pushes him up against a tree and kisses him with a desperate urgency, as if somehow it will give her strength. She closes her eyes, losing herself for a moment in the firmness of his hold, feeling the urgent pulse of his heart pressed hard to her breast, enveloped in the soft murmur of his breath. Tears suddenly surprise her, stinging behind her eyes. She allows them to come, in great sobs. Blount says nothing, just holds her tight until they have subsided. Then he whispers, 'Whatever happens, I am yours.'

December 1599

Whitehall

Lady Rich and her sister approach Cecil in the long gallery at a sedate pace. He is seated in one of the alcoves awaiting a summons from the Queen. Now Essex is in decline – three months of incarceration and no sign he will be forgiven – the Chief Minister of England must rise up and make his mark.

The women both nod, saying, 'Good day, Minister,' in unison, their insincerity not entirely hidden. They are both dressed in mourning, though no one in their family has died. It is a gesture of support for their brother who festers at York House and is said to be gravely ill. It has caused a great deal of gossip and a number of other ladies have taken to wearing black feathers in support. The Queen has assiduously ignored all the ersatz mourning, though when the bell at Clement Danes was erroneously tolled to mark the earl's demise and was the catalyst for a great outpouring of grief, she asked one of her ladies who it was that had passed away. Cecil watched the colour drop from her face, as the lady answered. Even the thick white paint could not hide her distress. She had to reach out to the back of a chair for support and pretend she was light-headed from lack of nourishment.

Where black drains the colour from most women's complexions, these two, who are so alike, are rendered quite lovely by it, Lady Rich in particular. Her sister, though undeniably beautiful, is like a copy of a great painting: delightful, yet lacking the perfection and depth of the original. Lady Rich seems not to care how she looks: her clothes, on close inspection, are carelessly put together, dirty hems and pulled threads; she goes unrouged, her ruff wilts and her nails are ragged, everything a little higgledy-piggledy, and all this conspires to confound a man like Cecil who strives for order.

Inexplicably, she still fascinates him as she did when he first laid eyes on her. Cecil reminds himself that they are the same age, but she wears her thirty-six years lightly and could be a decade younger. The exhausted reflection he encountered in the glass this morning bears testament to each and every one of his own years. Lady Rich's allure is a puzzle. Beauty alone means nothing in a place where loveliness is the currency, and her age cannot compete with the youthful flesh that adorns the privy chamber; her ruthless intelligence, too, ought to poison her charm, but somehow all these things conspire to bewilder convention. Even so, Cecil has long been baffled by the extent to which Blount has fallen under her spell. He could make a fine match, a great heiress, good blood, but he remains loyal to a woman he cannot wed and accepts having bastards for children. Cecil would never go *that* far.

He smiles at them, tilting his head politely. 'To you too, Lady Rich, Lady Northumberland.' To his surprise they stop, hovering over him, and out of politeness he makes to stand.

'No need to get up, *My Lord*,' says Lady Rich with a suspiciously warm smile, and her emphasis on 'My Lord' makes it seem as if she is mocking him for having a title only of office and not of heredity. It renders his recently acquired role of Lord Privy Seal seem somehow tawdry.

He picks a spot of dust from his sleeve, feeling, now, a little disadvantaged at being seated while they tower above him. 'You must be delighted by Lord Mountjoy's appointment to the Irish post, Lady Rich.' He cannot help himself. Blount has been doing everything in his power to convince the Queen that he is not cut out for the job and a little bird at Essex House has told him of Lady Rich's distress on hearing of her lover's appointment.

'Quite overjoyed,' she says without missing a beat. 'It is a consummate opportunity for him. One is always happy for the success of a dear friend. We are all delighted, isn't that so, Dorothy?' The sister nods in agreement. That smile is still spread over Lady Rich's face. 'You look tired, Cecil,' she adds, bending down to pick up the little dog that is at her heel. 'You have a wonderful estate at Theobalds. You might benefit from a rest there.'

Is she mocking him with a silken insult? All he wants to do is reach out and stroke her cheek to see if it is truly as velvety as it appears.

'The affairs of state do not wait for any man to rest.'

'Perhaps you should acquire a pet,' she says, stroking the dog's head. 'A little furred companion is most soothing for the troubled soul.'

He is wondering if his own troubled soul registers on his countenance and is framing a smooth smile in the hope of disguising it, when she plops her spaniel into his lap. Horrified, he pushes the filthy thing off. The sister puts a hand to her mouth, feigning a cough, which is surely laughter.

'Poor Fides,' coos Lady Rich, taking the animal in her arms, allowing it to lick her face. Cecil's stomach turns and he brushes at the white hairs it has left on his jet-black hose. 'He is not accustomed to rejection.'

'Nor is your brother, it would seem. He has been sulking for months.' As the words leave his mouth he regrets rising to her provocation, but he cannot stay them.

Lady Rich surprises him with another smile, entirely incongruous with the content of her words. 'My brother is gravely ill, he is under lock and key with Death knocking at his door and he is not even permitted a visit from his loving sister, nor his wife who has lately given him a daughter. I feel sure that with your influence' – she touches his shoulder, allowing her hand to rest there lightly for a moment – 'you could persuade Her Majesty to at least give me leave to see him.' Only then does the smile drop from her face. 'I truly fear for his life.'

'My influence is not so great in this matter as might be thought. I should like to see the earl released into more comfortable surroundings where he can regain his health, as much as you, but the Queen is quite adamant.' This is partly true. His conscience has been troubling him, but he has the upper hand at last. There can be only a single victor in his power struggle with the earl, and Cecil has discovered that his integrity is no match for his will to win.

She then bends forward to hiss in his ear. 'I know your game, Cecil.'

He feels himself hardening and a gush of heat rises from his groin to his face. Try as he might he cannot tear his gaze from the smooth white mounds of Lady Rich's bosom. He forces his eyes to the bland rush matting on the floor, focusing on the plaited weave, counting the rows and taking several steady breaths.

'If I were you,' he says, once he is composed and has managed to place his own disingenuous smile on to his face, 'I would take care.'

'Of what, exactly?' This is Lady Northumberland, who stands with her hands on her hips.

'Your sister's presence at Essex House seems to have become a magnet for disaffected supporters of the earl's cause.' Lady Rich appears not to be listening and stands cooing to the dog in her arms as if it is a baby. 'They seem to think she will take up your brother's part in his absence. The Queen senses the rumblings of rebellion in the air. She does not like it.'

'There are just a few waifs and strays gathering there,' says Lady Rich, looking up from the pet, not seeming discomfited in the slightest. 'Whether they are loyal to my brother is neither here nor there, and they are mistaken if they think I will take up any kind of cause. But they are welcome at Essex House. Did not St Peter himself tell us to be hospitable?'

He brushes at his hose again, plucking off another dog hair, while he tries to find a suitable retort. 'How can you be sure there is not a Judas amongst them?' He thinks of Francis Bacon who is, under his own commission, poring over that tract of under a year ago that compared the earl to Henry IV, scrutinizing it for any slight sniff of treason and the means to send Essex to the block. Bacon, the sly fox, had approached Cecil with the tract when the earl was leaving for Ireland, since when Cecil has done everything in his power to suppress the publication; the last thing he needs is the masses conceiving of the earl as some kind of heroic Henry IV figure. Next thing they would want to see him on the throne. More peculiar things have happened and Essex does have a measure of royal blood. Fortunately, Cecil had succeeded in keeping the tract from the general public. But now it might be of use to him if it can cast the earl in a light of treachery.

When Bacon had first handed it to Cecil he had made the gesture seem offhand, but Cecil sensed his cousin was ready to change his affiliation. He must be delighted now to have put his money on the winning cock. Cecil wonders if Anthony is aware of his brother's defection. Francis says not, but then he might be playing a duplicitous game – he is doubtless clever enough –

Lady Rich interrupts his thoughts. 'A Judas! One can never be sure. Besides, I will soon be at Richmond for Christmas so all my brother's admirers will have to gather elsewhere.' The way she uses the term 'admirers' makes the dissenting rabble sound like a circle of poets. Then, taking her sister's elbow, she turns and walks away towards the Queen's rooms, leaving Cecil straightening his collar and adjusting the lacing on his doublet, with the distinct feeling that he has been taken for a fool.

December 1599

Richmond Palace

The Christmas festivities in anticipation of the new century have an air of feverish excitement, more so than usual. It is as if the Queen must shore herself up with pleasure. There has been feasting of gargantuan proportions, at each meal course after course of poultry is served; every feathered fowl Penelope has ever heard of and some she hasn't, spatch-cocked, or spit-roasted, or boiled, or baked, or stuffed one inside the other and cooked in a coffin. And then the meat: entire sides of venison, great knuckle joints of mutton, hams as big as soldiers' thighs, suckling pigs, thick slices of beef served with indigestible vegetables from the New World, and salads and pies and tarts and custards and suckets and cheeses, until it seems there cannot be a bird or beast or plant left alive in the land.

The presence chamber is garlanded with decorations; the Queen sits in there every night and cannot be persuaded to retire until the last dance has been danced, the final song has been sung and the very dregs of the wine have been glugged back. Her older ladies sit in heaps on cushions, yawning, barely able to keep their eyes open, whilst the young ones skip about the boards until they have holes in their slippers and still the Queen cries out for more.

Penelope stands in the gallery with her sister, watching the revelries continuing below, sickened by it all, thinking of her brother, locked away at York House. He ails from something and can neither sleep nor eat. Penelope fears he will not live the week and still she has not seen him, despite trying every-thing. She even offered one of his guards an emerald hung from a string of pearls that had been a gift from Blount. The jewel almost persuaded him, he had it in the palm of his hand and inspected it with bright eyes, but just as the deal was about to be struck he had a change of heart; she supposed he had been threatened with dire consequences. She has pleaded with God until her knees are bruised but in her heart she knows it will take more than prayer to save her brother.

The worry is wearing her thin. Responsibility falls to her but she fears she has not the strength to hold up the Devereuxs alone. Dorothy provides a little moral support but, as when they were children, it is Penelope who is expected to engineer a miraculous solution. Lettice has taken a house in Richmond near the palace and has been pressing Penelope to do more to help her brother. 'You know how to deal with Elizabeth. *You* have had her favour for years,' she had said. 'Find a way.'

Penelope could hear the bitterness beneath her words, as if her mother were casting around for someone to blame. 'I am doing all I can,' was her reply.

'Anyone would think you cared nothing for your brother.'

Stung, Penelope said, 'We must not let this pull us apart. I love my brother as much as you do.'

'You are right.' Lettice slumped in despair. 'That woman means to take every last person I have ever loved from me.'

She spots Moll Hastings below, sitting to the side, and is flooded with memories of the maids' chamber, the gossip, the romantic intrigues. How straightforward life was then, though she hadn't thought it so at the time. Wild Moll leading them all astray, peevish cousin Peg – she died in childbed – and Martha, whatever happened to Martha? Moll has never wed, forced to live out her whole life at court. She remembers how their heads all turned like sunflowers as Sidney passed by, and lines of poetry alight in her mind: *Let my whispering voice obtain / Sweet reward for sharpest pain.* When she reflects on it with the wisdom of distance, she understands how Sidney recreated her with his poetry, formed out of the parts of her a woman who did not exist, yet one who still endures in words – will continue to do so after she is gone. That creation is a woman she is often mistaken for, but not by Blount. For Blount she is flesh and blood. Yet she feels Sidney's loss even now, even after so much else has come to pass. She will not lose her brother too.

Penelope has beseeched the Queen, countless times, to allow her a single visit to her sick brother, to no avail. And now it is Christmas, Elizabeth is in a frenzy of pleasure and will be petitioned no more. She considers the excesses of the season, wondering what God, who asks for moderation in all things, must think of such carousing. Looking down, she seeks out Blount, who is beside the Queen. She is laughing, her head thrown back. Penelope watches her lover recite a ballad, which has amused the Queen so greatly she wants to hear it over and over again. Penelope keeps herself out of the way. Her last encounter with the Queen was a frosty one indeed and she fears it will not be long before she too is asked to leave court – or worse.

A hurdy-gurdy starts up with a relentlessly jaunty Christmas tune and people line up on the floor to dance. The Queen claps along. Despite her merry mask – the elaborate dress cut obscenely low, the painted face, the ropes of pearls – she looks old. Her increasingly bad eyesight makes her seem befuddled as she confuses one person for another, and her intransigence has hardened as it does in the elderly. It is no wonder her subjects – the ordinary men and women who live outside the bubble of court – are apprehensive; no wonder there has been unrest. They are gripped with the fear, though no one dares say it, that she will die before she names an heir and chaos will reign – that has always been the fear but now she has passed her three score years the dread has hardened. The Queen still lives in her glory days but England is spent, her people are starving and the terror of Spanish attack lurks. The uncertainty is like a poison seeping into every crevice of the realm. It is no wonder men turned to her brother. He became a figure of hope, but now . . . it hollows her out to think of him in his lonely prison.

'Look,' says Dorothy, nodding her head to where the Queen has taken Blount's hand to be led to the floor, as the musicians start up another dance. All Penelope can think of is her brother last Christmas, dancing hand-in-hand with the Queen, as Blount is now. How they had all been teeming with optimism then – the favourite returned to the fold. Blount is dancing with her now and soon it will be *him* in the Irish mud.

'How history repeats itself,' she whispers. Unease sits over her, blocking her light.

She can see her husband down there too, wandering about, trying to ingratiate himself with a group of privy councillors – he has been less than useless in advancing Essex's case, but even he is doing his best. At least his coffers remain full and he hadn't lost that land dispute, thanks to her intervention. Cecil is lurking with his cronies; he glances up, catching her eye – she doesn't smile, and nor does he – before he turns away sharply. She remembers her encounter with him the other day at Whitehall with a shiver of disgust; the way he looks at her, as if she is one of those spatchcocked chickens on the Christmas table, makes her flesh crawl. As he swings high on fortune's wheel the Devereuxs are plummeting. That man's influence has become unassailable. She cogitates exhaustively on how to shift that wheel back in their favour.

She feels sure that it is Cecil behind Blount's appointment to Ireland. He had talked of it with such insouciance, as if they are all marionettes, there to enact his own drama while he pulls the strings unseen. But she girds herself with the thought that perhaps Cecil will regret giving Blount charge of the greatest army ever mustered. She absently touches her fingers to the thong about her neck that holds the leather purse hidden beneath her clothes. Cecil thinks he knows everything but perhaps there are things he will never know, until it is too late.

She can see him now, whispering something to Francis Bacon, who is folding and unfolding his delicate hands. She knows Francis Bacon can't be trusted, there is something sly-eyed about clever Francis – too clever for his own good – that always raised misgivings in her, and now she has proof. It was his brother, Anthony, who first discovered that Francis was now Cecil's ally. 'Do nothing, My Lady,' he had advised. 'We shall watch on, silently. We may be able to use this know-ledge to our advantage.' She saw then how deep Anthony's loyalty was to the Devereuxs, that he would put Essex's cause before brotherly love.

The hurdy-gurdy blares on, its insistent drone penetrating her skull. The beginnings of a headache descend, the slight burn of light at the edges of things that heralds hours of pain in a darkened room.

'Penelope!' her sister says, jolting her from her thoughts. 'I think Blount is trying to get your attention.' She looks down to see that he has been released from the Queen's clutches and is looking up towards her.

'Come up,' she mouths and he slips out of sight towards the steps.

'Do you think, if the worst comes to the worst, that Northumberland will take up our cause?' she says to Dorothy.

'The worst comes to the worst?' Dorothy's face is aghast. Dear Dorothy, who always believes things will turn out well.

'Best be prepared, that's all I meant,' Penelope says lightly, but her sister remains glum.

'My husband is barely speaking to me,' she confides. 'Says he wants nothing to do with my "family's troubles". Or that was how he put it.'

'Do you think he sides with Cecil?'

'To be honest, I think he wants no part of any of it. Besides, it will not come to that. The Queen will forgive our Robin, as she always has.'

Penelope wants to tell her that this time is different, but wonders then why she is even thinking of this when Essex lies at death's door. Perhaps it is that she cannot imagine a world without him in it. Her life has been defined by her family and with her brother at its helm. If only she could get him released into her care, she could surely nurse him back to health. Her throat begins to silt up with unwanted emotion.

'Yes, of course she will forgive him.' She does her best to give Dorothy a hopeful smile, thinking through what she truly means by 'the worst'. There are so many potential scenarios, and none of them good: Essex could die alone under lock and key; he could be sent to the Tower to rot; he could be tried and executed for treason. She remembers the feather that had lodged in his shoulder, just a stray plume from a pillow that had found its way beneath his skin like a splinter and drifted to the floor when she removed it. But now Essex has begun his own slow fall, she cannot help but think it was a sign.

A sharp flare of pain moves through her head. She can sense Cecil pulling the strings of the situation; the Queen, though she is entirely oblivious, dances to *his* tune. As long as she continues to refuse to nominate her successor, Cecil can play each potential heir off against the other and position himself to his own best advantage. If she didn't loathe the man so greatly she might admire him for his guile. She feels girded suddenly, committed to renewing her efforts to ensure the Scottish King is named, for England's sake as much as her family's, but she is bereft of influence now. Most urgently, she must secure her brother's release.

Someone takes her hand; she turns to see it is Blount and they sidle back into the shadows where they cannot be seen from below.

'I have persuaded the Queen to let me stay another month, until February,' he says.

'I should be thankful for small mercies.' She cannot allow herself to think of his departure, to see him in that hellish place her brother described, or she may lose her grip on things.

'I want you,' he says quietly, his voice rasping with desire, as if it is only in her arms that he can forget about the death and brutality he must face.

'If only Rich were not here.' They both know she must give the impression, at least, of being the virtuous wife. It would be going too far to spend the night with her lover whilst her husband was at court. They have both become used to their snatched moments of pleasure – it has been nine years, after all, that their love has been stretched and bent to fit other people's lives.

'We will carve ourselves out a few days together at Wanstead before I leave.'

She rests her head briefly on his shoulder. 'I hope –' she begins, but stops herself. She was going to say that she hopes circumstances involving her brother will not escalate and prevent them from having their moment together. It does not need saying, they all pray for Essex's release, for his recovery. 'I don't know what more I can do to help him.'

The hurdy-gurdy gives way to a pipe and fiddle, easing the discomfort in her head. She can hear the chink of the ladies' jewels and the thump of their feet as they dance.

'There is no doubt the Queen is acting on the counsel of your brother's enemies,' says Blount.

'Cecil,' she says.

'Primarily.'

'What if I were to write to the Queen and point out that there are those close to her motivated by private revenge and personal ambition rather than *her* best interests. Men who would rather bring down my brother than do what is right for England. I might remind her that Essex hasn't had the chance to defend himself.'

'You would risk a great deal. The Queen could take it in the wrong spirit and, as for Cecil . . .'

'It might unsettle him into an error,' she says. 'And I have an idea as to how to make sure he gets his eyes on it.' She has a spark of clarity.

'How so?'

'I will ensure Francis Bacon sees it. He is the hole in our ship.'

'Bacon has turned?'

She nods. 'I can only imagine he thinks the opportunities are greater on the other side. But he could be unwittingly useful.' She thinks of the man, his boyish face, a picture of innocence, and the way he punctuates his conversation with that sniff – the tic that gives him away.

Blount squeezes her waist, smiling. 'My God, Penelope, Cecil has a mighty adversary in you.'

'I simply work in my brother's interests. You know that, Charles.'

He leans in close. 'I have sent word to the Scottish King that once in Ireland, with the army behind me, I can secure your brother's release by marching into England and *forcing* the Queen to name James as heir. I suggested that his support would guarantee success.'

Her head begins to spin. The stakes have been raised to an unthinkable level and, rather than fear, her prevailing feeling is something akin to excitement. 'Have you heard from him?'

'I await his response. Such a plan would be suicide without his agreement.'

She has long stood on the brink of a precipice; now she must leap, and either she will fly or fall. 'Let us hope my letter to the Queen does its job and that it doesn't come to that.' She pauses, looking at him. 'We are up to our ears in danger.'

'Don't forget that I am yours, whatever happens, and that I have thirteen thousand armed men who will do my bidding.'

He pulls her into him, kissing her hard on the lips before peeling away and slipping off back down the stairs. She returns to Dorothy's side at the balcony, hooking an arm through her sister's and perusing the scene below. The dancers appear the worse for wear and the musicians are out of key. 'We Devereuxs will need to stand strong as ever these months to come,' she says quietly. In her mind she is already formulating her letter.

'That letter . . .' Cecil looks at Francis Bacon. His beard has been carefully combed and trimmed, his ruff is bright white and reassuringly well starched – Cecil supposes he must have a Dutch laundress. Francis Bacon blinks slowly, like a reptile, and Cecil asks himself, not for the first time, whether the man can be trusted. 'Lady Rich made all kinds of veiled accusations in it. The Queen was not at all pleased at the time. But its effect seems to have fizzled out. I thought we could make more advantage of the Queen's displeasure.'

Cecil walks over to the door, opens it far enough to put his head through and looks up and down the corridor. There is no one there. As he returns to the room he runs a hand along the hangings, just to be sure no one is concealed there. He can hear a gaggle of maids in the garden below, shrieking. There has been a late snowfall, several inches in an hour, and they are throwing the stuff at each other. He remembers snowball fights when he was a boy and Theobalds was filled with his father's wards, Essex amongst them. They were aggressive affairs; he can remember as if it were yesterday, as he listens to those girls' screams, the sharp, cold sting of compacted snow hitting hard, full in his face, and how he pretended to laugh when he was held down, so the stuff could be shoved inside his clothes.

'She *was* questioned over it, but it didn't achieve anything. The Queen seems reluctant to take things any further. She seems still fond of Lady Rich, despite –'

'I know.' Cecil is well aware that it is he, rather than Lady Rich, who has come off worse from that letter.

The Queen had shown it to him, unaware his eyes had already been all over it, thanks to Cousin Francis. It was an impassioned plea, all the usual metaphors about the sun departing into the clouds and divine oracles and suchlike. But there was more to it, that letter. In it Lady Rich implied that Essex's enemies were taking advantage of the Queen. By Essex's enemies she surely meant him, Cecil. Once they have done away with the earl, she wrote, they will 'make war against heaven', in other words push the Queen herself off her throne in favour of another. The message was clear and, though sufficiently indirect as to avoid causing trouble for him, irritating enough to get beneath his skin like an itching powder.

He has felt his luck shift on its axis since that letter arrived. The Queen has been cold and offhand with him for several weeks, made a number of spiked comments about trust. She had sent her own physicians to treat the ailing earl and had released him into his own house; he remains under guard without the right to leave, allowed only sanctioned visits and all the ladies have been shunted elsewhere, but even so. He has heard from one of the ladies-of-the-chamber that the Queen has shed tears often over what she described as 'the loss of her closest family', meaning, he can only suppose, Essex and his sister. Cecil fears he has been wrong-footed. Essex's trial was set for February in the Star Chamber – high treason. But Cecil had sensed the prevailing mood; he didn't think it politic to be seen to be the one pursuing the earl to his death, the Queen might turn on *him*, so on the eve of the trial he had paid the earl a quiet visit.

Cecil found Essex hunched over his desk with his back to the door, apparently unaware of his presence, though he had been announced. He turned, and Cecil was shocked to see the skin taut over the bones of his face, as if there were no flesh beneath it. His eyes looked dead, like dry stones. His prolonged illness had transformed him almost beyond recognition. He leaned heavily on the surface of the desk to stand and, clearing his voice, croaked, 'Ah, Cecil. Come to gloat, have you?' He smiled and Cecil caught a glimpse of the old Essex, haughty, insolent, impossibly charismatic, but only a glimpse.

He felt shame well up in him then. 'I know we have not always seen eye to eye.'

Essex laughed at this, a thin, hostile sound that churned up that shame further.

Cecil swallowed. 'You have no reason to trust me, but I do not want to see you tried tomorrow. I believe I can have the whole thing postponed; I know Her Majesty's heart is not in it.'

'Why?' he said. 'Why would you help me?'

He had known the earl would ask him this. 'Because I want what is best for England, for the Queen, and I fear your . . .' He searched for a word. 'Your demise . . . well, it would not serve any of us, least of all her.'

'So what do you propose?' Essex eased himself back into his chair, his raised eyebrows indicating disbelief.

'Write a plea, use all your charm; employ the utmost humility.'

'I have made humble pleas by the dozen.' He drooped, allowing his shirt to gape at his throat, offering Cecil a view of his jutting clavicles. He couldn't bear to look at them.

'If I deliver your plea myself, to Her Majesty, I believe she might relent. If people feel she is acting alone, they will think her weak, but if it is on *my* advice . . . well, perhaps then they will think her benevolent.'

'Quite a subtle mind you have, Cecil. I have always known it, since we were boys.' Essex pulled a sheet of paper from a writing box and began to pare a quill with a small penknife. Cecil was filled with conflicting emotions. Part of him felt truly sorry for the man and guilty for his part in reducing him to this. Another part of him felt disingenuous, because this dumbshow was for his own benefit, not the earl's, not even the Queen's – it was his own position he was shoring up with his show of magnanimity. He remembered then, his father's account of how the Queen had turned on him in the wake of Mary of Scotland's execution, which Burghley had orchestrated – *I did it for the security of her throne, but she did not see it that way. I feared I had lost her favour irretrievably*, is what he had said of it – and Cecil's position with her is far more tenuous than his father's ever was. But he also harboured a glimmer of triumph at his own cunning. It was a heady mix of feelings swirling about in him.

Essex sprinkled sand on his letter to blot the ink, tipped it away, folded it and warmed the wax cradle with a candle. 'I don't suppose you have the gall to ask me to show it to you before I seal it,' he said, dripping the wax on to the join and pressing his ring into it, without removing it from his finger.

It had done the trick – the hearing was cancelled, all the crowds and hangers-on that had gathered around the place of trial had been sent away and the earl now lives in limbo at his house, scratching the bottom of his pot for funds, for all his offices have been suspended and he has no income to speak of. It is like a long game of chess and Cecil cannot now plot his next move. He has found himself wishing that Essex had never recovered from his illness; that would have been the cleanest end to it all. And now there is the problem of Lady Rich. 'What do *you* think of her letter?' he asks his cousin.

Bacon seems to be collecting his thoughts before he speaks. 'It makes me wonder what she knows. If she has anything that might incriminate you.'

'Me?' Cecil's voice unwittingly rises, revealing his apprehension. His mind is turning on what Lady Rich might have in her arsenal of information. Has she somehow got wind of his correspondence with the Spanish court? He runs through the possible ways she might have discovered it. There is that

Pérez character, who tends to pop up in all sorts of places, at the heart of all Spanish affairs. Cecil knows he, for one, has been feeding the Essex faction with intelligence for years, and there is Francis Bacon's brother, Anthony, of course, who has feelers all over Europe.

It hits him with a force of dread then, the memory of writing a particular letter of his own, about the Infanta, to the Spanish ambassador. So much had happened in the wake of his writing it – the massacre in Ireland, Cecil's humiliation at court, renewed hostilities with Spain, the earl's eventful return – that he had not put his mind to that missive, hurriedly sealed and sent. He had assumed it safely burned by its recipient a year ago. But Lady Rich's letter, with its subtle insinuations, has pushed it up to the surface and he imagines it falling on to Anthony Bacon's desk via one of those shady contacts. What a fool he was to put such treason in writing, for in the wrong hands even ambiguity – and he is sure he had couched the proposal in sufficiently ambiguous terms – has a way of being manipulated into something it is not. He had been so caught up in his peace treaty he had dropped his caution.

'I have never understood what it is about Lady Rich that means scandal slips off her like water off oiled cloth,' says Francis.

'Yes.' Cecil can feel his grip on the situation slipping, as if his fingers have been greased. Going over and over in his head what it was exactly he had written to the Spanish ambassador – how had he worded it? – hoping to God the man had the nous to burn all their communications and not forward them to Spain. He never agreed definitively to champion the Infanta; it was a mere insinuation. But it is not what he actually wrote; it is how it seems that counts. He takes a deep breath and steps to the window, looking out to try to get a hold of his thoughts. The girls down there are red-faced now, lobbing snow with breathless verve. If you didn't know it was a game it might seem quite sinister. 'Tell me, has your brother had much news from the Spanish court of late, Cousin?'

'Anthony holds his cards close to his chest.'

He scrutinizes Bacon for any sign that he might know something, feeling the weight of his trepidation pulling him down. 'I need you to prove that you are trustworthy, Cousin.' He surprises himself by saying this, realizes that it is exactly the correct way to take the conversation under the circumstances.

'And how would you have me do that?' Bacon blinks slowly once more and gazes steadily at the other man, continuing before Cecil has formed a reply. 'I have an idea of what might cause trouble for Lady Rich in regards to her letter.' Francis Bacon wears a half-smile now and steeples his elegant hands together in front of his mouth as if about to pray. Cecil catches a whiff of hope and reins in his eagerness to hear this idea, waiting for Bacon to speak. 'Were the letter to be published, it might look as if Lady Rich was trying to muster *public* support for her brother –'

'It would appear to be propaganda rather than a private letter.' Cecil feels goosebumps run up his arms and through his shoulders. It is a devious idea indeed. He wonders momentarily if Francis Bacon was bullied in boyhood as he was. 'That would surely visit trouble on Lady Rich.' He imagines himself informing the Queen.

'Eliminate the lady and the knave will lose his lifeblood,' says Bacon. 'She is the heartbeat of the Devereuxs.'

Cecil's mind turns towards Lady Rich and his body responds without his permission. He forces his thoughts on to the Queen again. 'How will you ensure that nothing leads back to *my* door in this matter?'

'Leave it to me. The less you know the better.'

'I must say, I'm impressed, Cousin. I will see that this is all worthwhile for you.'

'I know,' says Bacon with a conspiratorial smile and no attempt to hide his flippancy. Cecil can only admire his audacity.

June 1600

Essex House, the Strand

'I have never eaten such a large portion of humble pie,' says Essex, walking in, flanked by Knollys and Southampton. A laugh rings out of him, as if his ordeal has been nothing. Penelope is feasting her eyes on her brother, revelling in the sound of his laughter, delighted to see that he has recovered some of his fortitude. They, as many of his family and friends as could be mustered, have waited for him to arrive from York House, where he has been grilled for a full twelve hours by the attorney general and his special commission. He is gaunt, his beard is unkempt and his skin as pale as the white satin doublet that hangs from his bones. He wears, beneath his bravado, the vestiges of that wild fearful look Penelope saw on him back at Nonsuch. 'I was on my knees a full two hours.' And there it is again, the chime of his laughter.

'It did the job,' says Lettice, 'for here we are, all together!' She places a palm to her breast. A cheer goes up outside in the Strand where the crowd that gathered to get a glimpse of Essex has not yet dispersed.

'But not quite free,' says Penelope, indicating with a nudge of her head the two guards who stand in the doorway, pretending to ignore this family reunion. Penelope waves at them. Neither moves a muscle, though their eyes pivot slightly. 'Are you to be dismissed?'

One – the older, bearded one – says, 'There are no orders to that effect, My Lady.'

'It's only a matter of time,' says Lettice, stepping towards her son. 'You must continue to seek the Queen's pardon. Once she gives you an audience' – she puts one hand on either side of his face as if he is her lover – 'well, who could resist this?' She stops short of pinching his cheeks and he sweeps her aside with a gentle but firm shove. 'You will be back at court in no time, my darling boy.'

'I should rather retire to the country,' says Essex. But they all know it cannot be. His debts are too great. 'Let's have a look at my new little girl,' he says then, taking the infant from his wife's arms, tossing her up into the air, until she squeals with either delight or terror. Frances blanches, unable to look, but says nothing and Dorothy puts a reassuring arm around her sister-in-law.

It is Penelope who stops him. 'Mind her, she is still a babe, you'll crack her little head.' He hands the baby to his sister and crouches down, opening his arms for his boy. Young Robert moves forward slowly, stiff like a wooden puppet, with his mouth clamped tight, as if to tell his father that he will have to earn back his love.

'Robert, my boy, how big you are. Eight years old. Look at you; you have become a man whilst my back was turned.'

The child removes his cap and bows formally. 'I am nine, My Lord.' Penelope can see that he doesn't know how to behave in the face of his father. Perhaps he thought he would never see Essex again and that he would have to become the head of the family. That memory returns, of her mother impressing upon Essex, when he was not yet eleven and their own father had died, that he was the earl now, head of the Devereuxs. The bewildered look on his little face was heartbreaking. But her brother's heir doesn't seem bewildered; he seems to be steeped in resentment, as if Essex has done him a great disservice in fleeing Ireland and getting himself arrested and losing royal favour. Or perhaps he is simply trying to hide his apprehension, as they all are. Penelope puts a reassuring hand on his thin shoulder; he looks up at her, smiling, suddenly relaxed, and she has a flash of him fearlessly brandishing that grass snake at Leighs. She has become close to her nephew since her brother's incarceration.

A page pours them drinks and they make several toasts. Penelope stands back, watching her family, wishing Blount were with them. Letters fly back and forth between them, he writing of life in the garrison, leaving out, she feels sure, anything that might cause her distress. She had written recently, telling him of the commission set up to try her brother. How relieved they all were that it was not to be the Star Chamber as they had feared, but that the attorney general was to be assisted as prosecutor by, of all people, Francis Bacon. She had confronted sly Francis about it.

'You, who have lived under our roof in the bosom of our family and benefited from the support of my brother – how can you live with yourself?'

'It is the duty of my role as Queen's Counsel. *Sniff.* I am not in a position to refuse.' He had at least squirmed visibly then, like a schoolboy caught pilfering from the kitchens. 'I will do my best to see to it that the judgement is lenient. *Sniff.* It could be a good thing that I will be in attendance. I did not seek this, *sniff*, but fully intend to put it to Essex's best advantage.'

The excuses spurted forth from him, with that telltale sniff making Penelope sure he was protesting too greatly. She knows Cecil wouldn't have allowed Francis Bacon to assist unless he could be sure of his allegiance. Bacon ought not assume her to be such a fool as to absorb his justifications like a sponge. But then he has always dismissed her for being female, as if she isn't capable of grasping things as men do. She asks herself whether Bacon secretly holds the Queen in equal disdain for the coincidence of her sex.

She had written a further letter to Blount only this morning. Her finger is still smudged black with the ink that wrote it. A quick scribble, penned as soon as word came that Essex was to be released – still banished from court and stripped of his offices, but free, nonetheless, and with his loved ones about him. Blount had no need now to march on London with his army, spring her brother free and deal with his enemies; which is just as well, for as far as she knows he has not yet had firm news of the Scottish King's full support. Without that it would have been too dangerous. But Blount isn't given to folly; he doesn't have the reckless streak of her brother. They had taken the utmost care to stress to King James that they did not seek to overthrow Elizabeth, simply to do away with the evil influences about her. She absently touches the black thong around her neck and imagines the messenger thundering towards Blount.

'Sis!' Essex jogs her out of her thoughts. 'You are miles away. Will you give us a song?' Someone thrusts a lute into her arms and she perches on the stone hearth surround to play, asking Lizzie Vernon to join her in a song of two parts. It is a merry tune and gets everyone clapping and humming along, but in spite of all the jollity Penelope cannot get her mind off Blount out there in the wilds. Life would not be so cruel as to kill both the men she has loved in battle – would it?

Anthony Bacon lumbers in on his gouty limbs, spilling into a chair with a great sigh, and someone brings him a stool for his feet. He beckons Essex, speaking to him in a lowered voice that cannot be heard above the music, pulling a pamphlet from a pocket, which Essex pores over, before announcing that he needs some privacy and nodding towards Knollys and Southampton to remain.

As they all file out he takes Penelope's elbow. 'Not you, Sis. I need you here.'

Lettice takes Frances and Dorothy, one on each arm, with a huff of protest at being overlooked in favour of her daughter, and sails towards the door in high dudgeon. 'I suppose you no longer value the counsel of your mother.'

Once the others have filed out they form a huddle about Anthony Bacon, turning their backs to the guards, who are not close enough to hear if they keep their voices down. Nevertheless, Penelope begins to strum her lute again to obliterate any words that might drift their way.

'So what is it?' says Knollys.

'This has been published and circulated.' He flattens the pamphlet on his lap.

Words jump out at Penelope – 'combined enemies', 'evil instruments', 'officious cunning' – her own words; it is her letter to the Queen of a few months past, in print.

'Does the Queen know?' she asks, forcing her fingers to continue plucking notes out of her instrument, but her heart has begun to beat out a hollow rhythm that is all out of time.

'I'm afraid so. My brother came to me with it,' says Anthony.

'Your brother can no longer be trusted, not since he chose to sit in judgement over Essex,' she says firmly, swapping a look with Anthony. They are the only ones to know the full truth of Francis's defection. She wonders how it is possible that siblings could be so different. Anthony loyal to the core and his brother, Francis, slippery as the muck at the bottom of a pond. Her tune begins to lose its way, becoming discordant. She stops playing, letting the lute drop into her lap.

'Whoreson,' says Southampton, hurling the word with force, causing one of the guards to turn and look.

'I *have* seen him lurking about Cecil's chambers at court lately,' says Uncle Knollys.

'No! Francis Bacon is loyal,' says Essex. 'I'm sure of it. He *has* to have dealings with Cecil. It is part of his duty as Queen's Counsel.'

'I'm afraid not, My Lord,' says Anthony. 'My brother has set his cap elsewhere. But we may be able to use his disloyalty to our advantage.'

Essex looks crestfallen and mutters something under his breath. A chant starts up outside: *Ess-ex, Ess-ex, Ess-ex*.

'But before we think about my brother I need to warn you, My Lady, that Cecil has sent Lord Buckhurst to interrogate you with regards to this.' Anthony taps the pamphlet. 'There is this for you too.' He fumbles in his clothes, taking out another paper, a letter with the royal seal. She tears it open, scattering red shards of wax over the floor.

Ess-ex, Ess-ex, ESS-EX.

'I am confined to my own house until further notice.' She rips the letter blithely, allowing pieces of it to fall like apple blossom. 'It's fortunate I have a number of houses, then, isn't it?' Her laugh cuts through the heavy hush, a lone chime, and she looks round at their faces. Southampton has a hand over his mouth, Anthony has a deep crease running vertically down his brow, Knollys stares at his bunched hands and her brother cannot meet her eye. 'Cheer up! Buckhurst is no match for me. I have already answered his questions with regards to my letter, back in the spring. He called it "an insolent, saucy, malapert action" and I told him he was wrong, that it was a heartfelt outpouring and demonstration of love to my beloved monarch.' Her laugh sounds empty now. 'In the end he could do nothing but agree with me. Buckhurst hasn't the stomach to bring me down.'

'But this is different, dear,' says Knollys. 'They will be trying to prove that you published this to incite rebellion. It could lead to . . .' He pauses, placing a hand on his forehead. 'It could lead to . . . to . . . more serious charges.' He is clearly loath to utter the word 'treason'.

ESS-EX, ESS-EX, ESS-EX.

'But *I* didn't publish it. They cannot try me for something I didn't do.' As she says it she realizes how wrong she is, that people are tried and convicted for things they didn't do all the time, and that if Cecil has decided he wants rid of her this is a golden opportunity. A sudden vivid memory of Doctor Lopez fills her head. 'I will fight this to the death.' The air in the chamber seems thin, as if it will not sustain her, and her head feels light. She takes up her fan, closing her eyes, gratefully breathing in the wafts of cool air it produces.

'Oh God!' says Essex, drooping with despair. 'This is too

much.' She wants to take him by the shoulders and shake him, force him to find his fighting spirit.

She stands suddenly and takes her brother's hand, leading him over to the window, flinging it open. A great roar goes up from the crowd outside as they see the face of their hero, the only man they trust to deliver them from the Spanish threat. 'See how you are loved.' She waves, causing another cheer to sound out, reverberating around the street. The guards begin to shuffle from foot to foot, presumably wondering whether they should put a stop to this. Penelope closes the window.

'We can try and find out who *did* publish it,' says Anthony quietly, once they are back beside him.

'That would be a start,' says Knollys.

'Meanwhile,' Penelope says to her brother, strumming once more at her instrument, 'you *must* petition the Queen to renew your sweet wines licence. Your rights end at Michaelmas, don't they?' He nods slowly as if he is under water. 'Without it, now you are stripped of your offices, you will have nothing and your debts are —'

Before she can say 'insurmountable' he interjects sharply. 'You think I don't know it!'

'She means to keep you in your place,' says Anthony. He is talking of the Queen, who knows well enough that if Essex has no funds he is nothing.

'It is as good as a siege. She thinks she will starve you into submission,' says Southampton under his breath; he is pacing up and down.

Essex has his head in his hands. They are still chanting outside.

'I see Cecil written all over this,' says Penelope. 'He is a snake. All that pretence at kindness, having the hearing postponed. It smelled wrong at the time and it stinks now. Write to the Queen.' Penelope says it like an order, looking directly at her brother. 'Convince her of your innocence. You *are* innocent.' She remembers his plaintive words that night at Nonsuch. 'All you did was what you thought was in England's best interests . . . just a six-week truce with Tyrone, until your troops had gained their strength . . .' Her voice trails off.

'That is why I refused to admit to insubordination at the hearing,' he says without lifting his face. 'I will not lie. I will not stoop to dishonour.'

'Your sister is right. It *is* Cecil who drives this. We all know that,' says Southampton. 'He has poisoned the Queen's mind.'

'I sought to articulate that in my letter,' says Penelope. 'And look where that's got us. We must fight fire with fire. Find me something against Cecil, Anthony – something that will truly incriminate him.' She is whispering. 'He cannot be entirely free from misconduct; he must have failed to cover his tracks *somewhere*.' She looks towards Anthony and thinks she can see a gleam in his eyes.

'Remember Pérez?' he says, one eyebrow raised. A thread of hope winds through her and the atmosphere in the room lifts minutely. They are all aware that Pérez knows the inner secrets of the Spanish court and if Cecil overstepped his mark with his Spanish dealings, Pérez will surely know of it. 'It is nothing definitive, but it is a possible lead.'

The guards both turn their way, as if they have sniffed intrigue in the air, and they peel themselves off the wall, moving slowly across the room with the thinly disguised pretence of going to look out of the window.

'How about a round of Primero?' suggests Southampton, producing a pack of cards from somewhere on his person. 'Will you join us?' he calls to the guards, who are clearly unsure how to react to this. 'A little enjoyment will do no harm.'

'I don't see why not,' says the bearded one, just as the other replies, 'I don't think so.'

'We shall have to toss a coin to decide,' says Penelope. Southampton produces a penny, handing it to her with a smirk. 'You call it,' she says to the more amenable of the pair.

'Tails,' he says tentatively.

She throws up the penny, catching it, clapping it on to the back of her hand. 'Tails it is.'

Anthony has already begun to shuffle the pack. Southampton drags over a small table and they pull up stools. Essex hasn't spoken a word for some time and that dark look which spells despair has intensified. Penelope sits beside him, taking his hand, kissing it, before wrapping it with both of hers and setting it into her lap. 'Do you have a headache coming on?'

He doesn't reply, as if he hasn't heard.

'I will mix you some of that tincture in a minute.'

Anthony is looking through the pack. 'What kind of cards are these? I have never seen this design. Look at this lady.' He passes a card to Penelope. It is the queen of spades. 'Is she not the spitting image of the Spanish Infanta?' He says it with a laugh, and the guards laugh too, but Penelope understands what lies beneath his little jest. The hope is that Pérez has dug up something on Cecil and the Spanish Infanta – that might be his 'possible lead'.

'Now you mention it,' she says.

Southampton is laughing, showing the card to the guards. 'Look, she even has a moustache.'

Uncle Knollys snatches it up with a chuckle.

Anthony Bacon is dealing now and they are placing their wagers, only pennies, but Penelope isn't thinking about the game, she has an idea formulating in her head.

August 1600

Whitehall

'I hope you have come to tell me that you have finally questioned Lady Rich, My Lord.' Cecil stands as Lord Buckhurst enters the chamber. He is utterly exasperated with the man and it peeves him to have to offer him the respect his title demands. The lady in question had managed to avoid Buckhurst for more than two months, moving between her houses. Such inefficiency rankles. The painting of his dead wife on the wall opposite is not quite straight and it adds to his irritation.

'I have, My Lord.' He is flushed and wheezy and he blots his damp brow with a square of linen. 'It is warm today. Would you mind if I were to undo my doublet a little?'

'You can strip naked for all I care as long as you tell me you have interrogated the lady.'

Buckhurst emits a guffaw of laughter at this. 'I see you are in good humour, Cecil.'

A couple of Cecil's pages are loitering in the doorway. He commands them to leave but when they are gone he wishes he'd asked one of them to straighten the painting, which he tries not to look at.

'Do please sit down,' he says to Buckhurst, who settles his large body into a chair with a sigh like a pair of bellows. 'So?'

'I questioned Lady Rich.' He says her name with a soft look about his eyes and Cecil has a bad feeling about this; he'd thought fusty old Buckhurst might be immune to her charms but apparently not. 'I tracked her down to her husband's house in Essex, where she was tending him. He had been struck down with some unknown malady. But by the time I arrived there she had departed for . . .'

Cecil wants to tell the man to get on with it, that he hasn't all day to listen to the story of his meanderings around the English countryside. 'And when you did question her, what were your findings, My Lord?' He is trying to keep a pleasant look on his face.

'I am entirely convinced of her innocence.'

'How so?' Cecil sighs in exasperation. Lady Rich seems to have a way of wriggling out of the tightest corner. An image of her pops into his mind unbidden, which he expels with a sharp intake of breath. He should have sent Bacon to talk to her; *he* wouldn't have been susceptible to her charms. But of course he couldn't, for Bacon is too tightly knit to the whole plan. At least Lady Rich has been away from court and without access to the Queen. So something has been achieved. Plus the earl's guard has been stood down and he has disappeared to the country, meaning the rabble of supporters has dispersed from the gates of Essex House.

There have been reams of letters from the earl to the Queen, all of which Cecil has intercepted, pathetic epistles pleading for her favour: *. . . for till I may appear in your gracious presence and kiss Your Majesty's fair correcting hand* – fair correcting hand, indeed – *time itself is a perpetual night . . .* All this, a thousandfold, in preamble to convincing her to renew his sweet wines licence. Cecil had been there when the Queen had read the most recent of them. She had let it flutter to the floor with the words: 'He cannot think me such a fool as to believe all this nonsense. All he wants is the means to pay his debts.'

It occurs to Cecil that perhaps he has already won. *Water hollows a stone, not by force but by falling often.* How right his father was.

Buckhurst is wittering: 'She acknowledged her follies and faults . . . her horror on discovering that her letter, a private letter (she truly seemed most affronted by it) had been made public . . . assurances that she would never again put pen to paper in such a way that might be exploited so . . . pleaded forgiveness for her insolence . . . said she would never enjoy a moment of comfort until she had the happiness to set her eyes once more upon Her Majesty . . .'

Cecil is barely listening. He is thinking about the gardens at Theobalds and how they have become neglected since he has been so taken up with this business concerning the earl. He is sketching out plans in his mind for a new series of knot gardens, each representing the rulers of England. At the centre will be the one devoted to Elizabeth. He imagines the blooms he will plant there, red and white roses entwined and exotic plants from the New World and those lilies the colour of flames to echo her hair.

'. . . and,' continues Buckhurst, 'she gave me a letter for Her Majesty – made me promise to deliver it personally.'

Cecil is jerked out of his horticultural reverie.

'A letter?' He tries to imagine what further slurs Lady Rich might have written against him. The idea swells once more that somehow that blasted missive of his has come into Lady Rich's hands. His old fears are renewed as if they had never gone. Why else would she be writing to the Queen if not to finish the work of her earlier letter and denounce him as a traitor? He feels desiccated, as if someone has thrust a handful of sand into his throat. He will make sure it doesn't reach the Queen. Before that thought has fully formed itself, he sees its essential flaw. He cannot suppress the letter, for Buckhurst is sure to mention it. Lady Rich is a shrewd creature indeed. A new idea drops into his mind; he will have it copied and any compromising material removed as a surgeon might purge a boil of pus. That is what he will do. 'Let me see it.'

'I am afraid that is not possible –'

'How so?' His smile is a rictus.

'I gave it to Her Majesty on my way here . . .'

He is finding it hard to breathe now.

'She was walking to chapel with her ladies. I have a niece amongst her maids. She stopped. I was most honoured . . .'

Suddenly the room is too close and it is *his* forehead that is slick with perspiration.

'I thought it a most excellent opportunity to hand the letter to her myself, as I had promised Lady Rich,' continues Buckhurst.

Cecil's mind is swirling out of control as he tries to remember once more exactly how he worded that letter to the Spanish ambassador. His wife watches him with bright accusing eyes, from her crooked frame. Surely he wasn't so rash as to make it explicit, or did his fervour for a treaty get the better of him? He struggles for breath.

'Are you ailing, My Lord?' asks Buckhurst. 'Are you in need of a physician?'

He pulls the fragmented parts of himself together sufficiently to say, 'It is just a little warm in here; that is all.'

'I will have one of the lads fetch you something to drink.' Buckhurst makes for the door to find one of the pages.

Cecil's mind is in chaos. He digs and digs to the very bottom of his being, to the place where he finally becomes aware that he *would* have seen that Spanish girl at the helm of England, had the circumstances been right for him, had he been placed to best advantage at the end of it. But did he ever say that? Worse: had he ever written it? He simply doesn't know any more. How is it that he, who prides himself on being so very orderly, never leaving any stone unturned, no thread out of place, could be so completely and utterly awry beneath his surface?

Cecil heaves himself out of his chair. His head spins and a moment of blackness drops over him. He clings to the edge of the desk to stop himself from falling and when he has recovered his equilibrium he walks calmly over to the opposite wall to straighten his dead wife. Buckhurst is fussing about, advising him to sit back down and worrying about the whereabouts of the page with his drink, when a lad in the Queen's livery arrives to inform Cecil that Her Majesty wishes to see him, once she is done with her evening worship.

Cecil scrutinizes the boy in the vain hope that his expression might reveal something of the spirit in which the summons was made, but his face is as bland as a turnip. He can hear the muffled hubbub of people leaving the chapel below and feels a pulse racing in the soft part of his neck, where it meets his throat – the place one of his henchmen pointed out once where, if you press firmly enough and in the correct manner, you can kill a man.

He turns to Buckhurst: 'I must take my leave. Her Majesty mustn't be kept waiting.' He is surprised there is no tremor in his voice and, collecting up a stack of papers from his desk, he leaves the chamber, indicating that the two pages should accompany him.

They make their way to the Queen's rooms. It is dark and cool in the back corridors where the only windows are small and set high up, so when they arrive in the long gallery it takes a moment for Cecil to adjust to the brightness burning through the vast casements, heating the place like a furnace and throwing sheets of light over the floors. Someone has recently strewn fresh lavender with rosemary and the smell, churned up by the milling throng of people, along with the intensity of the heat and light, assaults his senses. He is admitted without delay, though he would have welcomed a moment to collect his thoughts.

The Queen is seated and has several of her women close by; another group sit in a window seat, poring over what appears to be a book of images, and a few courtiers mill about. There is a fire burning in the great hearth in spite of the summer heat, though it is true these rooms face north, unlike the long gallery. She smiles broadly, saying, 'Pygmy, you look as if you have bad news. I sincerely hope you have not.'

Cecil, realizing only then that he must be wearing all his fears on his face, manages a smile in return, bows, and then straightens himself as much as it is possible, standing at his fullest height before her. 'No, no, Your Majesty. There is only good news. Lord Mountjoy is having great success at quelling the rebels in Ireland.' He proffers a paper from his sheaf: a letter from Blount telling of the progress he has made. 'He has established fortresses in Derry and Newry in the north and Munster has been brought under control.'

'Perhaps I should have sent *him* there at the outset.' She takes the paper and, holding her magnifier over it, scans the text briefly. 'He seems to know exactly what he is doing.' Then she turns to one of her women. 'Talking of letters, have you got Lady Rich's . . . the one Buckhurst delivered before chapel.'

Cecil feels his legs might collapse beneath him. She has called him in to explain himself here before everybody. His chest is tight as he watches the woman produce the letter. He recognizes Lady Rich's hand; he has intercepted enough of her letters over the years to be familiar with her untidy scrawl. But he notices, too, that it is unopened. So the Queen's smile and warm greeting were genuine. His mind flaps about like a doomed capon. Perhaps he could offer to take the letter off her hands: *Your Majesty needn't bother with such things. Let me see to it for you.* But he knows she would easily discern his purpose; why would he seek to relieve her of a private missive from her goddaughter? He fears he might vomit all over the polished oak floor, all over the carefully plaited rush matting, all over the Queen's embroidered buckskin slippers. The smile on his face feels wrought from granite and he keeps his eyes steady by focusing on those pretty shoes.

'What other matters concern us?' she asks.

The letter sits in her hand as he runs through the business

of state – the poor harvest, the dearth of corn, the prisoner (the author of the history of Henry IV) who still festers in the Tower – astonished he is able to do this.

'And there is the question of the sweet wines licence, Your Majesty.'

'Oh, that!' She sinks her chin on to her hand. 'I would rather ignore that for the moment.'

She lifts Lady Rich's letter, looking confused for an instant, as if she had forgotten it was there. Cecil cannot bear to watch but nor can he drag his eyes away. The seal breaks with a little crack and she unfolds the paper, reaching for her magnifier once more. He scrutinizes her while she reads, for clues as to the contents, but her face is a mask, entirely opaque. When she is done, she directs a look his way so icy it sends a shiver through him despite the sweat that is flowering in his armpits. He is thinking of ways he can discover what is written there, so he can at least arm himself for the possible eventualities that he is trying not to think about. There are a couple of the Queen's women who will do his bidding in return for a favour.

'Have Lady Rich informed that she is free to go where she pleases and may return to court if she so wishes.' Her voice is glacial and she balls the paper tightly before lobbing it into the hearth – a direct hit – where it flares up brightly until it exists no more.

January 1601

Chartley, Staffordshire

Chartley appears bleak and abandoned on its hilltop, surrounded by naked trees, and its windows are blank like the
eyes of a sightless man. A farmer is herding a large flock of
geese across the way and Penelope, who has ridden ahead
with Alfred, has to wait for them to waddle by at an interminable pace. Little do the poor creatures know they are destined
for the Epiphany table. She unpeels her gloves and rubs her
hands together in an attempt to warm them up but her nails
ache painfully where the cold has got beneath them, and she
tries to imagine herself beside a blazing hearth in the great
chamber.

Alfred calls out to the farmer to get a move on. They must
have waited a while for that condemned army to pass because
she can now hear the rumble of the luggage cart heralding
the arrival of the rest of their party. Lizzie Vernon is laughing at something, the geese perhaps, but Penelope doesn't
wait to find out what the joke is. She urges Gambit on to a
canter and then, once in the expanse of the pasture, speeds
up into a gallop until there is nothing in her mind but the
wind and the rhythmic thrum of hooves against hard Janu-
ary ground. The burden of worry that has been pressing
down on her for months has intensified on this approach to
Chartley, where her brother has holed himself away. She has
never seen an ostrich, there is not one in the menagerie at the
Tower, but she has worn their plumes and seen drawings of
them. It is said that they are tall as horses and as swift and
that they bury their heads rather than face danger. She might
say Essex resembled such a creature.

As she nears she can see her mother's dog scampering

about the knot garden and young Robert calling to him from the courtyard. Lettice must have arrived from Drayton Bassett yesterday. They had all planned to come here to prise Essex out of his torpor but as she nears the house Penelope feels increasingly filled with dread of her mission. She would love to leave her brother to his perpetual rustication but the truth is he cannot afford to retire to the country. His creditors have been knocking the doors of Essex House down day and night and Penelope fears they will not be kept at bay for much longer. She has teased a sum out of her husband but even Rich's wealth will go no way to solving this deficit. Besides, Rich seems to be a little less well disposed towards her brother since his fall from favour.

Robert sees them approach and waves, calling out a greeting; he looks taller, gangly, as if his limbs have grown too fast for his body. She thinks of her own boys back at Leighs. Hoby is thirteen now, on the brink of adulthood, and will soon be off to university. It strikes her with a pang of sadness that her girls will be wed before long. She has just turned thirty-eight and feels old, wonders where all those years have gone, drowned in the river of time. She returns Robert's wave; as he runs towards her he is transformed into her dead brother, Wat, and time has folded back on itself. Sidney is there, waiting in the orchard for her, just visible beyond the bare trees, and she is there with him, her younger self, sitting beneath that summer tree in his arms, as he whispers lines of heartbreakingly beautiful poetry in her ear. The memory is too much to bear and she forces it away, pushing her horse on and into the stable yard, where the grooms are forming a hasty line to greet her.

She comes to a halt beside the mounting block and is helped down by one of them, who says, 'Goodness, My Lady, your hands are like ice.'

She must have forgotten to replace her gloves at the top of the hill. She imagines them lying discarded in the cold mud and hopes they will be found by someone requiring a little warmth. There are plenty in need: they passed endless groups of pitiful souls begging a penny or a crust along the way. Another bad harvest and heaven alone knows what will become of them. At least there will be the leftovers of those Epiphany geese.

One of her brother's pages approaches, proffering a letter. It is from Ireland. Blount tells of the wild beauty, of the winter landscape and the quality of the livestock, sparing her the bloody details of his campaign, only saying he is gaining ground. But she knows well enough the danger of such an operation, the constant death and horror. He feels her presence close by, he says: *I am the wandering arm of a compass and you its still point.* That makes her sick with longing. *Victor is friendly,* he adds, hidden in a paragraph where he describes his favourite horses. Victor is her old code name for James of Scotland and, reading between the lines, she infers that James intends to send the Earl of Mar to court, to discuss the future. She feels a small flurry of hope – he will take her brother's part; all the more reason to get Essex back to the capital.

She tucks the letter inside her gown, already forming her reply in her head as she enters the house. How will she tell him that her brother is now in a slough of despond so deep she fears he will never find a path out of it? And how to describe the urgent press of Essex's disaffected supporters, who are waiting in the shadows for their champion to emerge and face down his enemies. She must tell him too that they have failed to find any hard evidence to bring Cecil down – how they had hoped that Anthony Bacon would produce something tangible out of his 'possible lead'. But it had all turned out to be little more than rumour and supposition.

Her mind twists and turns on the various ways of encoding all that information, hiding it within a simple message of affection, as she stops a moment at the portrait of her father.

There he is, still young and vibrant, armour gleaming, even behind the film of dust, as if he had never died in Ireland. That is a cursed place. It cost her a father and perhaps a brother; she cannot bear to think of what it might do to Blount. All she wants truly is to express her sentiments for him in her letter, to make him feel he is loved, to set the business of politics aside.

Lettice is in the great chamber. She looks old and afraid. Penelope has never seen her mother look afraid before.

'You are a sight for sore eyes,' says Lettice, by way of a greeting. 'Look, your habit is torn and you are covered in mud. I don't know why you didn't take the carriage.'

Penelope doesn't try to explain that she likes the feeling of her horse beneath her, the wind in her face, that it makes her feel alive. 'I am glad to see you too, Mother.'

'I'm sorry, my sweet!' Lettice says then. 'I have been beside myself with worry. I'm sorry.' She takes Penelope's hands and rubs them between hers. 'Come, you are cold, there is a fire in my privy chamber.' Lettice leads the way along the corridor to her own rooms.

'Where is Robin?'

'Abed. He hasn't risen for three days. He will not even look my way, let alone speak to me. I'm not sure it was such a good idea to bring young Robert with me. I should have left him at Eton. I thought it might cheer your brother up to see his boy so well.' The words are pouring out of her.

'I wasn't aware it was quite this bad. How long has he been like this?'

'Meyrick says he has been in and out of this state since he was definitively denied the sweet wines licence.'

'Since October! That is nearly three months. Why on earth didn't Meyrick tell us?'

'Your brother forbade him – didn't want to be seen in such a state.'

Penelope turns to the door. 'I will go to him now.'

'Wait awhile; warm up, Penelope. You catching a chill will do no one any good.' Her mother tugs at the sleeve of her riding habit. 'At least take this off and put on something of mine until your luggage arrives.' But Penelope has pulled herself free from her mother's grasp and is pacing fast to the other end of the house.

Meyrick is in the antechamber playing cards with a couple of fellows she thinks she has seen once or twice about Essex House. He heaves his bulk up to stand, smiling; his freckled face is creased and his marmalade beard is strung with grey. He introduces the men – Henry Cuffe and Ferdinando Gorges – who take her hand, each in his turn. Cuffe has a nondescript face save for a slight underbite and bad teeth, but Gorges must send the maids' hearts aflutter with his conker-brown hair and penetrating eyes, a little close-set, which only adds to the intensity of his gaze.

'Did you serve with Essex in Ireland?' she asks.

Meyrick interrupts them: 'I am afraid the earl is unwell. He needs to rest and has insisted I allow him no visitors.'

'He wouldn't mean me,' she says, walking briskly past him and into the bedchamber beyond.

The heavy curtains are all drawn tight, allowing barely a chink of light to breach the gloom, but a fire burns vigorously in the hearth, making the chamber stuffy and airless. Essex's hound unfolds itself and wanders her way, waving its tail half-heartedly, then stands before her with a mournful expression. He rubs his head against her skirts, pressing a wet nose into her hand, as if he's been starved of affection.

She pulls back the hangings that obscure the window, allowing in a stream of thin winter light, and stands for a moment looking out at the derelict fortifications of the old castle, remembering their childhood games. There is condensation on the glass, which she wipes away with her sleeve to better see the view. Robert runs across her line of sight and she hears Lettice calling him to come in before it rains.

There are heavy clouds looming and she hopes the luggage cart will arrive before the heavens open.

'Go away – leave me alone.' Her brother's voice emanates from behind the tightly drawn bed-curtains.

'It is I, Robin.'

'Sis?'

She swipes the drapes aside to find him half propped up on an elbow, blinking like a mole and shading his eyes with his forearm. He appears sallow and has dark rings beneath his eyes that make him look as if he has suffered a beating. She climbs up on to the bed, shuffling herself over to sit beside him.

'Thank God it is you, I thought it was that rabble out there come to hustle me into action. My dearest Sis.' He looks at her with lifeless eyes. 'You have to help me.'

'That is why I am here.'

'I cannot sleep for the terrible dreams and I am in the grip of this . . .' He stops. His breath is slightly wheezy. She notices the dark leather pouch she had returned to him on his release discarded amongst the blankets and picks it up. 'I fear I am losing my mind.'

'I hear that the Queen has not answered any of your letters.'

'I am an outcast, Sis.' He says this with all the drama of a player performing one of the great tragedies.

'Come on, Robin. You need to collect yourself.'

'Not you too – you're as bad as that bloody trio of ghouls out there.' He waves a limp hand in the direction of the door. 'Push, push; do this, do that; plotting my comeback. Henry Cuffe would have me on the throne if he had his way.'

'Well, Cuffe will not have his way,' she says, taking on the bossy tone of the older sister.

'They do it for themselves, not for me. I'm tired, Sis. I don't think I have it in me any more. There is nothing left, I am empty as my purse. And as for this.' He takes the pouch from her hand. 'I had such high hopes to see King James named as successor, England's future secured. I truly believed it was best for all. I used to be able to see it clearly. Now I can see nothing. If only I could sleep.'

'I have not come here to push you into anything. I have come to help you.'

'I'm beyond help – just want to sleep.'

She wants to shake some of his self-pity out of him, but it is more than that – his misery is indelible. 'You cannot hide yourself away here for ever. You must face your demons. And besides, you have responsibilities, duties – a wife, children. You are not any ordinary person, able to do as he pleases; you are an earl, and it comes with a price. Think of young Robert – your heir. Remember we are *all* but custodians of the Devereux name.' She wonders, though, if he is not irrevocably broken, whether something in him has shattered.

'Pity poor young Robert Devereux with me for a father.' His cynicism cuts through the air like a sword through flesh, and it is all she can do to prevent herself from snapping back a retort to quit his pathetic solipsism.

'Something I do know,' she says, 'is that this will pass.'

'Pass it may, but I shall still be as penniless as those beggars roaming the roads. Beggared yet an earl.' He emits a snort of derisive laughter. 'Have my creditors broken apart Essex House and sold it off brick by brick yet?'

'Enough.' Penelope cannot hide her impatience now.

She hears voices in the outer chamber and Lettice enters, closing the door firmly behind her, to stand at the foot of the bed. 'What's this I hear from Lizzie about Anthony Bacon? She says he has failed to get any hard evidence of Cecil's dealings with the Spanish.' She seems annoyed, directing what she says at her daughter. Penelope hadn't wanted to bring this up just yet, had wanted to lay the path for the bad news, to allow Essex to retain some sense of hope.

'What do you mean?' Essex says, his voice staccato.

'What she means,' says Penelope, taking her brother's hand

and trying to sound as soothing as possible, 'is that Pérez could only come up with anecdotal evidence of Cecil's meddling in the succession. There is nothing firm to make a case with.'

She feels Essex deflate beside her, as if punctured.

'But that's simply not true,' says Lettice. 'I have firm proof from another source.'

She can sense Essex perk up, like a hound with a sniff of a hare. 'What proof, Mother?'

'My brother once witnessed Cecil discussing the Infanta's eligibility for the throne. He saw it with his own eyes, heard it with his own ears. He told me so only the other day. If that is not evidence then I don't know what is.'

'Uncle Knollys?' says Penelope. 'Your brother told you he has heard Cec—'

'That's what I said.'

'When did this overheard conversation take place? Why did he not mention it before?' Penelope asks.

'Some time ago, I believe.' Lettice begins to fiddle with a tassel on her gown. 'Perhaps he thought Pérez might come up with something more tangible.'

'It is not written evidence but I suppose it is better than nothing,' says Penelope. 'Would he stand by it?'

'I can only assume so,' says Lettice.

Essex has flopped back on to the pillows.

'See,' Penelope says to her brother, 'it is not all bad news. Uncle Knollys is a trusted source. His testimony would hold weight.' She is trying to make it all seem less tenuous. 'Blount has developed a strong line of contact with Scotland. King James intends to send the Earl of Mar to London. He will touch favourably on *your* position too. See, this is *good* news, Robin. Our work is coming to fruition.' She tries to inject her voice with conviction, suddenly understanding what can be done to serve their ends. 'I think you should write to Mar and inform *him* of Cecil's underhand dealings. If Mar – a king's ambassador, a neutral party, as it were – cast a shadow on

Cecil it might cause the Queen to see things differently.'

'You mean she might be more favourable towards me?' he says, sitting up, a little more animated, and reaches for the discarded pouch, putting the thong over his head.

'That is exactly what I mean,' she says.

'However did I spawn such a creature as you, Penelope?' says Lettice. 'You would do well as a privy councillor.'

'Is that a compliment or a criticism?'

'Oh, a compliment, of course.'

Essex has got out of bed and is stretching. 'If you two ladies might give me my privacy I will dress and see you at supper. And I think we should plan my return to London.'

Lettice smiles at her daughter with a nod, as if to congratulate her on this transformation. 'I will send word to have Essex House prepared for your arrival.'

Penelope takes her brother's shoulders. 'Don't let your men get too ambitious.' She nods her head in the direction of the antechamber. 'They may become carried away and it will do you no good. Keep them well harnessed, for their aspirations could visit trouble on us all.'

February 1601

Whitehall

Cecil instructs his coachman to make a detour past Essex House. He wants to see for himself if the rumours are true about the earl's return. Court has been whispering of it and Cecil can sense the shifting of allegiances; it is as if everyone is waiting for a move to be made before they will show their hand. His clerk, who sits beside him, blows his nose loudly into a grimy handkerchief. Cecil shudders and sidles along the seat away from him, leaning out to see the gates up ahead, admiring for a moment the two pairs of glossy black horses harnessed to his carriage, each with perfectly matching white socks. Heads turn as they pass – that is the intention.

The Essex House gates open to let a group of riders pass out and Cecil can see a hubbub of activity in the yard beyond. Servants rush back and forth, clutches of men gather around braziers, smoking, talking, laughing; others are cleaning their muskets and some are practising their swordplay, shouting out as they score points. There is little doubt that the earl is in residence. Cecil scans the front windows and sees a woman looking out. It is either Lady Rich or her sister – impossible to tell which at such a distance. She waves in his direction. He is taken by surprise and jerks his head out of sight, then feels foolish. He should have waved back, or at the very least held her gaze.

The clerk sneezes loudly; Cecil puts a hand over his own mouth and nose, muttering, 'For goodness' sake.'

The man apologizes into the filthy square of linen.

'Find out exactly who is at Essex House,' Cecil demands. 'I want numbers of servants, hangers-on, everybody. Use whatever means you must.' The man looks at him gorm-lessly. 'Go on, out you get.' The clerk gathers his cloak about himself before jumping down into the street and Cecil taps the carriage roof to gain the coachman's attention. 'To Whitehall!' He is sure the rheumy clerk will be completely ineffectual in the task he has been set but at least the man is not still in the confined space of the carriage, spreading his contagion.

He thinks of that female figure in the window. Nothing has happened since Lady Rich's letter; none of his fears have yet come to pass, but that doesn't mean nothing is going on. He had a month of terror, jumping at every arrival, imagining himself arraigned and taken to the Tower, and several more months of a less intense fear, which still lingers. In his darker moments he has even begun to think about how he will form his scaffold speech, trying not to allow his mind to wander to the inevitable thoughts of what it might feel like, that noose tightening about his neck – no swift axe for one such as he, another reminder of his lack of nobility – struggling for breath, and, worse, the nothingness after, the not existing, or fac-ing eternal damnation, for surely that is what lies ahead. He has begun to pray with renewed zeal, collating his sins, hoping it is not too late for forgiveness.

Once at the palace he stumbles upon Knollys, who takes him to one side saying, 'I am glad to see you.' He kneads his hands anxiously, making Cecil wonder what is wrong. 'I have concerns for my nephew. I fear he is setting up his own court in opposition to the Queen and she is not happy, to put it mildly.'

'I have just passed Essex House – there is certainly quite a gathering.' Cecil has a vision of the Queen in a temper. It is a terrifying thought, even in the imagination.

'I have tried to warn him of the folly of allowing people to congregate in such a way.' Knollys continues to work at his hands as if making bread. 'He is so full of rage it is impossible to make him see sense.'

'Rage?' says Cecil, not sure what to make of it. The two men set off towards the steps that lead to the great hall.

'His sorrow has transformed to bitter anger. He raves; in my opinion he is not at all in his right mind. He believes he has enemies everywhere.'

'When did you see him?' Cecil stops short of pointing out that the earl *does* have enemies everywhere.

'I went there this morning. I tried to reason with him.'

Cecil is about to say that the earl needs bringing into line, but he stops himself. 'The poor fellow needs our help, I don't doubt. I will try to petition Her Majesty.' Knollys looks visibly relieved, allowing his hands to drop and swing at his sides. 'And who is with him?'

'Many . . . too many, and some who, I fear, are poisoning his mind. Men who served with him in Ireland . . . Henry Cuffe and Ferdinando Gorges seem to have attached themselves to his crowd, as well as a fair number of disaffected nobles; and the usual circle: Meyrick, Anthony Bacon, Southampton, you know the ones.'

'Is Gorges not a kinsman of Ralegh?'

'I believe so,' says Knollys. 'Has a wild streak, I'm told.'

'Ralegh will not appreciate one of his cousins taking sides with Essex.'

'No, indeed,' says Knollys. 'There has never been any love lost between Ralegh and my nephew.' He has begun to knead his hands again. 'I passed a virtual army of common soldiers gathering in his courtyard.'

'You have cause for concern.' Cecil strokes a reassuring hand over Knollys's shoulder. 'I will do my best to placate the Queen.'

In the great hall a group of players is rehearsing. One is dressed in a woman's garb and parping out a speech in a voice high as a pipe, with grossly exaggerated facial expressions and arm gestures. Knollys insists on stopping to watch for a full five minutes until the fellow collapses to the floor with a wail, apparently dead. Cecil finds the whole thing ridiculous, wonders how anyone could be moved by such a grotesque display and is about to say as much, when a slow handclap starts up on the other side of the chamber. He looks up to see the Queen with a clutch of women.

'Your Majesty,' he says, whipping his cap from his head and dropping into a deep bow.

'Up, up,' she commands, as if he is one of her hounds. 'What do you think of him?' Her arm sweeps round in the direction of the player.

Cecil inspects the Queen's face for clues as to how to form his response. 'Extraordinary, Your Majesty.' He has got into the habit of scrutinizing her forensically for signs of displeasure. She has been aloof these last months, that is true, but it is impossible to say whether this coldness is deliberately directed towards him, or is a more general distance.

'You are not so proficient at hiding your true thoughts as you might think, Cecil.'

He thinks – it is more hope really – that he can detect the ghost of a smile. 'There are many things I am not good at, Your Majesty. Alas, my failings are insurmountable. I find much drama beyond the limits of my narrow comprehension.'

'False modesty doesn't suit you.' Her look causes his insides to shrivel a little. 'Do you truly believe I would award you such high office if I felt your grasp of things was lacking? I am not surprised that someone of your pragmatism would find this kind of thing' – she nods towards the group of players – 'somewhat fanciful.' She returns that hard look back to him. 'I do, however, appreciate honesty.' She pauses, still holding him with her eyes, and he shuffles uncomfortably, noticing a trailing thread on her gown, which he longs to snip off. 'You know that well enough, surely?'

'I do, Your Majesty. If I am being honest, I believe drama can lead people into ill morals.'

'Ha!' she says, seeming amused. '*You* would know about that.' The shrivelling sensation returns to his gut.

'And it has the power to incite insurrection.'

'On that count you are right, but that is not a reason to dislike it; it is more a reason to respect it.'

'I cannot disagree, Your Majesty.'

'And talking of drama, what news of my favourite earl?' Her mouth turns down as she says this and Cecil cannot tell if it is in disdain or sadness. 'I understand he has returned to London.'

'He has, Your Majesty,' says Knollys, still kneading.

'I fear there are pressing things to discuss.' Cecil looks about the chamber and can count at least a dozen who are straining their necks to hear what is being said. 'Behind closed doors.'

'Understood,' she replies, proffering a gloveless hand for him to take.

He sees it as if for the first time, twisted and liver-spotted like an ancient piece of wood, traversed by a tangle of blue veins, knuckles painfully swollen. She had always had such beautiful hands, slender and silken. He glances over her, seeing the crêpe-like skin of her neck and breast, the sunken hollow of her throat, the lines carved into her face; and her eyes are filmy – the eyes of an old woman whose time has almost run through. He had thought he had time, time to form his allegiances, time to smooth his path to the next regime, but he has not. She snatches her hand away before he has a chance to take it.

They move slowly to the privy chamber, the Queen leaning heavily on Knollys, and when they are there she sinks into her chair, demanding a cushion for her back, which Cecil fetches for her. The two men hover, awaiting the command to sit, which does not come.

'So?' she says.

Cecil swallows. 'I fear the earl has become surrounded with bad advisors.'

'That is exactly what his sister says of me, that there are those about me who . . .' She stops in mid-flow, her eyes planted on Cecil. His stomach pitches. 'Oh never mind.'

'A great number of' – Knollys seems to search for the right word – 'disaffected men have gathered at Essex House and I fear they will incite the earl into some kind of rebellion.'

'Perhaps they have all been watching too much drama,' says the Queen, raising her eyebrows. 'Don't you think, Pygmy?'

On hearing that name, the tension drops from him instantly. He can only imagine that the sensation is something like being released from an hour on the rack. She is laughing with abandon at her joke. Cecil joins in. 'Yes, too much drama.'

Knollys doesn't laugh, he is taut as a bowstring, worried about his errant nephew, no doubt. 'If . . . if I might make a . . . a suggestion, madam.'

The Queen turns to him, shoulders heaving, wiping her eyes with the back of her hand, smearing it thickly with white make-up which finds its way on to her dark dress. 'You are right; it is no laughing matter. How many are there?'

'A good two hundred.'

'Oh dear,' she says, the mirth falling away from her face as if it never was. It is replaced not with anger, as Cecil expects, but a look of desolation. 'And what is your suggestion, Knollys?'

'It might be judicious to summon the earl – allow him to come and explain himself to Your Majesty personally. Perhaps if I were to go there with one or two others, talk some sense into him and bring him back to you?'

She turns to Cecil for his opinion. He nods. 'I think it the best course of action.' He is so accustomed to making the pretence of supporting the earl for the sake of his own reputation, he is quite surprised by the strength of genuine sentiment he has at the thought of giving Essex a chance. He would be in his rights to oppose the suggestion; after all, the hordes amassing at Essex House might well pose a serious threat to the safety of the Queen's person, to the safety of England. He cannot stop looking at the smear of white on the Queen's dress, wants to go at it with a wet cloth. This is his chance to topple his great foe and he is not taking it. 'It might defuse the situation.' He is thinking now of the Queen's old age and his own uncertain future.

He has long suspected that letters of friendship have continued, over the years, to pass between Scotland and Essex House, though he never did manage to get his hands on one, despite his best efforts. All the other possibilities – the Infanta, the Stuart girl, Lord Beauchamp or his brother – are freighted with problems. It is King James who holds all the cards in this game now: he is closest in blood, he has two boys and a fertile wife and, most of all, he is male – England has tired of having a woman at the helm; the small fact that James was not born on English soil has become a moot point in the light of all the advantages. If James favours Essex then so must Cecil, if he is to have a hope of surviving into the next regime. 'I truly believe the earl means you no harm, madam.'

'I sincerely hope you are right.' She takes a deep inhalation. 'And Lady Rich, is *she* there?'

'She is, madam,' says Knollys. 'With a number of women: her sister, Lady Southampton and Lady Essex.'

The Queen covers her face with her hands as if she is entirely spent. 'Penelope and her brother were the nearest I had to my own children.' Cecil is surprised to see her so wistful. It is not usually her way. 'But the fact can never be got away from, they were spawned by a she-wolf.' That's more like it, he thinks.

'I know they love you,' says Knollys, 'and would do you no harm.'

'Call a council meeting,' says the Queen, slipping her authority on like a cape. 'We shall see what *they* have to say about this.'

February 1601

Essex House, the Strand

Essex House is teeming. Penelope's only refuge from the unruly horde is in her private rooms, but even in that small sanctuary, where she sits with Dorothy and Lizzie Vernon, she can feel the atmosphere of suppressed violence and dissent pressing in on her. Her brother's supporters – the soldiers milling in the courtyard, the men swaggering about the great hall, the close friends in his privy chamber murmuring heatedly behind the closed door – are all in a state of high alert, like an army the night before a battle.

'I wish to God he had accepted the Queen's summons yesterday,' says Penelope. 'I have a terrible feeling about this.'

'My husband said Essex was afraid to go to the palace.' Lizzie has lost her usual ebullience. 'Thought it was a trick, that he would be arrested.'

'It's true he was afraid,' says Dorothy. 'He confessed as much to me.' She looks strained and Penelope sees for the first time the age on her sister's face, a certain gauntness behind her obvious beauty, and wonders if she too wears that same look.

'I tried to persuade him otherwise,' Penelope says. 'I showed him a letter Uncle Knollys sent to me, with firm assurances that the Queen would allow him to speak for himself. Even Cecil wants this resolved . . .' She was going to say 'peacefully' but can't bear the implication. 'Or so our uncle said, but Essex is driven by his suspicions –' She stops, meeting her sister's black eyes. 'I fear he is not quite in his right mind. There are people putting ideas into his head.'

'Which people?' asks Lizzie.

'What sort of ideas?' says Dorothy simultaneously.

'Nefarious ones.' Penelope wishes Blount was present, not only for the fact that the strings of her heart are tugged to breaking point with fear for his safety, but also for the fact that she has great need of his advice. He would know the best course of action. 'I overheard Gorges and Cuffe discussing –'

'Who *are* those men?' interrupts Dorothy. 'They hang around Robin constantly. Even Meyrick appears to be in their thrall.' She puffs out an angry snort of air. 'What were they discussing?'

'The fact that Essex's claim on the throne is greater than the Infanta's.' Penelope hadn't intended to divulge this, had feared fanning its flames, but it had been niggling at her for hours.

Her sister gasps and covers her mouth with both hands.

'You mean they would see your brother on the throne of England?' Lizzie's voice is shrill with shock. 'But that is *high treason.*'

'Oh, Lizzie.' Penelope rests her elbow on the arm of her chair and drops her forehead into her palm. Despair prods at her. 'It is all treason, if they want it to be, but, yes, *that* would be incontrovertible.' She glances over at her sister, who is like a woman drowning, her breath shallow, eyes flitting. 'A grab for the throne is altogether different from a desire to remove the evil influences on the Queen's council and insist that a successor be named.' She is aware that she sounds as if she is reading from a script. 'That is all we have ever wanted – the security of the Queen and England.' She knows she is being a little disingenuous, for truly what they have wanted before that is the security of the Devereuxs.

'But if it gets out amongst this lot,' Lizzie points out of the window towards the crowded courtyard, 'that the earl's inner circle are saying such things, it will . . .' The colour has fallen from her face. Lizzie's little dog, at her feet, seeming to sense the atmosphere, begins to whimper and scratch at her skirts.

'It will ignite them and start something that cannot be stopped,' says Dorothy; her hands are shaking slightly.

'It may well be too late already.' Penelope shuts her eyes and thinks of Blount, sending him a silent message of love. When he left it was *his* life she feared for and now she is not so sure it won't be hers hanging in the balance before the week is out. 'But even so, I think I will try and talk to them' – she thinks of Gorges with those close-set eyes, Cuffe's bland face and Meyrick hanging on their words like a lovelorn maid – 'make them see what danger they are visiting on Essex with this seditious talk.' She wishes now that she had pulled them up when she overheard their conversation, made them see sense. 'It is unlikely they are the only ones who think this, but I cannot sit here doing nothing.'

'Cuffe and Gorges are not here,' says Dorothy.

'Where are they?'

'I don't know, they said something about going to see a playwright with Meyrick and a number of others. They want him to put on a play tonight. All quite harmless.'

'Who was the playwright?' asks Penelope. The hairs on the back of her neck are standing to attention.

'I don't think they mentioned him by name.'

A well of dread opens up in her. 'Did they mention a particular play?'

'They did.' Dorothy pauses. 'The Life and Death of some king or other.'

'For God's sake, Dot, can't you be more specific?' says Penelope, regretting her impatience, for Dorothy looks as if she has been slapped.

'You know me. I do not have a memory for such things. Why is it so important, anyway?'

'Might it have been Richard II?' Penelope's tone is softer, coaxing.

'Yes, I believe it might have been. Which one was Richard II? Wasn't he the one that was usurped?' She looks across at Penelope. 'What is it? What's wrong?' Her eyes are glazed with fear.

'Listen, I think you should leave – both of you. Go home to your children. I shall tell your husband, Lizzie.'

'What is it?' It is Lizzie asking this time. 'You're frightening me. What's the play about, that it causes you such upset?'

'It tells of a weak king with no heirs, who is deposed by a strong pretender beloved of the people.'

'Oh!' Penelope can see understanding alight in both her cousin and her sister. Dorothy reaches out for Lizzie's hand, holding it so tight that the sinews in her wrist protrude.

'Don't be alarmed. I simply think it would be . . .' Penelope almost says 'safer' but stops herself. 'It would be better if you were at home.'

'But should *you* not also go home?' asks Dorothy.

Penelope thinks of her children, thankful that they are safe in the depths of Essex. Rich is there too. A realization strikes her now that Rich's departure yesterday was not, as he had said, occasioned by a tenancy dispute that needed his attention; he was a rat leaving a doomed vessel. He had not even tried to persuade her to go with him. She wonders why she is even taken aback by this.

'I cannot leave Robin. This is his hour of need and if I can limit the damage . . .'

'But *I* am his sister too,' insists Dorothy.

'Leave this to me, Dot. You go to Mother. She will be beside herself.'

Dorothy expels a slow breath. 'If you wish it so.'

Lizzie's face begins to crumble, her eyes spilling tears. Dorothy holds her, rocking slightly. Penelope watches them, her mind a whirr, planning what must be done.

'Go, before it is too late,' she says, once Lizzie's tears have subsided.

'What about Frances?' asks Dorothy.

'I imagine she will insist upon staying with Robin.' Frances has surprised her lately. That timid mouse of a woman has found her courage. She is reminded of her words at Sidney's funeral: *It was you he loved.* Those were not the words of a timorous creature; that stoicism was always in her; indeed, perhaps that is what Sidney admired. She has never really thought about that before, had always believed he'd married Frances through loyalty to her father; her jealousy must have clouded her perception.

The two women gather their things in silence. Lizzie picks up her little dog and heads for the door, turning back, holding a hand out for Dorothy. Penelope smiles and blows a kiss, making light of it, then stands a while at the window, glad they are gone to safety, yet wishing she did not feel so alone; even Fides is in the country with the children. She looks down at the courtyard, where someone is standing on a box, speaking to a gathered crowd. She cannot hear what is being said but judging by the fists punching the air it is a rousing speech. Her mind is turning over and over on what she can do to douse their misplaced enthusiasm.

Leaving her chambers, without bothering to put on her over-gown, she seeks out her brother, finding Anthony Bacon alone in Essex's privy rooms. He is jaundiced; his eyes a livid yellow, and seems in terrible pain, wincing when he shifts position.

'You are not well, Anthony,' she says needlessly.

'My health is the last thing that concerns me.'

'Do you have news yet from the Earl of Mar? Perhaps we can at least try and persuade them to see the sense in delaying things until Mar's arrival. Once he has spoken to the Queen in my brother's favour, things might look very different. Mar speaks for King James, after all.'

'I have word he is on his way but I'm afraid he has not

crossed the border yet. He is travelling slowly. It will be a good ten days . . .' He looks at her as if she might have an answer to this situation. 'I fear we do not have that much time.'

'Indeed, this lot will not be held at bay for long.' Realizing, with a shiver, that she is cold without her over-gown, she sits on a stool close to the fire. 'What do you know about this play?'

'Oh dear!' he sighs. 'They had the bit between their teeth. It was Cuffe's idea and he got a number of others behind them, Meyrick . . . that fellow Gorges too. Your brother did nothing to stop them – he seems to have fallen into a kind of . . .' Anthony looks at her again, pressing his lips together as if he doesn't trust what will come out of them.

'Madness,' she says. 'You may as well say it, Anthony. Everybody is thinking it.'

'It *is* like a mania.'

'Yes – a mania; he swings between that and complete inertia; in either state it is impossible to reason with him.'

'I wish Blount were here,' he says. 'Essex listens to Blount.'

'You are not alone in that.' She can't help the resignation in her voice and the distance of her beloved seems so great, as if he has travelled as far as the stars. She tries to think of his image of the compass's two conjoined arms, but it brings no comfort. 'So – the play?'

'They intend to pay the company forty shillings to put it on tonight. I tried to stop them.'

'Forty shillings, good Lord! That is a week's takings.'

'I imagine the deal is struck by now and word will be spreading already. They hope to generate further support for your brother. Get London on its toes in readiness.'

Neither of them needs to articulate what they are readying themselves for. All those years of quietly negotiating for the Devereuxs' future, she never truly imagined it would come to this.

417

'Do you think Cecil truly sought to put the Infanta in line as Uncle Knollys is supposed to have heard?'

'It seems like folly to champion a Catholic for the throne,' he says. 'But Cecil may have seen some political advantage there. It is possible, I suppose.'

They hear shouting on the steps outside and Essex bursts in with Southampton. The pair of them are flushed and high-strung with nervous excitement, pacing back and forth across the room. Essex is ranting about Cecil and sucking urgently on a dead pipe: 'We will remove him and all the others, by force if need be. That man seems not to care that people are starving on the streets. He persists in his evil policies. I will rescue her from him.' His eyes are rotating. 'They all want me dead: Cecil, Ralegh . . . all the rest . . .'

'Robin,' says Penelope, rising and attempting to place an arm about his shoulders.

But he shakes her off. 'You don't understand.' A shower of spittle lands on her face. '*You* have never had to wield a sword or fight for your life. You think you have the answer for everything but you are just a *woman*.'

She suppresses an angry retort, tempering her tone. 'There are peaceful means to achieve what you want.'

'You sound like *Cecil* now.' He throws his pipe across the room. 'I cannot even get satisfaction from that blasted thing.'

'This is folly, Robin. Can you not hold your fire until the Earl of Mar arrives, at least?'

'She's right,' says Anthony.

'It's true, she has a point,' says Southampton, upon which Essex grabs his shoulders and presses his forehead to Southampton's with a snarl.

'Not you too! Afraid, are you?'

Southampton shakes his friend off. 'Not afraid, no! I stand by you and fall by you. But your sister has wisdom to her fingertips.'

'My clever sister . . .' Essex begins to rant again, barely making sense, and Southampton tries to calm him, eventually luring him into his bedchamber with the promise of tobacco. Her brother seems to have regressed into childhood, has entirely lost control of himself.

After some silence Anthony adjusts his position with a groan. 'I think we have reached a point when we need to gather as much support from credible nobles as possible.'

'I will do what I can. Cecil has enough enemies to make an army.' She spits out a caustic laugh. 'Leave it with me.'

Whitehall

'It is only a play,' says one of the Queen's women, 'no cause for concern.'

The Queen lifts the edge of her headdress to scratch beneath it with a long finger. 'Do you not see, *I* am the second Richard.' She turns to Cecil, asking, 'Are you sure the deposition scene was left in?'

'Absolutely sure, madam,' says Cecil. He is weighing up how best to approach this. He has it from a good source that the performance was paid for by someone in the Essex camp.

The Queen lets out a frustrated 'Agh' and rips off her headgear – 'That thing!' – flinging it to the floor and going at her scalp, scratching hard with both hands. Pins scatter, the loudest sound in the room, and a couple of pearls break away, rolling over the floor. There is a moment's stasis; no one knows how to react until a woman crouches down to pick up the pearls. A maid follows suit, retrieving the hood and the pins, carefully replacing them one by one into a pincushion. She hovers with the headdress, waiting for instructions. The Queen looks up. Cecil has never seen her hair uncovered and is surprised that it is almost white, remembering then that she is nearly seventy. 'Just fetch me a plain coif. I've had enough of that discomfort,' she says to the waiting girl.

When the maid has gone she beckons Cecil to come closer and whispers, 'I know not what to do.' He is shocked to see her so forlorn. 'If only your father were here.'

He interprets it as a slight; the inference is that he is not up to the job. 'As do I,' he says, surprising himself with his own frankness. She is looking at him, waiting for a suggestion.

'Send Knollys. Let him gently persuade the earl to come to you.' He is thinking of the Scottish King. He will never forge those ties without the earl.

'Essex has twice refused my summons,' she mutters. 'Do you suppose him truly to be ailing as he says?'

'I think not, madam; I think he is afraid.'

She seems puzzled to hear this, sitting up straight with a quizzical expression. Perhaps she cannot imagine her warrior earl afraid of anything, least of all her; perhaps she cannot see that every last person here is afraid of her. He tries to imagine what it is like to be her, Elizabeth; how it must be to have everyone tread on eggshells about you out of fear, yet not know it. It makes him consider how entrenched people become, when they are old, in their ideas of others. It is as if she has a version of Essex in her mind and anything that veers from it is unrecognizable.

'Organize it, Cecil. Send Knollys, but not alone. Have Essex brought to me that he may plead his case in person.'

As he goes to leave, she calls him back. 'You stay here with me, Pygmy.' Adding very quietly at the end, 'I need you.'

A flower of satisfaction opens in him and he feels, for an instant, that he is what people think he is: the most powerful man in England. But the sensation is defiled by the realization that these words from the Queen, words that he has waited to hear for two decades, have come too late: everyone is looking to the future now and she is the past.

February 1601

Essex House, the Strand

It is not long past dawn and from her bed Penelope can hear men shouting down in the yard, a brutish sound that charges her with dread. Things have gathered their own momentum, there will be no waiting for the Earl of Mar to come from Scotland now; it is far too late for that. She had been there last night when the coordination of arms and forces was discussed. Her brother's close circle sat about the table in the great chamber; a number of nobles had joined their ranks by her careful persuasion. Their blood was up and Penelope was unable to turn them from their warmongering; none would listen to reason. Southampton had laughed openly at her suggestion that Essex accept the Queen's summons; only Anthony Bacon had been in agreement with her, though he sat with his head in his hands for most of the meeting.

'It is a trap, he will be murdered, or at the very least arrested if he goes anywhere near that place,' Southampton had said to her, enunciating as if she were a child who needed her Greek vocabulary explained.

There had been a dispute about what to do first: march on the court, muster supporters in the city, or capture the Tower with its arsenal and the mint. Southampton and Gorges came near to blows. Essex said almost nothing, just sat stiffly at the table's head wearing a blank expression, muttering about trust and jumping at the slightest sound. She quietly suggested he retire.

'To be murdered in my bed?' he replied with force and she understood, more from his wild expression than his words, that he had come to the very edge of his sanity.

She had tried to make a suggestion about flight, thinking the only way to prevent this rebellion – for that is what it has become, a monster that has crept up on them – was to get her brother away, abroad. She had been shouted down. There had been no agreement and tempers became frayed. When another messenger arrived from court with a further summons and was dispatched with the excuse that the earl's health would not allow it, she yet again tried to make her brother see the sense in going to plead his case at the palace.

'They do not seek to hear me – that council of varlets – they seek to silence me for good,' is what he had replied.

Later, in bed, it occurred to her that as long as they couldn't agree on the best course of action, there would be no action. She felt only slightly reassured by that and had barely slept, missing Blount desperately, trying to comfort herself by imagining she was at Wanstead with him, surrounded by their children. It would be just an ordinary day, unremarkable. They would ride out, see the early lambs and count the crocus heads piercing the earth in promise of spring. They would play cards on their return and then all gather for music; she would sing and the children would accompany her on their instruments. Then they would go to bed and she would lose herself in her lover's arms – a commonplace life.

She tried to remember what it was like to lie in Blount's embrace, the tang of him – sage rubbed between finger and thumb – the way he touched her, how his skin felt against hers, but she couldn't conjure up the remotest sense of him and began to ask herself if he existed only in her mind. Try as she might she couldn't keep her thoughts on happier things because she could hear the hubbub of the men in the courtyard, talking, making plots with her brother at their heart. She lit a candle and re-read all Blount's letters, though she knew them by heart, seeking succour in the sight of his script. When sleep came it was uneasy and too shallow to bring any rest.

Once morning has come they all gather again in the great chamber, to continue the heated disagreement about either taking the court by stealth or mustering men in London – there is some fellow named Smyth in the city who can bring a thousand men to their cause, or so Gorges asserts. Gorges, with those unnerving eyes, seems to have so many of them in his thrall.

But what *is* their cause, Penelope wants to ask, for there are some who seek only to be rid of the Queen's bad council, but others . . . She cannot even think the thought. Gorges's fervour and seeming eagerness for a fight is cause for grave concern.

She takes Meyrick aside and asks, 'Can Gorges be entirely trusted?'

'I shouldn't worry about that, he fought beside your brother in France . . . bravely, too.'

'You are sure of him?'

Meyrick places a vast steadying hand on her forearm. 'Absolutely.' She allows herself to dismiss her suspicions of Gorges, remembering Meyrick's years of loyalty to the Devereuxs and his uncanny ability to detect calumny. They watch in silence then as Gorges and Southampton descend once more into full dispute.

Southampton calls the other man 'dog-hearted', tossing his mane and adding, 'We march on the court, take them by surprise.'

'We are too few for that. A full thousand men await us in the city, if you would throw up that opportunity then you are more of a fool than I thought.' Southampton reaches for his sword, causing Gorges to puff his chest out and step forward to stand barely an inch away from his adversary. Penelope notices, for the first time, that Gorges's doublet is threadbare at the elbows, in contrast to Southampton's splendid damask. Meyrick tries to pull Gorges away but Southampton grabs him by the throat, ripping that worn doublet at the collar.

'Call me a fool, you miscreant,' Southampton spits. 'Think you can conjure a force of a thousand from nowhere . . . you, a *nobody* . . .'

Essex barely moves a muscle, just watches, stonily.

Penelope leaves the chamber and makes for the stairs, racking her brains for someone to turn to: her mother, Essex might listen to *her* at least. She dismisses the thought. It dawns upon her that Lettice has waited years for a moment such as this – bred them all to it. Lettice, in one sense or other, will achieve her own personal revenge if Essex pulls off his coup. She has never yet thought ill of her mother and hopes it is the lack of sleep and the relentless worry, rather than the blackness of her heart, that has infected her mind with such disloyalty.

She seeks out Frances, finding her at prayer in her closet, and stands quietly in the doorway, watching her. Her eyes are shut, her mouth moves and her head sways slightly from side to side as if she is in a trance. Penelope finds herself envious of the intensity of Frances's supplications. Her own faith is worn thin, like Gorges's doublet, and she cannot think of how to speak to God beyond the rote thanks for the health of her children. Her gratitude is threadbare too.

Frances opens her eyes and stands, turning towards her sister-in-law. 'Has he spoken to you? I cannot get any sense out of him.'

Penelope doesn't know what to say, just shakes her head and lifts her shoulders slightly.

'I know,' Frances says. 'He is in the grip of something.'

'Do you not want to leave, go to your mother and children at Barn Elms? You could take the barge.' Penelope goes to the window, from where there is a good view of the Strand. London seems to be going about its business: two women in high hats trundle along with a handcart, a boy kicks a ball aimlessly against a wall with a rhythmic *douf, douf, douf*, church bells chime out in unison for matins. The sky is clean and pale blue. It is a day too bright and pretty for a rebellion.

'I will stay,' says Frances. 'He does not know it, but he needs me – needs us – you and me.' Penelope can see, then, the depth of Frances's stoicism and that her anxious disposition is merely a veneer covering a loyalty that is solid and steady and rooted.

'You truly love him, don't you?'

She smiles with a little nod.

'Are you prepared for death?' Penelope doesn't know why she asks this but once it is out she feels she has released something dark into the room. Her mind goes over the possible outcomes of this day but none is happy.

'I am.' Frances's eyes flick up as if invoking God.

Penelope is distracted by a small procession of riders and a coach headed up the Strand from the direction of Whitehall. She watches as they come to a halt at the gates below. A page, in the palace livery, jumps down from his horse and for a moment she thinks it is the Queen herself come to see Essex, instantly reflecting on the stupidity of such a thought. The Queen would not visit a disgraced earl like that, though she did once, Penelope remembers. She came with physic when he was ailing – administered it herself. That was in the days when Essex could do no wrong and his disgrace was only ever paper-thin.

Frances, who has joined her at the window, says, 'Isn't that your uncle?'

She leans in towards the glass, close enough to feel the whisper of a chilled draught on the skin of her face. Uncle Knollys is being helped out of the coach, followed by three others: the Lord Keeper, the Lord Chief Justice and Worcester, who is a family friend. Penelope's spirits are lifted a little on seeing such a benign delegation.

This is certainly not an arrest — there are a number of servants with them but no guards. The two women exchange a hopeful smile and watch as the men walk towards the house. The main gate has been barricaded and several men with muskets can been seen on the inside of it. They shout that no one will be admitted without permission from the earl — Penelope hears it quite clearly from where she stands — and Knollys, who knows the house well, leads the way round to the east entrance. Penelope and Frances move into the adjacent chamber where there is a view over the wicket gate at the side.

There is no barricade there, only one of her brother's captains drilling a group of men, none of whom appear to be armed. She opens the window and shouts down, 'They are friends — family. Let them in,' feeling the smallest inkling of hope. The captain admits the delegation but stops the servants, save for a single pageboy, slamming the gate firmly, leaving them outside holding the horses. Essex's lurcher bitch bounds over to Knollys, greeting him exuberantly, and the consignment of men approach, gathering round the party in a hostile cluster, with more joining their ranks. They start to jostle and jeer. Penelope opens the window to try to catch what her uncle is saying but they are in a tight huddle and their words cannot be heard above the heckling.

The small delegation makes for the side doors, and the two women rush to the head of the stairs. They watch as the group is led to the great chamber and announced. It is only a few moments before Essex appears with Southampton and a number of others, leading the visitors up the first flight of stairs and along the gallery.

'To the study?' suggests Frances.

'I suppose so,' says Penelope. Hope takes hold in her. 'I'm going down there.' She descends the stairs two at a time and turns into the gallery, where the bright day lies in criss-crossed squares on the floor. Approaching the study, she has a sudden surprising memory of taking this exact path years ago in the dark, on the night when Sidney waited for her in that same chamber – it was used as a music room then and the house was Leicester's. She wonders if her life would have been different had she gone to him that night, whether it might have taken another path.

Her brother appears in the doorway with Southampton, barely acknowledging her presence. Meyrick and another man, both with muskets slung over their shoulders casually as if they are satchels, follow them out and the door is shut with a firm *thunk*. They stand one on either side of it, Meyrick bringing his weapon round to the front of his body, holding it now in both hands. Southampton turns the key and hands it to Essex who gives it to Meyrick. She tries to catch Meyrick's eye but he will not look at her. Her feeling of hope pops, like a soap bubble, to nothing. This is not right. She can hear her uncle shouting from within, 'For God's sake, Essex, do not do something you will regret!'

She turns to her brother who is striding towards her. 'What have you done?'

Knollys's desperate voice comes again. 'I will not be able to help you this time.'

Essex cannot meet her eye either, and tries to walk past but she grabs his sleeve and pushes him to the wall, surprised by her own strength. 'I hope you know what you are doing.'

'They think I will follow them to the palace like a puppy' – he jabs towards the closed door repeatedly with his forefinger – 'where Cecil and his cronies and that fiend Ralegh will be waiting to do me in. I would not survive five minutes in that place.' He is pent up, trembling beneath her hands, and his eyes rotate, making him look like a lunatic.

'It is Uncle Knollys in there.' She points towards the

guarded door. '*He* would see no harm is done to you. Worcester too, he is a friend. They are trying to help –'

'You seem to forget' – he has his face close up to hers but still will not meet her gaze – 'that the Lord Keeper in there was my jailer all those months at York House, and as for Popham . . .'

Penelope concedes silently that Lord Chief Justice Popham has never been a friend of the Devereuxs.

Southampton is hovering. She turns to him with a question on her face but he just makes a small shrug. 'I follow the earl's lead.'

'Were you truly his friend you would see that he is not . . .' She doesn't bother finishing, for they are not listening. Just says to her brother, 'It has gone too far. You cannot turn back. My only advice now is to find your courage and get the thing done properly.' She hardly recognizes herself.

He pulls himself free of her and puts two fingers to his mouth, whistling sharply. His other hand is on the pommel of his sword. Footsteps scurry on the stairs and a page appears.

'Fetch our breastplates,' Essex says to the lad. 'And my double-bladed poniard, the sharp one, and the short musket, you know the one. And pick a weapon for yourself.' His voice is smooth and calm, as if he is ordering meats for a banquet. The boy blanches a little. Perhaps he is imagining himself in pitched battle with grown men.

Essex is fondling his sword hilt as if it is a woman's hand. 'Not that,' says Penelope, pointing to it. 'Leave Sidney's sword out of this.'

Essex laughs, seeming now entirely in control of himself – not mad at all. 'You women can be so very sentimental.' He unbuckles his belt and swipes it off, handing the whole thing – belt, sword, scabbard – to her. It is not as heavy as she'd expected, not like that broadsword she'd tried to wield at the theatre. No, this weapon is slender and agile, a thing of great beauty. 'We will take all the men – how many have we – two, three hundred?'

Southampton is nodding. 'The Welsh force is not yet here. Shouldn't we await their arrival?'

'There's no time for that. Tell the men to prepare to march on London immediately. There shall gather Gorges's promised force of a thousand and any others who will join us.'

'At last you make a decision,' says Penelope, unable to hold her tongue. 'Sadly, it is the wrong one. If you had any sense you would march on the court while the council is in session. Get them all before they are prepared – Cecil, Grey, Cobham, Ralegh – in one fell swoop.' She looks to Southampton for support but he turns his head away.

Essex throws her a withering look. 'What would you know of such things?'

She is left standing in the long gallery holding the sword and, without thinking, she buckles it about her own waist, feeling then like an Athena or some other warrior queen from the myths. She runs her finger over the hilt, feeling the embossed initials PS, then draws it, enjoying the metallic swipe of sound, thrusting at an imaginary opponent, circling it through the air with a swish. It whispers a warning in her ear.

February 1601

Whitehall

'The delegation is being held at Essex House,' says Cecil, reading from a note that was delivered by one of his men.

'Under guard?' asks the Queen. 'They are held hostage?'

'I believe so. Essex is leading his men to the city to muster troops.' Cecil is afraid – there is a sharp sensation in his gut as if he has swallowed a shard of glass and it is lacerating his stomach. He tries to expel thoughts of Essex and his men hunting him through the corridors of the palace, cornering him, brutalizing him. He can feel their boots making contact with his skull; he can feel the sensation of the floor scraping beneath him as he is dragged by the feet; and he can hear the crunch of his bones as he is thrown into the bottom of a barge to be taken downriver to the Tower.

There is a clamour of voices as the council members all try to make themselves heard above each other, until the Queen thwacks the table hard with the clerk's ledger. They all turn towards her. She shows nothing of what must be roiling beneath her surface.

She points to Cobham. 'You first, what do you know?'

'I have word the earl has a thousand men at his disposal in the city.'

'I doubt he can gather those numbers,' says Ralegh, who seems unperturbed and is cleaning his fingernails with a toothpick.

'He is more beloved of the people than –' starts Cobham.

'More beloved than *us*,' the Queen cuts in. 'Was that what you were about to say?' She seems less troubled by fear for her life than the indignity of being thought less popular than the earl.

431

Cobham mumbles, flush-faced, wittering on about how of course no one is more beloved than she.

'Nevertheless,' says Cecil, 'we must ensure Your Majesty's safety.' He cannot get those thousand men out of his mind. They might well be bearing down on the palace already, brandishing their weapons, baying for blood. 'This is not a fortified place.' The Queen looks at him as if he is an idiot for stating the obvious. He sits on his hands to stop them trembling.

The Lord High Admiral suggests sending the Queen by barge with a consignment of guards to the safety of Windsor Castle. 'We simply cannot match the earl in men at such short notice.'

Another prefers Hampton Court, 'for they will not think to look there', and a general squabbling starts up about the best place for the Queen to go for her protection. Cecil stops himself from suggesting that he should accompany her, hoping she will want him by her side anyway.

'Enough!' says the Queen. 'We will not slide off to Windsor or anywhere else. We shall remain here, where we belong. We have faced worse than this.'

There is a moment's silence. Cecil wonders if they are all thinking, as he is, that she has not faced worse than this. There have been assassination attempts, some close calls, but never a usurping army marching on her. He is trying his best not to think of himself, trying to gather a few fragments of courage to face whatever it is that is on its way.

'Send Cumberland with a detachment of troops, the hardest men we have.' She is talking directly to Ralegh. 'Trap the earl in the city walls. And send someone into London with word that the men who stand down shall be pardoned.' She sinks back in her chair. 'Ensure the palace guard is on full alert.' She stops, looking round at the collected councillors dispassionately. 'We shall reconvene on the hour.'

Ralegh is the first out of his seat, barking orders at his

432

steward, who is waiting outside in the gallery. The others follow suit, bustling about, looking for their pages, calling for their weapons and armour. Cecil finds himself praying silently.

'Cards, Pygmy?' says the Queen. He must be staring at her open-mouthed, for she adds, 'Catching flies?'

'Cards?'

'Yes, I thought separating you from that purse of crowns I see nestling in your doublet might be a fitting distraction from the . . .' She pauses, seeking an apposite word, Cecil presumes, then adds, 'Anticipation.' She beckons a page, asking him to bring a deck.

Cecil admonishes himself silently for his lack of mettle, which contrasts starkly with the Queen's apparent nonchalance in the face of such great danger. Much as he tries to push the dark thoughts away, his wayward mind runs through all the possible disastrous outcomes of this situation, digging up the old anxiety (worn thin with over-examination) of that letter to the Spanish ambassador. Surely, he reasons, if the Queen knew of it I would not be at her side now, allowing her to win my bag of coin from me.

'God put me on this throne against all the odds and will ensure I remain here, if it is His wish.' Her eyes turn to the ceiling. She clicks her fingers, asking a page for sweetmeats, and goes back to her cards, as if the only thing that merits her focus in this moment is the game.

The page brings a dish of fancies; the Queen puts one in her mouth, licking the sugar from her lips with a darting tongue. 'Go on, Pygmy. They are delicious.' She pushes the plate in his direction. He helps himself, out of politeness. It sticks to the roof of his mouth and the extreme sweetness exacerbates a toothache that has been niggling for some time.

He lays down his hand: a desultory collection of mismatched threes and fours. Hers reveals a run of hearts – ten, knave, queen, king. 'I hope you're not letting me win. I wouldn't like that.'

He shakes his head, mumbling, his mouth too full of the gluey confection to speak properly. She picks out the queen of hearts, holding it face up to Cecil. 'Where is Lady Rich? Is she still at Essex House?'

'I believe so, madam.'

She flinches almost imperceptibly, as if a wasp has stung her but she doesn't want to show she is in pain.

February 1601

Essex House, the Strand

Penelope still hears the echo of her brother's shouts as he paraded down the Strand towards the city. 'For the Queen! For the Queen! A plot is laid for my life!' A lacklustre cheer had gone up in response, nothing like the great roars of support she has heard for him in the past, and she listened out for the chant of *Ess-ex, Ess-ex, Ess-ex* but it didn't come. She makes a silent prayer of thanks for Gorges's thousand men. In her mind that multitude has become like a biblical miracle – a horde from nothing. She hopes God is on their side, wishes she could feel sure of it.

Not knowing what else to do, she makes for the chapel, finding Frances there, hunched over the prayer stand. She looks up as Penelope enters; their eyes meet and they nod solemnly like mourners at a funeral. Penelope kneels beside her sister-in-law and, pressing her palms together, pours her heart out, beseeching God to save her brother, to save them all. She asks for a sign; but nothing comes, no ray of light falling through the window, no thunderclap, nothing, only one of her brother's guards who sidles in, standing behind them, clearing his throat to gain their attention.

She turns to look at him, struck by his youth – what is he: thirteen, fourteen perhaps? He carries a musket that dwarfs him and she cannot help but think of her own boys and young Robert, who stands to inherit this mess, thankful they are out of the way. But who will help *this* lad if it comes to the worst? She can feel tears smarting in the roots of her eyes for this boy she has never seen before.

'Your uncle requests that you go to him, My Lady.' He

blushes as he speaks – unused to women of rank, she supposes. She wants to tell him to leave, to go home to his mother.

The two women rise and follow the boy out. She slips her arm through Frances's. Her body is unyielding. The boy's feet whisper on the floorboards of the long gallery – he is not even wearing proper boots – and her slippers slap out a rhythm, whilst Frances, who must have on hard-soled shoes, in preparation for flight perhaps, makes a *tap*, *tap*, *tap*, like a little drum to accompany them.

Meyrick is at the study door and seems relieved to see her. 'See if you can calm them, My Lady,' he says, slowly closing his eyes, with their colourless lashes, and opening them again – a small gesture of hopelessness. 'They are becoming most agitated.'

'Why is my brother not back yet?' she asks. 'It has been almost three hours.'

'I have had no news,' is all Meyrick says as he unlocks the door and opens it. She supposes he is hoping that she will be able to negotiate them all out of this situation, but she fears it has gone too far for that. She sends the boy to the kitchens for food. 'The best our cook can produce. These are noble guests and ought to be treated as such.'

'How delightful,' says her uncle when they enter, as if this is merely a social gathering. He opens his arms and steps towards her with a smile that doesn't erase the crease of worry from between his eyes and, holding her hands in his, presses a dry kiss on each of her cheeks. She greets the others formally. Chief Justice Popham skewers the two women with a hard look and steps away as if they might give him the pox. His mouth is mean and his face is long, every plane and angle sharp.

'You are armed, My Lady,' he says, glancing towards her waist, with a look that suggests the world has been turned on its head. His voice is phlegmy, quite at odds with his angular face.

'Oh, this!' She touches the sword, had forgotten about it. 'I am wearing it for safekeeping. It is ceremonial – not really suitable for combat.' His look of distaste is impossible to misinterpret and were it another day she might have laughed at him, given him a gentle ribbing.

She can hear the few men who were left to guard the house down in the yard talking and laughing – she wonders what they can find to laugh about but supposes these men are battle-hardened from her brother's campaigns, not tight with fear of the violence to come. They are the disaffected who have put all their hope in Essex and today marks the possibility of fulfilment. No wonder, then, that they are laughing.

Knollys begins to talk, but Popham speaks over him. 'What do you say to your brother's treachery, My Lady?'

'I do not think he means to be seditious, Lord Justice. He merely intends to remove those who seek to ill-use Her Majesty.'

The man replies with a laugh. 'We shall see about that.'

Uncle Knollys asserts himself now, saying, 'We must do *all* we can to get him back here and disarmed. But I fear he has gone too far this time.'

She says nothing. There is nothing to say. Essex cannot return now; he must see this thing through, whatever its outcome.

'Aside from what Essex is up to in the city, you must be aware, My Lady' – Popham says 'My Lady' as if it is ironic – 'that you commit an offence of the highest degree to hold the Queen's envoys hostage. We bring the royal seal.' He points to the pageboy who stands to one side, holding a scroll of parchment carefully, as if it is alive. There are two large seals hanging from it. The boy's hands are chapped and he quakes slightly; she smiles at him. He drops his eyes.

'Hostages!' she says, as if the very thought is absurd. 'You are *guests*. The earl has merely asked that you wait awhile for his return.' Her voice is steady as the untruth spills out.

437

'My husband had urgent business in the city,' adds Frances.

Popham arches his eyebrows, as if surprised to discover she has a voice.

'So the musketeers at the door are there for decoration? Perhaps they are made of painted plaster.' He emits a gurgle that might be a laugh, but his mouth is turned down so it is hard to say. 'And the locked door is for our safety, I suppose.'

'I think it might be wise, My Lady, to tell the guards to stand down and allow us to leave,' says the Lord Keeper with a pained expression. Despite the fact that it is February and there is no fire lit in the room, his forehead is glossed with sweat. Worcester is nodding in agreement. 'I personally will vouch that we stayed here at Essex House of our own volition. That will be one less charge against him.'

'*You* may say that but I will not,' says Popham. 'Essex deserves whatever fate awaits him. It is simply a question of how deep he intends to dig his own grave and who he will drag down with him.' Penelope clenches her fists, imagines her knuckles meeting the sharp bone of his cheek. 'It is said that you have authority in this house, My Lady.'

She holds his gaze, saying nothing.

He adds under his breath, 'Only a fool would give such power to a woman, and one of such loose morals.'

She wants to pick him up on his mutterings, force him to explain himself, but it is Frances, standing quietly beside her, who surprises everyone by saying firmly, 'That is no way to address Lady Rich.'

Uncle Knollys pipes up too. 'Watch your tongue, sir. That is my niece you speak of.'

Popham ignores them both. 'Do as your uncle says and perhaps *your* role in this will be overlooked.'

'I have found,' Penelope says, speaking in general to the company, 'men of the law to be less loyal than most.' She is thinking not only of the Lord Chief Justice but also of fickle Francis Bacon.

Popham coughs pointedly as if he will not dignify her words with a response. She is glad to see the doors opened and three servers enter with the food she ordered. They are silent as the dishes are laid out on the table. The cook has done them proud; it is quite a spread. Frances comments on the temperature, asking if anyone is feeling the cold and insisting that a scullion be sent up to light the fire, also suggesting some music as a diversion. It is a futile attempt to make this incarceration seem benign.

Uncle Knollys takes Penelope aside to say quietly, 'Have us released. This is too great a folly. I cannot bear to watch this . . .' His voice trails off.

She thinks about it, but only for an instant. The idea of saving her own skin is tempting, but she gathers her fortitude. 'Uncle, my hands are tied. I can do nothing without my brother's permission.' He looks crestfallen, so she adds, 'But I will endeavour to contact him.' She will not, for she knows that these hostages give her brother traction in his struggle and she is not about to weaken his cause by feeling sentimental over a beloved uncle. They will be freed in good time and they are being well looked after according to their station.

Both women make their excuses eventually, after an excruciating hour of strained conversation and the enforced jollity of a musical interlude. They leave the chamber, walking in silence along the gallery before Frances gives Penelope's hand a squeeze and peels off back to the chapel. Penelope stands for a moment, looking out at the river, not knowing what to do with herself. She watches a bevy of swans glide eastward and a fat-bellied wherry lumbering slowly towards the south bank. Other little craft dip and duck on the surface of the water, transporting people here and there, unaware of the momentous happenings going on so close by.

She wonders about her brother, why he hasn't reappeared with his great army, keeps thinking she can hear the sound of a thousand pairs of feet marching along the Strand towards Whitehall. But hope is deceiving her. She supposes it must need time to muster such a multitude. On impulse she takes the back stairs to the courtyard, where the remaining guards greet her as if she is royalty, which niggles at her, for perhaps it is their foolhardy wish that she will be the King's sister by the end of the day. Her brother has never sought to take the throne but she has learned that the ambitions of those around him cannot be underestimated. She wonders, then, if perhaps Essex *did* dream of such a thing – after all, hubris can gather its own momentum; she dismisses the thought instantly.

'We are at your bidding, My Lady. How can we serve you?' says one of the guards, standing to attention with a stamp of the feet, his weapon braced.

'If you truly wish to serve me,' she says loudly, directing her voice up towards the study window above, 'then I would have the Lord Chief Justice's head on a platter.'

The men laugh and joke loudly about playing football with 'Popham's noggin', and Penelope instantly regrets her words, wondering if, at the end of all this, Popham will be sitting in judgement over her and her brother. It is a sobering thought.

There is a shout from beyond the riverside gate. 'Hoy, it is I, Gorges! Open up.'

Gorges is alone, though Penelope can see beyond the open gate that he has a boat waiting with a man at the oars, and another pair sitting in the back, both armed.

'What news?' she says, trying to interpret from his expression whether things are going to plan in the city.

'Essex has sent me to accompany the hostages to the Privy Council and negotiate on his behalf.' His collar is ripped from his altercation with Southampton. He smiles and she feels foolish for having judged him on the set of his eyes, as if that said something about what lies beneath.

'Thank God for that,' she says, feeling relief wash over her – he must have his army behind him now. 'It is best you refer to them as guests.' He nods, instantly understanding her meaning. 'And my brother . . . the men are mustered?'

'Some, some.' He seems to be avoiding a direct answer.

'Some?'

'It is taking longer than we thought, My Lady.' He has begun to stride towards the steps.

She follows him, running to catch up.

She is quite out of breath by the time they arrive at the door to the study. Meyrick, who is slouched on a stool, cradling his gun in his lap, stands. 'What news, Gorges?'

'I am to take them to Whitehall on order of Essex.'

Meyrick nods, standing aside, slapping Gorges's shoulder. 'Good man!'

Gorges is about to lift the latch when she grabs his arm and draws herself up to her full height, so he has to stop and listen to her. 'Leave this to me.' She holds him firmly with her look, remembering how forceful he was with Southampton. 'It needs careful handling.' What is it she sees flash over his face; is it alarm? She cannot tell, but it disturbs her nonetheless and she wonders what possessed her brother to choose this particular man for such a delicate mission.

They enter, with Meyrick hovering behind them. 'My dear guests,' she says, 'Gorges here has come from the city with news from my brother. It would seem he has been delayed and proposes that you reconvene at another time. He is most sorry to have inconvenienced you. Gorges will accompany you to Whitehall and the Privy Council by river.'

Popham releases an angry laugh. 'Inconvenienced!'

When they have left the room Penelope watches from the gallery window as they emerge into the courtyard. She can see a consignment of mounted guards from the palace in the Queen's livery, moving along the Strand towards them. Her heart sits high in her throat, making it difficult to breathe. From the south side windows she can see the delegation take

441

the steps down to the pier with Gorges behind them. He helps them, one by one, into the waiting boat, which tips and bucks under their weight. The oarsman casts off and they move away into the river, circling round to travel upstream in the direction of Whitehall. Penelope feels her insides shrink. Meyrick comes to stand beside her. They don't look at each other.

'I am uneasy about that,' she says, nodding her head in the direction of the boat that is moving at a fair pace now.

'How so, My Lady?'

'Is Gorges loyal?'

She realizes she has asked Meyrick this before, but this time his answer is less certain. 'I hope so.'

On the Strand the troops are nearing, the thrum of hooves becoming louder. There is a drummer with them, matching the beat of her heart.

'You should leave, My Lady, there is not much time.' Meyrick still doesn't look at her. 'With Lady Essex. Take one of the boats, before it is too late. I fear things will become . . .' He stops, wiping a hand through his hair. 'I fear for your safety.'

'Meyrick, what do you take me for?' She keeps her voice light as if she is jesting. 'You have known me for years. I am a Devereux.' He looks at her then and she beams at him. 'Don't worry about me, and Lady Essex has more nerve than you think.'

The troops have begun to surround the house, posting sentries at all the gates.

'Look!' he says, pointing towards the east where the river bends. 'I think it is your brother with Southampton. Do you see it?' He opens the window and leans out. 'Do you see his scarlet cape?' He is indicating a flotilla of small boats; the kind of mean craft that ferry folk across to the Southwark bear pits.

'But where is his barge?'

'I'm sure it is them. Yes, it is.'

She is thinking that if he is not in his own barge, and has been reduced to cadging a wherry the size of a beer barrel, then something is amiss. But Meyrick is right. Her brother *is* aboard one of the boats, she can see him quite clearly now, and Southampton in his red cape. They are all pumping urgently at the oars, even the earls.

'Something is wrong, they are retreating,' Meyrick says.

She glances west towards Whitehall, and sees, inevitably, a number of barges bearing the royal colours headed their way too. They are further away but are upstream with the current behind them. She wills the odd little armada on, as it bobs towards them at an excruciatingly slow pace. The fleet from Whitehall is bearing down. They hear an ominous thud and, turning towards the Strand entrance, see that while they have been watching the water a battering ram has been prepared to break down the gates. It meets its mark once more with another almighty thud but the gates hold.

A terrible female screaming starts up from somewhere and Penelope imagines the effect it must have on the troops out there, knowing there are women within. Perhaps that will give them a soupçon of bargaining power; God knows they need it. The men in the yard are preparing to fight. There are precious few of them and one is that young lad who came into the chapel earlier. An agonizing pang strikes her as she realizes that her own children may well lose their mother on this day.

Leaning from the window, she orders the men inside. 'Get all the furniture, anything heavy you can lay your hands on. Barricade the house.' It is only a matter of minutes before the gates will give way and those few in the yard are no match for the troops without. She turns to Meyrick. 'You go and take charge down there. Make sure Essex can gain entry, then, once they are in, seal the place.' She is silently urging her brother on. 'Find out what we have in the way of weapons and make sure each entrance is well guarded with as many armed men as possible.'

Meyrick has already charged the distance of the long gallery and is at the head of the stairs. 'Ensure all the female servants are sent up to me.' She refuses to entertain the fact that Essex in his upturned barrel might not reach them, but takes a last look out to gauge their progress, willing them to find some hidden current that will speed them upstream before the looming barges, with six oarsmen apiece – she can see them quite clearly now – find their rhythm.

She can already hear the scrape of furniture being dragged across the flagstones downstairs, with Meyrick barking out orders. Tearing herself away from the window, she rushes to the chapel, dragging Frances from her prayers.

'Gather all his papers, everything there is, letters, documents, books – anything that might incriminate him. We must burn every last scrap. You take the bedchamber and I shall deal with the study. Bring it all there, for the fire is lit.' She is trying to keep calm, her mind focused on what she must do right now, and not on what might happen in the near future. But she can feel a flush of fear crawling up her body.

Frances nods, making for the door. 'He has the Scottish letters on his person.'

Penelope looks at her sister-in-law, wondering: if he has told his wife about those letters then who else? 'You are sure of that?'

'Absolutely.'

'Let's hope to God he has the good sense to get rid of them if he's captured.'

'It will not come to that.'

Penelope doesn't mention the collection of boats out there and the royal barges bearing down on them. There is no point in bursting Frances's optimism at this stage; it will all unfold soon enough.

As she enters the study she realizes the enormity of the task in hand, more than a decade's worth of secret diplomacy – heaven knows what might be written there that could be turned against them. Aside from the two chests filled to bursting, one with correspondence and the other with legal papers, there is a wall of books. Many of them have notes and pieces of paper between their pages, any of which could be incriminating. She starts with the chests, pulling out bundles of letters and throwing them into the fire, waiting until they have caught before adding more.

Four servant girls arrive from downstairs. One is a buxom, practical lass who seems unperturbed by the situation, one is older, thin as a wraith and wears her dread in a pair of startled eyes, the other two are very young, and are clinging tightly to each other. She sends two of them to help Frances search every cranny of the house and sets the other two to work on the trunks, while she pulls the books down from the shelves, flipping through the pages of each one to see what might be hidden there. It is slow work, for some of the vellum documents do not burn easily and they have to take the utmost care that no fragments are left.

Frances returns, brandishing a fistful of letters, and begins to feed them into the fire. 'God only knows what they are,' she says, her mouth set in a thin line. 'Letters from his mistress in the main part, from what I can tell.'

'Best be rid of everything,' says Penelope.

Glancing from the window, she can see the fleet from Whitehall has drawn up beside the river steps, forming a line, so they are surrounded entirely. To her relief, though, she spots a few of the small wherries drifting off back down the river unmanned. She doesn't say anything in case she is mistaken and asks Frances to continue with the books so she can investigate. Out in the gallery she runs, calling for Essex, finding him eventually in the great chamber with a wild-eyed

Southampton and a desultory group of men. She can hear Meyrick by the main entrance, keeping things in order.

'Oh God, thank God,' she says, rushing towards her brother, who seems, despite being filthy and dripping in sweat, surprisingly assured. 'What happened to all the rest?'

'Half of them fled at the first sign of trouble,' says Southampton. 'Your stepfather is wounded badly. Some stayed to treat him.'

'Will he live?' she asks, thinking, with a hollow in the pit of her stomach, of their mother widowed for a third time.

'Hard to say,' Essex replies. 'We couldn't get everyone back here.' She can see his eyes flare in anger as he adds, 'Others are seeking Smyth and his thousand men. We couldn't find him. Something must have happened. But once the force is mustered they have orders to make haste and join us here.'

'Then we will have a real battle on our hands.' It is Southampton who says this, causing a general exclamation of agreement in the chamber. But Penelope is thinking about all the men who used to turn out in support of Essex, lining the streets thirty deep in places, waving his colours, boys brandishing wooden swords and hanging from parapets to get a better look at their hero. Where are they all now? They were gone for hours in the city and returned with fewer men than they left with. She supposes that Essex is operating under a delusion. Time has moved on without him noticing.

She is about to ask if he has a contingency plan when Essex says, 'How are our *guests*?'

Time stops as the realization dawns on her: he believes the delegation is still safely ensconced in his study. So that is why he seems so full of bluster.

She girds herself. 'They are gone.'

He looks at her as if he doesn't understand what she means. 'Gone?'

'Gorges came. He said you had charged him to accompany them to the Privy Council and plead your cause.'

446

Essex expels a cry, a bestial sound.

Southampton winces loudly with an expletive, as he smashes his fist on the wall. 'He had no such order.'

The chamber falls silent and Penelope supposes they are all coming to the understanding, as she is, that Gorges has betrayed them, not only by releasing the delegation, but also with the fiction of the thousand men. Without such a lure Essex would have marched on the court, not into London, and the cankered future spread out before them might have looked entirely different.

'It can't be helped now,' she says, taking charge. 'We have set to burning all your papers. Give me the Scottish letters.' Essex is standing as if in a trance now, dead eyes staring straight ahead. 'Robin!' she says with force, but gets no response. 'For God's sake, Robin.'

Without thinking she slaps him sharply across the face. Someone amongst the company gasps. Essex looks at her in shock. 'The Scottish letters.' She holds out her hand and, like an obedient boy, he lifts the thong over his head, handing over the pouch without a word. 'Now pull yourself together, take charge. Your men need ordering.' The whole room is suspended in silence, watching. 'What are you all gawping for?' She is shouting now. 'Ensure the house is secured. We must prepare for a siege, at least until all the papers have been destroyed.' She throws the black pouch into the hearth: fifteen years of careful negotiating up in flames. But the allegiances are tied fast now between the Devereuxs and King James, written proof or not. The acrid smell of burning leather fills the room.

A violent crash sounds outside. It must be the breaching of the gate, and the dreadful female screeching starts up once more. Only then does Essex seem to come to his senses and make for the window, saying with a bitter laugh, 'She has sent them all, I see,' and begins listing: 'Nottingham, Cumberland, Lincoln, Howard, what great numbers they have

447

rallied, and look,' he slaps Southampton on the shoulder, 'it is your dear friend Grey.' His voice is seething with sarcasm. 'See all my old comrades – there is Robert Sidney . . .' His voice trails off.

The screaming woman will not desist.

Penelope watches Robert Sidney. He is walking towards the house alone, unguarded, and she is reminded of his long-dead brother, who had exactly the same way of holding himself – the straight posture, the long stride, the upward tilt of the chin that was so often misconceived as arrogance. She only then notices two great cannon on the Strand, a pair of chilling black eyes, trained directly on the house. There are men scurrying about them – loading them, she supposes.

The screaming goes on.

'Someone find that woman and shut her up,' snaps Essex.

'Leave her,' says Penelope. 'That woman's screams will prick the conscience of the army without. If they have any sense of what is right, they will not want to bombard a house full of women.'

'I beg of you, Essex, give yourself up!' shouts Robert Sidney, from beneath the window.

'I'm going out to talk to him,' says Southampton.

'It's too dangerous; you will be shot sooner than listened to,' says Essex, who seems to have found his resolve. 'Get on to the roof; from there you will be out of range.' He grips his friend's upper arm, speaking quietly and insistently. 'Buy me time. Penelope is right; the papers must be disposed of. I have some hidden that I must deal with.' His expression is flint-hard. He rattles off orders for the others in the chamber and then plants a hasty kiss on his sister's cheek with a murmured 'Thank you', then leaves the room with the others, their weapons clanking.

Only moments later she can hear Southampton shouting down to Robert Sidney from the roof directly above.

'For pity's sake,' Robert Sidney is saying, his hands either

448

side of his head in a gesture of despair. 'Give yourselves up. Nottingham will not hold back. Those cannon will demolish the place with all in it.' He points towards the twin black beams that hold Essex House in their deadly gaze through the gloaming, and she is assaulted by a fragment of memory. She can feel the rough kiss of parchment beneath her fingers as if time has collapsed and she is that young woman once more. She runs her eyes over the remembered inky lines. The words are engraved on her soul: *When Nature made her chief work, Stella's eyes, / In colour black why wrapped she beams so bright?* She can sense the warmth of Philip Sidney's body beside her.

She hears those lines in Blount's voice then. Time is playing tricks on her, for now she is momentarily at their first meeting – when he had wounded Essex in that ill-advised duel – in this very chamber over eleven years ago. She feels Blount's kiss on the back of her hand; she smiles; her heart pitches and she is back in the present with those twin cannon staring, unblinking, her way.

Southampton is saying something but his words are taken by the wind and the continued screaming.

Robert Sidney replies. 'At least let the ladies out before the house comes under fire.'

Penelope forces herself to look at him, to see the ways in which he is not like his brother: his hair is darker, he is not quite so long of limb and he is older than his brother ever was. That thought is a punch to the heart but she cannot allow herself to be overwhelmed by old emotions. She is not the same woman now. She opens the window. 'I stand or fall with Essex!' Robert Sidney looks devastated and she refuses to consider whether she is afraid. 'Perhaps I can persuade some of the other women to come out to safety; there is but a handful and I doubt Lady Essex will leave my brother's side.'

She turns to the man who was assigned to protect her,

whose name she doesn't know, asking him to relay Robert Sidney's message to the women. 'Tell them no one will think any the less of them if they choose to leave.'

Leaning back out of the window, she can hear Southampton more clearly now; the wind must have changed. There is a desperate tone to his voice. 'Send in a delegation, and we will thrash out an agreement.' He talks like a man who has something to bargain with. He must know their case is hopeless; there is no getting away from it. She wishes he would cease his foolish talk. She looks out at all the men gathered.

They have encircled the house entirely. Darkness is descending fast and torches have been lit, bobbing about like fireflies. To one side she can see shadowy rows of halberdiers and there is a line of men kneeling in the knot garden with muskets held to their shoulders. On the Strand mounted men mill about, she can hear their horses' hooves clattering on the cobbles; several torches light the black eyes of the cannon, which continue to stare their way – she assumes their fuses will be lit from those lights. The air is thick with impatience. She knows that once the order is given to fire, there will be no stopping the bloodbath. She must not let herself think of that.

'Sir Robert,' she calls, drowning out Southampton's voice, 'relay this to Nottingham. It will take us some time to dismantle the barriers at the doors. Ask him to give us two hours' grace to free the entrance, allow the ladies, who so wish it, to leave and then rebuild the blockade. Beyond that, it is a fair fight.' She hopes to God, as she says this, that two hours will be sufficient time and thinks of the women in the study feeding papers into the mouth of the fire – in her mind it is the mouth of hell.

Someone has handed Robert Sidney a torch and its russet light kisses the edges of him and catches the gilding on his breastplate as he goes to pass on the message to his superior. Penelope cannot see Nottingham; he is doubtless keeping himself at a safe distance. Despite the fact that he is kin – he is wed to their cousin Kate – and he has fought alongside Essex on more than one campaign, Nottingham has never liked her brother. She recognized him years ago for one who carefully managed to stay upwind of foul odours. While she waits for a reply she thinks of Cecil at the palace, imagines him rubbing his hands together, revelling in his imminent victory, for that is what it is.

They have been picking up and putting down cards for years but they are near the end of the game now and Cecil holds all the trumps. But there is one card he has not been able to take and that is the Scottish King. King James does not trust Cecil. Though what advantage, she reasons, can James's favour bring them in this moment? She tries not to think of what might have been, had the Earl of Mar arrived with James's support for Essex. Then Cecil might have been left with a dud hand.

She cannot see much outside now, save for the glow of the torches moving about, and is glad not to be able to see those twin black holes holding her in their gaze. But the impatience still hangs ominously in the air. Her stomach flutters in anticipation of death, just as it would were she awaiting a lover. Her hands are icy on the window sill and she fancies she might already be dead. She hears a call from below. 'You are granted your two hours' grace, My Lady, by word of Nottingham.'

'I am ever in your debt, Sir Robert,' she says, wondering if her words have any meaning, for her 'ever' may not be so long.

'Good man, Sidney. You always were true,' comes Southampton's voice from above.

She closes the window and moves to the fire to warm herself, taking up a writing box. Her fingers are too cold to hold the pen properly but she finds a way, nonetheless, to scratch by the light of the fire a note of love to Blount. She refuses to think more deeply on him for fear of losing her courage, but is unable to prevent herself from imagining her note being found amongst the rubble of tomorrow's dawn. *Be sure that our children are cared for, my love*, she scribbles, *and forget me. Find love elsewhere. I cannot bear to think of you alone.* Though she has yearned to have him by her side for months, has desperately needed his counsel, now she is glad that he is far away, safely distanced from this chaos, and that none of the Devereux soot will rub off on him. She is surprised to see a tear blotch her words, had thought herself in control of her emotions, but she takes a deep breath, folds the paper, seals it, writes on it: *For the eyes of Charles Blount, Lord Mountjoy*, and slips it in the frame of the great painting of Leicester, where it will not be missed. She meets Leicester's supercilious gaze and briefly wonders, as she leaves the chamber, what her stepfather must think of all this, if indeed he is able to bear witness from beyond the grave.

In the study, all is industry. A laundress and a seamstress have joined Frances in feeding the fire and searching the books, and the younger maidservants are in the corner trying to calm the older, who is no longer screaming but moaning and flailing like a terrified animal. 'Where is Essex?' she asks.

'Scouring every inch of the place for anything that might incriminate him. We are nearly done. I cannot imagine there is a scrap of paper left in this house that has anything written on it.' Frances takes Penelope's hand, holding it tight, as if she needs the reassurance of human touch. She is steady, though, not trembling. They say nothing for a moment as they watch the fire and Penelope is struck by the futility of it all. There is nothing that will save her brother now. He has raised an army against the Queen's authority and they will not need incriminating letters to send him to the block.

'I have managed to buy us a little time and I think we

should use it to persuade Essex to surrender rather than . . .'
She lets her voice drift off, thinking in particular of that
young boy from earlier. Somehow he has come to represent
to her the senseless carnage that might come of this lost
cause.

'Rather than fight to the death and take several dozen
souls with him?' says Frances. 'Has it come to that?'

'I'm afraid so.'

Frances just nods in response. They all knew how high the
stakes were.

'The earl has surrendered, madam,' says Cecil to the Queen. 'Without bloodshed.'

'Where is he?'

'Lambeth Palace – he will be transferred to the Tower at first light.' He says this quietly, bracing himself for an outburst of regret from the Queen, but she seems not to react at all, not the slightest flinch. She sits straight with no sign of tiredness, despite the fact that it is well past nine at night and she has been in and out of council meetings since dawn, with the whole palace on tenterhooks. Cecil himself is aching with exhaustion – his back is in spasm and he longs to lie down and close his eyes even for half an hour. He is bracing himself for the slanders that the earl will surely make against him.

'And Lady Rich?'

'I sent orders for her to be held at Sackford's house. She was taken wearing a sword.'

'Goodness! A sword! So she was armed.' The Queen seems delighted by this detail and Cecil cannot tell if it is because she is impressed at the idea of Lady Rich wielding a weapon, or because it sanctions her to condemn her goddaughter as a true threat. 'Henry Sackford, he is a friend of yours, isn't he?'

'He is. And at Sackford's house, at least, Lady Rich will not hold sway over the staff.'

'People are easily wrapped around those dainty fingers of hers. I am well aware of that.'

'Besides, I know I can trust Sackford implicitly,' adds Cecil.

'Trust is a most elusive quality, I have found. But I can trust *you*, can't I, Pygmy?'

454

'Indeed you can, madam.' He wonders if her question means she doubts it.

'And Southampton, the others?'

Cecil begins to recite the names of prisoners who have been taken and their whereabouts. 'I have drawn up a list, madam.' He hands her a leaf of paper.

From the corner of his eye he can see Ralegh sharing a joke with his kinsman, Ferdinando Gorges, who is snorting with laughter, sputtering: 'Completely and utterly taken in.' Ralegh lifts his cup to touch the lip of his cousin's and they both take a swig. Gorges wipes his mouth on his sleeve, leaving a dark wine stain on his linen. His doublet is torn at the neck and the elbows are almost worn through. Cecil knows that Gorges has been part of Essex's inner circle for some time now. He feels his annoyance rising because momentous things seem to have occurred about which he knows nothing. He adjusts his cuffs, tugging them down so they are even and straightening out the ruffles, admiring the velvety surface of his best slippers, his smooth inky stockings, and the discreet shimmer of his black satin hose; he is somehow reassured by the sight of such order.

'Lady Essex, where is *she*?' asks the Queen.

'With her mother at Barn Elms. She has taken all the other women with her.'

'Apart from Lady Rich.' The Queen taps at the paper in her hand. 'I want you personally to question her, Pygmy. At least *you* might be immune to her famous charms.'

'If it is your wish, madam.' Cecil's mind is whirring, wondering if there might be something to be gained from such an interrogation – something to his own advantage.

'I don't want you going soft on her.' The Queen's voice is tight and clipped. 'If she is at the heart of this, then she must go to the block like her brother.' She sniffs sharply and gives her head a little shake as if to rid herself of a memory. 'I want this dealt with quickly, before the month is out.'

*

455

The chamber is gloomy, with dark unpainted panelling and nothing to cover the ancient oak boards that creak beneath his feet. There is a small hearth, playing host to a diminutive fire that goes no way to cutting through the February chill. Cecil notices clumps of dust in the corners and a layer of it lies over almost every horizontal surface. It makes him absently brush at his clothes, though he has not yet touched anything.

Lady Rich sits with the small window at her back so Cecil cannot make out her features – it is an old trick he learned from his father, designed to unsettle interlocutors – but she surprises him by rising and coming to the centre of the chamber, offering her hand and a smile. Cecil removes his hat and takes her proffered hand. It is cold like marble and as smooth. He would like to allow his grip to linger there; he cannot remember the last time he touched an ungloved hand, a woman, skin to skin.

'I would like to offer you something to drink but the servants here are . . .' She stops with a look of amused indignation in her black eyes. 'Well, they are not exactly forthcoming. Perhaps if *you* were to ask for some wine they would be more willing to accommodate us.' Only then does she allow her fingers to slip from his clutch and moves towards a table where there are two mismatched chairs. 'Run to the kitchens,' she says to Cecil's boy, who is standing by the door, 'and tell them that your master requires refreshments.' She seems entirely unperturbed at the idea of being left alone with him – something he finds quite thrilling; he has never been alone with Lady Rich. In all his years at court that opportunity has never arisen.

Cecil, still standing, is inspecting the dust on the chair and casts about for something to remove it with, seeing nothing suitable and eventually resorting to his own silk handkerchief, wiping the surface before lowering himself on to it. He notices that there are lines of grime edging Lady Rich's cuffs and collar – of course, she must have been arrested in this outfit and no one will have had the decency to offer her a change of clothes in the three days she has been here – even so, the impression she gives is dazzling. It was ever thus. His eyes rest on her breast; she catches him with a ghost of a smile and covers her bare flesh with her shawl. Heat wells in his groin. 'I shall see to it that your husband sends you anything you might need in the way of clothing and sustenance.'

'Good,' she says, 'but we both know that the Queen hasn't sent her foremost councillor here to procure comforts for me.' She smiles, broadly this time; her teeth are even and unspoiled.

Cecil inspects his fingernails, as if he is entirely oblivious of the disarming qualities of that smile, waiting for her to speak, hoping his silence will unsettle her a little, but her confidence remains undented.

'Is this to be an unspoken interrogation?' she mocks him. 'Perhaps that is best, for I would be very surprised if you could find a way to condemn me.'

'It would not take much. Your signature on a letter to . . .' He pauses for effect. 'Let us say – the King of Scotland.'

'You will not find any letters. All the earl's papers were burned.'

'What, everything?' She is smiling. Why is she still smiling? 'Every last scrap?'

Cecil is thinking of that letter to the Spanish ambassador which he feared had found its way to Essex House – the greatest error in his game – going up in flames. A wash of relief breaks over him. He hadn't realized the extent to which that letter was still oozing poison at the back of his mind. It may well come up at Essex's trial – the earl is sure to fling some mud about – but without hard evidence it will be difficult to make it stick.

'It wouldn't need written proof to convict you, My Lady. You were armed when you were arrested. There are plenty who will bear witness to that.'

457

'That! Sidney's dress sword? You are being ridiculous.'

'A dress sword is as sharp as a battle sword,' he replies, interlacing his fingers, grasping that it must have been that very same sword her brother almost drew on the Queen. 'You know as well as I do that if Her Majesty wants rid of you then it will be done.'

'Of course,' she says. 'I understand how these things are.' He is impressed at her mettle; her composure remains entirely intact. 'Are you afraid to die, Cecil?'

He does not know how to respond and drops his guard a little. 'Well . . . well . . . That has nothing to do with this.'

'I think everyone is afraid to die, even those few who are truly pious and without sin. And as for the rest of us . . .' She lets her voice fade.

Fear flaps in his gut. Her ruse has worked, for he is rattled by this talk of death.

'I have a proposition,' she says, regarding him with those inky eyes.

'A proposition? Do you truly feel your situation offers opportunities for bargaining?' It is taking all the composure he can gather to keep himself together. He imagines her pulling a letter written in his hand from beneath her gown. It is addressed to the Spanish ambassador. He tries to reassure himself: if what she said is true, then his letter may well be nothing but ashes.

She doesn't answer, just continues to hold him with her eyes, and slowly understanding alights – a proposition. He cannot forget that this is a woman who defies all the laws of decency with her lover, and seems not to care for her reputation. He reaches out, a fingertip grazing the soft flesh of her throat.

She flinches as if he has burnt her, moving back abruptly out of his reach, the legs of her chair screeching against the floor.

A servant interrupts, entering with an array of dishes, followed by his boy carrying a gilded jug.

'I see they have brought out the plate in your honour.' She

sniffs at the jug. 'Good red wine – I have been drinking watered ale from a leather cup since my arrival.' She makes an exaggerated scowl and picks up a small pie from a platter, sinking her teeth into it without ceremony. A flake of pastry clings to her lip. He imagines removing it with his tongue.

The server hovers. 'Do you require –'

'Leave us be,' he says, indicating for his boy also to wait outside.

When the latch has fallen with a click he stands, taking a step towards her. His mouth is arid, making words impossible. Snatching up a trailing corner of her shawl in his fist, he whips it away from her body. She pulls it back smartly.

'Not that! Did you think *that* was my proposition?'

He is rigid with shame, horrified by the way his desires had taken hold, confused him, disrupted his composure.

She is laughing at him. 'I have something better by far for you than my body.' She is still laughing. Cecil's face is pulsating with heat.

'So what, then?' he says when he eventually finds his tongue, his mind returning to that blasted letter. 'Do you have it?'

'It?' She is half turned away from him, seeming distracted by something beyond the window.

'The letter.'

She spins towards him, her eyes grabbing him sharply, like the claws of a cat. 'A letter? No. I'm talking of . . .' She stops. 'Sit down, for God's sake.' He does as he is told, like an obedient dog. 'I believe there are always opportunities to strike agreements if both parties find it to their advantage.'

He collects himself, understanding only now that this is not about anything he might have written, his emotions adjusting like a compass to the north. 'You have my ear.'

'I want to talk about the succession,' she says. 'You must be aware that the Scottish King is the only truly suitable candidate.'

A shiver runs up his spine, for he suspects he is about to hear the resurrection of something he'd thought lost with the demise of her brother. She might be on the brink of making the very proposition to him that he might have made to her, had it occurred to him first.

'Perhaps,' is all he says.

'There is no perhaps about it. The Infanta was a pipe dream all along. Not a soul within these shores would accept a Spaniard, and a woman to boot. We all know that. And that Stuart girl, the Scottish King's cousin who has been groomed for the throne – she's half mad from what I hear; and the Beauchamp claim – well that's run dry. James of Scotland is as near in blood as it is possible to be, he has a son and a fertile wife. Do you think England would turn away from a chance like that?'

'And your point is?' He keeps his voice steady, not wanting his eagerness to show. She is right, of course, but he will not give her the satisfaction of agreement.

'Mark my words: James of Scotland will be named successor, I have no doubt about it.'

'I still don't see why this is relevant.'

'James of Scotland is a dear friend to the Devereuxs, to me in particular and to Lord Mountjoy.' She pauses, for effect he presumes. 'But I know he is not enamoured of you. Indeed, he believes you to be – what was the word he used when he last wrote to me?' She stops again, and licks her lips, scooping the fragment of pastry up with her own tongue. 'Ah yes, "devious", that's what he said of you. "I would not want *devious* men like Cecil advising me. He would be the first I'd be rid of."'

She plants her eyes on his once more, seeming to challenge him, and must be aware that she is admitting, here and now, to having discussed the succession with the Scottish King. That alone is enough to send her to the block. But she has the confidence of knowing that Cecil wants to feather his own nest for the future – he feels as if she has peeled back his soul and taken a good look inside.

'King James will know you are the instigator of my brother's downfall. He will want revenge once he is in power.' She pauses as her point strikes home. Cecil feels himself shrink. 'But I could tell him he has misunderstood you, Cecil. And your mercy with regard to me shall be proof of that. Deliver me from the block and I shall deliver you James of Scotland. I will convince him he needs a man like you at his side. I fancy you could see yourself as Chief Minister in the new regime.'

His mind is stirring. If he agrees to this, it means he is tied to Lady Rich by their shared treachery. But he can see his future, an infinite vista of glory, of riches, something his father would have been proud of, a legacy to pass to his son. It is that, or his destruction.

He is trying to calculate the best way to package this to the Queen, when like a mind reader she says, 'Tell the Queen you are convinced of my innocence, or if that's not enough then remind her that Lord Mountjoy has an army thirteen thousand strong who will do his bidding, and it is not worth the risk of raising his ire by doing away with his wife.' She says the word 'wife' with defiance, as if challenging him to contradict it. 'Besides, in Ireland Lord Mountjoy has achieved in months what a string of others did not manage in three decades. The Queen needs him and if a hair on my head were harmed I am sure Lord Mountjoy would . . .' She doesn't finish, just leans back in her chair and stretches her arms up above her head with a little moan of satisfaction. 'You will think of something, Cecil, a man of your ingenuity.'

'You will be brought before the Privy Council for your part in your brother's folly.'

'The Privy Council – I think I am quite able to deal with them. I have done it before.' She tilts her head to one side and lifts her tone to a high-pitched simper. 'I was enslaved by my blind love for my brother.' She flicks her head back to upright and holds out her hand. 'Do we have a deal?'

He looks at her hand and then back at her face; she reveals nothing in her expression that tells him if this is a bluff of the highest order. Perhaps the Scottish King said nothing of the sort . . . *Devious* – pah! Perhaps this great friendship between him and the Devereuxs is a fabrication.

That marble hand is still held out.

Cecil peeps through a crack in the hangings. From up in the gallery he has a view across Westminster Hall. Below sit Essex and Southampton. He cannot see their faces, only the tops of their heads. They sit before the men of law: the Lord Chief Justice in his scarlet robes with his eight judges and Lord Buckhurst presiding. On either side Cecil counts out the nine earls and sixteen barons – the peers who will pronounce the verdict; one of them is Lord Rich. Opposite the judges sit the Queen's Counsel with Francis Bacon amongst them. It must curdle the earl's insides to see a man who has been privy to so many of his secrets seated there with his prosecutors.

Cecil is reminded of Doctor Lopez all those years ago – that poor man hounded to the scaffold; in his mind he has erased his own part in the doctor's downfall, attributed it entirely to Essex. Bacon was one of the prosecutors then, at Essex's behest, if Cecil's memory serves him well, which it does. Cecil pushes Lopez from his thoughts before he has another crisis of conscience. He has not been able to shake away Lady Rich's question: *Are you afraid to die, Cecil?* He is afraid of the day of reckoning. But sometimes he receives signs of God's mercy, indications that perhaps God understands a ruthless man if his actions are for the higher good, and what has Cecil done but serve his Queen and country?

He had one such sign only this morning, a happy discovery that laid a foreboding of two years' duration to rest. As a result he sits behind his arras light as a cloud. He had need to refer to an old ledger on a point of governance and, flicking through its pages, came upon a folded leaf of paper, recognizing instantly his own tidy hand on its surface, a particular line popping out at him: *I feel sure some kind of accommodation can be arrived at in respect of the Infanta* . . . A wave of euphoria caused him to exclaim, 'Thanks be to God!' so loudly, his scribe had come in to ask if all was as it should be. 'Oh yes, indeed,' he replied, tearing the letter into several pieces and scrunching them in his fist. How memory can play tricks on the mind; he'd felt so sure the offending item had been sealed and sent, it never occurred to him to look for it in his own study. 'The entire universe is correctly aligned.' His scribe had looked his way askance, making a last perturbed glance back towards him as he left the chamber. Cecil skipped across the room and dropped the torn fragments into the fire, watching the flames devour his words for good. He has a fancy that God was teaching him a lesson with that letter.

Bacon is speaking now, tearing strips out of the earl with his rapier intellect. Cecil likes his vantage point and the fact that no one is aware of his presence. He is neither a peer of the realm nor a man of law, so he is not required to attend the proceedings and nothing would have made him sit with the rabble. If he cranes his neck he can see the public gallery. He supposes Lady Rich would be there were she not still incarcerated in that grim chamber at Henry Sackford's house.

He can still feel the marble-cold clasp of her handshake and the arousing sense of trepidation that came with it. He is working on the Queen with respect to that business – that handshake, that deal struck – she is coming round; he has seen the glimmer of forgiveness in her eye when Lady Rich is mentioned. The same look he used to see so often in respect of the earl. Not this time, though. The earl is as good as done for but Lady Rich's slender neck will remain intact. And he, Cecil, has begun to sow seeds for James of

Scotland's succession. Subtlety is what's required, and that he has in abundance. He has wondered, though, in the black of night, if he hasn't made a pact with some dark force; after all, he has betrayed his Queen. He stops his thoughts before they fall to wondering if that means he has also betrayed God.

For the first time today Essex is becoming riled under the questioning of his one-time ally Bacon. He has sat through testimonies from Popham, Ralegh and a squirming Ferdinando Gorges. Not once did the earl lose his composure. But now he is twitching visibly as he listens. Bacon is armed with a depth of knowledge; he and Cecil had questioned all the main players in the affair. In the most part they had confessed like papists. Only the stepfather, Sir Christopher, half dead from a pike wound to the face, had refused to speak. He had spat on to the filthy floor of Newgate prison, saying, 'You will get nothing from me.' He was hanged the next day with Meyrick and Cuffe. The Devereux women were really most unfortunate in their choice of husbands.

Bacon continues his prodding, describing each point with a wave of one of his graceful hands like a choirmaster.

Essex gets to his feet, shouting now. 'You want to hear about rebellious intent and treason? Well I have a story about how the crown of England was nearly sold to the Spaniard. It was told to me by a loyal source, that one of my fellow councillors heard with his own ears. *His own ears*,' he repeats loudly, his voice ringing round the rapt hall. 'Robert Cecil, the Lord Privy Seal, was heard to say that the Infanta's claim was as valid in the succession as any other.'

Cecil draws in a sharp breath, racking his mind to remember saying this and to whom. He may have vaguely alluded to such a thing in passing in the confines of a private meeting with the Spanish ambassador, as a way to tease out that thwarted peace treaty, but to a member of the Privy Council, never!

Essex is still shouting. 'If that is not a plausible reason for me to wish this evil influence from Her Majesty's orbit, then I do not know what is.'

The earl collapses back into his seat and the place falls silent. Cecil garners his courage and, thinking of that burning letter, stands and draws back the curtain that conceals him in a single swift movement. It makes a loud metallic swish, like the drawing of a sword, and a gasp goes up through the chamber. Cecil stands erect, feeling for a moment, with all those faces turned his way, that he is acting a part in a play. He then takes the wooden stairs slowly, his uneven footsteps ringing out through the hush. As he makes his way over the vast expanse of floor towards Buckhurst, he can sense his anger brewing, as if he is a pot left too long on the heat and his lid will burst off. But he keeps his mind on that burning paper and on Lady Rich's marble handshake, reminding himself that he has complete control over the game.

He drops to the floor before Buckhurst, something he has only ever done for the Queen, but it seems an appropriately overblown gesture for the occasion. 'I beg permission to answer this false accusation, My Lord.'

'Permission is granted.' Even Buckhurst, leaning forward in his seat, is unable to hide the eagerness, spread over his baggy face, to hear what Cecil has to say.

Cecil turns to his adversary, speaking slowly and clearly. 'My Lord of Essex, the difference between you and me is great. You surpass me in wit, and in nobility, and at the sword, of that there is no doubt.' He pauses, locking his eyes on to the earl's. They do not have the beguiling intensity of his sister's and, despite his appearance of absolute confidence, Cecil can see something else there, something resembling doubt. He has seen it often enough in the looking glass. 'But I have innocence, conscience, truth and honesty to defend me against this scandal, and in this court I stand as an upright man, and your lordship as a delinquent. Had I not seen your ambitions inclined to usurpation, I would have gone on my knees to Her Majesty to have done you good; but you conceal a wolf's body beneath a sheep's robe . . .'

Essex wears a smile and has a haughty tilt to the head as he replies, making no effort to hide his sarcasm. 'I thank God for my humiliation, that you in the ruff of all your bravery have come here to make your oration against me.'

Cecil will not be cowed. 'I beg of you, enlighten this court as to which councillor has heard me speak of such intrigues. Name him, if you dare.'

'It is no fiction,' says Essex. 'Southampton here, he heard it as well as I.'

Southampton, who looks green with trepidation, mumbles out that he has it on good authority that Sir William Knollys said such a thing.

'Bring Sir William Knollys forth,' says Buckhurst.

An usher is dispatched to hunt down Knollys, who has kept a distance from the proceedings. After all, he risks much if he tries to save his nephew. A chair is procured for Cecil and they wait. He straightens the pleats in his cuffs, though they are already aligned to perfection, while his mind churns over the possibilities of what might be about to happen and the old fears return. Has Essex concocted a trumped-up charge with his uncle; will they produce faked documents to support their words; has Essex decided that if he is to fall he will take Cecil with him?

After what seems an interminable time Knollys arrives and is sworn in. He looks towards Cecil and then to his nephew, before beginning a lengthy preamble. It takes all Cecil's control to stop himself from interrupting and insisting he cut to the heart of the matter. Then: 'I did indeed hear Mister Secretary utter such a thing' – Cecil feels his insides crumble, his bowels loosen – 'but it was in the context of a discussion by some members of the council on a tract entitled

Conference on the Next Succession, which we had been charged with looking into.' Cecil slowly expels a long breath, as relief washes over him for the second time today. 'Mister Secretary had remarked, "Is it not a strange impudence in that the author gives equal right in the succession of the crown to the Infanta of Spain as to any other?" There is no corruption there, I think.' Knollys glances wistfully at his nephew, blinking slowly and pressing his lips together with a slight hunch of the shoulders, as if to say he has no way of saving him from his inevitable demise.

'The remark was reported to me in another sense,' says Essex lamely, completely deflated. The final moves have been made and the pieces are being cleared from the board.

The verdicts are pronounced: each peer speaking in turn: 'Guilty, My Lord, of high treason, upon my honour.' Lord Rich twists his eyes up and away as he says it. Cecil wonders, briefly, what is going on in *his* sorry mind. Essex, maintaining his composure, makes a plea for Southampton to be spared; it is a gesture that reminds the entire company of his nobility. Southampton loses his legs beneath him and has to be propped up as he implores Buckhurst for mercy in a quivering voice.

As Buckhurst announces the sentence all Cecil can hear is his father's voice: *Water hollows a stone, not by force but by falling often.*

The Sword

For sweetest things turn sourest by their deeds;
Lilies that fester smell far worse than weeds.

William Shakespeare, Sonnet 94

'Why?' asks Penelope.

Essex looks back with a perturbing gaze that follows her about the room. He is dressed in white, a tight doublet of notched satin the colour of spring clouds, stockings like swans' down, a snowy ruff frames a face that wears a small smile which cannot quite disguise a tiredness about the eyes. He is wearing Sidney's sword; only the hilt is visible. She thinks about young Robert, her fearless nephew who is now an earl, riding into London a month ago ahead of the newly crowned King James, as his sword bearer – how he looked like his father. But it was not King James's sword he carried. Before the procession, in the chaos as everyone was dressing in their regalia, Penelope had slipped Sidney's sword into the King's scabbard, pressing a finger to her lips when her nephew opened his mouth to question her actions.

For her that sword had come to represent the spirit of something intangible, the elusive standard Sidney had stood for, of goodness and rightness and chivalry. By the time Robert was mounted on his father's favourite horse and came to draw the sword, holding it up vertically before him, no one could see that beneath the boy's hand were the inter-twined initials PS. All eyes were on the new King. Seeing the splendour of it all, the crowd abounding with hope, she'd thought of the old Queen; in those two final years of her life she had seemed made of straw.

Penelope rode behind, with Lizzie and the newly par-doned Southampton, his prettiness a little soured from a brace of years in the Tower but reanimated by his freedom nonetheless. He didn't mention her brother and nor did she.

As they turned a bend Robert glanced back and caught his aunt's eye with a smirk; Penelope felt herself ring with pride to see a Devereux back at the head of things, the future secured.

'Why?' she asks her brother again.

His painted face, with its half-hidden smile and tired eyes, is mute.

'*Why?*' She shouts it this time, feeling an eruption of anger, imagining gouging out splinters from the panel that bears his portrait with her fingernails, but her voice echoes aimlessly about the Wanstead gallery.

Cecil had come to her again, on the day of her brother's execution. He was the only one. She supposed no one else could gain entry to Sackford's gloomy house. She thought she might receive a letter from her mother, though Lettice was mourning the loss of both a husband and a son.

But Cecil visited and was kind. 'I'm sorry it came to this,' he had said. His spindly legs and hunched torso, clad in shimmering black, gave him the appearance of a crow. He had removed his hat; even the servants didn't bother to bare their heads for her in Sackford's house, not that she cared particularly.

'You are sorry?' she said. 'But this outcome was your life's work, surely.' His face crumpled then and she thought, strangely, he might cry.

'I believed it was what I wanted,' was his reply. 'I was wrong.'

Something had changed in Cecil; he had never been one to admit his mistakes. And the way he had always looked at her, that wretched leer that made her feel like a sweetmeat, was gone, replaced by a look that seemed full of respect – as if she were not a woman at all.

'Did you see him die?' Her voice was small and fractured from holding back her grief.

He nodded. 'He died well . . . bravely.'

She remembers the sense of desolation coming to her violently, like a bullet to the heart. She had refused to entertain, until that moment, the thought of her beloved brother meeting his end. He had seemed at once so fragile and yet invincible and somewhere deep inside she harboured the belief that he would be pardoned. She looks again at the painting, imagining a different world, a world in which her snow-white brother had a stay of execution, stewed in the Tower for a couple of years, to be released by King James. It would have been he, not Robert, carrying the King's sword. She will never become accustomed to his absence. A soldier once told her that years after losing his leg in battle, he still felt pain in the place where it had been.

She had asked Cecil what were his last words.

'He begged forgiveness, said he never intended to harm Her Majesty, and when he knelt there was not so much as a tremor in his hands.' Cecil held out his own hands in imitation but they trembled horribly, like a drunkard's, and he tucked them back beneath his robe. 'He cried, "Executioner, strike home!" Then it was done.'

She felt herself collapse inside as her imagination conjured the scene, her brother courageous to the last. Cecil didn't tell her then that it had taken three strikes of the axe to sever his head. She discovered that later. It was the Queen who told her, seeming horrified by what she had done, desolate with grief. The Queen never fully recovered her strident demeanour, as if her regret had opened a fissure in her, through which her life slowly ebbed away. She was like a wraith for those two final years. Penelope wondered if the Queen had thought of Essex on her deathbed. It is remorse that does for you in the end.

Her painted brother watches her still. 'Why?' she asks again, whispering this time, but there are no answers to be had there.

She is back in that grim room with Cecil, learning of her

brother's death. Cecil seemed uncomfortable, twisting his hands, unable to look her in the eye.

'And the Queen?' she asked. 'How did she respond, once he was . . .' She couldn't put it into words. 'Once it was done?'

'She cannot speak of it. Is shut away in her bedchamber. She wept and cared not who saw.'

Penelope tried to imagine that – the Queen weeping – but couldn't.

'There is something else,' she said to Cecil, 'something you are not telling me.' She could see it in his posture, his arms crossed over his body.

He shook his head minutely and they were silent for a moment.

It was Cecil who spoke eventually. 'I should tell you he denounced you.'

'What do you mean?' she said. 'Who denounced me?'

'Your brother. He gave testimony that it was you who pushed him into rebellion, that you were the source of the whole affair. Said you told him his friends all thought him a coward, that it was your idea that he should march on the court – to "get the thing done properly", is how he put it.' It seemed Cecil, having decided to speak, could not get his words out fast enough.

'My brother said those things?' She was hollowed out; the brother she had cared for, nursed through melancholy, supported, loved – how she had loved him – had denounced her in a futile attempt to save his own skin. It was difficult to breathe, as if there was not enough air in the entire world to keep her alive, and she had a picture in her mind of his head struck from his body, repeating over and over again.

Her eyes return to the painting, and his face is that of a stranger. 'Was it easy?' she asks that face. 'Would you have rather seen *me* go to the block? You would have been eaten away with guilt, Robin.' She can feel her throat clog and her eyes begin to smart, but shakes the feeling away.

She wanted to quiz Cecil, ask him for each and every detail of her brother's damning statement, but didn't, for neither could she bear to hear more of it. She looked to her hands, only then realizing that they had been fisted so tightly her nails had drawn blood in the soft pads beneath her thumbs. She clasped them together so Cecil would not see the depth of her anguish. 'Why do you tell me this?'

'In the spirit of honesty,' is what he said.

A snort of disbelief had escaped from her. 'Honesty?' She was clinging to the last shreds of her self-control.

'Yes, now we have an agreement, it seems right to start from a place of truthfulness.'

'I wonder if I have not made a pact with the devil,' she said, making it sound like a jest, somehow able to disguise the profound loathing in her voice.

'As do I,' he replied with a smile. 'You will find I am a man of my word.'

That has turned out to be the truth – she has her life, her freedom, an elevated place at court, and he is chief advisor to the King – they both kept their promises.

Once Cecil was gone the surge of anger surprised her; it took hold of her body with a force she could not control and she picked up a chair, hurling it at the wall, then the other chair, then the table – terrible sounds came out of her, sounds that might have raised the dead, and still that image remained: scarlet blood streaming from his severed head, a river of blood. She broke every last object in that room of Henry Sackford's and collapsed on to the floor, entirely spent.

She leaves her brother's portrait and wanders about the house, with Fides trotting in her wake, his claws clicking rhythmically on the floor. Wanstead is filled with memories; its very walls seem to whisper to her of Blount and their snatched assignations. The gardens are overgrown, as if they have refused to be clipped into submission, and the summer blooms make bright splashes of colour, serenaded by the humming of bees. She presses her face to a rose, feeling its velvet petals touch her lips, breathing in its glorious scent. She throws her head back and arms out, circling like a child, feeling, for the first time in all her forty years, a sense of true liberation, or at least the possibility of it.

Rich has announced in a letter she received lately that he intends, 'now our children are grown, to untie what God has put together'. That is how he described it, as if he could not bear to defile his pen with the word 'divorce'. She wondered, only for the briefest moment, how he was going to reconcile it with that stern God of his. He will find a way. She has barely seen Rich these last years. She was of no use to him after the demise of her brother. Their paths did cross once, at Leighs, as she was arriving and he leaving. She was glad, for she wanted to tell him she held no grudge.

'Why do you not hate me?' he asked.

'You have been a good father . . .' she began, but stopped herself, not wanting to rub in what he well knew, that three of the children in the nursery were not his. 'But, more than that, hatred makes you weak.'

She had never thought of it until those words left her mouth, but it was true. She'd watched the way the Queen's hatred of her mother, and all those other disobedient maids who had incurred her wrath, had eaten away at her and left her empty. Her brother's hatred of Cecil, too, had been his undoing. She had seen enough hatred and needed no more.

She looks back at the golden stone of the house which will soon, finally, be her true home, imagining the sound of her children inhabiting it. There is music drifting from the windows and laughter in the garden as she thinks of them playing chase and catching butterflies on the grass.

Hearing the sound of horses in the distance, she picks up her skirts, running down the drive. And there he is, mounted comfortably on his horse as if in a chair, his reins held loose, wearing an easy smile. She feels strangely shy. It has been three full years since they were last together. He vaults down and they stand several feet apart, scrutinizing each other. His hair is newly cut, his moustache and beard trimmed and his earring is missing; there is a little rent where it must have been torn from his lobe, which makes her wince inwardly and a tender feeling wells up in her.

'Your poor ear.'

He puts his hand to it, shrugging. 'Oh, that.'

There is a new hardness about him. War changes a man – she knows that only too well.

To combat her shyness, she resorts to humour, dropping into a curtsy with a smirk, saying, 'My, if it is not the Earl of Devonshire, the great conquering hero, he who quelled the Irish rebels.'

He laughs, and she can see he has lost a tooth at the back of his mouth. 'If it is not His Majesty's favourite lady, muse of poets, she with the finest mind in all of Christendom, she with the voice of an angel, she who holds my heart.' She laughs too now; and then they fall into an embrace that dissolves those three years of absence to nothing.

Author's Note

In telling the story of the remarkable Penelope Devereux I have adhered closely to historical fact, drawing on primary sources where possible, but it must not be forgotten that this is a work of fiction and so my Penelope Devereux, with her complex inner world, is a character of my own invention. Penelope was an intriguing woman, living life on her own terms in a time when it was almost impossible for women to take such freedoms.

There are many well-documented truths that form the basis of the novel. It is fact that Penelope was Sidney's muse and the model for 'Stella', and though we don't know whether their relationship was consummated in the traditional sense, it is clear from reading Sidney's sonnets that his feelings for her were profound. It is also documented that Penelope was betrayed by her brother after he was condemned. We cannot know what Essex's motives were in doing this but we do know that Penelope was not only the sole woman on the list of rebels handed to the Queen, but also the only person whose name was on that list who did not stand trial. This made me wonder if she might have somehow negotiated her freedom, for there is no doubt she was deeply involved in her brother's insurrection and had been in contact with King James for many years.

We also know that she gave birth to at least three children with Blount, though she was still married to Rich. It seems her adultery was an open secret and, given the morals of the times, and the Queen's particular distaste for such things, it is remarkable that she was able to get away with it for so long. For me this fact is testimony to her strength of character. Her marriage to Rich is interesting because he seems to have been aware of her behaviour and yet did nothing. We know he was a man who was rather disliked and also of little courage. He did, indeed, have to be put to shore due to seasickness when he had been supposed to join one of Essex's military campaigns. What is known about him led me to imagine he held a shameful secret that gave his wife a hold over him. In the novel it is the secret of his attraction to young men, but this is pure speculation.

There are also elements of Penelope's story that I had no space to explore in the novel, which are nonetheless fascinating and somewhat poignant. Penelope was eventually divorced from Lord Rich but a condition stipulated by King James stated that she was not to remarry during Rich's lifetime. She and Blount (by then the Earl of Devonshire), perhaps believing themselves to be held in sufficiently high esteem by the King to avoid his wrath, married anyway. This resulted in Penelope's fall from grace; she, like her mother before her, was banished from court, publicly disgraced, and James famously referred to her as 'a fair woman with a black soul'. As Penelope fell from favour her great adversary, Cecil, rose to become the most important advisor to the Stuart king.

In a tragic twist of fate the couple, though they had lived 'in sin' at Wanstead for two years or so, only had a short period of wedded bliss, as Blount became ill and died in her arms. He, as the great victor of Ireland, was awarded a triumphal state funeral and was buried in Westminster Abbey. In the aftermath Penelope struggled to have her marriage legally recognized and Blount's relatives mounted a challenge to the will that he had carefully drawn up to provide for Penelope and their children. Blount's great wealth was sequestered and Penelope lived in poverty during a protracted legal battle in which she faced charges of adultery, fraud and forgery. In the end she won, but at devastating cost to her reputation, and her victory was to be short-lived as she fell ill and died just months later aged only forty-four.

There are always curious challenges that arise in writing about the sixteenth century, not least that of characters' names. It was customary for children to be named after their parents, or godparents, so often they not only share a surname but also a Christian name, which could be most confusing for readers. In the story there are no fewer than six Roberts and all are important to the narrative; indeed, Essex, Cecil and Rich are all Roberts, and this is why I resorted to Robin for Essex (and young Robert, where necessary, for his son), but Penelope's eldest ended up as Hoby, which is an unusual early diminutive of the name. I will not even begin to go into the number of girls named after Penelope and Lettice. Scholars of Elizabethan fashion will note that I have revised the contemporary spelling 'bodies' to the slightly later but entirely unconfusable 'bodice'.

I must confess to extreme use of poetic licence in the scene in which the young actor/poet recites a sonnet. I was indulging playfully with ideas about Shakespeare's mysterious dark lady, whose identity has been much speculated upon over the years. Some have suggested she was Penelope Rich, others the poet Aemilia Lanier, and there are several more candidates, but the truth remains elusive. It is, though, almost certain that Shakespeare was familiar with the Essex circle. It is thought that *Love's Labour's Lost* was loosely modelled on their set, and it is known that his *Richard II* was performed at the request of Essex's men in a bid to generate support for the earl on the eve of his fateful rebellion.

For those interested in further reading about Penelope Devereux, I recommend Sally Varlow's *The Lady Penelope: The Lost Tale of Love and Politics in the Court of Elizabeth I*, a thorough and fascinating biography of a woman whose story has been largely overlooked. Varlow attributes Penelope's disappearance from history to a Protestant propaganda machine seeking 'blameless heroes of the reformed faith' that worked to whitewash the names of Sir Philip Sidney and the Earl of

Devonshire (Charles Blount) by erasing all memory of their liaisons with a woman who marched to the beat of her own drum.

I referred to many works in my research, too numerous to mention here, but a few I recommend are: Philip Sidney's sonnets (the edition edited by Peter C. Herman has a good introduction, and if they leave you dry-eyed, then you have a heart of stone); Katherine Duncan-Jones's *Sir Philip Sidney: Courtier Poet* is another excellent source of information on one of the foremost Elizabethan poets. For Shakespeare's sonnets, I like the Arden edition for its extensive introduction. Robert Lacey's book *Robert, Earl of Essex: An Elizabethan Icarus* is a good place to start with the earl, and David Loades's *The Cecils: Privilege and Power Behind the Throne* offers much about a father and son who, between them, held the reins of royalty for more than half a century. There is a multitude of books about Elizabeth, but a rich source of inside information on her private life is *Elizabeth's Bedfellows: An Intimate History of the Queen's Court* by Anna Whitelock, and for extensive detail on Elizabethan life look no further than Ian Mortimer's *The Time Traveller's Guide to Elizabethan England.*

Acknowledgements

This novel may bear my name but there are many who have contributed to its genesis and to whom I would like to offer my thanks. I am truly grateful for my agent, Jane Gregory, whose support and belief is a blessing, and Stephanie Glencross, whose ability to negotiate a chaotic first draft is invaluable; the team at Michael Joseph – Louise Moore, Maxine Hitchcock, Liz Smith, Hana Osman, Clare Parker, Francesca Russell and Francesca Pearce, to name only a few – whose enthusiasm and encouragement know no bounds; also the endlessly patient Emma Brown and Trevor Horwood, who is the most tactful and subtle copy-editor known to man; and always Catherine Eccles, whose friendship and advice I couldn't do without.